An Idler's Life

ORLA KELLY
PUBLISHING

Éamonn MacCionnaith

Dedicated to Noel McKenna

Chapter 1
Reality Awaits

The pair of alluring temptresses were sitting at the bar, giving me a look that indicated their intentions. One was white, blonde, and had legs as long as the Nile. The other was black and had curves that were a perfect complement to her companion's slender frame.

I mused over the most advantageous response to their leers.

Subtlety was the most effective weapon in my modest arsenal. After sipping my pint, I offered them a nod and maintained eye contact to assure them that my own thoughts were similar to theirs. The two swooped from their nest, their balletic movements and predatory eyes transfixing me.

The two of them then walked towards me and sat on stools beside me. They said hello in posh British accents that enhanced their seductiveness, while their lustful eyes said much more than just the one word they'd uttered.

"How are yis?" I replied in an Irish brogue that I hoped would pleasure their ears as I tried to hide my boyish excitement.

I learned that their names were Barbara and Linda, and that they were over for the weekend. They'd probably slept with every man in Britain and needed to travel abroad to make more conquests.

The conversation flowed and with each round of drinks I felt my confidence surge, returning their flirtatious mannerisms twofold. They spoke of what they did for a living, while enquiring as to my own profession. I conceitedly informed them of my recently acquired, highly lucrative, promotion in the bank.

As the night went on, Linda, the darker of the two, became impatient and whispered into my ear, "Do you fancy a threesome?"

Never had an arrangement of words incited such an explosion of dopamine within me, nor had there ever been a question asked with such a ludicrously obvious answer.

I sought to respond in a manner that would portray me as nothing other than a seasoned campaigner of such shenanigans, an internationally renowned lover, a sexual messiah whose mission in life was to enrapture women through fornication, a folk hero whose nights of debauchery would become fireside tales for generations to come.

"Ah, I don't think yis would be able for me, girls. I've a bit of an appetite."

"So do we," Barbara replied. "Come on, let's go."

She took me by the hand and escorted me up the stairs to the room they were staying in. My excitement built with each step that I climbed. This was the stuff that fantasies were made of.

Once inside their room, I immediately stripped off and lay on the bed, watching with lust as they unfettered themselves from their clothes, like two escaped prisoners freeing themselves from their shackles. As they climbed onto the bed, the four walls could hardly contain my exhilaration. I was about to discover the meaning of life!

EEERRRHHH!

EEERRRHHH!
EEERRRHHH!
EEERRRHHH!
A sudden noise. Sharp. Loud. Perplexing.

Startled, I looked to my left and to my right. Neither girl lay with me. Beside me lay a phone. The grating sound of its alarm ringing out was like a saw cutting through my foggy head. When I turned it off, the ensuing silence gave rise to an awful realisation.

"Ah, bollocks!"

It had been a dream; a fleeting glimpse into a different life before my own life saw fit to remind me of its dreary existence.

Alas, I wasn't a renowned lover, nor did I have a career that was carrying me towards a wealth-ridden utopia. Such a life was far beyond my paltry expectations.

I was nothing more than an unemployed twenty-one-year-old lad from Bray, named Paddy Dempsey, who spent his waking hours idling away the life he'd been given.

Why was that the case?

To answer that question, I must recall a time in my life when I was a young daydreamer. That epoch, as care-free as it was directionless, was instrumental in the creation of my future troubles.

Chapter 2
The Irish Empire

"Ye look like ye know the answer, Mr Dempsey?" said Mr McMahon in a tone suggesting he thought the opposite.

Teachers had a peculiar habit of addressing you as 'Mr' before they unleashed their wrath upon you, scolding you with the utmost respect.

McMahon wasn't the worst. He was strict but fair, one of the more approachable teachers in St Brendan's College. He was unique in that he was a teacher you could converse with beyond the lexicon of his profession. With an adoration for the country's sporting exploits, you could derail his lesson plan for a few precious minutes, by mentioning the exploits of the Dublin football team or the fortunes of his beloved Shamrock Rovers. His digression would always end with the line, "Anyway, I'm after going off on a tangent. What was I saying to yis before that?"

His sporting passions were only surmounted by his passion for the Irish and English languages. He taught both, lamenting the omnipresence of English to the detriment of the native tongue, while being enamoured with its literary offspring. He had a particular fondness for Irish writers, who, in his opinion, had made Ireland the mecca of literature. He believed that the country was so beset by contradictions, that it was no wonder that so many of its people had been inspired to write about it over the years. He once spoke of how it had a proud but depressing past, a national identity that was alien to some of its own people, and its own language that most of whom couldn't speak; that it was a country that had fought to end British rule, only to then allow itself to be ruled from Rome; that its greatest export was people, through whom it had built its own empire, colonising half the world without firing a single bullet. "The Irish Empire is the most impoverished empire in history," he once said jokingly, "but it still survives today, long after all the other empires have been consigned to the history books."

With such fervour came an unwavering intolerance for anyone acting the *amadán*. So, after I unwisely decided that a pinch of comedy was the appropriate remedy for my boredom, he saw fit to make an example of me.

"I don't know the answer, sir," I said meekly, bracing myself for the approaching avalanche.

"*Tá fhios agam sin*, Dempsey. *Agus inis dom, cén fáth nach bhfuil?*"

"Why *don't* I know the answer, sir?"

"*Cínte*. Has it anything to do with ye not even knowing the question, Dempsey? *An bhfuil?*"

"Eh, I didn't hear ye, sir."

"Well, that's understandable, seeing that ye were so engaged in your humorous conversation with Mr Pope. Why don't ye share the joke with us, Dempsey."

The age-old 'share the joke' conundrum. As old as teaching itself.

I'd remarked that McMahon's fantasy was to be ridden by Oscar Wilde while reading one of his poems. It was unlikely that he'd find the joke amusing.

I could've strangled Popey for getting caught laughing over such a daft line, but boredom tended to amplify jokes. The class was a desert, humour an oasis, and when you stumbled across it, you drank every drop of its filthy stagnant contents as though it was the freshest water you'd ever tasted.

Alan Pope or 'Popey' as he was known, was an integral part of my school life. He was great craic, easy-going, and he had no problem with me copying his work. He was all you could ask for in a classmate. When McMahon caught him laughing, Popey's chubby red face being hard to miss, he knew the source of the gaiety.

"*Seas suas*, Dempsey. Stand up and tell us," he insisted, his patience dwindling.

"Eh… It's about me ma, sir," I lied.

It was a canny move that I hoped would deter him from continuing with his interrogation.

"Your mother, is that so? And what hilarious antics does your mother be getting up to that warrants being shared with Mr Pope?"

Shite! He's called me bluff!

"Eh… eh… she… she… she fell down the stairs last night, sir."

"Your mother fell down the stairs! How'd she manage that, Dempsey?"

"Eh… eh… She was carrying clothes for the wash, sir, and she didn't see the dog in front of her. She tripped over him and fell down, sir."

"All the way down?"

"Right to the bottom, sir."

"*Máthair Dé*, and what about the *madra*, what happened to him? *Cad a tharla dó?*"

"He ended up falling too, sir."

"Both o' them were tumbling down, good God Almighty! *Agus an raibh sí gortaithe?* Was she injured, Dempsey?"

His pseudo concern was a shrewd attempt to derail me, but I was well able for him, I thought.

"Eh… no. She was awright, sir. The dog broke her fall."

"She fell on the dog? *Agus an raibh an madra gortaithe?*"

"Eh… no. The pile o' clothes broke *his* fall, sir… but me ma landed on his belly."

"So, the clothes fell first, then your dog on top o' the clothes, and then your mother on top o' the dog! Is that how it happened, Dempsey? *An bhfuil?*"

"*Tá.* Yes, sir."

The exclusion of the dog falling down the stairs might have made for a more credible anecdote, but at the time I felt that believability lay in the minute details of the affair.

"Good God! That's an incredible story! So, if I rang your poor mother, would she confirm all that cock and bull?"

"It's true, sir. I swear!"

"Would she confirm it, Dempsey?!"

Christ, this bollocks will probably ring her right now.

Think fast, faster, even faster!

"Well, she'd probably be too embarrassed to admit it, sir."

Lovely hurling!

"And the poor auld *madra* wouldn't be able to confirm or deny it either, Dempsey, would he?"

"No, he wouldn't, sir."

"*An bhfuil sé an mhór?*"

"No, sir. He's just a little fella. He's a Jack Russell."

Hands covered mouths throughout the class. Popey looked like he was suffering from cardiac arrest.

"*Suigh síos le de thoil,* like a good man, Dempsey. I'll tell ye what, you've provided us all with such entertainment, I'll repeat the question for ye… What is the meaning behind Emily Dickenson's poem, *I heard a Fly buzz - when I died?*"

Christ, did she even know what she was shitting on about?!

"Eh… There's a fly buzzing around the room, has her driven demented, sir."

"You take it as a literal statement, Dempsey?"

"Yes, sir."

"I see. Do ye not recall our last class in which we discussed metaphorical meanings in poems?"

"I do, sir."

"Do ye not think that applies to the poem in question?"

"Eh… Perhaps, sir."

"Perhaps in what sense, Dempsey?"

Fuckin' hell, he won't let up. It would've been less painful to share the joke!

"Well, maybe she's not real, sir… or the fly's not real… or her and the fly are real but she's not dying… or maybe the fly's buzzing like a mad thing 'cause *he's* dying… I think the poem's open to interpretation, sir."

"With an interpretation like that, it bloody well must be, Dempsey!"

I looked to Popey for a dig out, but he was too busy choking on his own laughter to come to my aid.

Fuck ye anyway, Popey. You're as about as useful as a stitched gee!

"Okay, Dempsey, I'll tell ye what ye can do for me. Reread your notes from the last class and tomorrow you'll quote me five metaphors from any o' the poems in the book. Also, as punishment for your lack of attention, ye can write a six-stanza poem about your mother and dog falling down the stairs. Have it for me by tomorrow."

"Yes, sir," I replied, grateful that the interrogation was over.

To be fair to McMahon, he wasn't without a sense of humour.

"Have ye your masterpiece ready for us, Dempsey?" McMahon asked me the next day.

"I do, sir. I spent all last night writing it."

"Well, don't leave us in suspense, Dempsey. Let us all hear it like a good man."

"In front o' the class, sir?"

"O' course, Dempsey. Isn't that the audience ye usually like to entertain? Come on, up on your feet. We're all waiting. *Cad is ainm don dán?*"

"It's called 'A Day in the Life of Buddy Dempsey,' sir."

I stood up, cleared my throat and reluctantly read:

"Clothes, worn and casting a smell,
were being carried to their destination.
My mother, the bearer, arrived at the stairs;
a chippy's sturdy but steep creation.

She took a step forward, beginning her descent,
probably thinking about having to clean the house.
With her mind elsewhere, she didn't notice the dog.
Buddy was on the next step, as quiet as a mouse.

Suddenly, she tripped, having no idea why,
as the pile of clothes was flung aloft.
She fell down the stairs along with Buddy,
hoping to land on something soft.

She got her wish, as her fall was broken
by the pile of clothes and the poor Jack Russell.
She lay on the floor, uttering every curse she knew,
but hadn't the strength to move a muscle.

When my mother rose, she sought revenge.
Buddy could see the writing on the wall.
She gave chase as he fled the scene,
ignoring her thunderous, unceasing calls.

From room to room, he scampered for his life
as my mother threatened to show him no mercy.
Both had danced this routine before.
Just another day in the life of Buddy Dempsey."

My reading was greeted with apprehensive silence as
the class awaited McMahon's next move.
"A big *bualadh bos* for Mr Dempsey, folks!"
On cue, there was an eruption of sarcastic applause,
before McMahon held his arm aloft, silence immediately
reintroducing itself.

"Well, I think that cleans your slate, Dempsey. Don't be expecting me to be teaching that to students in twenty years' time though. Now, sit down and pay attention, there's a good fella. And Pope, if I see that face o' yours change colour or move one inch away from the book in front o' ye, you'll be the class's next poet. Is that understood?"

"Eh, yeah."

"*Arís*, Pope!"

"I mean, *tá*. Yes, sir."

"And don't be distracting Yeats beside ye either!"

"Yes, sir."

Chapter 3
The Foundations of Failure

"Me da told me last night that technology will have advanced so much by the time we're his age that everything will be done on computers," Popey said. "Paper will become extinct. Can ye believe that, Paddy?" he asked, looking perplexed by the proposition.

"No, I can't. Your da's so full o' shite, he could feed a pig."

"Well, what would *you* know?" "What does *he* know?"

"More than *you*."

"Awright, so paper's extinct, is it? Everything's computers? Well then, what would ye wipe your arse with? The mouse?"

"I never thought o' that."

Popey became preoccupied with his ham and cheese sandwich, forcing it down his gullet as quick as he could so he could voice whatever else was on his mind.

"Paddy, what's the standard way o' measuring your knob?"

"What do ye mean?"

"Well, do ye measure it in centimetres or inches?" "Well, I suppose if you're Irish ye measure it in centimetres."

"Well, that's better, isn't it? 'Cause it'll be a bigger number."

"Why, are ye lacking inches? Ha ha."

"No, I'm just saying… And do ye just measure the length?"

"I suppose so."

"Do ye round it off to the nearest whole number?"

"If ye want to, I suppose."

"What about the width? The circumference of it?"

"Well, that too I suppose."

"I reckon ye'd multiply the length by the diameter to get your proper measurement."

"Jesus Christ, Popey, you're measuring your knob, not going on a mission to fuckin' Mars! Ye don't have to multiply it by Pi or find its square root, for fuck's sake!"

Popey's discourses were as integral to my lunchbreaks as the butter on my bread.

"Ye know what me da told me last night, Paddy?"

"Him again? Do you pair just spend all night talking shite?"

"He told me that if you're ever looking for work, use your initials for your name. It makes ye sound real important."

"What?"

"I'm Alan Matthew Pope, right? So, I'll introduce meself as A.M. Pope. Doesn't that sound impressive?"

"A.M. Pope? Sounds like you're saying, 'I am the Pope.'"

"Sure, no better man! What's yours?"

"P.J. Dempsey."

"Ah, that has a great ring to it. If Paddy Dempsey came to me looking for a job, I wouldn't give him the whiff o' me own shite, but P.J. Dempsey, I'd buy a second-hand car off him!"

I wiped the last of my sandwich from the side of my mouth as I smiled at the absurdity of such advice. Popey's affability endeared him to all, particularly me.

We had the good fortune of encountering one another in primary school and our friendship had grown steadily in the years since.

We were now two fifteen-year-olds in possession of adolescent minds that had a hankering for a bit of devilment. School and its rigid banality couldn't cater for our ilk.

We had begun to hear teachers casually refer to our futures, taking an interest in them that we, or at least I, failed to reciprocate. We were growing up in the company of the illustrious 'Celtic Tiger' economy. It was 2003 and the tiger's roar was at its loudest.

Ireland's economic performance was being marvelled at around the world. We had record low unemployment rates, a skilled workforce, an abundance of foreign investment, record earnings and banks nonchalantly giving money to anyone in need like acts of philanthropy. Property had become the national pastime. The country was getting richer and richer and richer. The recessions of the past, the emigration of yore was that of a foreign country to the opulent, opportunity-laden land we found ourselves to be citizens of. The country was invincible. The prosperous life it offered us was our birthright, our future inheritance. We didn't need to worry about such frivolous concepts such as 'our futures.' For the time being, 'having the craic' was the only thing we cared about.

Popey and I were two of a gang of lads who'd befriended one another in St Brendan's.

Rory Davin rarely spoke unless he was spoken to. His vow of silence could be broken from on occasions, revealing a wealth of knowledge which he hid behind his apparent shyness.

Gary Keating was rarely referred to by his Christian name. He was given a nickname in primary school after he ran out of the classroom one day to get away from a small mouse that he saw under his desk. The speed of his dash to the door and the panic in his voice as he told the teacher what the matter was, ensured that from that day forward, he'd be known affectionately as 'Mousey.'

Ciarán Talbot had a father who was worth a few quid, which led us to re-christen him 'Richy' when we were younger. By the time we'd realised that he revelled in the moniker, it had unfortunately already stuck. Despite his haughtiness, Richy's company was always welcomed for its entertainment value, as he adored a good wind-up and was quite skilled at executing them.

Mick Dolan had a less fortunate family background, with a father who was locally renowned for breaking out in a rash at the mere mention of work, known to all as 'Doley' Dolan. Mick rarely minced his words and could slice you in two with a well-timed venomous retort or with a demonstration of his sometimes-volatile temper.

Seán Walsh and Paul Murphy were two lads who were able to attract the interest of many of the girls. Hearing them bragging about the girls they'd been with, was always a source of irritation and envy for the rest of us.

Then there was Popey, who despite never having to fear accusations of being anorexic, actually fancied himself as a footballer, aspiring to play for Bray Wanderers one day, considering it a more achievable ambition than his previous aspiration of playing for Liverpool.

There was camaraderie galore and with a group of adolescent males, the line between banter and insults was often crossed and a fistfight was sometimes required to settle the matter. Naturally, such occurrences didn't derive from disagreements as to who was the more erudite philosopher between Plato and Aristotle. Comments about one's family would often form the nucleus of such disputes.

"Here, Mick, I heard your da Doley's in trouble with the social welfare," said Richy Talbot, as he nudged and winked at Rory Davin.

Rory, knowing what was to follow, true to himself, stayed quiet and let the champion of wind-ups perform his act.

Although christened 'Doley' locally, none of us referred to Mick Dolan's father by his derogatory moniker in the presence of his son, for fear of the possible repercussions. But Richy Talbot never hesitated in using the name in Mick's company if he reckoned there was a decent laugh to be had from it.

"What the fuck are ye talking about?" asked Mick hostilely.

"I heard he was doing a bit o' work on the side."

"Where did ye hear that?"

"A lad from your estate."

"It's bullshit. Sure, who would *you* know from *my* estate?"

"Nobody, thank God. Friend of a friend, that's all."

"Why, what's wrong with me estate?"

"Nothing, if ye like that sort o' place," said Richy, smirking.

"Sure, when was the last time you were even in me estate, Richy?"

"Why the fuck would I wanna be going into that kip? Ye can't walk down the street in that place without stepping on syringes and being chased by junkies and their mangy dogs," said Richy, laughing.

"Yeah well, it's better now. That was the Flanagan and the McCarthy families causing all the trouble. Most o' them are locked up."

"Well, your da better be careful or else he might join them. He'll be Eddie Flanagan's bitch. He'll end up with an arsehole so big, with a bit o' luck he might fall into it and save the country a few quid. Ha ha."

"If you shut your mouth, ye might save yourself a slap! It's all horseshite anyway. He hasn't been doing any work."

"Ah sure, that's always been his problem. Ha ha."

"Ye know what I mean. He hasn't been doing any-thing on the side. And me da's always looking for work. As soon as they see his address, they lose interest," Mick protested.

"I'd say as soon as your da sees the hours he has to work, *he* loses interest. He knows he'll be missing races down in the bookies! Ha ha."

"Shut up, Richy! What does *your* da do anyway? Sits on his fat hole in a bank, doing fuck all!"

"Ah, but it's not what he does, it's what he earns that's important," Richy informed him, rubbing his thumb and two fingers together. "The only time auld Doley earns anything is when his horse comes in first. Ha ha."

"I swear, Richy. I'm gonna…"

"Does he still blow all his dole in the pub like he used to, talking the ears off everyone? Ha ha."

"Right, you're getting a fuckin' smack, ye cunt!"

"Awright, relax for fuck's sake, will ye! I'm only winding ye..."

Before Richy could finish his sentence, Mick punched him under the eye. Richy, slightly dazed, swung back and missed, before Mick hit him again, at which point the rest of us got between them. Richy, whose mouth had earned him the digs, was still talking, saying, "Ye caught me off guard, ye prick! Go on, try it again! I dare ye!"

At an age when we were most conscious about how our peers perceived us, questioning one's sexuality was a slight on that lad's masculinity that demanded a stringent response.

"I bet ye didn't know this, Seán," said Rory, indicating that he was about to bestow a snippet of his general knowledge on his friend.

What would follow could be any piece of random information, ranging from the world's longest piece of string to the average number of shites that can be had using one toilet roll.

"There's more cows in Ireland than there are people," he told Seán.

"And?"

"What do ye mean 'And'? Do ye not think that's incredible? I mean, if there's that many, where are they all? Why aren't we bumping into them on the street?"

"Are ye expecting to see them out and about getting their shopping? They live down the country."

"Where?"

"In the fields. Where else?"

"But most o' the fields are empty. If there's that many o' them, the fields should be jam-packed with cows. Ireland should be like one giant cow housing estate. See what I mean?"

"They probably hide as soon as they see you coming! That's why ye never see them!"

"Isn't it amazing though?"

"Ye know what's even more amazing, Rory?"

"What? What?" he asked eagerly, expecting another quirky fact to be offered in reciprocation.

"Do ye see that Tara O'Toole one over there?"

Tara O'Toole was the protagonist of many a schoolboy fantasy. She accompanied us in our thoughts before going to sleep at night, and then again in the morning and maybe even at break time. She was the one girl we all unanimously craved.

"What do ye think of her?" Seán asked.

"She's awright."

"Awright?! I haven't been pulling the hose off meself night and day 'cause she's just awright! That one's a work o' fuckin' art! What's amazing is that you're more interested in cows than her! You're a bit queer."

"Who the fuck are ye calling a big queer?"

"I didn't call ye a big queer. I said you're a bit queer."

"Oh, so I'm a part-time queer, am I?"

"No, ye fuckin' gobshite! I meant as in…"

"Love a bit o' mickey on the weekends, do I?"

"Well, you'd know more about that than me, mate."

Rory drew himself closer to Seán until their noses were nearly touching. The two stood awkwardly, locked in a staring match, neither wanting to back down or throw the first dig.

"Come on, lads," Mousey Keating encouraged. "Yis look loke yis are about to fuckin' tongue each other! Give him a belt, Rory. Knock him out, Seán!"

A couple of pushes ensued, followed by the obligatory threats.

"I'll kill ye!" "Go on then!" "I'll kill ye!" "Go on then!" "I'll kill ye!" "Go on then!"

The action reached its zenith with Seán grabbing and yanking Rory's tie like he was trying to train an unruly pup.

"Jesus Christ, lads. I've had better fights trying to squeeze out a shite," Mousey complained.

The two were separated to save them further embarrassment, each of them pleading, "Let me at him!" like archetypal pub fighters in the making.

With girls having become an integral part of our adolescence, they had also become a source of conflict.

"I heard ye went off with o' the girls on Friday night, Paul," said Popey.

"Yeah, Tara O'Toole," he triumphantly replied.

"No, not her," Popey responded, smiling.

"I was with her mate too. Your one with the big jugs."

"No, not her either. Come on, Paul, ye know who I'm talking about. Don't be shy," he said as his smile widened.

"Sandra Lynch he's talking about!" Mousey blurted, his head like a nodding dog's in laughter.

Sandra Lynch was a girl whose obesity deterred lads from taking any interest in her. To counteract her lack of male attention, she'd play the hunter instead and would pounce on any potential prey in her vicinity. Those who had a chance with any of the other girls, repelled her advances, while the weak and desperate had no choice but to capitulate to her. To be one of her victims was to be branded for life; an embarrassing tattoo that a hundred bars of soap couldn't wash off. You'd be the butt of countless jokes that would never grow old. It would be talked about at your funeral. God himself would crack a joke about it upon entering the pearly gates, just when you thought that the one perk of death would be finally seeing the back of it. For a ladies' man like Paul Murphy, being accused of having 'gone off' with Sandra Lynch was the ultimate insult.

"What the fuck are yis talking about?! I wasn't near her!"

"That's not what I heard, Paul," said Popey.

"I don't give a fuck what ye heard, Popey. She'd be more your type!"

"Well, I wasn't the one going off with her, mate. Ha ha."

"Even *she* wouldn't touch *you*, ye fat tub o' shite!"

"She doesn't need to when she has you feeling her up. Ha ha."

"Who the fuck told ye I was with her?"

"Mousey did."

"Mousey, who told *you*?"

"Ah now, I've to protect me sources, Paul. Ye know me, I don't rat on anybody."

"Ye'd rat out your own ma if the price was right!"

"Ye better watch out, Mousey. He'll be after your ma next," said Popey, laughing.

"You shut your fuckin' gob, Popey! His ma's the only one you'd have a chance with!"

"Here, what are ye saying about me ma?" Mousey interjected.

"Who told ye, Mousey?"

"Sure, it doesn't matter, everyone knows now. The damage is already done, mate."

"Who started spreading it?"

"Seeing that you're a mate… I'll tell ye for a fiver."

"A fiver?! I've only got about three quid on me."

"Ah, that'll do… Right, hand it over then and I'll tell ye."

"Ye swear?"

"On me ma's life."

Paul grudgingly handed over the money to Mousey.

"Right, who was it?"

"It was me! Ha ha!"

"I'm gonna fuckin' kill ye, ye prick!"

"Ah come on, Paul! It was just a joke, mate!"

"Come 'ere to me, wait till I catch ye! You're fuckin' dead!"

Mousey scarpered as Paul gave chase to the amusement of the rest of us.

As innocent as all the horseplay with the lads was, it also had a pollutive effect on me. It steered me away from the idea of school being something that needed to be taken seriously. What I didn't realise then, amid such larks, was that the foundations of failure were being laid, and the sound of my own laughter was preventing me from hearing the concrete being poured.

Chapter 4
The Rambling One-Man Band

Although I revelled in the laughs that the gang in St Brendan's provided, I was always an outsider looking in, enjoying the play, without wanting a starring role in it myself. I began to keep my own company to that of my peers as I approached my teens, and noticeably drifted from the local youngsters who I'd shared my formative years with. This burgeoning fondness for solitude soon supplanted any diminishing yearning I had for the fruits of companionship. I no longer possessed the appetite to initiate a friendship, nor the patience to maintain one, at an age when the lives of others were being built upon them. Invitations to social gatherings were ignored continually before I eventually stopped receiving them. My cohorts indulged in the archetypal adolescent lifestyle, while I found greater stimulation in my growing interest in music.

I devoured albums and began to teach myself to play some of their easier songs on a guitar I'd found in a skip which I had restrung. Fanciful ambitions of replicating my idols weren't long in shaping my outlook.

While others in St Brendan's conversed about their weekend hijinks, I silently listened, physically present but mentally adrift, the tales of their humdrum reality unable to haul me from my absorbing fantasy. My aloofness quickly spread to the classroom. I was too intrigued by my daily musings to be burdened with Pythagoras and his infamous theorem or Emily Dickinson and her buzz-ing fly, or the shackled existence that school life offered. Each was met with an indiscriminate apathy.

I portrayed my detachment as quiet diligence with my indolence hidden behind a concentrated countenance. Others in the class had the decency to make a nuisance of themselves which enabled me to escape the attention of the teacher. My physical universe stagnated, as its intellec-tual counterpart expanded rapidly, superseding it.

However, I viewed St Brendan's as a prison. Inside its four walls, allies were imperative. Six years spent in solitary confinement could break even the most ardent loner. To survive, I needed laughter. It was like a drug that offered a temporary high, just enough to take the edge of the monotony, and that drug was inaccessible without the gang.

My lust for life beyond its confines, inevitably led me to start mitching. I'd treat myself to the odd day off, walk-ing halfway to St Brendan's before returning home when I knew Ma and Da had left for work and my younger sister Claire had left for school herself. We attended the same school, but St Brendan's was big enough for my absence to go unnoticed. If she caught me, she'd main-tain her secrecy until the time came when she sought a favour and found blackmail to be a foolproof tactic to attain her requirements. Sibling loyalty had a price.

Da drove for Dublin Bus and Ma worked in the local corner shop. As their hours varied, the house wasn't always empty. When it was, the music blared in tune, I strummed along out of tune, singing on an imaginary stage, performing to the masses, as I spared a thought for

Popey and the rest, slowly and cruelly being zombified,
all in the name of the Irish education system.

I even penned my maiden song while mitching, *The Rambling One-Man Band.*

Ye hear me here, ye see me there,
banging out a tune, often out of time.
Not a note in my head, nor a permit to play,
but till I'm handcuffed, I'll be playing hail, rain or shine.

Endless complaints and thieving galore
is all I get when all I wanted was a few bob.
So, I find a new street and a new clientele,
somewhere I can play in peace without being robbed.

I'm rambling, rambling, rambling round.
I'm the uncrowned musical king of the town.
Spare me your coppers and give me a hand.
I'm the rambling one-man band.

The same auld heads every day,
nine to five grinders, winos, junkies and all.
Rarely a cent, never a smile,
"I'll catch ye on the way back," I do hear them call.

I've heard that line a thousand times,
but I'm still standing here by my empty hat.
Love me or loathe me, you have to admit,
I'm part of the scenery and a character at that.

I'm rambling, rambling, rambling round.
I'm the uncrowned musical king of the town.

Spare me your coppers and give me a hand.
I'm the rambling one-man band.

Seasons have come, years have gone.
Age has ravaged the tools of my trade.
I may have played my final tune.
Early retirement is looming, I'm afraid.

But I have a think, "That's it!" I say,
as the solution comes to me in a snap.
I'll sing sean-nós or opera instead,
and for extra variety, I'll even rap.

I'm rambling, rambling, rambling round.
I'm the uncrowned musical king of the town.
Spare me your coppers and give me a hand.
I'm the rambling one-man band.

I'll start a new fund, no time like today,
saving every penny for my brand-new kit.
Seeing that they thought the noise was gone,
when it makes its return, they'll throw a fit.

It's finally time to debut my new gear.
Thanks be to God, for everyone's sake,
because despite their moaning, deep down they know,
the place wasn't the same without the racket I make.

I'm rambling, rambling, rambling round.
I'm the uncrowned musical king of the town.
Spare me your coppers and give me a hand.
I'm the rambling one-man band.

On the days when Ma or Da were home, I'd resort to wandering the streets of Bray, before coming home for four o'clock, exhausted from my day of self-schooling, having learned how many miles it took to kill seven hours. It made for a painstakingly long day, but still trumped the endless hours in St Brendan's.

Bray was the supposed gateway to the 'Garden of Ireland' that County Wicklow was hailed as being. 'Little Bray' was like a village within the town, situated beside the Dublin border, and separated from the rest of the town by the River Dargle. Its various roads and housing estates branched off from the main thoroughfares of Castle Street and Dublin Road, giving way to a maze of back roads, cul de sacs, and alleys. Next to the river was the local park where we spent much of our childhood playing whichever sport was being shown on television. Back then, our kingdom stretched from Bray Bridge in the south, to Cork Abbey in the north, and from the back-strand in the east, to Fassaroe in the west. There were schools, corner shops, chippers, a supermarket, playing fields, bookies, barbers, pubs, our mates' houses – the lot. We even had a sex shop and dared each other to run in the front door, our intrigue of all things sexual growing at a supersonic pace. A gang of us once gathered all our pocket money together and voted on who'd go in to buy a dirty magazine. Little Roy O'Keeffe was unwillingly elected, and no sooner did he cross the threshold than we heard him being ordered to leave.

"Get out, ye little dirty git, before I smack ye one!"

"But Mr, Mr… I have the money!"

"Give it to your auldfella. *He* can buy it for ye!"

An unwavering sense of community held the predominantly working-class area together, creating an identity that refused to be either patronised or gentrified to the social tastes of others. We lived on Dargan Street; a narrow street comprised of two rows of terraced houses within such proximity to each other that they looked like they were squaring up for a fight. Privacy, therefore, was in short supply. Your own business wasn't long becoming everyone's business.

As architecturally indistinguishable as it was from its neighbouring streets, its uniqueness lay behind the generic bricks and mortar, in the benevolence of its residents. The street's sustainability was seemingly built on the trading of favours. Any monetary deficit was balanced by a surplus of goodwill. If we were stuck for a bag of coal, the Donoghues next door would be quick to offer a couple of shovelfuls. If Conor Donoghue was short the price of a pint, Da would buy another round. On the other side we had the McLoughlins. Christine McLoughlin would bake a cake for us whenever Ma looked after her two sons. The fact that her cakes always looked like they'd been rescued from a burning house never detracted from her kind gesture. A couple of doors down were Frank and Ann Griffith. When we were younger, Frank would lecture you to clean behind your ears, pulling a pound coin out from behind them to prove his point, whenever he heard the ice cream van approaching in the summer. I was once close with their son Graham and the McLoughlin twins, but different schools and diverging interests saw us amicably drift apart in the coming years.

At the corner house was an elderly lady named Mrs Cooper. I never knew her first name. Mr Cooper had died a few years prior. He was a cantankerous man who'd moan about what shade of green the grass was, but also the respected patriarch of the street. His musings on life were now remembered fondly, now that they were all that remained of him. When we were young kids, we all used to knock on Mrs Cooper's door, enquiring if she needed anything in the shop, knowing she'd let us keep the change for a couple of tenpence toffees. Frailer now and housebound, it was Ma and Christine McLoughlin who catered for the ever-increasing challenges that age and widowhood were presenting to her. With her still razor-sharp mind, she scoffed at any suggestions of a nursing home, despite her own children's pleas.

Henry McCabe was the street's eccentric. He was a bachelor in his mid-fifties who worked for the post office. He had a habit of divulging his life story to anyone he bumped into on his morning rounds. Upon each retelling, another quirky anecdote seemed to have been included. If all was true, Henry had sailed the seven seas before finding his fortune in America. This apparently was all lost in a game of poker before he returned to Ireland to join the IRA in Belfast and fight the Brits. Captured by the enemy, he supposedly then escaped the Maze Prison and fled to Dublin with a gorgeous blonde who he soon had to dump upon realising that she was a British spy. Somewhere in the midst of all this, he managed to squeeze in a successful career as a lounge singer and was the uncredited 'real singer' of many famous recordings. His British arrest warrant prevented him from travelling to London to sue the respective record company for the lucrative royalties he was apparently owed. His appointment to the post office was supposedly the Irish government's way of thanking him for his patriotic service up north, and it had promised him it would investigate the matter of his unpaid royalties on his behalf. Henry insisted he'd be handing in his resignation to An Post once he received his royalty cheque.

As kids we used to be enthralled by his stories, never doubting their veracity. There was God, there was Santa Claus and there was the life of Henry McCabe! Nobody was more fascinated with his yarns than Da, who was never short of ways to describe his neighbour.

"He's madder than a house full o' monkeys, that fella!"

"Ah, he's a gas character, McCabe, give him his due."

"He's a total spacer. Away with the fairies!"

"He's a fuckin' gobshite and you're a bigger gobshite, son, for believing him!"

I'd inform him of the latest riveting chapter that Henry had told us of his epic adventures, only to be met with a belly laugh.

"The seven seas?! That fuckin' eejit hasn't even set foot in the *Irish* Sea. Ha ha."

"But he lost it all in a game o' cards, Da!"

"He lost his marbles awright, about the only thing he lost. Ha ha."

"Then he said he escaped the Maze Prison, Da!"

"The M… M… Maze… Ha ha… Escaped the fuckin' loony bin more like! Ha ha."

"And they're still looking for him, Da!"

"I'd say they are awright, the men in the white coats. Ha ha."

"And he says he'll leave the job once he gets the money he's owed from the singing!"

"Auld McCabe, he's some man for one man. Ha ha."

In such a close-knit community, wandering through the local streets during school hours would've been idiotic. I had to traverse further afield by crossing the bridge into 'Big Bray.'

The main street of the town wasn't without risk, but the throngs of people shielded me from sight. I'd browse the aisles of the music shop and the book shop. The staff undoubtedly knew my motive but didn't let on. I'd then go to the library on Eglington Road, an ideal place to hide, pretending to be studying on my lunchbreak.

I'd often head down to the seafront, finding a seat on its quaint Victorian promenade, at risk of arousing the suspicions of the odd passer-by. But the only attention I ever garnered was from the foraging seagulls who fought over the crusts that I'd throw to them. Even their loud squawks couldn't diminish the sense of tranquillity I'd feel as I watched the ebb and flow of the sea, despite my undoubtedly sullen appearance suggesting otherwise. If only I could've bottled such a frame of mind. But if I could've, I probably would've sold it for half its value to the first bidder, naively assuming its possession to be surplus to my needs.

It was on such an occasion, when I had a chance encounter with a man, the memory of whom, would one day be unearthed.

As I sat, arms and legs stretched, yawning into the afternoon air, I heard a voice.

"How are ye, son?"

A scruffy, middle-aged man stood hunched over me. He wore faded jeans that were stained at the knees and a damp-smelling brown coat. He had a scraggly greying beard, frayed eyes and hair that had lost its battle with age, his few surviving hairs brushed across in some haphazard attempt at a combover. The almost comical combover was his most respectable feature.

"Do ye mind if I sit down beside ye?"

"Work away."

His movement was laboured. If by appearance he was middle-aged, his body was that of an old man. As he nestled beside me, the overpowering smell of drink wafted up my nostrils.

"Nice day, son?"

"It is," I replied cautiously, a pinch of apprehension in my words.

"What's your name, son?" "Paddy."

"Pleased to meet ye, Paddy. I'm Barry." He offered his hand.

It dangled in the air, tremble slightly, before I shook it.

"What brings ye down here, Paddy? Are ye mitching?" he asked, breaking into a hoarse laugh that degenerated into a cough.

"Well, I'm eh, I'm…"

"Don't worry, son. I'm not gonna squeal on ye, you're grand," he said, smiling, still unable to shed the look of sadness from his tired face.

"I used to do the same thing meself when I was a young lad. Ye picked a good spot here. Grand place for it, isn't it?"

"I suppose, yeah."

"And now you're thinking, what in the name o' God does this pain in the hole want with me? Just a bit o' company, son, that's all."

He coughed again, this time, pulling his 'medicine' out of his inside coat pocket. He drank a mouthful and put the bottle back in his pocket as I silently watched a couple walking along the beach.

"Ye don't say an awful lot, Paddy, do ye?"

"What's there to say?"

"Ye know what? You're dead right! Wise words for a young man. What is there to say? Nothing that either of us will remember, that's what."

He reached for his inside coat pocket again, then thought twice and retreated from it.

"What has *you* down here?"

"Me? Ah, I'm always here, son. I live here."

"Whereabouts?"

"Here, on these benches."

"Oh... I see," I said awkwardly.

"That's me dining room table you're sitting on, ye bollocks." He tried to laugh again but the cough broke through. No hesitation this time. The bottle was opened, gulped and put back in his coat. I looked off into the opposite direction as if to afford him some privacy. His discretion was peculiar given there was nobody around bar me. An age-old habit perhaps.

"How long have ye been living here, Barry?"

"Too bloody long, son."

I waited for an answer that never came. His mournful eyes stared blankly ahead at nothing.

"Must be rough?"

"That it is. The weather can test your spirit, awright. That little shelter over there does the job normally, once it's not too bad. The bang o' piss off it would keep ye up half the night, but sure if it keeps the wind and the rain off me back, I'm a happy man. It's quiet down here at night. No rowdy eejits taunting ye, throwing shite at ye. I've gotten a couple o' hidings. Lads with bellyfuls o' drink looking for trouble. Jesus, I wish I had that much energy with drink on me. Then again, I'd be happy just to have the bellyful o' drink… Ye wouldn't believe some o' the characters I've come across. They wouldn't spit on ye if ye were on fire, but they would if ye weren't! I'm left alone here, nobody bothers me, apart from meself."

He held back the laugh this time, swallowing hard instead.

"Have ye nowhere to go?"

"Do ye think I'd be here if I had?" He winced, before he spoke again. "Well, that's not entirely true, son. I've a wife, ye know, but she… she had her fill o' me." He paused.

I said nothing. He looked off into the distance, as if pondering whether he'd said too much.

"Even when I was your age, I used to make the odd bet here and there. I was too young to go into the bookies meself, so I'd get an older mate to go in for me. When I became old enough to place the bets meself, it wasn't too long before me gambling became a problem.

O' course, poor auld Catherine only found out about it after we got married. She caught a glimpse of a bank statement, and when she found betting slips in me pockets doing the washing, well, she put two and two together. Then one day I came home with only me P45 to show for me day's work."

"What…" I said, before I hesitated in asking.

"What happened? Well, I gave meself a little loan from the till. I was gonna pay it back. Figured I'd be over to the bookies and back with me winnings before anyone would notice the money was gone."

"And they noticed?"

"Ah, they noticed awright – when a week later it was still gone. The fuckin' horse finished last! They weren't long sussin' out who had the sticky fingers either. Without the job, I started gambling more, trying to earn a few quid for her, ye know? Blew it all o' course! No money for the mortgage or for the nipper that was on the way. We lost the… I lost the house and had to move in with her mother. Ye can imagine what that was like. Jesus, we argued about everything. Money, jobs, babies, flats and that was only with the mother-in-law!"

He paused, staring blankly again.

"Well, I legged it. I went off on binges to numb the guilt and to get away from the pair o' them. Anyway, the last straw was when I got back one night with a bit of a head on me. The mother-in-law was all over me like a fly on a fresh shite. I was a this, a that, you name it… Anyway, I gave her back as good as I got, the auld cunt. I fell asleep. When I awoke, the place was in a right state and I had two bin bags o' clothes packed for me and was being shown the door. I could've argued with her, but I didn't bother. I hadn't the energy. I just left."

"What happened then?"

"Ah, I was gambling worse than ever 'cause I didn't have to hide it anymore. I got me dole and crossed the road to the bookies every Wednesday and lost it. I started sleeping rough to save money for bets. Then the dole cut me off and… Well, that was that. That was a year ago, and I've been out here since. I was staying in a homeless shelter for a while, but the place was the pits. Junkies, needles and all that shite. Ye'd be sleeping with one eye open. I get a better night's kip out here."

"Would she not take ye back?"

"Well, I haven't spoken to her since that night. If she knew I was here she probably would. Can't say the same for her auld one now, mind you. I'm not arriving at her door like this anyway, without a penny. I've still a morsel o' self-respect. I'm embarrassed – no, ashamed, ye know? I wouldn't give the mother-in-law the satisfaction either! The next time I see that auld bat she'll hear the money jingling in me pockets from a mile away."

"Does your kid not miss ye?"

"Don't know. Never met him… or her. It'd eat away at ye, knowing you've an auld sprog running around who doesn't even know ye. It's for the better though, for the time being at least."

I didn't have any advice nor believed that he'd want to hear advice from a youngfella.

"Listen, I better get going, Barry."

"Yeah, no worries, son. Listen, thanks for the company. I didn't mean to be boring ye with all that depressing shite. Ah, I just fancied talking to someone, just one o' those days, ye know? You were the first poor unfortunate that I laid eyes on, so ye can blame either me or your own luck." His sad smile returned.

"Yeah, no problem, Barry."

"And get yourself into school, Paddy, or ye could end up like me."

"Yeah, will do," I replied unconvincingly. "Sure, I'll see ye around."

"Ah, ye probably won't. I'll either be back with herself or dead. God knows which is worse!"

The bluntness of his reply startled me. Not knowing what to say next, I asked him the first thing that came to mind.

"What's your second name, Barry?"

"Why, are ye gonna keep an eye on the obituaries?" This time, the sad smile was absent. "Cunningham, Barry Cunningham."

On that morbid note, I turned and walked up the promenade. My earlier euphoria was a distant memory. It seemed almost inappropriate to try to resurrect it. As I cut across the grass on to Strand Road, I glanced back to get one last look at him. He was already gone.

Chapter 5

The Certainty of Uncertainty

School life was unremarkable in the following months, so much so that my attendance suffered. By sixteen, I'd mastered mitching to such a degree that I began to think I had a God-given talent for dodging, hiding, lying and secrecy, ensuring my future would lie in the criminal underworld or in the houses of parliament. Amidst the tedium, I was drawing the blueprints for my escape plan. Mick Dolan was leaving school early to start a plumbing apprenticeship. I was keen to get in on the act, fancying myself as a carpenter. If it was good enough for Jesus of Nazareth, it was good enough for Paddy of Bray. I'd have a trade to my name, a few quid in my pocket, and St Brendan's as only a memory. If there was a drawback, it was too shy to introduce itself to me.

With Ireland's building boom showing no signs of abating, a trade was a job for life. There was but one flaw in my plan. I needed a tradesman in search of an apprentice. Mick was taken on by one of his father's friends. I had no such luck.

"Da, do ye know any carpenters who'd take me on as an apprentice?"

"Nope."

"Any plumbers?"

"Nope."

"Any tilers?"

"Nope."

"Jesus Christ, Da. Do ye know anyone?"

"There was a fella up in Palermo that I knew. He was an electrician."

"Really, yeah? Would he take me on?"

"Ah no, sure isn't he dead a long time."

"Why are ye telling me then?!"

"Ye asked, didn't ye?!"

The employment gods were against me, or the educational gods were with me. I believed in the former as I surrendered to the prospect of serving the remainder of my sentence in St Brendan's, my hope of parole flung into the bin along with my blueprints. To my vexation, some of my classmates already had their whole lives planned out. The girls were only short of drawing up their wills.

"What are ye gonna do, Ellen?"

"Hairdressing."

"Then what?"

"I'll become the manager of a salon."

"Then what?"

"I'll buy the place."

"Then what?"

"I'll get married."

"Then what?"

"We'll buy a house."

"Then what?"

"I'll have kids."

"How many?"

"Three."

"Then what?"

"I'll raise me family, then retire."

"Then what?"

"I'll become a granny."
"Then what?"
"I'll get a disease."
"Then what?"
"I'll organise me funeral."
"Then what?"
"I'll die."
"Then what?"
"I'll go to heaven and meet God."
"Then what?"
"I'll give him a trim and a shampoo."
"Then what?"
"I don't know. I haven't thought that far ahead yet. What about you, Paddy?"
"Eh… I think I'm having chicken for dinner tonight."

For their male inmates, the future was opaque. Bar Richy Talbot who wanted to study business and follow his father's career path, and Rory Davin who bizarrely enough wanted to be a teacher, the rest of us were bereft of any such clarity. We were jumping out of a plane without a parachute, praying we'd land on something soft. We made sure to dish out slaggings to Richy and Rory, but the jibes hid an underlying jealously and concern that we all secretly held, but never spoke of.

"Business, is it? Sure, what in the name o' God would you know about that?" Popey asked Richy.

"Me and me da do talk about that stuff all the time. He reckons I already know more than half o' the crowd working in his bank."

"Oh, does he now? Ha ha."

"Sure, the reason ye go to college is to learn about it, Popey. If I knew everything, I wouldn't need to be going in the first place, ye sap."

"I bet you'll only last a few months. Sure, they'd be all boring arseholes doing that, there'd be no craic. They're all just bread heads."

"I'd be in the right company so. After six years with you lot, four years with a few breadheads would go down a treat. It'd be nice to be around people who I've something in common with."

"Like what, Richy?"

"Money! Ha ha."

"Your da's money, ye mean?"

"Ah, it'll be mine someday, Popey. I'm his only child."

Richy often referred to his future inheritance. It seemed to be his destiny, his goal in life, to get his hands on it. That the death of his father was required for it to come into his possession, seemed a minor hindrance.

"I'll drive up to the front door in the car me da'll get me for me eighteenth and let them know I've arrived."

"They'll know you've arrived when they get a whiff o' bullshit. Ha ha."

"Bullshit, says you? What about your football career, Popey? I haven't seen ye lining out for Bray Wanderers yet. When are ye making your debut?"

"Ye know very well I got a bad injury last year."

"A swollen gut isn't an injury, Popey. Ha ha."

"Me knee, ye sap. I twisted it badly. I need to let it heal."

"What about the few extra pounds ye have jiggling about?"

"Once me injury heals, I'll lose that no bother. Wait till ye see me in a year's time. Ye won't recognise me."

"You're right, I won't, 'cause you'll be fuckin' twice the size. Ha ha."

I butted in, Richy's path to wealth intriguing me.

"So, when are ye gonna make your first million, Richy?" I sarcastically asked

"Same time you make your first hundred, Paddy!"

"Smart bollocks, aren't ye? Ha ha. Will your da have something lined up for ye when ye finish college?"

Richy's father was a bank manager, which in his son's eyes, made him an infallible creator and possessor of wealth in the town. In retrospect, Richy's estimates of his father's wealth, and our own notions of it, shared little in common with reality. But in St Brendan's, just a kitchen extension or a spare bedroom was enough to achieve promotion into a higher social class.

"He probably will, but between me and you two boys, he'll wish he never hired me. Once I get me feet under the table in there, I'll be eyeing up his job. By then, he'll be getting on a bit, they'll want some fresh blood, and I'll be there waiting in the wings. I'll get him to show me all the tricks o' the trade, then take over the reins when the time is right. Sure, he'd be near retirement age anyway, he could do without the stress. Play a bit o' golf or something."

"You're un-fuckin' believable, Richy. Ha ha."

"Then once I'm the manager, I'll arrange a nice fat loan for meself to get me own business started and give meself a big mortgage."

"So, you've it all planned out then?"

"To a tee, Paddy boy. I'm the cutest hoor in the brothel!"

Our attention turned to Rory.

"So, Rory, what in the name o' God makes ye wanna be a teacher?" I asked, dumbfounded.

"He's become institutionalised, Paddy," said Mousey. "He's spent so long in this kip that he can't handle life without it. It's all the poor chap knows. He's like one o' those prisoners that serve their life sentence, can't hack it on the outside when they're released, so they rob a shop to get back in. They've destroyed him!"

"Will ye shut up, Mousey," Rory protested.

"Well, what is it then?"

"I just think it'd be an interesting job."

"How?" I asked. "You're just gonna be reliving the last six years for the rest o' your life!"

"Lads, its different if you're a teacher."

"How?"

"Well, number one, you're getting paid to be there, and number two, it's like the difference between being a prisoner and a prison guard."

"Sure, who'd want to be a prison guard?" I argued. "They have it worse. At least the prisoner does his sentence and then he gets out, the guard spends his whole shaggin' life in the kip!"

Rory was getting nowhere with us.

"Aw, I give up on you lads," he said, shaking his head in amusement.

Mousey, who was sitting next to him, said, "God, I feel like I'm stuck sitting beside Judas at the last supper. Anyone wanna swap seats, lads?"

The school afforded us all a one-to-one meeting with the career guidance counsellor, a friendly man named Mr Fahey. He would direct the students with a career path in mind down their chosen route, while trying to help find a route for those of us who didn't have one.

Before meeting him, I tried to think of what I could say that would give him something to work with. The coming end to my schooldays created a troubling paradox. I couldn't wait to escape the zoo, but I also feared how I'd survive in the wild.

"Come in," said Fahey, after I knocked on his door.

I felt a slight sense of unease as I entered his office. Doing so was a sign that I couldn't ignore my future for much longer. I would have to confront it as if it was the school bully.

"Close that door behind ye, Patrick, like a good man… Have a seat."

I sat in the seat next to him as he tidied up his paperwork.

"Okay, Patrick. The first question I always like to throw out there is, 'What would ye like to do when ye leave school?'"

When he threw out the question, it went over my head and out the window, up into the sky, through the atmosphere and into outer space. I hoped that aliens might stumble across it, beam me up into their spaceship and let me copy their answer.

"Eh… I don't really know, sir."

"That's fine, that's fine," he said reassuringly, with a hand on my shoulder, like a doctor who'd just told his patient he had six months to live.

"Well, what interests ye?"

"In school, sir? Eh, not a lot to be honest. Well, I love the auld game o' football in PE."

"I've just spoken to Alan Pope about the chances of becoming a professional footballer. Not to say it's impossible but ye'd really want to have an alternative plan as a backup."

"Ah, I don't expect that to happen, sir, it's just something I like."

"Anything else?"

My silence was compounded by the cluelessness that was no doubt painted all over my face.

"What about outside o' school?"

"Em, the usual stuff, sir."

"What's the usual stuff?"

"I watch a bit o' sport, listen to a few tunes, strum a few chords, read bits and bobs, watch the odd film."

"Ah, okay. And is there anything in those areas that would interest ye?"

"I'd like to be a musician. I could see meself doing that. Travelling round, pub to pub, town to town, working me way up."

"That wouldn't be a very steady job. If music's your passion, ye should think of studying it in college."

"Ah, that wouldn't be very rock 'n' roll, sir. I'd have no credibility. Ye can't play the blues with a diploma on the wall behind ye."

"Well, there are various avenues ye can go down. Ye could be a sound engineer or a..."

He rattled off a handful of music related occupations. Being 'involved' in music held no interest for me.

Pressing buttons and twiddling knobs on a switchboard didn't equate with my romantic image of the bohemian artist, penning the lyrics to his latest masterpiece, four minutes of ingenuity from a virtuoso of the craft. It was all or nothing with me. It was already looking like the latter.

"So, what do ye think o' those options?" Fahey asked.

"Yeah, they're great," I lied.

"Now listen, you'll need decent points in your Leaving Certificate if ye want to study any o' them at third level. That means getting the head in the books and knuckling down…"

I'd already stopped listening. For the rest of the meeting, I pretended to be paying attention, nodding when it seemed appropriate to do so. Before I left his office, he handed me printouts of music courses that I could consider doing and told me if I ever wanted to chat again, his door was always open. I didn't. I'd already closed mine. His printouts weren't long getting lost either, but not as lost as the person who lost them.

Chapter 6
The Murky Waters of Femininity

By seventeen, I was in my final year in St Brendan's, and despite further distractions from my schoolwork being the last thing I needed, I naively dove into the murky waters in which swam the strange creature known as the female. Her name was Rachael Dowling. I sat beside her one day out of necessity after I forgot my history book. Having never properly spoken to her before, I found that I was able to converse with her easily. When I made her laugh, I noticed a prominent gap between her two front teeth, which she caught me staring at. As if trying to compensate for me noticing it, she then took off her black-rimmed glasses, showing me how she looked without them. The exchange was enough to make me intentionally leave my book at home the following week for another opportunity to sit beside her. None of the lads were interested in her, but with each conversation, I found *my* interest in her growing by the day, thankful for their lack thereof.

Asking her out was daunting, so I opted instead to cautiously steer the conversation in that direction in the hope that she'd discern my intent and be willing to ask the question herself instead.

"So, do ye be up to much on the weekends?" I asked her.

"I hang around with the girls. You?"

"I...I..."

Teach the girl Morse code why don't ye!

"I… I do be out and about… here and there… doing this and that."

Jesus, you're making it sound like ye go out robbing houses on the weekend!

"With who?"

"Ah, this person one day, that person the next, ye know yourself."

Christ, will ye give the girl a straight answer! Ye sound like you're in the witness protection programme.

"I *don't* know, that's why I'm asking."

Cheeky bitch.

"Ah, ye wouldn't know them."

You don't even know them. Ha ha.

"I might. What's their names?"

"Eh…"

Don't Eh! Who's Eh when he's at home? Say anybody for fuck's sake. Tom, Dick or Harry, one o' the twelve Apostles!

"One o' them is Peter."

"Peter who?"

"Thomas, Peter Thomas."

"Never heard of him. Is he in a different school?"

Yes, yes, yes, yes.

"He is, yeah."

"Do ye drink?"

O' course ye do!

"Ah yeah."

"Where do ye go drinking?"

Hold on, think carefully now. If ye mention Peter's house, she'll want to know where he lives next.

"In Peter's house. He has it free on the weekends."

"Where's that?"

CLAP CLAP.

Bravo! We're plummeting fast here. Ye better turn this round before we hit the ground.

"Eh..."

Is Eh back again? Ah, long time no see, Eh.

"Ah, just nearby. What about you?"

You've turned defence into attack, nice move! We're back in the game!

"I usually have a few drinks in Laura's house when her ma is out... Sometimes I stay over, and I see her ma when she gets back drunk. She's gas. Ye wanna see her. She does be dancing and singing like a mad thing. It's a howl."

"It sounds like great craic."

Does it fuck! Some menopausal auld one gyrating around the place. Sounds like a night in the madhouse!

"I'm going over to Laura's tomorrow night. Ye can come over if ye want and have a few drinks with us. Unless you're planning to go over to your mate Peter's house?"

We're in here! Tell Peter to fuck off. Kill him and bury him. He'll never be heard of again.

"No, I've nothing planned... Yeah, I'd like to."

"Great. I'll say it to Laura."

"Sound. See ye tomorrow night then."

I arrived at Laura's house feeling excited and somewhat nervous. My previous experiences with the fairer sex were limited to 'going off' with them behind the school. There was a modus operandi that had to be strictly adhered to when 'going off' with a girl. A friend of the girl would act as the 'agent,' making the offer to the lad on her client's behalf. Upon acceptance, the time and place of the meeting would be discussed. The whole time, the 'agent' would be the lad's only point of contact. He'd only meet her client after the negotiations were completed, by which point any flames of romance would be long extinguished. Knowing nothing about each other, they'd sit in lingering silence until one plucked up the courage to make the first move, leading to an inevitable clash of styles. The girl would gently press her lips against the lad's, resting a hand on his nape, attempting to reclaim some of the lost romance. The lad, however, would seize the girl in a mugger's grip and open his mouth as wide as possible, unleashing his lizard-like tongue as far into her mouth as he could, wreaking havoc with repeated revolutions of his weapon until she submitted while she still had half a face left. It wouldn't be without its romantic climax as the lad finally released the girl to ask, "Did ye like that?"

Like my contemporaries, I too had been a practitioner of the 'Attack of the Lizard' and my victims are probably lying down on a couch somewhere today, telling the sordid tale.

But this was different. This was the much sought-after duo of girls and drink. I was still unacquainted with the latter half of that duo, having only ever drunk the dregs of Da's cans on the sly. Properly introducing myself to alcohol, and doing so in the company of girls, was something to eagerly anticipate.

I knocked on the door.

God, I hope that auld one isn't here.

There was a short, tantalising wait before the door creaked open.

"Ah, how are ye, Paddy?" Laura greeted.

"Awright, Laura. How's things?"

"All good. Come on in. The girls are inside."

"Who's here?"

"Just meself, Rachael, and Sandra."

"Sandra. Sandra who?"

"Sandra Lynch."

Oh fuck, what's she doing here?! She's bad enough sober. What's she like with drink on her?

You'll be grand, relax!

I was guided into the sitting room where the other two girls were already enjoying themselves, if the sight of drink and the smell of hash was anything to go by.

"Hi, Paddy," they both greeted.

Lynch looked like she was already on the back nine of her session. She dragged her half-gargled body off the sofa and embraced me with a hug that I thought would snap my spine. I was ready to tap out before she released me from her bear-like grasp.

"Did ye bring any drink with ye?" Laura asked.

Was I meant to?

Good man, Paddy. Great start! Make yourself look like a cheapskate. That'll earn ye brownie points.

"No, I couldn't get me hands on…"

"You're grand, there's plenty here," Rachael said.

The girls had bottles of lager aplenty. I didn't wait to crack one open.

"We were just talking about what we're gonna do after school," Racheal added.

Jesus Christ, a busman's holiday!

"What about you, Paddy?" she asked. "What are ye thinking o' doing?"

I'm thinking o' how to best bullshit me way around this question.

"What am *I* gonna do?"

"Yeah."

No messing around now. Think o' something impressive. No hesitation.

"I want…"

Don't say something stupid like an astronaut.

"… to be…"

Or an archaeologist.

"… a door-to-door salesman."

A what?

It popped into me head.

Ye need a fuckin' bullet popped into your head. Even an archaeologist was a better option!

"Ye mean one o' those annoying eejits that call to your door selling shite?" Lynch asked.

"Yeah… kind o'…"

The three girls giggled. Lynch exhaled the hash from her fat lungs.

"What would ye sell?" she asked, laughing.

Meself, to randy auld ones! Ten quid an hour, half-price on Wednesdays, free trial session! There's a career plan for ye, Fahey!

"What I meant was, I'll be setting up me own business. I'll start with door-to-door sales, just to get the name out there before I can invest properly in advertising once I have a substantial flow of revenue."

Where did ye find that little gem? That'll be hanging proudly in the museum o' bullshit one day. We're back in the race!

"Oh, very good. What course will ye take for it?" asked Rachael.

Now, nice and easy, think business, think money, think Richy.

"I wanna do a business degree in UCD."

Bingo!

"Would that be your thing?" asked Lynch, looking somewhat puzzled.

What's that supposed to mean? Is she having a dig?

"Well, making money is me thing, so… yes."

Ha ha. You're on a roll. You hit that one out o' the ballpark!

Having survived the initial onslaught of conversation, my nerves eased courtesy of another few bottles and a few drags of a joint that was being passed around, all availing of its mood-altering properties bar Rachael. My virgin lungs repelled my first drag with an abrupt cough.

"First time, Paddy?" Lynch enquired.

"No, it's just heavier than me usual stuff."

As I rose high into Happy Paddy Land, I slouched back in the sofa, as the girls chatted amongst themselves. Listening to them talk was an education. They discussed relationship problems, as if to do so was a cathartic experience. Their 'feelings' lay at the root of every conversation. They had their own vernacular. This was conversing in a way I'd never heard. I tried to follow the thread of the conversation, but it was like they were speaking in code.

"How's things going with James?" Rachael asked Laura.

"Well, not great at the moment. We had a big argument the other day."

"Aw, what happened, hun?"

"Well, we were supposed to be meeting to go to the cinema on Monday. I was looking forward to it. Then that afternoon, he asked me if I minded if he went to play football with the lads instead. So, I said go ahead."

"So, what did he do?" Rachael asked.

"Oh, you won't believe it! He actually went to the football!"

"Ah, you're joking?"

"Nope, I was fuming!"

Hang on, didn't she tell him to go ahead?

"He called over to the house the next day. Not a bother on him. He asked me how I was. I said I was okay. Then he started telling me some stupid joke he'd heard from the lads. He sat there laughing his head off at it. I wasn't laughing at all. So, he asked me if I was sure I was okay. I told him I was fine."

This lad sounds like a decent skin.

"So, then he says, 'You're very quiet today.' I said, 'I'm just tired.'"

"Did he apologise then?" Lynch asked.

Apologise for what?

"Nope."

"Unbelievable!"

What's unbelievable?

"Then he asked me if I wanted to go to the cinema next week. I just said, 'Whatever.'"

Is that a yes?

"So, then he asked me if that was a yes or a no."

Good question.

"So, I asked him, 'Well what do *you* think it is, James?'"

He doesn't know does he, hence the question.

"He said, 'Well, I think we should go, seeing as we didn't go yesterday.'"

Good idea. This fella has his wits about him.

"I said, 'Can ye go back in time? No? Then, ye can't make up for what happened yesterday?' Then he goes, 'What happened yesterday?'"

Another good question.

"So, I asked him, 'Well, what do *you* think happened?'"

He doesn't fuckin' know! That's why he's asking! This lad must have the patience of a saint!

"He goes, 'Eh, I don't know.'"

Ah, I see good old Eh is back. He gets around a good bit. Busy man.

"Oh my God, that was his answer?" Rachael asked, seemingly perplexed.

"Yep, I couldn't believe it. Me blood was boiling!"

Wait a second. I don't know either. What answer did she want?

"I said to him, 'James, if you can't figure out the problem, then we have an even bigger problem.'"

What? Now there's two problems? Where did the second problem come from? What's the first problem?

"Then he asked me if it had something to do with the football."

What could it have to do with the football?

"Oh my God, finally the penny drops!" said Lynch.

What Penny? Where's it dropping?

"So, I asked him if *he* thought it had anything to do with the football."

Aw, not this shite again! We've already been through this.

"And he goes, 'Well, I think it might be related to it, maybe…'"

How's it in any way related?

"I shouted at him, 'O' course it's to do with the bloody football!'"

The football? What's that got to do with it? Am I the only person not keeping up with the plot here?

"'Do I have to spell it out?!' I said."

Hmmm, it seems so. Or ye could just speak in plain English, woman!

"Then he started complaining, 'Oh, you said I could go blah, blah, blah.'"

That you did.

"I said, 'Yeah, I told ye you could go, but I didn't want ye to go!'"

What?

"Then he looked at me with a stupid head on him, and he goes, 'What? Is that a riddle?'"

No, mate. A riddle ye'd have some chance o' fuckin' solving!

"I lost it with him when he said that. I said, 'Listen, if ye don't understand me and ye don't understand me feelings, then maybe we shouldn't be together.' Then he goes, 'Eh...uh...eh... right.'"

Eh always pops up at the worst times. He's like the bearer o' bad news. And who's uh? Is that eh's brother?

"Then he said, 'I like ye, Laura. I want to be with ye. You're deadly. I mean, I'd apologise to ye if I knew what I was apologising for.'"

The other two girls looked at her in disbelief.

"I just shouted at him to get out o' the house. He walked out in a sulk. He texted me today. He wants to meet to have a chat."

He probably wants to have a chat about having ye committed.

"Well, that's something anyway," Rachael cheerfully remarked.

Yes, that would be something. A padded cell. Nice and cosy.

"What do ye think of him, Paddy?" Laura asked me.

How'd ye get dragged into this?

I don't know. I've been sitting here quietly, making sure I wasn't dragged into it.

Well, you're in it now, mate. You're knee deep in it. Take the girls' side. Don't screw up your chances with herself by defending some eejit.

I agree with him though. I don't wanna throw him under the bus.

Are ye mad? Ye don't even know him. Fuck him under the bus and don't think twice about the bollocks!

I suppose...

There's no supposing. And don't invite Eh or Uh into the conversation either. Pair o' scoundrels those two!

"Ah, he's acting the eejit, Laura. He should apologise."

"Thanks, Paddy. At least some lads understand."

Ten out o' ten, me boy. Ye just need to listen to me more often.

Later on, Lynch and Rachael retreated into another room, leaving me alone with Laura. She opened another couple of bottles and nestled beside me on the sofa.

"There's another bottle for ye, Paddy... You've been very quiet. I suppose ye can hardly get a word in with us. We love a good auld chat... I've been waiting to get the chance to speak to ye on me own all night."

"Really?"

"Yeah. You're not seeing anybody, are ye?"

"No, why?"

"Well, let's just say one of us here tonight really likes ye and... I shouldn't be saying this, she'll kill me!"

Say it, say it, say it.

"Who'll kill ye?"

"Don't play innocent. Ye know who, Paddy. Are ye interested in her?"

"Yeah, o' course I am. That's why I came."

"She's been looking at ye all night. She's afraid to make the first move in case ye turn her down."

"I won't."

"That's what I said to her. Will *you* make the first move?"

"Yeah, okay."

"But don't tell her I said anything to ye!"

"Yeah, yeah, no problem."

"I'll get her to come in and leave yis alone."

When she left the room, my intoxication heightened my anticipation.

Right, this is it. Any second now.

A minute or so later, the door opened, only for Lynch to walk into the room.

Aw, fuck off, Lynch! So much for being left alone! Laura, where are ye? Get this gobshite out o' here! She'll fuck everything up with Rachael!

She came over to the sofa and sat uncomfortably close to me.

"Laura said ye wanted to talk to me, hun?"

What?! Oh fuck! She thinks… Laura thinks…

"Eh…"

Not Eh, he's barred!

"Yeah, I wanted to talk about…"

Quantum physics, horoscopes, the Russian revolution

"… about…"

Greek mythology, South American politics, algebra, the Dutch Royal Family

"About what, Paddy?"

Endangered species, climate change, gynaecology, arachnophobia, will ye pick one o' them for the love o' God!

"… about…"

"Listen, it's okay. I saw the way ye were looking at me."

In revulsion?

She placed her hand on my thigh.

"I know ye want me."

Like an incurable dose of diarrhoea.

I felt movement in the nether regions of my anatomy.

Oh no! Not now! Control that fella down there, will ye! If she sees that, you're done for!

I can't.

Don't be so weak, man! O' course ye can!

Here, what in the name o' God do ye think you're doing poking your little head out?! Get your head back in your house, ye little shite!

Resist the urge, resist, resist. Think o' the consequences!

She began to slide her hand towards my mischievous friend, who despite my desperate efforts to control him, continued to disobey me.

What are ye playing at down there? I'll be scarred for life.

You'll be the ruin o' me, ye little pink-headed bollocks!

Just as Little Paddy had proven himself to be too strong an opponent for my resolve, and as I cherished the last moments of the life I knew, the most unlikely of saviours came to my rescue.

The front door opened before I heard a woman say, "Laura, I'm home!"

"Aw, shite! Laura's ma is back," Lynch whispered. "Quick, hide the bottles."

As we frantically hid the evidence of our night's drinking under the pillows, Laura's mother entered the sitting room and stood unsteadily before us.

"Hi, Sandra," she said labouredly, before collapsing into a seat, exhaling in exhaustion. She was a right sight. She had somehow squeezed herself into a red dress which showed off every roll of fat and was short enough to allow me to spot that her knickers were a matching colour. Accentuating such 'elegance' was a coat of makeup so thick that it had probably acted as insulation to keep her face warm while she had waited for her taxi. From her glassy eyes, ran her mascara, offering an indication of how her night had gone.

"Hi, Mary… You're back early."

"Who's…your friend, Sandra?"

"This is Paddy."

"Hiya, Paddy… Oh, San, he's a cute little thing… I'll rob him on ye… I love…younger men."

"How was your night, Mary?"

"Men are…bastards…pricks…selfish…arseholes!"

A good night then.

"Aw, what happened?"

"That, that…bastard!"

Yeah, we got that bit.

She covered her mouth, swallowing hard, before informing us of the night's drama.

"I bumped into Anthony, me ex… He was parading round the pub with some…slag! A young one! He came over to me with her to show her off… I told the pair o' them to fuck off! So, we started…arguing… He called me all sorts o' names… I slapped him. Then *she* slapped *me*… We were kicked out… The bouncer was a…"

"Aw, a real prick, was he?"

"No…he was a fuckin' ride! Dark lad. I gave him… me number."

Laura and Rachael re-entered the room.

"Ah, Ma! The state o' ye!"

"Ye wanna see…the state o' your father's…new girlfriend, Laura. His fuckin' mid-life crisis…that's what she is!"

"Ma, I'll take ye up to bed, come on."

"Paddy's coming…with me. Come to bed, Paddy… I'll make a fuckin' man out o' ye!"

"Paddy has to go home, Ma."

"Not before I…ride him!"

"Ma, will ye shut up! You're making a show o' yourself!"

"If he gets a young one…I want a youngfella!"

"Bed, Ma. Come on, I'll help ye up. Paddy, we'll have to get her to bed. Listen, thanks for coming over, awright. Girls, give us a hand, will yis?"

As they helped the mother up the stairs, I left the house and headed back to Dargan Street. Along the way, amidst the tranquillity of the night, I made a defining discovery. I liked drinking. I enjoyed being drunk, even more so than the heights that a carefully rolled joint took me to. It rid me of inhibitions, heightened my confidence, made me more appreciative of who I was or who I wished I was. The rest of the world no longer mattered. It was a glorious self-indulgence. I knew I'd want to feel the sensation again and again thereafter. A relationship had been formed, and I wouldn't wait long before dropping to one knee and asking my new companion for its hand in marriage.

Chapter 7
The Burgeoning Romantic

By Monday afternoon, I still hadn't heard any talk of the incident with Lynch. I was careful to avoid her until she found her next victim. Meanwhile, after much procrastination, I decided to make a proposition to Rachael Dowling, feeling something akin to courage trying its best to imbue me.

What's that?

Courage.

Courage? I'd have thought courage would feel a bit more...

Encouraging?

Yeah.

Nah, that's as good as it gets. You're on your own.

"Rachael, I've to ask ye something."

"About Sandra?"

"No, not her. She's not the reason I went to Laura's house on Friday."

"I thought ye fancied her. That's why I asked ye to come over."

"No, I don't! What made ye think that?"

"She told me ye kept staring at her."

Staring at her! The girl's so big, no matter which way ye look you're staring at her!

"What?! When? Anyway, it doesn't matter... I only went because... I like ye... ye know."

"I know?"

"Yeah… ye know."

"What do I know?"

"Come on… I know ye know."

"I don't know if I know what ye think I know."

"I know ye know enough to know what I think ye know."

"If I knew enough to know, what you say ye think I know, why would I say I don't know?"

Scintillating conversation.

"Well, because… maybe… you're playing hard to get… ye know?"

'Ye know' must be the halfwit cousin of the Eh and Uh brothers.

"Hard to get? Ye reckon?" she said, smiling.

"Well?"

"Well what?"

Oh God, not another round!

"Are ye?"

"How could I be? Ye haven't asked me anything yet."

Jesus, Mary and Joseph, will ye ask the poor girl before she dies of old age!

"Oh right… Would ye fancy doing something with me?"

Bloody hell, ye left that open to interpretation. The last girl to hear that line was a whore!

"Sandra wouldn't be too pleased."

"Don't mind her. I mean, yis aren't close mates, are yis?"

"Well, not really."

"Well then, what's the problem? So?"

"Yeah, I would."

Ah, you scored the winner in the last minute! A cracker!

"What would ye like to do?"

"Well, as it happens, me ma and da are heading out this Friday for me da's birthday. They won't be back till late. And me sisters will be staying over with one o' their mates, so I'll have a free house. Ye could come over. We could watch telly, listen to some music, have a few drinks."

"Yeah, great."

"Will you sort out the drink?"

"Yeah, will do."

"I'll look forward to it."

"Me too."

I now had the ominous task of getting my hands on drink, but I knew exactly who to turn to.

"What do ye want and when do ye need it?" Mick asked me.

"Not a lot, just a few cans o' lager. Nothing major. Eight's enough, four each. I won't be there too long. I need them by Friday."

"What brand?"

"Whichever's cheapest."

"Ye don't wanna go too cheap now. She mightn't be too impressed if ye arrive up with eight cans o' rat piss."

"Well, I'll leave it up to you then, you know best."

"What do ye mean by that?"

He shot me a look of irritation.

"Nothing, I mean, whatever ye think."

Mick Dolan had acquired a reputation in recent times as a lad who could get things for you. Whether it was drink, smokes, hash, a fake ID, or a counterfeit football jersey, you name it, and he somehow got it. His estate was the arsehole of the Celtic Tiger. All it saw of the booming economy was an increase in its local drug trade. With cocaine becoming the fashionable drug of Celtic Tiger Ireland, purchasing it was a sign of prosperity. One line snorted up the nose was one rung climbed up the social ladder. The local dealer was now the most successful entrepreneur in the area, his profits making a laughingstock of his law-abiding neighbours. In contrast, the estate was now being ravaged by junkies and by the crime that financed their addictions. Its respectable residents could only watch apathetically when the Gardaí made arrests, knowing the vacancy left would be filled before dinnertime. In such an environment it was a doddle for Mick to build up a network of contacts who he could call upon when required. Mick was very protective of his sources. Most of them were either in prison, just out of prison or soon to be in prison. It was all very clandestine. At seventeen, I was still too young to be served, so Mick became my 'go to' man.

"I'll mix and match. A few o' this, a few o' that. How's that sound?"

"Yeah, grand. How much?"

"Call it a tenner."

I handed him the money, curious as to whose hands it would end up in.

"Do ye want anything else? Smokes, hash?"

There was impatience in his voice.

"The cans'll do, Mick. I don't think she's the smoking type."

"Right, meet me here at seven on Friday. I better go, the lads over there are waiting for me."

"Sound, see you then."

As I watched him walk away towards his new-found comrades, a far cry from the St Brendan's gang, I thought of how he had changed since he left school. His once admirable traits seemed to have succumbed to a gruff persona, one that undoubtedly was a prerequisite when associating with the who's who of future offenders. I'd heard one of the lads mention something about him, but none of us ever bothered to spare him a thought. Whatever concern we had for him was far outweighed by our need for his cardinal services.

As I walked through the last of his estate's shabby streets, I felt like the place was dragging him down with it. He seemed to now blend in seamlessly with the boarded-up houses, graffitied walls, littered gardens, and with the women traipsing around in their pyjamas. He was as much a part of the scenery as he was a product of it. As I left the estate, it occurred to me that I'd never asked him how he was faring in his apprenticeship. The honest reason was that I didn't care. I'd stopped viewing Mick as a friend. He was a necessary acquaintance now. Our meeting was a transaction. Nothing more.

I arrived at Rachael Dowling's door armed with my bag of cans.

Get stuck into these straight away, settle the nerves.

I rang the bell and waited. With no answer, I was about to ring again when I heard her coming down the stairs.

Finally, the door opened.

"Hi, Paddy. Come on in," she said. "Go into the sitting room. Make yourself comfortable. I'll be into ye in a second. I'm just getting a glass."

While she was in in the kitchen, I opened my first can and guzzled it like I'd just discovered the cure for thirst. When she came into the sitting room, she sat down beside me, poured herself a glass of lager, and sipped it slowly. We watched television and chatted as I drank as quickly as I could, searching for the chap I remembered so fondly from my previous alcoholic soirée. I was soon laying into my second can, wanting each mouthful to land a jab on the face of my inhibitions. By my third can, I could feel myself becoming more relaxed and confident. I was awakening from my sober coma. She chatted away as I feigned interest in the conversation, my attention being given to the comedy being shown on the television, which my buzz was making funnier.

"So, what do ye think?" I heard her ask me.

"What do I think?"

What the fuck is she on about?

"Well, should I get them done or not? It costs a fortune. I'd have to save up. Maybe get them done in a couple o' years' time when I've more money. I hate the way I look now."

Bluff.

"Would it be worth it?"

Safe question.

"Well, I'd be more confident in me appearance. I'd feel more attractive. I'd be happier, so yeah, I think it'd be worth it. I've been thinking about getting them done for a while now. You're the first person I've said it to."

Fuckin' hell, she's talking about getting a boob job!

Well don't sit there with that gormless head on ye. Offer her some support.

"Well, if it makes ye happier, I'd say go for it."

"Yeah, you're right."

"You'll be getting a lot more attention from lads."

"Ye reckon? I'm doing it for meself though, not for that."

"Ah yeah, that's fair enough. You'll look great… I mean ye look great now, but you'll look even…"

"I know what ye mean, Paddy. You're very sweet."

What's that sound?

It's the sound o' me rubbing me hands together. Ha ha. Ye play your cards right here, buddy, and in a couple o' years' time you'll be surveying the landscape of her gargantuan bosom!

"You'll look different, awright."

"Ye mightn't recognise me."

Oh, I'll recognise ye, like a vulture spotting his prey!

"Ah, Rachael, ye'd look great with big ones."

"Big ones?"

"They'll be bouncing up and down when you're walking down the road."

"What'll be bouncing, Paddy? What are ye on about?"

"Your boob job."

"Me what?!"

"Your boob job. What you've been talking about."

"What *I've* been talking about? Paddy, I was talking about getting laser eye surgery, so I wouldn't have to wear me stupid glasses anymore!"

Oh… We're after driving off a bridge! Boob job? Gobshite!

What's the plan now?

"Oh, I see… I thought… ye meant…"

"A boob job, Paddy?"

"Me mind just ran away there a little bit. When I let it off its leash, it goes where it wants."

"Yeah, it did Paddy."

"I mean, like, ye don't need one… I did say ye look great as ye are…"

Oh God, we're in damage limitation territory now.

She looked unimpressed. I knew of only one way to salvage the situation.

Go all in. Black or red, place your bet now.

"I love the way ye look. I fancy the arse off ye."

"Aw, Paddy."

The sternness softened on her face.

Keep going, we're not dead yet.

"I always have. I love your boobs too… You've a deadly pair. I think about them… you… all the time."

"Paddy Dempsey, when did you become such a romantic?"

Since that boob job howler. I took a crash course in chivalry!

I held her hand and leaned in closer.

"I'd love to be more than just friends," I said.

"Me too."

We kissed. I tailored my technique to suit the occasion, favouring a subtler approach than the 'Attack of the Lizard.' My new technique, the 'Titillating Tongue,' was debuted. After the kiss, we gazed into each other's eyes. As she basked in the romantic ambience, I desperately tried to think of something to say.

"Jesus, fierce weather this week."

"What?"

"The weather, it's been atrocious."

"Paddy, will ye shut up and don't be ruining the moment."

"Oh right, sorry."

She leaned into me. We cuddled, watched television, and drank.

"So, am I your fella now?"

"I suppose I'll have to put up with ye," she joked.

And with that, I was in my first relationship. She was now my other half, the person in whom I'd share my life with.

Where do we go from here?

How often will she wanna see me? Am I in over me head?

Am I ready for this?

Did I think this through?

Why am I having doubts already?

By eleven o'clock, conscious of her parents' imminent return, we said our goodnights at the doorstep, reluctantly parting company. My alcoholic high ensured that any doubts were deported from my mind, at least temporarily. All I could see was the procession of jubilance ahead.

I returned home and lay on my bed. Drowsy from the drink, my thoughts couldn't keep me awake for long. I was awoken the next morning by the sound of a text message.

"Morning hun, heading out shopping with Ma, chat later, love you xxx."

Love you? Where did that come from? How did we make that jump? Did I miss something while I was asleep?

Sobriety embraced the doubts that had been spurned the night before.

Love you?

One half of me liked it, the other half of me hated it.

Fuck. What have I done?

Chapter 8
The Last Meal Before Execution

As I tried to decide which one of my feet to leave in the relationship, and which to leave out, the next blight-ridden crop sprouted alarmingly from the ground.

"Me ma and da would like to have ye over for dinner," Rachael said to me.

Hold your horses! One minute you're dining with the family, the next minute you're married into the family!

"Why?"

"What do ye mean 'why'? To get to know ye, why else?"

To hang, draw and quarter me and leave me remains outside the town hall for all to see!

"Do they know about us?"

"Yeah, o' course. I told them."

"Oh."

"Oh what?"

"Nothing, just… Oh, that's nice."

"They're dying to meet ye. I've been talking about ye and…"

"You've been talking about me? What have ye been saying?"

"Nothing bad! I've mentioned ye, Paddy this, Paddy that, but they still don't know ye from Adam."

Auld Adam, now there's a fella I envy. Nobody bothered him with dinner invitations.

"It'd be like a job interview or something."

"Don't be daft! They just wanna talk."

Yeah, right. They want to interrogate me!

"It sounds a bit…"

"A bit what, Paddy?"

"A bit…too much, too soon."

"A bloody dinner?!"

"Is that not a big thing?"

She rolled her eyes. "No, it's not a big thing, Paddy. It's not any kind o' thing. You're making it into a thing… You're impossible, I swear!"

"I don't think I'm ready for that, Rach."

"What's the problem? Me ma and da are sound."

Sound? Like the sound of a drill boring through your brain.

"Come on, Paddy. I've been putting this off 'cause I know what you're like."

"What's that supposed to mean?"

"Nothing, just, I know ye don't like these sorts o' things, that's all. It'd mean a lot to me."

She held my hand, a manipulative tactical switch that she knew would be my undoing.

"I don't know… How long would I have to stay?"

"Couple o' hours, I suppose."

"Could I bring Popey with me? For moral support?"

"God, no! I'm not having that eejit in me house!"

"Will there be any drinks?"

"No, me parents wouldn't allow that."

"So, I've to march into battle unarmed?"

"March into… Paddy, what image do ye have in your head o' me family?"

One that's probably nowhere near as bad as the actual reality.

"I'm sure they're a lovely bunch."

"Well?"

"Oh awright, I suppose I could. I won't be any use though. I'll be like a fish out o' water."

Don't worry, there'll be great white sharks circling to drag ye back in!

"You'll be grand, hun. It'll be great."

You'll be destroyed. It'll be the death o' ye.

"When?"

"I'll ask me ma. I'll text ye later."

Suddenly the idea of us breaking up before the dreaded date had a certain appeal.

We were sitting at the kitchen table, eating a roast pork dinner. Six of us. Rachael, her parents, her two sisters and myself. The conversation was sporadic. Short spurts of chatter were followed by the sound of the ticking clock on the wall. The chatter provided a welcome respite from the daunting silence and vice versa. With each break in the conversation, I readied myself like a boxer awaiting the next round.

The kitchen was spotless. The family photos hung on the walls, creating the image of the perfect family life. The father's weight and hairline were documented in the photos, showing off his younger days before recession and inflation formed a poisonous marriage, giving way to the bald, fat middle-aged man sitting at the end of the table.

"I told ye we should've bought the bigger one, Brenda," he observed.

"What's the matter with ye, Ray?"

"The roast… I told ye we should've bought the bigger one. There's hardly enough to go around."

"A smaller portion won't do ye any harm, Ray. You're not getting any thinner."

Tick tock, tick tock, tick tock, tick tock.

"Patrick, Rachael tells me that ye wanna do a business degree in UCD," the mother said.

What?

I'd been spewing so much waffle regarding the heights of my entrepreneurial ambitions that I'd forgotten half of it.

I'm stepping in me own bullshit here. I must start keeping account of it.

The table talk had been unremarkable up to this point. The last thing I wanted was for this topic of conversation to be brought up, for I feared it would be my undoing. The mother, however, seemed eager to find out what my career plan was. The father was more captivated by his roast potatoes.

"Oh yeah, that's right," I said.

"Are ye confident you'll get the points?"

"Not if he eats your roast potatoes, Brenda. He won't live long enough to sit the bloody exam!"

"I am, but I'll have to put in the work."

"Like *I* have to with this poxy roast potato!"

The mother shot the father an angry look.

"How many points would ye need for it, about four hundred?"

Trick question?

"Yeah, about that, about four hundred."

"Brenda, ye must've roasted these potatoes at four hundred!"

"It'd be well worth your effort though, Patrick."

"I hope your spuds are worth the effort, Brenda."

"Ray, please, if ye wouldn't mind… And Rachael was saying ye'd want to start your own business?"

"Yeah."

"Doing what, Patrick?"

Being a bullshitter for hire. Mother o' Christ! She could've warned me her auld one would cross examine me. I could've prepared better material.

"Selling… selling stuff… electrical goods…"

"It might be hard to get that off the ground. Have ye a backup plan?"

"I… I… well…"

"It couldn't be any harder than this roast potato, Brenda. Ye could kill a man with this thing."

"God Almighty, Ray! Will ye stop going on about that shaggin' roast potato!" she barked.

Silence. She rediscovered her composure as quickly as she'd lost it.

Tick tock, tick tock, tick tock, tick tock.

"Sorry, excuse me, Patrick. Where were we?"

I was experiencing my first taste of Rachael's mother and I had an educated enough palate to know I was tasting something rotten.

"Jesus Christ, Brenda, will ye stop grilling the lad! He only popped over for a bit o' grub, not to meet the Irish branch o' the Spanish Inquisition!"

"Well, excuse me for taking an interest in the young man, which is more than can be said for you, Ray!"

"The lad doesn't wanna be talking shop. Amn't I right, Patrick?"

Don't answer!

"Well, ye know… I, em… Is there any more gravy?"

"Hop up there, Hazel, and get Patrick some gravy," the father instructed.

"There's none left, Da."

"Ah, ye didn't make enough, Brenda."

"I made plenty, Ray. If ye hadn't turned your plate into a swimming pool, there'd be more for others!"

Tick tock, tick tock, tick tock, tick tock.

"Paddy plays guitar, Ma," said Rachael, attempting to both ease the tension and change the subject.

"Do ye, Patrick? I had a hunch ye were creative. It must be hard to find the time for it with all your study?"

She spoke with a look of suspicion which she made no effort to hide.

"Well, I can strum a few chords."

"Sure, that's all most o' them can do, Patrick," her father said. "The music industry's full o' chancers. It's tailormade for ye. Ha ha."

"Da!"

"I'm only pulling his leg, Rachael. He knows I am, don't ye, Patrick?"

"Eh… yeah," I replied, half-smiling.

"So, what brought me daughter to your attention, Patrick?" he asked.

"Ray, what sort o' question is that?"

"I forgot me book one day and sat beside her. We started to get to know each other from there."

"Ah, so your negligence is to blame, is it? Ha ha."

"I suppose, yeah," I agreed, laughing awkwardly with him.

"Ray, enough o' your jokes."

Somewhere amidst the conversation the mother and the father had seamlessly switched roles. Or perhaps his intolerance to me was catching up with his wife's.

Tick tock, tick tock, tick tock, tick tock.

I began to wonder whether my dinner invitation was an offer given to Rachael or an instruction; a means by which they could inspect me and decide if I met the requirements that they probably had for any of their daughters' boyfriends.

The tension hastened my eating, her father taking note.

"You're finished you're grub already, Patrick! Jesus, ye were like a savage the way ye wolfed that down. I hope you're not like that with me daughter! Ha ha."

"Da, will ye stop! Ma, tell him!"

"Ray, you're embarrassing her!"

"I'm only codding, love."

Tick tock, tick tock, tick tock, tick tock.

"Do ye work, Patrick?" the mother asked.

"I've a paper round. The money's not much."

"Ah, so you're good for a free newspaper at least," the father replied in a half-joking tone.

Yeah, I've plenty for ye to wipe your fat arse with!

"He's looking for other work too, aren't ye, Paddy?"

"Yeah, yeah. Keeping me eyes peeled."

"If I hear of anything, I'll pass it on, Patrick," said the mother, "provided I'm hearing good reports from Rachael, that is."

Her words were accompanied by something masquerading as a smile, an expression as transparent as the glass of water she sipped.

I was like a tennis ball being volleyed up and down the court as each of them tried to outscore the other. Her mother didn't speak to me, she addressed me. She had an ulterior motive for her every question. Her father said everything she dared not say, disguising his words behind a veil of laughter. If they felt that they already had me sussed out, the feeling was mutual.

By eight o'clock, I felt my required shift had been completed and glanced at Rachael and down at my imaginary watch.

"Paddy needs to head off now," she informed them.

"Okay, Patrick. Well, thanks for coming over," the mother said, without leaving her seat.

"Nice to meet ye, Patrick," said the father, as he stared at the cigarette he was rolling.

I said goodbye to her two sisters who hardly said a word all night, before Rachael walked me out.

Stepping out into the cold air was a relief.

"That wasn't too bad, was it? I told ye they're sound."

Is she for real?

"Yeah, they are… What do ye think they made o' me?"

There was a slight delay in her reply.

"I think they liked ye. I told ye they would… Come 'ere to me," she said, as she leaned in to kiss me.

I wanted to tell her what I thought of her parents, and to excoriate her for having subjected me to them, but I found restraint.

Don't prove them right!

"Goodnight, Paddy."

"Goodnight. Talk to ye tomorrow."

I drifted home from Upper Dargle Road, my body sauntering as my mind raced at breakneck pace.

Never fuckin' again!

Chapter 9
The Crusade Against Virginity

By the end of 2005, my expectation of our relationship's duration had been surpassed, despite my commitment to the cause being questionable at times. It was harder work than I'd contemplated. From the outset, I hadn't accounted for the needs of the female in her teenage years. The endless messaging, the mundane conversations and her sometimes suffocating presence, gave rise to a sense of tedium that I tried my best to subdue. Nothing, it seemed, came without a cost. An 'Attack of the Lizard' kiss would require me to compliment her appearance. A fondle could only be acquired after spending an hour listening to that day's all-important issue, and a well-earned disappearing act would be met with unmerciful repercussions.

"Where were ye yesterday, Paddy?"

"I was…"

"Mitching?"

"Ah, don't start that, Rachael."

"Start what?"

"Grand for you, ye love this kip. Doesn't mean we all have to."

"Our Leaving Cert is just around the corner, or have ye forgotten?"

"How could I forget?! Ye go on about it every five fuckin' minutes!"

"I rang ye three times."

"I missed the calls. I hadn't any credit to ring ye back."

"Ye never have credit when it suits ye."

"Well, I'd no money to get any 'cause I had to spend what I had on that poxy concert ticket for your birthday!"

"Oh, I'm so sorry it was me birthday, Paddy. I should've done ye a favour and not reminded ye about it!"

"Ye didn't have to remind me about it! I…"

"I did so! And if ye don't wanna go to the concert with me, well then fine, ye don't have to! Me ma would love to go."

"Good, I'm delighted. Go with *her*. Yis are well matched!"

"And what does that mean?"

"You're beginning to sound like her!"

In my youthful naivety, I dropped the atomic bomb of insults. The 'You Sound Like Your Mother' line. I unleashed it without fully appreciating its power to offend, without realising the magnitude of its impact or the consequences of it. Its blast wave tore through Little Bray, uprooting every tree, demolishing every house and reducing everything in its path to ash. A whole civilisation was wiped from the face of the earth in one sentence. I watched its mushroom cloud rise above the town as I reviewed the sagacity of my words.

She stormed off.

After the argument, we left each other alone for a few days which allowed me to rediscover a life that was awaiting my return with open arms, ready to forgive me for abandoning it, delighted to pick up from where we had left off. During this hiatus, I began to reassess my suitability to be a girl's 'fella' and questioned the legitimacy of our compatibility, which I'd previously thought of as being beyond doubt.

Maybe it's not for me?

Maybe she's the problem?

Maybe I'm too harsh on meself?

After much consideration, I felt I knew what the problem was. We had been seeing each other for a few months but still hadn't consummated our bond. We hadn't loved each other physically and it had made the relationship stagnate. I had the solution. I rang her without further hesitation.

"Hello."

"It's me, Rach."

"What do ye want?"

"I wanted to talk."

"Ye took your time."

"I wanted to give ye some space."

"Is that so?"

"Listen, I've been thinking… and I know what's wrong."

"Do ye now?"

"Yeah… We haven't taken the next step, and because o' that, we've gotten stuck between a rock and a hard place."

"And what's your next step?"

"Sex."

"What?!"

"I think the line is bad, Rachael. Can ye hear me?"

"Oh, loud and clear, Paddy!"

"I was just saying, I think we should…"

"You are unbelievable, Paddy Dempsey! Ye don't bother talking to me, ye disappear for days, then ye ring me out o' the blue 'cause ye want a lash!"

"No, hold on, Rachael. I didn't mean it like that!"

"You're a fuckin' selfish prick!"

She hung up.

Hmmm, maybe it's her hormones.

I gave her ten minutes and rang again.

"What?"

"Listen, just hear me out for a minute, will ye? Forget about sex. What I mean is, what I'm trying to say is… Sex is just a metaphor for what I mean."

Sex is a metaphor. Brilliant. McMahon would be proud o' ye!

"What are ye shitting on about now, Paddy?"

"I mean, we've hit a pothole and we've to get ourselves out of it. Sex is just a metaphor for the solution."

What?

"I think we're lacking intimacy, Rach. We should have an auld chat, about everything. Put everything on the table. Lay ourselves bare. Open up to each other. It'll have the intimacy of sex, without the physical bit. We'll get the same results without actually having to – ye know… do it, and before ye know it, we'll be sucking diesel."

Ha ha! I like it. No, I don't like it, I love it! You're a genius!

"Okay, Paddy. I'll talk to ye at big-break tomorrow."

We were sitting at the foot of the school's back wall, the unofficial smoking and smooching area.

"You start," I suggested.

"Okay. Well sometimes, Paddy, when I don't hear from ye, I think you're giving me two fingers. I think that ye forget I'm your girlfriend. I think ye forget that what I give you, I need in return. I think that ye don't realise that kissing and drinking and all that only makes up a small part of it. There's more to it than that. I want to talk to ye, share stuff with ye."

"Okay, well, that's awright. I want to do all that stuff too. It's just I'm not as good at all that shite as you are. I need a bit more practice at it."

"So, what do we do then?"

"How about I'll make a big effort to do all those things, if you give me more time to practise?"

"Fair enough."

"Are we okay then?"

"Yeah, o' course we are. Give us a hug."

That was easy. I should work on a suicide hotline.

You'll either save them or push them over the edge.

Now that I was on good terms with her again, my thoughts turned back to a matter that I was eager to discuss with her.

With Paul Murphy and Seán Walsh bragging about their sexual exploits by this point, I was getting antsy for a bit of action myself. Even Popey was having his carnal needs attended to. I'd assumed that having sex was a concomitant of having a girlfriend; that the former was the one perk that made all the drawbacks of the latter tolerable. But apparently not. The female was a slightly more complex creature than what I had first thought. She was making me wait. She wasn't ready. The Virgin Mary was a hussy when compared to Rachael Dowling. I opted to try to slip it into a conversation.

"Did ye hear about Popey, Rach?"

"No."

"Him and your one he's seeing, the fat one, Sharon, were at it the other night and her ma arrived home."

"Oh really?"

"Yeah, she went upstairs to hear what the noise was. Popey threw himself under the bed. He could hardly fit his fat arse under it."

"What happened?"

"The ma burst in the door and Popey's mot was lying in bed, sweating. She told her ma she had a fever and wanted an early night. So, her ma asked her what all the noise was. She said it was a dirty scene in the film she was watching. Ha ha."

"And she believed it?"

"Yeah, yeah. Then the ma sees his clothes on the ground. The mot says they're her da's clothes and that the dog had dragged them into her room. Then the ma starts rambling on forever about where the neighbours are going on holidays while Popey's stuck under the bed. So, she eventually fucks off, but Popey can't go downstairs. The only way he can get out is climbing out her bedroom window. So, he gets his clothes on and climbs out onto the kitchen roof. He reckons he can jump it. So, he hops down, lands wrong and sprains his ankle. He's roaring in agony, lying on the grass. The mother must've heard him 'cause he sees her staring out the window at him. So, he hobbles around the side o' the house on his banjaxed ankle and out the side gate."

"So, he got away with it?"

"Well, not quite. Ha ha. Just as Popey's halfway home, the guards pull up alongside him. They start questioning him 'cause he fits the description of a burglar they'd received a call about. He starts trying to bullshit them that he was just on his way to the shop as they're throwing him into the back o' the car."

"Oh shit!"

"So, they bring him back to the house and the mother identifies him. Popey pleads his innocence but she's having none of it. 'That's definitely him!' she says. "That's the gouger that was trying to break into me house!' Popey's shitting a brick at this stage and goes, 'Ah no, I swear. I wasn't trying to break into your house – I was trying to break out o' your house!' Ha ha!"

"So, what happened in the end?"

"Him and the mot had to confess everything to the ma. Ha ha."

"That lad is something else."

"Gas chap. Ha ha."

My laughing fizzled out as I tried to gauge her reaction.

"I'd say I could've made the jump if that was me. What do ye think?"

"Maybe. But don't go jumping out any windows on my behalf."

"What would ye say to your ma if that was you?"

You've thrown in the bait, now just wait for her to bite.

"I'd probably come clean."

"Really? And what would your ma say?"

"She wouldn't mind too much if it was in me own room and we used protection. She knows I'm old enough now and all that."

She sees the bait. She's closing in on it.

"So, ye think you're old enough?"

Bite, bite, bite.

"I suppose I am now."

Ah yes! She's on the hook. Now just slowly reel her in.

"So, would ye be ready to take that next step?"

"Ye mean?"

"To have s...well, to develop our relationship into an adult relationship."

"I'm ready for an adult relationship, Paddy. Are you?"

"Yeah," I replied, looking at her like a dog being teased with a biscuit.

"Are ye sure you're ready for an adult relationship, Paddy, or do ye just want the perks?"

"Like what?"

I put on a face that had all the innocence of a new-born baby.

"Ye know very well what, Paddy... Sex," she said in a hushed voice, like it was a dirty word.

"Well, it wouldn't be an adult relationship without it, would it?"

"That's ridiculous, Paddy. Are ye telling me ye can't commit to strengthen our relationship unless I ride ye?"

"No... yes...well, kind o'. Ye wouldn't expect a car to make it up to Belfast without giving it a drop o' petrol, would ye? I'm running on fumes here, Rach. I'll be a virgin pensioner at this rate!"

"Okay, Paddy. If ye can promise me that if we do it, you'll see me as maybe more than just your girlfriend in the future, then I will."

She wants a husband in return for a lash?

Take the deal! The 'maybe' clause can be enacted any time.

"I promise."

"Ye swear? Look into me eyes and say it."

"I promise."

"Do ye love me?"

"Ye know I do."

The words were emphatically spoken, making them sound like they meant something. It was the last obstacle, and I would've said anything to get past it. But I figured that engaging in what was supposed to be the ultimate expression of love, would be the very thing that would make me love her, and that I would therefore arrive at the same destination.

She placed her small hand over mine.

"Will ye get the protection?" she asked.

"Do I have to? Will you get it?"

"Ah, Paddy, give over, that's the lad's responsibility."

"I don't wanna be lurking round the chemists looking for girls' pills."

"Pills?! Ye think I'm taking pills?! G'way out o' that, Paddy! Buy yourself a packet o' condoms."

"Condoms? Nobody uses them these days, Rach. There's too much faffing about with them."

"Is that right, Paddy? Well, you can be the chap to make them fashionable again."

"It's embarrassing having to… I'll give ye the money to get them."

"Paddy, it's your knob, so it's your job!"

"It's just…"

"It's just nothing, Paddy. It's either a condom or no sex. Your choice."

"Yeah, but, if I had a disease, ye'd know about it by now."

"I don't bloody care, Paddy! Get the condoms! End o' story!"

At seventeen, buying a packet of condoms seemed a daunting task. I imagined the awkward conversation I'd have to have with the woman in the local pharmacy.

"Hello, what can I do for you, young man?"

"Em… I'm looking for something."

"What?"

"Something for…"

"What's your ailment?"

"Not exactly an ailment… I need the things to put on ye… so ye can…"

"I'm sorry, I don't follow."

"For himself."

"For whose self? A family member?"

"Eh no… Me own member."

"I beg your pardon?"

"I want to… love me girlfriend… but I don't wanna be a daddy…"

"Oh, I see. Condoms?"

"Eh… those things, yeah. How much are they?"

"Well, the prices vary depending on what type ye want."

"There's types?"

"Oh, yes. I'd recommend starting with these basic ones and ye can discuss using other types with her…or him, later on."

"It's a her."

"Well, these ones are five euros."

"Five balloons for a few… balloons?!"

"It's a small price to pay for your peace o' mind, not to mention the alternative costs involved in rearing a child."

"True, I suppose… What if one o' them bursts when I'm using it and she ends up getting pregnant? Will yis cover the cost of all the nappies if I still have the receipt?

It wasn't a conversation I was willing to subject myself to. I tried to think of another way of getting my hands on one. I could've robbed one of Da's, but he probably would've noticed it missing. He'd have had a search party scouring the streets of Little Bray for it. I would've been the first suspect to be brought in for interrogation.

"What did ye do with me last rubber?"

"Wasn't me, Da!"

"Well it didn't climb out o' me drawer and run down the shaggin' road, did it?"

"Maybe Claire took it."

"What are ye saying about my little girl? Ye saying she goes around town throwing it about?"

"No, Da."

"Well, I haven't used it, so that leaves you!"

"I wasn't near it. I swear!"

"Listen, I've been working all week and I've been looking forward to a night with your mother."

"Ye could buy another packet, Da."

"Oh, another packet, he says. Do ye think they grow on trees? Ye need to start appreciating the value o' things, Paddy. I suppose I'll have to send himself in naked, will I? The last time I did that I had you dropped in me lap nine months later! And who's the poor girl that's having to suffer being on the receiving end o' your langer anyway?"

"Nobody, honest!"

"We're gonna sit here till ye own up to robbing it. I don't care how long I've to wait!"

I thought of who else could help me.

Popey. He'd have a spare.

"Popey, I need a favour. You're having sex with Sharon, right?"

"Having sex? God, you're making it sound very formal, Paddy. I'm giving her a lash."

"Whatever, listen, would ye give us a loan of a condom?"

"A loan? Are ye planning on giving it back to me afterwards?"

"No, ye know what I mean."

"Why, are ye gonna have a posh wank?"

"No, I'm not having a bloody posh... I need it for Rachael."

"Oh, so she's doing the deed, is she? Are ye not man enough to buy them yourself? Ha ha. Ye know what they say – if you're not big enough to buy 'em, you're not big enough to ride 'em."

"Yeah, yeah, whatever. Are ye gonna give me one or not?"

"You're asking me to make a big sacrifice, Paddy, but seeing that it's yourself, I'll give ye one… I'll bring it in tomorrow."

"Sound, Popey."

The next day, he handed it to me during little-break. I stared at it like I'd discovered the Holy Grail.

With a girlfriend ready to unfetter herself from her innocence and a condom to my name, the slaying of my virginity was now an inevitability, but more waiting lay ahead. She'd pencilled me in for a night over the Christmas holidays when she'd have the house to herself.

"Sure, we could do it somewhere else, Rach."

"Where Paddy?"

"In a field somewhere."

"A field?"

"Yeah. I'll bring a blanket and a pillow and a flask o' tea. It'd be like a picnic under the stars. It'd be real romantic."

"I hope that's a joke!"

"Well…"

"Paddy, ye needn't think I'm lying in some damp field! And what if it rains?"

"I'll keep an eye on the forecast. We'll postpone it if the weather's bad."

"Get offside, Paddy! Ye can wait a little longer."

I tried to hide my exasperation.

"Are we getting each other Christmas presents?" I asked furtively.

"Why wouldn't we be?"

"Well, I'm just asking for your sake," I lied.

"For my sake?"

"Yeah, I don't wanna embarrass ye by giving ye a present if ye haven't got me anything."

"I've already got yours."

"Oh... I'll pick up something for ye on the weekend so."

"We can exchange them on the night ye come over to me house... before we go upstairs. That'd be nice, wouldn't it?"

"Ah yeah."

Great. A ropey present could see me virginity survive for God knows how long!

My paper round was always more hassle than it was worth. Every week I delivered hundreds of copies of the free local newspaper for the purpose of cleaning windows, picking up dog shite, painting and wiping arses. Rarely was it ever actually read by anyone. The tedium of the job had me keeping an eye out for any alternative work. However, the money I received from it ensured that I could get her something that would keep her happy.

What'll I buy her?

Clothes? Don't know her size.

Money? What are ye, her uncle?

Bra and knickers? Is it for her or for you?

Voucher? Looks like ye weren't bothered.

Jewellery? Can't fail with that.

I arrived at Gleeson's jewellers on Castle Street, the local treasure chest that had recently been robbed. Its stolen merchandise was probably being worn by local residents, having been bought for half the retail price. When I entered the premises, the first thing I noticed was the view of the sex shop across the road; an amusing counterbalance to the plush jewellery surrounding me.

The man behind the counter looked at me suspiciously, as if I was on a reconnaissance mission for the next robbery.

"Can I help ye, young man?"

"I suppose so. I'm looking to buy something for me mot. I was thinking o' getting her a gold ring... One that's reasonably cheap... The cheapest one ye have."

"I see. Well, I've a lovely set o' gold-plated rings which should be within your price range," he said, before directing me over to them. To the untrained eye they looked identical to the rest of the gold rings that were on display, but they undoubtedly had more in common with the jewellery that Mousey and Popey wore.

"Gold-plated rings? What are they, fake yokes?" I asked.

"Oh no, not fake. They're rings that have been coated in gold."

So, in other words, fake.

"The cheapest of them is this one here," he said, taking one of the rings out of the cabinet.

"How much is it?"

"Forty euros."

Forty quid for a fake gold ring!

"How about if we agree on twenty?"

"I'm sorry, but the price is the price."

"Twenty-five?"

"I don't negotiate prices."

"Thirty?"

"I'm afraid you've got the wrong idea. I'm not selling from a market stall. This is a high-end jewellery store, dealing in merchandise of only the finest quality... So, are ye interested or not?"

As he posed his question, I thought of an alternative means of acquiring his merchandise, at a cheaper price, but knew nobody who had such clout to be in possession of it.

Mick Dolan?

"Ah, not really. There's cheaper gold doing the rounds in Bray."

I couldn't resist the parting remark. He had the face of a man trying to hide his anger.

"I'm trying to get me hands on a cheap gold-plated ring for herself," I told Mick. "I know Gleeson's was robbed a few weeks back..."

"I know nothing about that!"

"I'm not saying... Would ye know someone who might?"

"What if I did?"

"What could ye get me for twenty quid?"

"I'm not sure. You'll have to give me the money and I'll see what I can find."

"Sound, Mick." I entrusted him with a twenty euro note.

A few days later I received a text from him.

"Got one. Meet at Flynn's shop @ 6."

"Jesus, that looks the business, Mick, fair play."

"Ye didn't get it off me though, understand?"

"Understood."

I thanked him before making off like a squir-rel frightened of larger rodents stealing his collection of nuts. The ring was so hot you could get a tan from it, and I had a paranoid fear that a Garda was waiting around the corner of Flynn's to snatch me; that I was the target of a sting operation. The area was clear, and I cleared myself from it.

The long-awaited night had finally arrived.

I was sitting on Rachael's couch with only one thing on my mind.

"Do ye want your present," she asked.

"Yeah, sure," I said, not particularly caring about it.

She reached under the Christmas tree, pulled it out and handed it to me. I tore off the wrapping paper. She'd gotten me an assortment of books and albums.

"Aw, nice Rach, thanks."

"That's the sort o' stuff ye usually read and listen to, isn't it?"

"It is yeah… Here's yours," I said, taking the box containing the ring out of my pocket and presenting it to her. Her eyes widened when she opened it.

"Oh, Paddy, it's gorgeous! Is that real gold?"

"Is Santa Claus a fat bollocks? Absolutely."

"It must've cost a few quid."

"Ah, don't worry about that. I shopped around."

"Will ye put it on me?"

"O' course."

As I slid the ring onto her finger, she looked like she'd just accepted a marriage proposal.

If this doesn't get me a ride, I'm out o' ideas.

Any hopes I had of the ring being the catalyst that would lead me to her bed, proved to be misplaced. It earned me no more than a kiss and a lousy cuddle. Half an hour later, I was starting to become impatient, and I didn't have any cans to make the waiting more bearable. I had decided against bringing any with me, wanting to be in tip-top shape on the night, treating the occasion as if it was a match.

"Rach, when do ye wanna go upstairs?"

"When I'm ready, Paddy."

Another twenty minutes passed.

"Rach, when will ye be ready?"

"I don't know. Whenever I get into the mood."

I'll be getting into a fuckin' mood if ye don't open those legs o' yours sometime this century!

"So, when will ye get into the mood?"

"In a while, maybe. Don't rush me."

I ended my line of questioning. It seemed that asking about 'the mood' was the very thing that would prevent her from getting into 'the mood.'

Then, only fifteen minutes later, she got up from the couch, held out her hand for me to take, and said, "Come on."

"Ye mean...?"

She nodded with a look that confirmed what I thought. Just as I'd been fearing that 'the mood' was going to scupper what I had been looking forward to, I suddenly saw the personification of it staring me in the face, wanting my attention.

I took her hand, and she led me up to her bedroom.
Here we go, full steam ahead!

She turned on a lamp and closed the curtains. We kissed and began to take off our clothes. When she pulled down my boxers, Little Paddy popped up, ready for action. I then went about putting on the condom but found that doing so was not the simple task that I had assumed it would be. I fiddled with it as Rachael lay on the bed, looking on.

"What's keeping ye?" she asked. "Just roll it down."

"I can't just roll it... It's stuck."

"Did ye not read the instructions?"

"The instructions?! I didn't think I *had* to read instructions! I didn't think it'd be this fuckin' awkward!"

"Your losing your…"

"I know, I know. I'm losing me fuckin' patience too!"

"Here, give us a go."

Through a collective effort, we eventually managed to dress Little Paddy for the occasion. Without further delay, he entered her and discovered a world of delight.

After five minutes of exploring, he was eager to finish the job. I held him on a lead, pulling him back from sprinting over the finish line. I waited to see how far behind Rachael was in the race. I wanted her to have a respectable second place finish, not lagging a mile behind. She oohed and aahed, making cute little noises to harmonise with my aghs and ughs. When I felt her creeping up on me, now just on my shoulder, I let go of the lead, and allowed Little Paddy to finish the job.

I took him out and whipped off the condom as he began to collapse in exhaustion. A proud moment. He'd proven his worth. He'd delivered on the big day when called upon.

You take a rest now, buddy. You've done your shift.

She rested her head on my chest as we lay there in silence for a few moments.

"Do your bits and bobs feel awright?" I asked.

"Me bits and bobs are still in one piece," she answered, staring adoringly into my eyes. "What are ye thinking, Paddy?"

Give her the answer she wants.

"I was just thinking how special tonight's been, ye know?"

"Aw, Paddy, I love ye, hun."

"Come 'ere to me," I said before kissing her. While doing so, I wondered if this would be as good as it would get between us.

Chapter 10
The Lethargy of the Drunk

Returning to school in the new year brought a swift end to the harmony that Rachael and I had enjoyed over the previous two weeks. I wondered why, before realising that the Christmas holidays had offered me time and space without her, which I had welcomed. Being around her all day again was enough to make me fall back into my old habit of distancing myself from her. Phone calls would be ignored. Excuses for not being able to meet up would be invented. By the end of January, the night we first had sex felt like a century ago. Nevertheless, we persevered as best we could.

By March however, the problems between us were becoming harder to ignore. Now eighteen, I could whisk myself away on an alcoholic adventure on a whim and did so when my appetite demanded it, indulging in the perks of my new-found adulthood. In contrast, Rachael had her head stuck in the books, scrupulously planning for her life after school. With increasingly disparate outlooks, an argument was only ever a sentence away.

"What time do ye wanna meet on Paddy's Day, Rach? I wanna head down to the seafront early, spend the day on the tear. It'll be great craic."

"I can't. I've to study for a French test next week, and I was gonna go to the parade with me family and have dinner with them."

"Study? On Paddy's Day?"

"Just for a couple o' hours before we head out."

"Fuckin' hell, Rach, it's Paddy's Day for Christ's sake! Can ye not knock that shite on the head for one day?"

"Why, so I can spend the day watching you getting pissed, like your birthday all over again?"

"When did ye become a nun?"

"When did you become a pisshead?"

"Well, half the town will be down there, so I'm not gonna miss out. Jesus, you've become a right boring pain in the arse. Would it kill ye to take your halo off and put it in the wash for one day? With a bit o' luck it might shrink!"

"Excuse me?!"

"Yeah, ye heard me!"

"You've some nerve, Paddy! I never hear from ye half the time, but then as soon as *you* want something, ye magically appear on the scene!"

"Anytime I *do* see ye, you're never up for doing anything, like now!"

"I've a mountain o' work to do, Paddy. I'm not gonna apologise for wanting to do well in me exams. Some of us have ambition and want to do something with ourselves after school. I need a rake o' points to do psychology."

"Since when have ye wanted to do that?"

"Since when are ye interested?"

"God, ye couldn't make it up!"

"And what does that mean?"

"You've to do some course to figure yourself out and yet I'm supposed to be able to figure ye out! Fuckin' hell, they could use ye as their test subject!"

"The course isn't about *me*, Paddy! Nor is it about you either, but ye somehow manage to make it be about you! And tell me, what's *your* plan? Go gargling for the rest o' your life?"

"It's Paddy's Day!"

"Yeah, and I'm going out for dinner with me family. Ye can come along if ye want but I'm sure ye don't want to."

"You're too fuckin' right I don't want to! If ye think I'm spending Paddy's Day with your auld one, ye can think again. I'd rather castrate meself with a rusty knife. It'd be less painful!"

"Well, me ma thinks…"

"Ye hardly think I give a bollocks about what your ma thinks?!"

"Oh, don't worry, I don't! Nor does she!"

"Is that right now?"

"Yeah, it is. I'll tell ye what, Paddy. Ye can either come to dinner with me or go off on the lash. It's your choice. I don't give a shite either way!"

"That's grand. So, you're not gonna be moaning about me heading out then?"

"You're not worth a moan, Paddy!"

"And you're not worth the hassle!"

"Oh, I'm hassle, am I?"

"When ye go on like your ma, ye are!"

"Aw, fuck off, Paddy! I mean it!"

"Gladly. Ye can stay here with your poxy schoolbooks! Fuckin' miserable auld cunt!"

"Fuck you, Paddy!"

As her eyes welled up, I left her in haste and in a huff.

Maybe I should go back and talk to her?
No, fuck her. Ye were dead right.
Maybe 'miserable auld cunt' was too far?
Nah, had to be said. She doesn't like hearing the truth.
I don't like seeing her upset.
I'm fuckin' delighted she's upset.
It'd be a shame if it's over.
Good riddance to her if it is.

March 17th, 2006 – St Patrick's Day

In high spirits, and with a sense of liberty that I'd acquired from the row, I found myself sitting amongst the throngs outside the Waterfront Lounge on Strand Road, the nucleus of Bray's social scene, with Popey and Sharon - the girl who inspired his leap off the kitchen roof - for company. The lounge was thriving, helped by the good weather and by the fact that it was a Friday, which for most of us meant that there wouldn't be any school or work the following day to curb our intake of alcohol.

The parade's array of local clubs made their way along the road, much to the indifference of the lounge's patrons who were immersed in their carousing. The scene would make even the most stubborn atheist believe that there was a God, and he was Irish.

We drank from our own supply of cans that we'd smuggled past the bouncers in backpacks, buying one pint and then furtively refilling the glass beneath the table.

"Where's herself, Paddy?" Popey asked.

"Up her own arse, Popey. The best place for her!"

"Jesus, this place is black! She doesn't know what she's missing. That Leaving Cert will be the death of her!"

"Maybe. At least it'll put her out of her fuckin' misery!"

A group representing the local Brazilian community went past, led by two scantily clad dancers. For the first and only time, the parade attracted our attention.

"Holy fuck, Popey, look at those two!"

"Which two? I can't see… Here, mate, get your head out o' the way!"

"The two wearing next to nothing!"

"Next to nothing?!" Popey frantically moved his head left and right like a boxer dodging jabs.

"I see them, Paddy! Holy shit! I'd wear more having a shower!"

"Look at the arse on her!"

"And the jugs on the other one!"

"They're not real lads," Sharon insisted. "Will yis relax, for fuck's sake, before yis make a mess o' yourselves."

"We're just appreciating the culture on show, Sha-ron," Popey assured her.

"Here, listen you, I didn't come out to watch ye gawking at Brazilians. Ye may gawk at *me*!"

Popey's face had a smart retort written all over it, but he wisely resisted the temptation to say it.

"Are ye going for a closer look, Paddy?" he asked as I rose from my seat.

"No, I'm going for a piss. Mind me cans."

Inside, a couple of St Brendan's lads I hardly knew nabbed me for a chat and I happily obliged when a round of pints was ordered with my name on one of them. Then another round and another pint. Certain that Popey was keeping vigil over my cans, I felt no urge to leave their company until my round was nearing, at which point I made another trip to the toilet before discreetly sauntering back outside. I returned to the table to find Popey and Sharon in the middle of a heated row over Popey having drunk more than his fair share of their cans.

I tried to play the role of peacemaker by offering Sharon a couple of mine, before she promptly told me where to shove them.

"Here, ye needn't think ye can talk to Paddy like that!"

"Fuck Paddy and fuck *you*, Alan!"

She left our table abruptly and charged out of the Waterfront.

"Fuckin' cow, Paddy! I mean, I told her to take them while they were there… I better go after her."

Left alone, I began to listen to a conversation being had between two middle-aged men at the table next to me.

"I can't drink in Boland's anymore," one of them said.

"Why, did ye drink the place dry?" the other one asked jokingly.

"'Cause o' the brother."

"What did he do?"

"He offered to buy the missus a drink."

"'Cause he offered…"

"It was the la-di-da way he offered it, ye know? Ever since he got that new job, he's been rubbing me face in it, throwing the bread around. His missus is forever onto mine about their holidays, their car, their kids' school, it's always something. Anyway, me and herself were out with the pair o' them. It was my round. Herself asked me to get her some fancy cocktail, and then the brother jumped in like a shot, going, 'Oh, I'll get this round.' I said, 'Like fuck ye will.' He says, 'What's your problem?' I said, 'Ye know me problem. I can buy me own wife a drink.' He says, 'Right, go on then. Ye might as well. It's about the only thing ye can buy her!' I fuckin' decked him. Now they won't serve me anymore. All because o' that git!"

Our patron saint then became the topic of conversation between them.

"Ye know it's all a myth, don't ye?"

"What?"

"The story o' St Patrick."

"What do ye mean?"

"All that business about him using the shamrock to describe the holy trinity and converting all the chieftains. It's all codology. There was no mention o' shamrocks in the story until centuries after he popped his clogs. And the shamrock was a Celtic symbol years before he ever arrived on the scene. He's not even really a saint. He was never canonised."

"Well, we're all Catholics, aren't we? So, somebody must have converted us at some stage?"

"He converted people yeah, but the other stuff..."

"So, he didn't invent Catholicism?"

"Who says he invented Catholicism?"

"Is that part o' the story not true either?"

"That was never part o' the story in the first place. He didn't... He brought Christianity to..."

"Was he not the first Pope?"

"No, he wasn't the first shaggin' Pope! He wasn't even Catholic!"

"You're saying he was a Prod?!"

"He was neither. He was a Christian."

"Ye just said that was all codology."

"Not that part of it... The other... Aw, never mind."

"Sure, aren't ye getting a day off because of him all the same, so what are ye moaning about? Ye owe the man a drink and all you're giving him is lip!"

The conversation then returned to familial matters.

"How was the daughter's wedding? Good night?"

"A long night... The first dance was a disaster. The fella's equipment kept stalling, so they had to keep restarting. I swear, amateur hour at the comedy club. Then some fella puked his ring on the dance floor and one o' the bridesmaids slipped in it. She was destroyed. There was uproar... The best man's speech had to be heard to be believed. He gets up and says all the usual stuff, then before ye know it, he's giving racing tips."

"Racing tips?"

"No word of a lie."

"Did he pick any winners?"

"He may have for all I know, but I wasn't gonna be betting anything based on what that clown was suggesting... Trust the auld son-in-law to have picked some eejit like that to be his best man."

"You're not a fan of him? The son-in-law, I mean."

"I haven't decided yet. There's something about him that won't let me make up me mind."

"Well, he's family now."

"Then he'll fit right in. I still haven't made me mind up about half o' them. Ha ha."

A girl of a similar age to me approached where I was sitting.

"Sorry, hun. Do ye mind if I squeeze in beside ye?"

"Work away."

"Ye looked like ye could do with a bit o' company, so I thought I'd come over."

"Ah, I don't mind being on me own."

"It's not a night to be on your own, hun... I'm Saoirse, by the way."

"Paddy."

Two 'huns' and an introduction. This is leading in one direction.

Let it.

What about Rachael?

Rachael me hole! If she gave a shite about ye, she'd be here.

"So, tell us, have ye no girlfriend to keep ye company?"

"Well, I have, but she wouldn't come out."

"She sounds like great craic altogether."

"I know. She wanted to go out with her family for dinner."

"On Paddy's Day?"

"That's what I said."

"And?"

"There was war."

"So, are you still seeing her?"

Yes.

Yes? It's over. The auld one's in her ear as we speak.

It was just an argument.

Nah, it's done. Move on.

"Well, I don't know," I answered honestly.

"One o' those ones… I understand." She smiled, pushing her black hair over her shoulder in a flirtatious manner.

We ordered another round. A voice in my head asked what Rachael was doing, but with each pint, the voice became ever fainter, before becoming inaudible.

By the early hours, the effects of the day of drinking were on show. People danced, sang and 'got off' with one another, while others looked on wearily, concentrating solely on keeping themselves from throwing up. Around them, there were glasses smashing and insults being traded as bouncers dragged lads who'd been fighting from the premises. St Patrick's Day in all its glory.

"Let's get out o' here, Paddy. This place is getting messy."

"I can hardly stand straight."

"Ye better hold my hand then, come on."

She led me across the road, over the seafront lawn, where we sat on the promenade. Speaking had become laborious, or more accurately, had become unnecessary. She put her arms around me. I felt the need to make a half-hearted protest.

"I can't…"

"Ye can."

"But Rach…"

"Forget about her. She's forgotten about you," she said damningly.

It was neither the 'Attack of the Lizard' nor the 'Titillating Tongue.' I'd inadvertently discovered a new technique, the 'Lethargy of the Drunk.'

Hearing the rowdiness of the lounge's closing time exodus a while later, she got up off my lap.

"I better go, Paddy. Me friends will be wondering where I am."

"Okay… I'll see ye so," I replied tiredly, too drunk to care whether she stayed longer or left.

Without as much as a parting kiss, she was gone.

The short journey to Dargan Street seemed like an epic hike across the Great Plains without the use of my legs. That warm drunken glow had been superseded by a state of near paralysis as my brain and limbs struggled to communicate with each other. Everything swirled around me. I threw up onto the footpath. As I reached my front door and opened it, I greeted the awaiting staircase with horror, before trudging up each painful step with legs devoid of strength, feeling like Jesus Christ climbing the hill of Calvary. Only in Ireland could religion lead you to such a state. Perhaps we showed our devotion to God by being willing to endure the consequences of having drunk ourselves into stupors on behalf of one of the saints. But there would be another consequence of St Patrick's Day that I was still ignorant of as I lay down on my bed.

Chapter 11
Saint Patrick, Patron Saint of Hangovers

Unable to remember getting into bed, I awoke in it, feeling like a dying man. I craved water as if I'd gone without it for days. My head felt like somebody was hitting it with a mallet. I tried and failed to raise myself from the bed. Sausages were being cooked downstairs, the smell hurrying up the staircase and invading my nostrils. It motivated me to reach the kitchen by whatever means. Four of them with a cup of tea was the medicine I knew I needed. I managed to get out of the bed on the second attempt, and still clothed from the night before, I gingerly made my way out to the landing and inched my way down the stairs. The enticing smell became stronger and the sizzling louder with each step that I took down the hallway. I was being drawn to the kitchen door as if in a trance.

"Morning, love. Did ye have a good night?" Ma asked before she turned away from the cooker and saw me. "Ah, for God's sake, look at the state o' ye! How much did ye drink?"

"Too much."

Please not a hundred questions, Ma.

I navigated my ragged body to the kitchen table, and sat, placing my heavy head in my hand.

"What time did ye get back at?"

"Aw, I don't know… It was still dark anyway."

"Here, get a cup o' tea into ye… John, the sausages are ready!"

Da came in for his breakfast and found amusement in my appearance.

"Now there's a sight for sore eyes," he said. "Jesus Christ, son, you've a head on ye like a sow in labour. Ye know, you young lads are bloody amateurs. Yis are useless at drinking."

"Well, he hasn't had as much practice as you, John."

"Is she having a pop at me, Paddy boy? Do ye have me auld breakfast, Aoife?"

"Here ye go."

"Yum, yum… Christ, ye look like someone's put ye through a shredder and taped ye back together again, Paddy. You'll put me off me sausages. Doesn't he look a right sight, Aoife?"

"He does. No worse than you though after you've been on one."

"A chip off the old block then, eh? Like father, like son. I suppose you'll be looking to claim me throne now? No chance, son. You've a lot o' drinking to do before ye catch up with your old man. See this gut?" Da pulled up his shirt and grabbed a fold of flab. "A lot o' time and effort went into creating that, son."

"Ah, John, pull your shirt down. Nobody wants to be looking at your belly at this hour. Leave him be, will ye."

"Says the woman who does have me tormented whenever *I'm* feeling a bit worse for wear after a few drinks… I'd say ye weren't cutting such a sorry figure with that mot o' yours last night. Ha ha."

"I wasn't with her. I was with Popey."

"Pope? What use is he to ye after closing time when a man needs to unburden himself of his woes for an hour or so?"

"An hour, John? Ye'd be doing well to last ten minutes."

"I wasn't with him at that stage, Da… I was… I was…"

"Ah, don't tell me ye were moping about on Paddy's night with only your neglected pecker for company? What are ye like, son? What breed o' eejit have I raised at all? I blame your mother," he said jokingly. "Ye should've seen *me* in me day on Paddy's night, son. In me element, I used to be. That's how I met your mother. Remember that night, Aoife?"

"I remember trying to get ye home when ye could hardly walk."

"Yeah, it was very romantic."

Da pondered his next thought as he chewed on his sausage sandwich.

"Where was herself anyway?"

"She didn't wanna come out."

He covered his smiling mouth with his cup of tea. "Oh, do I dare ask why?"

"No, ye don't, John. Mind your own business."

"Where were ye anyway, Paddy?"

"Down the seafront. In the Waterfront."

"The Waterfront? Ah, sure it must be wall to wall young ones down there on Paddy's night. By the early hours, I'd say they'd throw themselves at anything with two legs and a pulse."

"What's your point, John?" Ma interjected bluntly.

"All I'm saying is that it's an awful auld place for a man who's spoken for to find himself in… Temptation would crawl up the leg o' your trousers in that kip."

"Oh, is that right, John?"

"So I've heard, Aoife."

Da dunked his next sausage sandwich into his puddle of brown sauce.

"I've more respect for ye now, Paddy. You've inherited the Dempsey trait of loyalty. A good woman is like this sausage. You've to enjoy it, value it, and by Jaysus, don't let anyone else take a bite out of it."

After breakfast, I lay abjectly in front of the television with a fractured memory of the previous night. By the afternoon, still feeble but over the worst, the phone rang. Rachael's number.

Oh God, she's ringing to brag about the great night she had with the family.

Maybe she's ringing to apologise.

"Hi, Rach."

"Ye fuckin' arsehole!"

Not the strongest apology I've ever heard.

"What?"

"Ye know what. Don't even make me say it!"

"Say what?"

"Her."

"Who?"

"That bitch ye were with last night!"

"A bitch?"

Is this how she starts all her apologies?

"Rach, I haven't the energy, just get to the point. What are ye raving about?"

"Ye know very fuckin' well what I'm raving about, Paddy! Don't you dare play innocent with me!"

"Play innocent about what?"

"I know ye were with another girl last night!"

Another girl?

"Who told ye that?"

"One o' the girls saw ye with her on the promenade."

Hang on… The promenade? Why does that ring a bell?

"Ye were eating the face off her apparently!"

"Who? What did she look like?"

"A tart, Paddy. She looked like a fuckin' tart!"

A tart on the promenade?

Oh shit! Your one! Bollocks!

"Oh yeah, her. Listen, Rachael, I didn't want anything to do with her, but she wouldn't leave me alone. She was just some slapper looking for a bit."

"And you gave her a bit!"

"I didn't… I just kissed her."

I think.

"Oh really, are ye sure? 'Cause a minute ago ye couldn't even remember doing that!"

"It was just a kiss, honestly."

Was it?

"You're a prick, Paddy! I leave ye alone for one night and ye cheat on me!"

"I was thinking about you, wishing it was you I was kissing."

Good line.

"Oh my God, don't even try to weasel your way out of it!"

Change of tactics required.

"Sure, what are you moaning about?! If ye were that bothered about me, ye would've come out with me!"

That's it, put her on the backfoot.

"Just because I wasn't out with ye, doesn't give ye the right to…"

"Well, this time yesterday, ye didn't give a shite about me, so why should I have given a shite about you?"

"Fine, Paddy, if that's how ye feel!"

"That's exactly how I feel!"

"Right, then it's over, Paddy!"

"Fine, it's over!"

"It was nice while it lasted."

"Yeah, but now it's over, so goodbye."

With that, my first relationship had come to an end. Half of me regretted it after the time and effort I put in. The other half of me was elated. I was a free man again.

That night, having recovered from my hangover, I went to O'Connell's on Dublin Road to celebrate and to rid myself of any pangs of guilt. I thought of Rachael. I knew she'd be upset.

She'll find someone else anyway.

The thought struck me that without a girlfriend, I'd now have more time to concentrate on my schoolwork with the exams only a few weeks away. I quickly dismissed the ludicrous thought as I signalled for another pint.

Chapter 12
The Gallant Martyr

Old habits endure the most prolonged deaths.

With the exams upon me, my perfunctory endeavour at studying was of the utmost importance, a token gesture that would grant me the gall to claim that I had made a heroic effort, that I was the gallant martyr of the Irish education system. It would be inscribed on my headstone lest anyone doubted my good character.

Here lies Patrick Dempsey, beloved son of John and Aoife,
cherished brother of Claire, despised ex of Rachael Dowling.
He tried, made an honest effort, and did his best.
Forgotten in life, remembered in death.
May he rest in peace.

Two weeks later, after a fortnight of unexceptional performances in the exams, my time in St Brendan's came to an end. They had taught and prepared me as best as they could, and were now releasing me into the world, posing the ludicrously ominous challenge to me, of making something of myself. The old building, for all my notions of escaping it, wasn't without its sentimental value, as reluctant as I was to admit it. As I walked out its front gate after the last exam, I imagined the bustling corridors, the banter in the canteen, the mischief in class, and the games of football in the sport's hall. Such visualisations were already beginning to take on a deeper meaning as I now faced the reality of the life I knew being over, while still not knowing what would replace it.

Elation, apprehension and bafflement were all sitting round a table discussing my future as I attempted to chair the meeting, affording each of them equal speaking time. I opted to ignore their conflicting voices. A celebratory drink would quench their tiresome bickering.

I headed for the Waterfront Lounge, the staff of which already knew me by name.

"The usual, Paddy?"

"When you're ready, Eoghan, thanks."

The voices were silenced bar one.

Drink up.

A summer of decadence which saw my emancipation degenerate into two months of exploring Bray's motley array of drinking establishments, came to an abrupt cessation.

I traipsed up Dublin Road to St Brendan's gates, glee passing me on arrival, ecstatic voices trading results, only serving to exacerbate my sense of impending doom.

I reached the office. There was a queue as the woman behind the desk shuffled through the multitude of envelopes. Four lads stood in front of me. Each of them I knew, but the anxiousness of the moment ensured that an eerie silence prevailed.

We were standing on the gallows, nooses tightened, waiting for the hangman to release the trap door.

"Ye'd need a spare pair o' jocks for this, lads," Brian Hogan said, breaking the silence with an ill-timed quip. "I'll tell ye what…"

"Don't tell us what!" Finn Rafferty replied. "I'm not interested in you and your cacks!"

"I'm just trying to lighten the mood, chap."

"Jesus, Mary and Joseph!" said Finn. "How long does it take this auld one to find a fuckin' envelope? I'd shuffle through them faster with me arse cheeks!"

The wait was excruciating, but part of me didn't want it to end. It was a delightful ignorance to be unaware of bad news. After the other lads received their envelopes, I approached the desk.

"Name?"

"Patrick Dempsey."

"Darcy, Deasy, Donoghue, Dwyer… Dempsey, ye say? Dixon… I can't find a…"

Good God Almighty, give me the strength to beat meself to death!

"Ah, Dempsey. There ye are, love."

I grabbed it and shot out the door. Fearing the worst, I avoided everyone else outside, not wanting them to witness what I thought would be my imminent failure. I quickly left the school grounds and tore open the envelope with all the finesse of a bulldozer. I knew the results wouldn't make me. I just hoped they wouldn't break me beyond repair.

I stared at the grades on the page. Cs and Ds. I neither rejoiced nor was crestfallen. My results were devoid of drama. They were the definition of mediocrity. My fingerprints were all over them. They could've been better, could've been worse. I was unsure how to gauge it. Either I'd succeeded in passing all seven or I'd missed a great opportunity to do better. Hindsight was pointless. If I sat the exams again, my approach would've been no different.

What now?

The results didn't provide any clarity or point me in any direction. If anything, they left me feeling even more lost than before. Without consciously deciding to do so, I had walked down to the park on Lower Dargle Road, mulling everything over. I sat on a bench in the shade of a sycamore tree, pondering what to do next.

Well?

No answer.

I sought any happening that would offer me a distraction from my troubling thoughts. I watched an old man totter slowly across a football pitch as his dog unloaded its bowels in the centre circle. As the dog sprinted back to its owner, part of me envied the animal's free spirit, its lack of responsibilities. A young girl pushed a pram past me. Following behind her were two women speaking animatedly about piddling matters unworthy of animation. From the pavilion, a man emerged with a bucket of white paint. I stared in fascination as he painted a goalpost, the wet paint glistening.

Well?

Still nothing. I was flummoxed.

I deemed it time to wander home, but something held me to the bench. I knew, once home, the real world would come knocking loudly on the door and I'd pretend I wasn't in.

"Grand morning, isn't it?" the old man said to me as he approached the bench. He sat down beside me, placing his cane between us.

"The auld legs are begging for a rest… That's a heavy looking head ye have on your shoulders, son, if ye don't mind me saying so."

"I just got me Leaving Cert results."

"Ah, I see."

He threw a stick, sending the dog off on another dash.

"And now you're wondering what to do next, am I right?"

"Yeah."

"That can be a tricky one."

The dog returned and he wrestled the stick out of the animal's mouth. He appeared in his early seventies. He was in possession of an impressively thick head of grey hair for his age. He brushed it from his brow as he spoke.

"It can take ye twenty years before ye know your place in the world. I had to see half of it before I found mine."

"Where'd ye go?"

"Here and there. London first, then New York, Germany, Australia, Canada. Same gig everywhere I went, just doing whatever odd jobs came me way. Ye know what I learned on me travels? Ye can leave everything behind ye – your possessions, your family, your girl, everything, but not your troubles. They'll follow ye to the four corners o' the earth. I left 'cause I thought that this place was the problem. I reckoned a bit o' travelling would do the trick. It took me years to realise that the problem was in me own head. It was meself that I was trying to escape from."

"What made ye come home?"

"Would ye believe it, a woman of all things. I met an Irish girl in Canada. I go to the other side o' the world and who do I get in with? A young one from Finglas. Anyway, she'd had her fill of living abroad by then and wanted to come home. I had no intention of returning, but she wasn't one to let slip away, ye know? She was adamant she was leaving, without me if needs be. I said to her, 'Sure, I'd have no job back home, nothing.' She said she was going back to school. Then she started convincing me to do the same. Sure, I hadn't seen the inside of a classroom since I was fifteen. And ye know what?"

"What?"

"I came back with her, and within a few days she was already on the phone to some relative, getting me sorted for an apprenticeship. Some bloody girl."

"Did ye do it?"

"I did indeed. Four years later I had a trade, a wife and a couple o' kids. That's the women for ye, son."

"Ye still…"

"Married? I like to think we are… Are ye a religious man?"

"Don't know."

"I probably would've said the same thing when I was your age, but when your missus dies, it can make a believer out o' ye. Better to think of her up there than in a box," he said abjectly.

Unsure of how to respond to his revelation, I nodded solemnly. The silence was more fitting than any words that I could string together.

"I've had plenty o' days, son, when I've seen your face in the mirror. I recognise that face, even without me glasses… Anyway, the reason I'm saying all this to ye is just to let ye know that we've all been there, not knowing what to do next. But you'll soon find your own path. Give it time, I say. Be patient. Whatever's on that sheet isn't important. It won't define ye as long as ye don't let it… God Almighty, if she heard me giving advice, she'd get some laugh. She'd be telling ye to run a mile from me before any o' me gibberish starts making sense!"

The old man threw the stick again, sending the dog away and hoisted himself to his feet with the cane.

"Anyway, I better be off. I'll end up yapping all day if I stay any longer. Look after yourself, son, won't ye?"

"Yeah, you too."

He slowly plodded up the footpath before stopping to look back at me.

"Rita, that's her name."

Ma, Da and I were sitting round the kitchen table. The autopsy was underway.

"I've never seen the letters C and D written so many times on a page," Da remarked. "What do they stand for – clever dosser?"

"Ah, John, give over. He did his best."

"I know he did. I'm only pulling his leg. Ye passed it, son, fair play to ye. That's the main thing."

Da's words were providing solace but no answers.

"What are ye gonna do now, love?"

"I don't know, Ma. I'll give it time, I suppose."

"Ye don't wanna be giving it too much time," Da advised. "Employers wanna see that you're keen to work."

"There's courses ye can do to further your education," Ma said.

"Further it? I've just seen the back of it. I'll try to get a job, make a few quid."

"Well, it's your life, love. You're old enough now to make your own choices."

"I can get ye on a driving course, son. I might be able to put a word in for ye with Dublin Bus."

"I don't wanna be a bloody bus driver, Da."

"What's wrong with being a bus driver?! It's fed ye and put a roof over your head, I'll have ye know!"

"Nothing, Da. I just don't wanna do it."

"Well, you're gonna have to do something," he said. "Ye can't wait around forever. You'll get lapped."

"I was talking to an auld lad. He reckoned the best thing to do is to be patient."

"An auld lad? Are ye hearing this, Aoife? He won't take advice from his own father, but he listens to some auld codger. And who's this sage when he's at home?"

"I don't know. I just got talking to him."

"And what wise words did this character bestow on ye, that your own father couldn't?" Da enquired.

"Well, nothing. He was just going on about giving it time and that."

"The best thing for ye to do, Patrick, is to go down to the job centre tomorrow."

"Yeah, I'll do that, Ma."

"So, you're definitely not interested in the bus driving then?" Da asked.

"No, Da. I'm not!" I replied impatiently.

"Me apologies for offering! Christ, do ye buy your knickers with the twist already in them?!"

All three of us sipped our tea.

"I'd be the proudest father in Ireland to be handing me one-four-five route over to me own son one day. It'd bring a tear to me eye. We'd make that route our own. Stamp our name all over it. The Dempsey dynasty o' Dublin Bus!"

I basked in the headiness of the obligatory binge to celebrate my results, never questioning what it was that I was celebrating.

"So, what's the plan, Paddy?" Popey asked.

"The plan? I was gonna ask you first and rob yours!"

We laughed, as if the topic was unworthy of serious discussion.

"Same again, Popey?"

"Yeah, Paddy. Thanks."

As I walked to the bar, I toyed with the old man's advice. I also speculated as to where the line between 'not chasing it too hard' and 'dossing' lay. I knew I'd probably soon discover where and would most likely cross it.

Chapter 13
The Merits and Pitfalls of Charlatanism

I walked listlessly round the room, inspecting the lack-lustre vacancies on the walls, hoping to spot a well-hidden nugget that I'd missed on the previous lap. The job centre, it seemed, wasn't quite the career starter that I'd naively assumed it would be.

The Celtic Tiger was running wild round the country, making the poor rich and the rich richer, such was the ubiquitous claim. But I questioned if the Celtic Tiger had ever visited Bray on his travels, judging by what I had to choose from.

Cashier required for MacBetting Bookmaker Ltd. Must have previous experience.
No go.

Commis chef in O'Brien's Restaurant. Hourly rate based on experience.
What in God's name is a commis chef?

Second-year apprentice carpenter needed.
Typical. I can't find anyone looking for a first-year apprentice.

Office administrator needed. Competitive salary. At least one year's experience necessary.

A year's experience just to shuffle papers! What are they doing in the office, planning a space launch?

Warehouse operative needed. Minimum wage. No experience needed. Forklift license essential.
Forklift license? Ye need a license to drive a poxy forklift? How hard could it be? Would they even check? I'll take that one.

Back home, I set about writing a CV.
Education?
I knew my exam results would negate anything positive on the rest of the CV. I could've written the cure to cancer below them and even that wouldn't have drawn employers' attention away from the Cs and Ds on the page. I decided to do what any self-respecting jobseeker would do. I changed the grades, I exaggerated my performance, I transcribed the biggest, foulest heap of dung this side of the Curragh.
Work history?
My paper round was accompanied by a much-heralded stint in a hardware store that saw me become the recipient of their much lauded 'Employee of the Month' award for a record, four consecutive months. If I was to be a charlatan, I'd strive to be the finest artist of the craft.
I augmented my CV with a mention of my voluntary work in the local community and of the interest I had in contemporary social issues such as homelessness and drug abuse, not failing to note my substantial charitable donations in their regard.
References?

Conscious of how suspicious it would look not to have a referee from the hardware store, I added Popey's phone number and cast him in the role of the fictitious manager of the local DIY City store, Jack Harrison. I had no doubt that Popey would give a sterling performance as the astute, talent spotter that I imagined Jack Harrison as being - effusively lauding my work ethic and lamenting my departure from the store - if he received the call.

I read over the CV, admiring the socially conscious, ambitious, philanthropist that jumped from the page, and found no difficulty in seeing myself as him.

I posted my application. Some days later, I still hadn't heard a reply. Curious and impatient, I rang them.

"Hello, Tiernan Storage. Emma speaking. How may I help you?"

"I'm just ringing about a warehouse job I applied for."

"Hold on two seconds, I'll put you through to the manager."

Elevator music played down the phone.

"Hello there, Gavin O'Rourke speaking."

"Hello, Gav– Gavin. I was just wondering if ye received a job application from me?"

"Your name?"

"Patrick Dempsey."

"Yes, we have an application from a Patrick Dempsey here."

"Am I, ye know, being considered?"

"I'm afraid, Patrick, we need a qualified driver."

"Oh, I've a forklift license."

"Ye do? There's no mention of it on your CV."

Of all the things to leave out!

"Yeah, I got it just last week. The CV's out o' date."

"I see. Why don't ye meet me and we'll discuss whether you're a good fit for the job."

"Yeah, that'd be great, Gavin."

"Is half nine on Wednesday morning okay for ye?"

"That's sound, mate. I mean, that's ideal, sir."

"Perfect. I'll see ye then."

My walk into O'Rourke's office was that of a man with a purpose, albeit not knowing what that purpose was.

"Hello, Patrick. Nice to meet ye. Have a seat."

He looked different than I'd imagined. He was a small man with a horseshoe hairstyle, glasses, and a belly that asked a lot from the buttons on the lower half of his shirt.

"I've a busy enough diary, Patrick, so I won't keep ye long. Tell me, what made ye apply for a job in our company?"

"Well, 'cause I need one."

"Well, yes, I understand that, but what I'm interested to know is why you chose our company specifically?"

"I saw your ad in the job centre."

Simple questions so far. I'm flying!

"Yes, yes, again, I understand that much. I suppose, what I'm trying to ask is what would ye bring to the role in question, bearing in mind your lack of experience in this area?"

Ouch! And ye were going so well. Okay, think, Paddy.

"Well, I mightn't have the experience, but I'm sure this is a well-run business that has plenty o' capable employees who could show me the ropes for the first few days. Plus, at my age, I've a huge appetite to learn everything about the role, and my ambition is to progress further up the ladder in the company. I've a huge passion for warehousing - doing paperwork on boxes, moving boxes…"

Opening and closing boxes? Christ, stop talking!

"I see. It's good to hear someone with such passion. Most o' the people we get in here are happy to go through the motions. Their only ambition is to out-whinge each other about their wages." He let out a pompous laugh. I deemed it appropriate to laugh with him.

This guy is a magnificent prick.

"To be honest with ye, Patrick, I like your CV. Ye seem to have a great work ethic, and I have a lot o' time for someone who helps out those in need."

Those in what? Oh, the philanthropy!

"Ye remind me o' meself when I was your age; full of ambition, wanting to take on the world."

Ye'd be better off taking on less burgers!

"I love seeing those traits in a young man."

God, this cunt is insufferable.

"I notice that one o' your referees is Jack Harrison, manager o' DIY City. Is the manager not Bobby Maloney? I know him well."

Aw, for the love o' God! Of all the places ye could've picked.

That lady luck is a right trollop!

"Eh.... Bobby left there recently. He got a promotion to one o' the bigger stores in Dublin."

"Ah, I wasn't aware. I must congratulate him the next time I see him."

"And would ye see him often?"

"Ah, rarely these days. We're both too busy raking in the profits."

Watch out for the bullshit you're raking in with them.

"Well, o' course. No quarter given in the auld rat race, is there?"

"Certainly not, Patrick. But I can't complain. That's an unavoidable consequence of success, isn't it?"

Is it?

"Isn't it just."

As he continued to speak, he averted his gaze to a framed picture of himself receiving an award and a handshake from some local politician who had the appearance of someone who was well-versed in the dispensing of such awards.

"Anyway, I need someone asap, so seeing that ye have the license, and in light of your CV, your willingness to learn and your ambition, I'm offering ye the job, Patrick."

"Great, thanks very much!"

"You'll start on Monday morning at nine o'clock."

"Perfect, Gavin. I'll see ye then."

I left his office feeling relieved that Popey wouldn't be offered the opportunity to display his acting credentials, as having met O'Rourke, he struck me as the type of person who would see right through such a performance. Lady luck, it seemed, was a trollop trying to change her ways.

Monday morning. O'Rourke barked his orders, delegating as much of his job as he could to his underlings. He would've had you hold his one-eyed associate while he took a widdle if it didn't breach employment law.

"Right, lads, that's today's work. I've to head off to a meeting. I want a good chunk o' that done by the time I'm back. Dumitru and Slaven, I want you two on admin duties. Matas and Paddy, you two on the forks. Get to work, lads."

I waited until he left the building before climbing onto one of the forklifts.

Accelerator, brake, steering wheel… Simple.

I turned the key in the ignition and pressed a pedal.

Nothing.

The brake?

I placed my foot over the other pedal and charted a short course in front of me. I wanted to get a feel for it before I attempted moving the forks. With my course set, I readied myself and stamped on the pedal. The forklift shot backwards at speed. I heard the shouts of my co-workers as they jumped clear of its trajectory, cursing me in their native tongues. Their shouts were accompanied by a horrible crunch that emanated from behind me. The crashing sound brought me to my senses. I took my foot off the pedal and looked behind, fretting about what dismal scene awaited me. I had driven the forklift through a door, knocking it off its hinges.

Oh, bollocks!

"My arm, my arm! You breaked my arm!" Matas, the Lithuanian, said angrily.

He'd had to perform an Olympic standard long jump to avoid being run over and landed awkwardly in the process.

"Ah, if it was broken ye'd know all about it. Relax, will ye!" I said brusquely.

Dumitru, a Romanian, then got involved. "You no drive, you danger! I tell Gavin."

"I can drive it. Some eejit left it in reverse!"

"No, no, no. I tell Gavin!"

Knowing my rebuttals were futile, I opted for a different approach. "Listen, Dumitru, I'll be honest with ye. I've no license. If he finds out it was me, I'll be out on me arse. What if you or Slaven took the blame for it? I'll give ye some o' me wages. Just say the forklift was acting up. He'll believe you pair."

Slaven shook his head in disapproval of the idea. Dumitru wasn't as dismissive.

"How much?" he asked.

"A hundred quid."

"One week's pay," Dumitru haggled.

"Get offside, Dumitru!"

"Then I tell Gavin."

"Okay, okay, one week," I said, reluctantly relenting.

Just as the deal was finalised, Matas butted in.

"My arm, my arm breaked. I want money. I want one week's pay too!"

"Your injury will be covered by the insurance, Matas, you'll be sorted," I told him, trying to silence him.

"No, no. I want money too!" he demanded.

"For what? Dumitru is taking the blame, so he gets the money. You're not doing anything. Why should you get any money?"

"My arm!"

"What did I just tell ye about the insurance? And your arm's not broken anyway, would ye give over!"

"I get money Dumitru get, or I tell Gavin."

"Why don't yis split it?" I suggested.

"I no share money," Dumitru said.

"Well, I'm not paying another week's wages to Matas. And if he's gonna spill the beans anyway, well then, I'm not paying a week's wages to you, Dumitru."

"Matas, stay out my business," Dumitru instructed.

"I get what you get, Dumitru."

"No ye don't, because you're not doing anything," I remonstrated. "Ye want money for the dirty work that others are doing. You're a Lithuanian Fagin, Matas!"

"No insult my country!"

"I'm insulting *you*!"

As we quarrelled, O'Rourke arrived back unexpectedly.

"They've cancelled the meeting," he informed us frustratedly. "Ye'd think they'd give me more notice! I'm up to me eyes as it is and… What happened to the door?!"

"He crash machine, Gavin!" Matas told him, pointing at me. "He breaked my arm!"

"That man, he no drive," Slaven said, wagging his finger.

Dumitru said nothing as O'Rourke surveyed the damage.

"Patrick, come into me office now!" he ordered.

I stood in his office like a guilty man awaiting sentencing from a judge.

"Sit down, Patrick... What in Christ's name were ye up to out there?"

"Someone left the forklift in reverse, Gavin."

"And did a licensed driver like you not notice that it was in reverse, Patrick?"

"I learned on a different model."

"A different model? Ye must think I come from a different planet! I took your word that ye were licensed!"

"Well, I did say I'd need to be shown the ropes for a few days, but sure those three clowns out there couldn't teach a dog to take a shite!"

"Those three clowns that ye so eloquently refer to are licensed drivers, Patrick! The only clown here is you! Ye lied to me about being licensed, then ye destroy a door *and* injure an employee, all in your first hour on the job!"

"Well, it's not the most ideal start I will admit, but it can only get better from here on in."

"It can't, because you're sacked!"

"Ah, Gavin, sure I've only started! I've just to iron out a few creases, that's all!"

"Well, ye can iron your creases out on someone else's ironing board!"

"Ah, that's fierce harsh, that is!" I protested.

"Harsh?! Ye should never have got the job in the first place. Pick up your belongings and be on your way!"

Knowing that a final plea for clemency would be pointless, I left his office and exited the building, saying everything to myself that I wished I'd said to O'Rourke.

Fuck him anyway! Fuck all o' them! He can shove his poxy forks up his arse, the fat bollocks! With a bit o' luck he might puncture himself! Fuckin' shite job anyway!

I thought I was going forward when I was going backwards. It was true in more ways than one. My first proper job hadn't even lasted one day. I hadn't even made it to the tea break. I must've broken the world record for the quickest sacking.

As I headed home, my receding anger offered me a sense of perspective. The moon hadn't crashed into Earth. I'd chanced my arm to get a job and supposedly broke a Lithuanian's arm to lose it. There was a certain karma tangled somewhere in that. I was in no worse a situation than I had been a few days prior. I just needed a new plan; one which I'd try to formulate at the Waterfront bar, staring into a pint glass.

Chapter 14

The Queen is Dead, Long Live the Queen

I reacquainted myself with the job centre, more out of a sense of duty than any hope of finding whatever it was that I was looking for. There were jobs, but I was either unqualified for skilled labour or too inexperienced for non-skilled labour. It was now September. Ma and Da's patience with me was on the wane. If they'd known about the forklift fiasco, their patience would've been long depleted. I had been prudent enough to not mention a word to them about the job, and to refrain from resigning from my paper round, as if having foreseen the approaching buffoonery. Claire was already planning for college, ready to overtake me. Bereft of ideas, I was becoming increasingly conscious of the fact that time was passing as I remained static.

One evening, all four of us were watching an Ireland football match on the television. Ma and Claire were talking about the latter's exams. Knowing that such a conversation could lead to Ma wanting to know what *I* was planning on doing with my life, I made sure to have no part in it, opting to discuss Ireland's two goal lead with Da instead.

Over recent weeks, they'd had the pleasure of seeing me getting out of bed at eleven to spend a few hours delivering newspapers, only to return afterwards and spend the rest of the day in front of the television. They were probably perplexed by my indolence, now that they were witnessing it in its full glory, butchering any notions that they may still have had that the teachers had been wrong about me.

"Da, can we watch something else?" Claire asked. "This match is over."

"No," Da responded curtly. "I've a few quid on Ireland to win by three, so I'm not missing the end of it."

"Sure, you'll find out the result later, Da," she said, persisting.

"I can find it out in a few minutes if I keep watching it, Claire. Why, what do ye wanna watch?"

"Brides and Grooms is starting."

"Brides and… Fuckin' tarts and twats, more like!"

"I saw it last week. It was gas."

"A lethal bloody gas!"

"Ah, go on, Da," she pleaded.

"We're watching the match, Claire, end o' story."

"Love, will ye let your father watch the match in peace," Ma interceded.

"Load o' shite," Claire mumbled.

"Excuse me! What was that, young lady?" Ma asked sternly.

"Nothing, Ma."

"Well, you're making a lot o' noise for someone who's saying nothing!"

"How much would ye win, Da?" she enquired.

"Not enough for whatever it is ye want, Claire," he replied bluntly.

"Love, don't be scabbing off your father."

"Why not? Paddy does all the time."

"Yes, you're right, Claire. Patrick, will ye stop milking your father for money and get out o' this bloody house and do something with yourself!"

The words were fired at me with a ferocity she rarely employed.

The two women have united against me! It's an ambush!

"Here, I haven't said anything!" I protested.

"Nor are ye doing anything!" Ma replied.

"I am!"

"And what's that?"

"I'm watching the match, Ma."

"And after the lousy match?"

"I've a busy round o' papers tomorrow afternoon."

"So, is that all ye wanna do, is it? Deliver shaggin' newspapers for the rest o' your life?"

"I've been applying for lots o' things, Ma."

"They're not gonna be interested in ye unless you've some qualification. I said to ye about doing a course."

"Yeah, well, I thought I could find a proper job, didn't I? Mr Celtic Tiger and all that crap."

"John?"

"What?"

Da's attention was solely focused on the match. He was oblivious to the conversation being had beside him as he kicked and headed every ball on the pitch.

"What do ye think, John?"

"About what?"

"About what we've been talking about."

"Ah, I'd be hopeful. There's still time."

"Exactly, Da," I concurred.

"Well, it's not getting any earlier, that's all I'm saying."

"Relax, will ye, Aoife. There'll be about four minutes of injury time. They'll get another chance."

"Ah, for God's sake, John! I'm not talking about your poxy bet! I'm talking about Patrick!"

"Christ alive, Aoife! I stand to win a few quid here and you're hassling me about Paddy! What about him?"

"What do ye think he should do?"

"I agree… Go on, go on… I agree… Will ye cross the shaggin' thing! I agree with what you're saying, love."

"Thank you, John," she said with a hint of sarcasm. "Patrick, ye should meet with one o' the case officers down in that job centre. They'll tell ye what options are out there for ye."

"Yeah, yeah," I muttered.

"Don't 'yeah, yeah' me, Patrick! And don't even think o' coming back from your meeting without something in mind. Do ye hear me?"

"Yeah, I hear ye, Ma. Jesus."

"And John?"

"What now, Aoife?" he asked, exasperated.

"No more handouts to Patrick."

"Yeah, I– Go on, go on, go on…couldn't agree… Hit it, hit it…with ye more… Yes!"

Da leapt out of his chair in celebration as Ireland scored a late third goal, before standing at the fireplace to give an impromptu rendition of *The Fields of Athenry* as he awaited the final whistle. When the match ended, he went out to the hall, grabbed his coat and came back into the sitting room.

"Paddy, come on. We're heading down for last orders."

"Ah, John, what did I just say?"

"Ah, come on, Aoife. It's not every day I take the bookie to the cleaners."

"Oh, awright, go on," she said, relenting.

"Do ye have any idea what ye'd be interested in doing, Patrick?" Shay Daly, my appointed case officer, asked.

The age-old question had returned to torment me again. I tapped my fingers on his desk, trying to think of something.

"Em… I could be a handy man, Shay."

"A handy man?"

"Yeah, ye know, doing the odd job here and there."

"Like a caretaker? Have ye any relevant qualifications for that?"

"What qualifications do ye need? I'd only be opening up the place, doing a bit o' painting, unblocking the bog if there was a monster log stuck in it. There's not much to it, is there?"

"More than ye think."

"What about me age? Doesn't being young mean something? Energy, ambition and all that stuff?"

"Well, unfortunately, Patrick, to most employers, being young means being inexperienced. How much work experience do ye have?"

And here it comes over the horizon, the torrent o' codology, destroying everything in its path, heading in your direction.

"Well, I've a paper round for what it's worth. I worked in a warehouse too."

"Well, that's something. For how long?"

Be vaguely specific.

"Well, I was in a transitional phase. I was taking stock o' things at the time. I was reassessing me career options…"

"A year?"

"No."

"Months?"

"No."

"Weeks?"

"No."

"Days?"

"No."

"A day?"

"Nearly. A few hours."

"A few hours! What happened?"

"I was sacked. Can ye believe it?"

I'm sure he can.

"Why were ye let go?"

'Let go.' That has a nicer ring to it.

"Ah sure, the boss was looking for any auld reason to get rid o' me. He said I lied about being able to drive a forklift, destroyed a door and injured one o' the staff. But sure, if it wasn't any o' that, it would've been something else. I reckon he was afraid I'd get them all to go on strike."

"Ye reckon?"

"Would I have a claim for unfair dismissal? Is it worth chasing?"

"Let's not go down that road. It's a competitive employment market out there. We'd be better off concentrating on finding an alternative career path for ye."

"Where's that Celtic Tiger geezer?"

"Well, that geezer is everywhere, Patrick, but *he* won't come to *you, you* have to chase *him*. Ye have to make the effort to get a qualification. Once ye do that, you're in the race."

"What about courses? Me ma has me head done in yapping about them. Anything worth dipping me auld toe into?"

"I'm glad ye asked. I was just about to recommend ye go down that route. There's a wide range o' full and part-time courses that ye can avail of locally. I've a brochure here that ye can cast your eye over and see if anything tickles your fancy… Here, take this home with ye."

"Sound."

"And workwise, try the hospitality sector. With the economy booming, pubs, restaurants and hotels are forever looking for staff." He rose from his seat and shook my hand. "I've other business to attend to, Patrick, so best o' luck."

I headed home down Quinsborough Road, leafing through the brochure diligently, as if somewhere hidden in it, was the meaning of life. Perhaps, amongst its pages, I'd find a meaningful life.

Despite the numerous full-time courses available, I opted for an evening bookkeeping course. I figured that it was one which wouldn't demand a level of commitment from me which I was certain I didn't possess and would provide me with a quick fix qualification, the credentials of which, would hopefully lend themselves to the Celtic Tiger's playground.

No sooner had I arrived in the college on Navaro Road for my first evening, when I found my attention distracted by a girl across the room. Stephanie Heffernan. She was attractive enough that I fancied her, but not so attractive that I wouldn't have a chance with her.

The course's duration allowed me to plan a strategic approach, one that relied on steadily building a friendship to the point at which an invitation for a drink would be accepted without hesitation.

One evening in the canteen, I sat with the women in the hope that I'd get to converse with her. It was my first experience of being in the company of a group of mostly middle-aged females, and it was quite an eye-opener. There was no end to the conversation. Blokes could sit together and pass a few remarks, crack a joke now and then, or occasionally air a grievance. The conversation would come and go as it saw fit. These women, however, were a different animal. Silence was strictly forbidden. One topic of conversation would stream seamlessly into another, and when one stopped talking to chew her food, another would instinctively jump in and take over, each contributing their shift. The conversation transitioned between light-hearted observations to depressing sob stories without a key change being audible. I hoped that I wouldn't have to contribute to this linguistic marvel as a ritual of an unwanted initiation. But any such impromptu contribution made by me, would surely have had no less merit than the rest of the blather I was hearing.

"They sell the best tea bags. I do me shopping all the way over on the far side o' town just to get their tea bags.

Derek is forever moaning about wasting petrol, but sure isn't that what the car is for?"

"You're dead right, Nuala. Sure, why else would ye be going across town?"

"Ah, ladies, don't mention anything about a car to me. Kevin was trying to teach me to drive the other night and didn't I drive it into the neighbour's wall."

"Ye did not?!" one of them asked.

"I did. Kevin has to get the car fixed, pay for the neighbour's wall, and pay the vet's bill."

"The vet's bill?"

"The neighbour's dog was behind the wall having a shite when it happened. One o' the blocks fell on his paw."

"Ah, you're joking, Joan? How was himself afterwards?"

"Ah, he had a head on him like a constipated ape."

"Ye mean Kevin or the dog?"

"Both! Ha ha."

"If I was you, I'd let that husband o' yours chauffer me around. Put him to good use."

"Ah, it was a new year's resolution I made. It was either that or giving up the smokes. After that incident with the wall, I'm convinced the smokes are less of a hazard to me health. Ha ha."

"Ah, Joan, ye shouldn't be making light o' those shaggin' things. Me da was diagnosed with lung cancer last year because o' them."

"Aw, God love him. How's he getting on, Liz?"

"The treatment has him worn out but he's trying to keep his head up."

"Well, that's good to hear."

"He had me driven demented the other day when I was driving him into the hospital."

"Ah, ye can forgive him for that. Sure, his poor head is probably all over the place. He wouldn't be himself."

"No, I was delighted. He *was* being himself, for the first time in ages. Arguing with me about me parking technique. That's Da of old to a tee!"

"Tell him, next time you'll get your friend Joan to drive him in and he can critique *her* parking instead! Ha ha."

"Ah, girls, the man has cancer, not a death wish. Sure, if I drove him in, cancer would be the least of his worries. They'd have to cut him out o' the car. He'd go in for treatment and come out with his legs amputated!"

"Lisa, you're being very quiet today," one of them mentioned. "Are ye tired? Tell that fella o' yours to start doing more around the house."

"Ah, don't get me started on him, girls."

"Oh, tell us."

"He wanted us and the kids to go camping on the weekend. Now, what Cormac knows about bloody camping is anyone's guess, but he's seen enough o' the shows on telly to make him think he's some sort o' expert. So off we went, down to the back arse o' Wicklow. He had the whole route planned. We'd get the bus to such a place, walk a few miles to another place, until we'd get to some shaggin' forest in the middle o' nowhere. So, o' course, what happened?"

"What?"

"We arrived at his camping spot, having walked half o' Wicklow, only to find it was already taken by a bunch o' teenagers. So, Cormac started moaning, 'Ah, we're not staying here. They'll be drinking and causing trouble.' So, he wanted us to head further off the beaten track. We eventually found a spot that he was happy with, so we set up the tents and collected wood for the fire. But o' course, Cormac being Cormac, forgot to bring his flint stick thing. So, we were sitting there for the whole night, freezing our arses off, watching Cormac rubbing sticks like an absolute fuckin' eejit!"

"Aw, he wouldn't last the night with me. I'd be strangling him!"

"Aw, the best is yet to come, girls. When we packed up on Sunday to go home, he had no idea where we were or how to get back onto the main road. So, there we were, walking around in circles for hours. I swear, we must've passed the same stream a dozen times. I was pissed off. The kids were moaning. O' course Cormac saw it all as some sort of adventure. 'Part o' the experience,' he said."

"So, what happened then?"

"We were blessed. It was only by pure luck that we eventually bumped into a couple, and they told us which way to head. Mind you, only 'cause I asked them. Cormac didn't want to ask them. Ye'd want to hear him, girls. He goes, 'I'm not asking for directions. That's the height o' femininity. That's why women have never been to the moon. They'd get lost and start looking for an alien to show them the way.'"

"Aw, for heaven's sake! The aliens may abduct him!"

"That's my Cormac, ladies."

"Ah, they're all useless, girls. But if they were any way useful, ye wouldn't know what to do with them. Ha ha."

As Stephanie became an integral part of the women's yapping, having a conversation with her away from them was proving difficult, so I caught up with her one night when she was leaving the college.

"Hi, Stephanie."

"Ah, how's things, Patrick?"

"All good, all good… So, where are ye from?"

"Bray, just up on Boghall Road. You?"

"Little Bray… I don't be up your way too often."

"Ah, sure you Little Brayites get homesick if yis cross the bridge," she joked.

"We're not that bad," I said, laughing. So, what has ye doing the course?"

"Well, I work as a receptionist but I wanna go to college. The problem is, I don't know what I wanna study. So, I figured I'd do this course for the time being. You?"

"I just wanna get some sort o' qualification to help me find something."

"I know the feeling."

At the end of Navaro Road, our journeys homeward split off in opposite directions.

"I'll see ye Thursday, Steph?"

"Yeah, see ye then."

I turned away from her and waited a few seconds before I looked back to get one last glimpse of her, only to catch her doing the same thing. We smiled at each other before I turned back around and headed home.

When I arrived back at the house, I was already relishing Thursday's arrival.

Rachael Dowling had lingered in my thoughts in recent weeks – what she was doing, what might have been. The curiosity had tempted me to make contact. Only my stubbornness had restrained me from doing so. Now, my thoughts of her could be laid to rest.

The Queen is dead, long live the Queen.

Chapter 15
The Good Ship Employment

I was sitting on the toilet, leafing through the local newspaper.

Sham Door-to-Door Fundraiser
Found Guilty of Fraud

Damien Greene of 150 Oldcourt Avenue, stood trial in Bray District Court last Wednesday on a charge of fraud, which Mr Greene pleaded not guilty to. Garda Gerard Taylor, who presented the prosecution's case, claimed that Mr Greene had carried out door to door collections throughout Bray, in which he pretended to be fundraising for the Society of St Vincent de Paul. It was stated by Garda Taylor that the defendant was not an employee, nor a registered volunteer of the charity, and that the charity didn't have any knowledge of Mr Greene or any of his activities. Garda Taylor also stated that the defendant had fraudulently collected over 1,000 before the Gardaí arrested him. Mr Greene's barrister Simon Mulvaney said that despite not being an employee or a registered volunteer of the charity, his client had been genuinely fundraising for it, and that he had been planning to lodge the sum of money in his possession to the charity's bank account upon the completion of his work. Mr Mulvaney also said that his client had intended to register as a volunteer with the charity, but because of his work commitments, he hadn't had the time to do so. Judge Andrew O'Neill refused to accept Mr Greene's defence and found him guilty, describing him as 'a vulture who preyed on the good nature of the town's residents.' The judge, taking into consideration that Mr Greene had no prior convictions, imposed a 2,500 fine on him, and a six-month suspended sentence.

Owner of Chinese Takeaway Denies Poisoning Customers

The owner of the Beijing Kitchen, Yao Chen, has insisted that a rumour that some of his customers have suffered food poisoning as a result of eating in his establishment on Vevay Road is completely untrue. Mr Chen stated that he has seen a decline in business in recent weeks, which he attributes to the rumour; one that he refuted as being, 'a terrible, terrible lie.' He insists that he has not received a single complaint regarding his food and that he will happily comply with an inspection from the health authorities to try to repair his business's damaged reputation.

Mr Chen believes that the rumour was started by his competitors, in response to his expanding clientele, which was to the detriment of nearby takeaways. He has threatened to sue those responsible for slander, in the event of discovering their identities.

He also stated that he has become aware of a second rumour that he is serving fried dog in his establishment and masquerading it as pork.

Mr Chen said that the situation has become very stressful, as along with his financial worries, he cannot attend the local pub without fellow customers barking and what he described as 'howling at the moon' upon his arrival.

Neighbours in Street Brawl Over Extension

The Gardaí were called to Wolfe Tone Square North last Monday because of a brawl that had broken out on the street between two of its residents. It started after Stephen Dowie and his neighbour, Luke Purcell, became involved in a heated argument that related to the latter's house extension, for which no planning permission had been sought. It is alleged that Mr Purcell said to Mr Dowie, 'F**k off if you know what's good for you.' It has also been alleged that Mr Dowie replied to Mr Purcell's threat in a frank manner, saying, 'I'll beat six shades of sh*te out of you!'

There were conflicting reports as to who made the initial assault. The fight was believed to have ended when neighbours managed to separate the two men. But minutes later, Mr Dowie emerged from his residence equipped with a sledgehammer and was quoted as saying, 'I'm going to knock some sense into Purcell before I knock down his extension!' Mr Dowie then began hammering on Mr Purcell's front door as screams were heard emanating from the house. The Gardaí arrived at the scene just as Mr Dowie had bust the lock of the door and gained entry to the house, in what one witness described as being like a scene from a horror film. They rushed into the house

after him, emerging minutes later
with Mr Dowie handcuffed and being
led away. Mr Purcell was heard goading
Mr Dowie as he was being seated in
the squad car, saying, 'I'd be more
worried about my wife if I was you,
Dowie. From what I hear, there's no
permission required!'

Each page was ripped out and put to good use between my two cheeks.

VACANCY: Bartender required for O'Connell's Public House

Bar tending experience an advantage
but not a necessity. Training provided.
Competitive salary. Candidates must be
able to work flexible hours.

The advert caught my attention, saving itself from an arse-wiping, U-bend travelling, sewer-dwelling fate.

I applied for the job. A week later I heard from David Doyle, the manager of O'Connell's. The dreaded interview was arranged.

Lacking the experience that other candidates would probably possess, I felt I needed something else to make me stand out. Over the coming hours, I devised a plan which I became in awe of.

I'd bamboozle him with a linguistic feast, serving him a series of rehearsed phrases that would leave him dazzled by the extent of my intellect.

"Tell me a little about yourself, Patrick. What would make ye the right candidate for this job?" Doyle asked, looking as unimpressed with me as I was with him.

"Well, I'm not known to be a fanfaron, David. I'm more of a pauciloquent type o' person to be honest. But I suppose many people would say that I have an argute business acumen and a supererogatory work ethic."

He narrowed his eyes in bemusement.

"I see, and you've no prior experience working in a pub?"

"No, but the multitudinous experiences that I've had beyond the pub trade have afforded me a certain eruditeness, which I believe can be applied to the job in question, given that there's a level o' homogeneity between bartending and me previous employments. Wouldn't ye agree?"

"Yes, yes indeed, and…"

"And at risk of coming across as a blatherskite, I have to say that I've never been accused o' being a mendacious person. In fact, I'm quite trustworthy."

"Em, yes… Em, I suppose I'm looking for certain qualities from each candidate. I need someone who can take the heavy workload in their stride, while being able to have a chat and a laugh with customers."

"Oh, I can mirthfully expatiate upon multifarious topics of conversation."

"Sorry, I didn't quite get… Em… Are ye a good team player? Teamwork is key to running a successful pub."

"Well, I'm quite an altruistic individual. I'll vivaciously work extra hours when required, and I'm not known to absquatulate at the end o' me shift."

"Absqu...? Yeah, em... Do ye think it would take ye long to settle in, to get used to the way o' doing things?"

"No, not at all. I'm an equanimous sort o' fella."

Doyle fell silent. He clasped his hands and tapped his thumbs for a few seconds.

"I won't beat around the bush, Patrick. I think that ye have the necessary skillset for the job from what ye... from what I think you've said. I'm going to offer ye the role on a two-week trial basis. Now, don't worry, I won't be nitpicking everything ye do. Once ye don't blow the place to smithereens, you'll have the job permanently. Ye can start next week."

I rose and shook his hand. "Thanks, David! Ye won't regret it."

As I exited the premises, I expected to feel an urge to laugh at my successful stunt, but instead, I felt relieved. Words shot through my head, one after another.

Purpose, worth, meaning, money, job, somebody, life, future, ladder, rung, step, direction.

At home, the news was greeted enthusiastically.

"Ah, good man, Paddy! You'll own the place next," Da joked.

"I'm delighted for ye, love!"

"Thanks, Ma. Thanks, Da."

"Ye better not be expecting any tips off me, Paddy. And I want none o' that 'You've had enough' malarkey," Da quipped again.

"At least now I'll have someone to keep an eye on ye, John," Ma remarked, before the pair of them became engrossed in the programme on the television. I was elsewhere, sailing away on the good ship employment, a one-way voyage to a money-laden destination.

Television, politics, the perfect pint, history, balding, marriage, scams, horses, children, wages, who's riding who, who's robbing who, who owes who. Nothing occurred in the country without it crossing the bar of O'Connell's. No issue, no matter how great or small, escaped their collective expertise. They were a think tank, a gambling committee, a comedic group, a band of balladeers, an assortment of whingers, they were whatever they wished to be on any given night. Their frivolous conversations never failed to amuse me.

"So, your man comes knocking on me door," one of them at the bar said.

"Right," the man beside him replied.

"Says to me, 'That little brown dog is yours, isn't he?' I said to him, 'Why do ye ask?' He says, 'Because he's after doing the business with my yoke, and now isn't she about to drop a few nippers because of him.' So I said, 'What's that got to do with me?'"

"And?"

"'Well, he's your dog,' he says. I said to him, 'Listen, he lives with me but he's not mine. What he does in his own time is his own business.'"

"So, what did he want?"

"Ah, that's the best bit. He wanted me to take a few o' the pups off his hands. I said to him, 'I will in me hole!'"

"And?"

"He says, 'Your dog's the father!' I said, 'He may be the father, but *I'm* not the father. I'm not rearing a pack o' hounds just 'cause your bitch can't keep her tail down!'"

"So then what?"

"He says to me, 'That little mut o' yours has been running riot round the streets. God only knows how many other dogs he's impregnated!' I asked him, 'What do ye want him to do, wear a condom? Pay child support?'"

"Ha ha. What did he say?"

"He says, 'I want you as the legal owner of the dog to take responsibility for his actions!' I said, 'Sorry, but did *I* personally give your dog a lash? Furthermore, how do ye even know that my fella's the father? Your yoke would throw herself at anything at the wag of a tail. If ye had any sense ye'd have her on the pill.'"

"So then what did he say?"

"He says, 'Yours is the only one prowling the streets at all hours.' I said, 'What can I do? The dog has a better sex life than meself.' 'Get him neutered,' he says. So I said, 'I'll get *you* fuckin' neutered!' 'You're taking three,' he says to me then."

"Three no less? The bang o' shite would be something else! Why doesn't he sell them?"

"He hasn't the heart to supposedly. He wants me to take a few o' them so that they're with their auldfella, just up the road from the other half."

"Ah, have ye ever heard the likes?"

"Mind you, if I take them off him, then they're mine. I can sell them if I want to. They'd make a decent Christmas present for someone. Would your young lad be interested in a dog?"

"I'll make sure he is if the price is right. Cheaper than a bloody computer!"

"Jesus, maybe I'll try to get the whole litter off him. Sell them all off before he's any the wiser. Sure, I'd be doing him a favour. He doesn't need the hassle. And as for me own dog, what would he want with pups? They'd only interfere with his social life."

"You're as bad as your dog! Ye never miss an opportunity. Ha ha."

Two weeks of cleaning tables, collecting glasses, pulling pints, and suffering the odd sing-song, saw me land the job permanently.

"Ye can thank me for himself keeping ye on, Paddy," one of the regulars informed me. "I gave ye a cracking reference. 'No better barman,' I said. 'He pulls a pint like he pulls his knob; slow, with lots o' care, and with special attention given to the head.' Ha ha."

After my two-week initiation, my name was inseparable from the punters' orders for drinks. For the denizens of the twenty-foot long mahogany bar, the pints greased their throats as they spouted their wisdom and their grievances, garrulously giving voice to the random thoughts that occupied their inebriated brains.

There was Willie Clarke, whose booming voice never seemed to fit with his short stature. Beside him usually sat Pete Robinson, Clarke's foremost sparring partner in all things nonsensical, who possessed a nose like Munster and a political mind fixated with Ulster. Denis Duggan was the unofficial referee who sat next to them, while Glen Duff threw in the odd remark from the flanks. Niall Kenny and his wife, the sole female representative, ignored their ramblings, only allowing themselves to be drawn into their squabbles occasionally, when their opinions were sought to settle matters. A few other blokes, as misanthropic as their brethren were gregarious, warmed stools and emptied glasses, exercising their elbows as the others exercised their jaws.

"What do ye think yourself, young Paddy?" Robinson asked.

"What's that?"

"Clarke here with his West Brit cap on, insisting the Brits have given more to the world than the Irish."

"And ye don't agree?"

"Any self-respecting Irishman wouldn't!" insisted Robinson. "Ye have what they call an inferiority complex, Clarke."

"Inferiority complex, me bollocks, Robo! Sure, didn't the sun never set on their shaggin' empire. And isn't it still shining in the north o' this country!"

"It's only a matter o' time before our teddy bear gets his head back. And anyway, it's a culturally bankrupt country that has to rely on imperialism to argue what it's given to the world."

"And what in the name o' Christ would you know about culture, other than its spelling? What about Shakespeare, Dickens, Lennon and McCartney, and all the rest o' them?"

"Ye could go to the heart o' Africa and there wouldn't be a word o' Shakespeare to be found, but I'll tell ye what, ye'd still find a decent pint o' Guinness."

"Me arse! And wasn't Guinness himself a unionist?"

"Well, he was still Irish, even if he didn't want to be."

"The submarine!" said Glen Duff.

"Indeed, Duffer. An Irish invention," Robinson concurred.

"And why was it invented? Clarke asked. "Only to get as far away from the place as possible!"

"As unpatriotic a sentiment as you'll hear this side o' Shankill Road, Clarke! Amn't I right, Duffer?"

"Dead right, Robo."

"What about English?" Dennis Duggan interjected.

"Spot on, Den! Aren't we having this conversation in English? Have ye ever heard a Brit having a row in Irish?"

"Ah, English is like the cheap cutlery, ye use it all the time. But the expensive cutlery, Irish, that's saved for the special occasions."

"You're some man, Robo, for arguing the toss! Ye can hardly write a word o' one language or speak a word o' the other."

"I don't have to be a great songwriter to appreciate a good tune."

"And I don't have to be Arthur Guinness to appreciate a good pint," said Duggan. "Same again, Paddy, good man."

"Sure, they built this country, Robo," said Clarke.

"Built it?! Fuckin' destroyed it!"

"And didn't they give us our patron saint, him a Brit."

"Ah, would ye give over, Clarke! He was hardly parading round waving a butcher's apron and singing *Rule Britannia*. And didn't he have to come over to Ireland to find a civilisation to his liking."

"What are ye on about? Ye'd swear he came over for a holiday to get a break from herding the fuckin' sheep. He was kidnapped and brought here as a slave!"

"Ah, those were the days. When *we* were enslaving the Brits! When did it all go wrong?"

"When the first pub opened, Robo… Another one for me, Paddy."

Away from the banter, slouched over a corner table, was the silent, lonesome and apathetic alcoholic, Billy Hughes. He sipped his pint slowly, knowing he wouldn't be served another.

"Come on, Billy. Finish that one up and be off home," I said. "She'll be wondering where ye are."

"She knows...where I am."

"Well, she'll be wondering when you'll be back then."

"I'm not able for the walk… I'll kip here."

"I'll get one o' the others to help ye."

The noise of the hoover at one in the morning could always be relied upon to rid the pub of its last stragglers.

"Time, folks," I shouted, as I gave the carpet a once-over.

Duggan and Duff escorted Billy Hughes's lifeless limbs to the front door.

"Polio Hughes, here! Will ye use your legs, Billy!" Duff instructed.

"Demented I am, men," he said, as his head dropped.

"Christ, we'd mistake ye for someone else if ye weren't," said Duggan. "Come on, time to go."

The door closed behind them, creating a priceless silence.

Billy Hughes. The butt o' jokes. The target o' scorn. The victim o' drink. Former tradesman. Had his own business. Now look at him. How do ye end up like that?

I poured myself a well-deserved drink as I pondered the thought.

Chapter 16

The Introvert and the Extrovert

In the following weeks, I tried to speak to Stephanie as often as I could. I'd seen her one Saturday night in the Waterfront and had gone over to her to say hello, but I'd found myself competing for her attention with half of the people there. Stephanie, I'd discovered, was an extrovert, and was well-known. It had seemed that her night out wasn't complete unless she talked, sang and danced with every person on the premises. I was relatively unknown in comparison, and I never made much of an effort to change that fact.

Although her gregarious personality was the antithesis to my own, it didn't dissuade me from her. So, I'd decided that night to step out of the queue for her attention in the Waterfront and wait for a more opportune time when I could have a drink with her alone.

My chance came on the final evening of the course. Before our exam was due to start, I went over and spoke to her.

"Ye fancy a drink after the test, Steph?"

"Yeah, why not. Where?"

"What about Mullin's?"

"Yeah, grand."

Having breezed through the rudimentary exam with time to spare, I found myself in Mullin's on the main street awaiting her arrival. I necked a couple of pints to craft a bit of swagger as I compiled a list of conversation topics.

I'd start off by asking her about her plans. That would be followed by the ever-reliable topics of hobbies, family and holidays. Then, when she'd be more relaxed after a few drinks, I'd carefully enquire as to the type of lad she'd like to meet and gain priceless inside information from her.

When she arrived, I caught her attention from the bar and beckoned her over.

"You were finished early, Paddy."

"Ah, it was a doddle. What are ye having?"

"A white wine."

We headed to a quiet table in the corner.

"So, ye enjoyed the course?" I asked.

"I'm glad it's over. You?"

"Same. So, what's your plan?"

"I suppose I'll keep tipping away as a receptionist for the time being. You?"

"O'Connell's is awright. The money's not bad. I'll keep me eyes peeled, but if it ain't broke, don't fix it, ye know?"

Ten minutes later, I moved on to the next topic on the list.

"So, what do ye do in your free time?"

"Meet up with the girls, go shopping, ye know yourself."

A real culture vulture so.

"What about you, Paddy?"

"I'm fairly big into music…"

"Ye play any instruments?"

"A bit o' guitar. I've written a few songs."

"Wow, really? What will it take to get ye to sing me one?"

Don't answer that question honestly.

After an hour I could feel the chatter rolling off my tongue with less effort. I advanced to the third topic on my list.

"So, how many of yis are there in the family, Steph?"

"Five. Me, me two brothers, and me ma and da."

"I've a sister… Yis all get on?"

"Me and Ma have our fights, but that's the norm, isn't it? We weren't talking for a while 'cause o' the last fella I was with."

"What about him?"

"Ah, I don't really wanna get into it…"

She's dying to get into it.

"…Well, we got back from the pub one night. He was off his head on a cocktail of all sorts. He went into the kitchen to get another drink and saw Ma there in her nightgown. She'd come down to get a glass o' water. He went up to her from behind and squeezed her tit. Ma told me about it the next day, but I didn't believe her 'cause I rang Deco straight away and he said he was only reaching across her to get the bottle opener from the drawer. He said he may have brushed against her accidentally. But Ma was adamant. It ended up in a big argument. I called her a jealous cow and told her to get over herself thinking a young lad would have any interest in her. We weren't speaking for days after that. Then I was with Deco one night in the back of his car going at it, and he starts talking dirty, saying this and that. Then he goes, 'Aw, you're so sexy Steph. You and your ma can have me anytime.' I was like, 'What?!' I said to him, 'Ye fuckin' lying bastard, Deco! Ye *did* grope me ma, didn't ye?!' Then he goes, 'Ah, I didn't mean it like that. It was just dirty talk, that's all.' I was fuming. I told him to take me home. I didn't say a word to him the whole way. When I got out o' the car he asked me if we were finished. I said, 'What the fuck do ye think, Deco?!' And here's the best bit. He goes, 'Well, if we're finished, will ye let your ma know we are – just in case she's interested in me?' Can ye believe the nerve of him?!"

I wish I had balls like that.

"Aw, the cheek of him!"

"Put yourself in my shoes, Paddy. Could ye imagine bringing a girl home and she starts trying it on with your da?"

"Oh, I could. His only problem would be trying to keep up with her."

"Anyway, I had to apologise to Ma. It was a lesson learned… I'm pickier about fellas now."

I was eager to capitalise on what she'd told me and skip to my fifth topic, but I felt another round of drinks was needed first.

"So, any holidays planned?" I asked.

"I'm a bit cash-strapped. The girls are at me to go with them to Ibiza in a few months. We were there last summer. We had an amazing time. I hardly knew me own name after two weeks."

I'd say the fellas ye were riding didn't know it either.

"I'm in two minds about going over again though. What do ye think?"

Tell her not to! She'll go over there and meet some suave Spaniard who'll introduce her to 'Little Pablo'!

"I'd save me money. Ibiza will still be there in a couple o' years time."

"Yeah, you're dead right, Paddy."

She told tales of holidays past, before I ordered another round.

"Have ye been out much lately?" I asked, hoping to use the question as a bridge to get me to my fifth topic of conversation.

"I've been trying to cut back on the nights out. They were getting too expensive. Coke is such a rip off."

Wish I never asked now.

"I saw ye in the Waterfront recently."

"Why didn't ye say hello?"

"Ah, I was with me mates. I couldn't get away from them. Ye seemed to have a few admirers in that place."

"Well, obviously not enough, seeing as I'm single."

"So, tell us then, what sort o' fella are ye after?"

"Hmm... Someone who's charming but not cocky, funny but not always trying to be funny. Laid-back but not lazy, open but mysterious, fun but not a dosser. Loves his ma but isn't a mammy's boy. Ambitious but not smug. Loving but not smothering, romantic but not too girly, chatty but needs to know when to shut up. Oh, and all the girls should fancy him, but he's only interested in *me*. Do ye think I'm too picky?"

"Ah no, ye just know what ye want."

So did Stalin!

"What about you, Paddy? What kind o' girl do ye like?"

"Well... Someone who has...

Big tits.
… a big smile…
A lovely arse.
… a lovely personality…
A similar sex drive.
… similar interests… and is
Kinky.
… fun…
Great in bed.
… great company…
Bi-curious.
… and adventurous."

"I see. And tell us, how's your search for that girl going?"

"Well, you'd probably tick a few o' those boxes," I said daringly.

"Only a few?" she asked flirtatiously

"Well, the jury's still out."

"Fuck off with yourself! Ha ha. And I was just about to say ye tick most o' mine!"

I'd be doing well to tick one! Do I even want to be ticking one?

"Is that so?" I asked, smiling.

"Yeah, it is… Come 'ere to me."

She leaned into me, and we kissed. It was the culmination of my meticulous planning, and I savoured every second of it.

Later, as I walked her home, we shared a bag of chips while I listened to her re-enact an argument that she'd had with her father about where to buy the best bag of chips in Bray, which somehow led to her storming out of the house and not returning for three days.

We reached her estate on Boghall Road.

"I'll text ye tomorrow," I assured her.

We had a salty, vinegary kiss, before I headed back to the north side of town. A dead Bray Main Street offered the inescapable company of my own thoughts. They questioned her personality, our likely incompatibility, and the wisdom of getting involved with her. I didn't disagree with them. I just ignored them.

Chapter 17
The Misadventures of
an Irish Rover

By the following week, Stephanie and I had become a couple, and a romantic walk down Bray beach one night, led to kissing, fondling, and to Little Paddy discovering a new land to add to his growing map. I soon realised that she possessed a significantly sized libido which helped to maintain our interest in each other.

But by summer 2007, little wrinkles began to appear on the once youthful face of our relationship. Petty squabbles were arising regularly as the stark difference between our personalities became increasingly problematic. Her gregariousness, which at first I found somewhat intriguing and refreshing after suffering Rachael Dowling's prudish disposition, was now staler than a month-old loaf of bread left sitting on a shelf. Likewise, she sought a similar personality in me, which even with my greatest efforts, I couldn't summon. Sensing that we'd reached an impasse, a brainwave was born in my head that I was convinced would see us negotiate it.

With a few quid in the bank, and a few days leave at my disposal, I felt a holiday was the ideal solution.

With her birthday looming, I found a discount deal, and a month later we were in Dublin airport, leaving the dreary Irish weather behind for the blue skies of

Majorca, not before raiding the duty-free shop for half of its drink.

Almost from the outset, I felt like the holiday had been ill-judged. The plane had only lifted off the ground when the bickering started.

"I hear the clothes are real cheap over there," she said.

If she thinks I'm spending a week shopping, she can think again.

"Is that right? I've heard the drink is dirt cheap too."

If you think she'll let ye go on the piss for a week, ye can think again.

"Paddy, I'm not going to another country to go on the piss for a week. If ye were planning on doing that, ye might as well have stayed in Bray."

I should've. A week away from you would be more of a holiday!

"Well, I wouldn't have the sun in Bray, would I? It'd be nice to drink outdoors for once without freezing me arse off... And I'll tell ye something else. I'm not going to another country to go shopping for a week either."

"Ye won't be. I wanna see all the sights."

"Where do ye wanna go?"

"Everywhere, but I don't wanna be stuck on a bus in the middle o' the day when its roasting."

"What do ye mean ye don't... So we'll go everywhere without going anywhere?"

"I didn't say that. At the peak hours I'm gonna be working on me tan by the pool."

"So, you're just going over there to shop and get a tan? Jesus, I could've got ye a shopping voucher and half an hour under a sunbed back in Bray and saved meself a fortune!"

"Says you, with your piss up abroad!"

The captain's voice came over the intercom.

"Apologies to all passengers. We may be experiencing some turbulence in the next few minutes."

Turbulence? Ye don't know the meaning o' the word, mate. If ye wanna see turbulence, hang around with us for the next week!

When we arrived at Palma airport, one of Stephanie's suitcases was nowhere to be seen.

"They better not have lost it, Paddy! I swear, I'll go mad!"

"Well, what do ye expect when ye bring so many? There's a fair chance one o' them will go missing."

"Aw, seriously, Paddy! I'm not in the mood o' listening to ye right now!"

"It pays to be low maintenance, that's all I'm saying."

"Low maintenance? More like no maintenance! A fuckin' tramp would travel with more clothes than you!"

The wait continued. Finally, her suitcase arrived, and we hopped on board the bus.

Our journey took us through quaint villages that were settling down for a night's sleep, tourist-infested towns that were awakening for the night, and miles of unspoilt countryside that the tourism industry had yet to scar. The bus made its scheduled stops at each picturesque hotel along the way. When we eventually reached our own hotel in the resort town of Cala Millor, the reason for the discount became abundantly clear. It was dilapidated. The pool smelled like a dead animal was floating in it. The lobby had stained garish wallpaper and tattered furniture. When we reached our apartment, we found that that it hadn't been cleaned since the previous guests left. Along with that, the toilet wouldn't flush, and there was a hole in the bedroom wall which ants were crawling in and out of.

"Fuckin' hell, Paddy! This place is a kip!"

"It's not that bad. We've had a long day. It'll look better in the morning."

"Look, there's ants on the bed and everything!"

"You're in a different country, Steph. That's probably normal over here. It's a different culture. Next, you'll be complaining about the sun."

"Normal, me arse, Paddy! The place is a shithole. Sort it out, will ye!"

"What do ye want *me* to do about it? Fix the jacks and re-plaster the wall?"

"Get us a different apartment!"

"Why do *I* have to get us a different apartment? You're the one that has the problem!"

"'Cause you're the one that picked this kip 'cause ye were looking to save a few quid!"

Never mind saving a few quid. I should've got the holiday for free if I've to listen to you moaning for the next week.

"I'll have a word with the manager in the morning, awright?"

"In the morning? And what am I to do in the meantime?"

"What do ye mean?"

"If I want to use the loo."

"Ye can use the jacks down in the reception."

"Oh, great! So, I'll be up and down like a yoyo all night."

"The bit o' exercise will do ye good," I said jokingly, trying to lighten the mood.

"Well, you can sleep with the ants. I'm taking the couch."

Gladly. I'd rather sleep with the ants. They're less of a nuisance.

"Yeah, yeah, yeah. Grab that bag o' drink, Steph. Let the holiday begin!"

The following morning, I got out of bed at around eleven and stepped out onto the balcony to see Stephanie down below, sunbathing by the pool. I made a fry, the ingredients of which I'd made sure to bring over with me. Halfway through eating it, the apartment door swung open.

"Have ye spoken to the manager yet?"

"Good morning to you too. No, I haven't."

"Ah, Paddy!"

"Don't 'Ah Paddy' me. I'm only out o' bed two shaggin' minutes."

"I'm gonna go to the pool o' the hotel next-door. That one down there is rotten. It smells like someone's had a shite in it. Are ye coming down or what?"

"Yeah. Let me finish me bit o' grub first."

Having eaten, I went down to the lobby to speak to the hotel manager regarding the apartment. His name was Alberto Torres; a charming man who seemed to be constantly smiling when he spoke to guests.

"*Señor* Torres, I have a problem with my apartment."

"*Problema, Señor?*"

"Yes, big *problema.* Toilet not working."

"You, eh… break toilet, *Señor?*"

"No, it was broken already. It won't flush, so I can't… do me business, *Señor* Torres."

"Business?"

"I can't use it… I can't…take a shit," I said discreetly.

"Oh, *Señor,* you need doctor! I get you doctor."

"No. Not a doctor. I need a new apartment. My woman is not happy. She won't sleep in the bed because there's ants in it. So, we have no… night-time fun… So I'm not happy either."

"Ah, *sí. Entiendo.* Don't be, how you say – embarrass, embarrassed. I have answer, *Señor.*" He reached into a drawer. "These help *problema, Señor,*" he said, handing me a packet of Viagra.

"No, not that *problema!*"

"It's okay, *Señor.* I say *nada* to *señora.*"

"I don't want them."

"No price. They a gift, *Señor.*"

Well, in that case, take them.

"Thank you, very kind. But my *problema* is my apartment."

"I no understand, *Señor.*"

"Listen, *Señor* Torres, I think your English is a little better than ye let on. I want a different apartment, and ye can understand exactly what I'm saying. What's the Spanish for 'acting the maggot'?"

"*Señor,* we are a cheap hotel. You pay cheap, you get cheap. Sometimes there are problems with the apartments, but that's why we are cheap."

Incredible how he's managed to squeeze in a few English lessons since his last sentence.

He was smiling at me like he was awaiting the punch-line of a joke.

"I'm not expecting the Taj Mahal. I just want an apartment where I can use the toilet and not have to sleep in the middle of an ant colony! That's not asking for much, is it?"

"*Sí, sí.* We have a spare apartment that hasn't been booked. You can move in there. Is that okay, *Señor*?"

"Does the toilet work?"

"*Sí, sí…* But I think there is a problem with the cooker."

"Fuckin' hell… I'll take it."

After switching apartments, we lounged on the local beach. Stephanie barbecued herself as I began to get restless.

"How long can ye lie there before it gets boring?"

"Hours, Paddy. Why, ye getting bored? Go for a swim."

"Ah, I'm still a bit delicate from last night."

"Suit yourself."

I surveyed the scantily clad women around me.

"Look at that auld one over there topless."

"Don't start perving on her, Paddy."

"I'm not, I'm not. I'm just saying. Fair play to her."

"The fuckin' state of her! If they sag any lower, she'll trip over them. If mine looked like that, I wouldn't be flaunting them around."

"Yeah well, that's normal over here, isn't it? Anyway, how come women can go topless and its acceptable?

What if I wanted to get me kit off, give himself below a bit o' colour, get a bit o' sun on his face. The poor fella's never seen the sun in his life. Sure, I'd be arrested."

"Don't dare take it out, Paddy!"

"Well, obviously I'm not gonna. Sure, I guarantee ye if I did, some geezer with the leg of a table between his legs would sit down beside me."

"If he does, let me know."

"When do ye wanna go for a stroll round town?"

"When it cools down."

"God Almighty, Steph! Your one's rubbing sun cream on them now. I'm either horny or horrified."

"Will ye stop gawking at her! She'll think ye fancy her."

"She's looking over this way, I swear! And still rubbing… I think *she* fancies *me!*"

"Christ, she's welcome to ye."

There was little jest in her words.

Over the first three days, a mutual irritation of one another slowly festered. Beneath the one roof, we were discovering infuriating traits in each other which separate living quarters had previously left us ignorant of. Disagreements and petty squabbles were becoming as much a part of the holiday as the warm weather.

We sat in an Irish bar on the fourth evening.

"What's the matter with ye?" I asked.

"Nothing, Paddy. Why?"

"Just wondering, 'cause you've a bit of a head on ye."

"Is that so? Ye should see the one I'm looking at. You've a head on ye like a ball sack!"

"Well, I've spent half the day on the bog, so I'm entitled to look like a ball sack."

"And whose fault is that, Paddy? Didn't I tell ye not to go near that bloody curry! And did ye listen?"

God, she's unbearable when she's right.

"Aw, I've an arse on me like Powerscourt waterfall, Steph. I nearly had to do a fuckin' handstand earlier to keep it in, I swear. You're lucky to even have me out tonight."

"Oh, lucky, am I? To be sitting here with your mouldy head and your leaky arse."

We sipped our drinks in silence, scrupulously avoiding eye contact as I imagined the argumentative cogs turning in her brain.

"Ye know, now that ye mention it, Paddy, I *do* have a couple o' things I wanna get off me chest."

Is that right?

"Well, I've a couple o' little things lingering on me own chest too."

"Oh, is that so, Paddy?"

"Yeah, it's very fuckin' so! Every time I leave ye alone at that pool for two minutes, ye start chatting with the lads, shoving your tits in their faces!"

"Get the fuck out of it, Paddy! I'll talk to who I want! I'm surprised ye even noticed I was talking to them, seeing that ye pay no attention to me anyway. I wore that new dress yesterday, and ye never once complimented me!"

"That's your big problem, Steph, is it? Your poxy fuckin' dress!"

"Not the dress, Paddy. *You!*"

"Me?!" I asked indignantly.

"Yeah, you! The only time ye compliment me is when ye want a bit."

"Ah, would ye go away, Steph! You've been moaning since we got here."

"Yeah, 'cause you've been pissing me off since we got here!"

"Ye'd piss yourself off!" I barked.

"Says you! You've been a moody pain in the hole over the last couple o' days."

"Moody? I've had the trots, for fuck's sake! If you were in my state, I'd never hear the end of it. Ye'd want me wiping your arse for ye."

"Well, ye won't be getting anywhere near me arse tonight."

"Fine. I don't care. You're not half as much as ye think ye are in the sack anyway."

"Says you! I can hold me breath longer than you can last."

"Ah, whatever the fuck! I can't be bothered with ye," I said apathetically.

The silence returned, offering a ceasefire to the proceedings.

"Fancy another drink, Steph?"

"Yeah, go on. Order a bottle o' wine. Ye can plug your arse with the cork."

Our unabating bickering continued until it reached its long-awaited climax.

After enduring an excruciating boat trip on the penultimate day, in which the surrounding Mediterranean Sea denied us the escape from each other that we both

craved, we wisely decided to entertain our own prefer-
ences once we set foot back on land.

I explored the region, being thankful for my own
company, while Stephanie divided her time between
burning herself on the local beach and burning her
money on a shopping spree.

By that evening, having arrived back at the hotel rejuvenated after my excursion, I figured we'd spent sufficient
time apart to have allowed our appetites for each other's
company to be replenished. In my buoyancy, I made the
calamitous mistake of insisting that we should compensate
for our time apart by heading out that night when neither of us was in the mood for it. I envisioned a romantic
night which would assuage the hostility between us, thus
allowing us to leave for home the following day somewhat
besotted with one another, despite the week that had been.
The plan was working reasonably well until our consumption of alcohol began to take effect.

We'd decided that we'd have a meal and a few drinks
in a nearby restaurant, before heading over to one of
the late-night bars in the town centre. With the drink
flowing, the conversation was slowing. Both of us were
already finding each other's company challenging.

"Are ye not enjoying yourself, Paddy?"

"I am, yeah."

"Ye don't look like ye are."

"What am I supposed to look like when I'm enjoying
meself?"

"I don't know… Happy, perhaps?"

"Well, I'm happy, very happy, awright. You worry
about your own happiness."

"Well, I might as well forget about me own happiness when I'm with a fella who can't even enjoy himself on a night out."

"Christ, are we back to that again? How could I be enjoying meself when I've to listen to this?"

"So, you're not enjoying yourself then?"

"Well, I fuckin' was enjoying meself before ye started asking me if I was enjoying myself!"

She rolled her eyes before looking at her watch. I tapped my fingers on the table, envious of the happy couples surrounding us.

"A girl in the toilet told me I've a lovely colour."

"Well, I hope ye do. You've spent enough time lying around to get it."

"I'll spend the week getting pissed instead, Paddy, will I? Only have a beer belly to show for me holiday?"

"Well, at least a beer belly would last longer than your poxy tan!"

"I'll tell ye, if I was here with the girls, I'd be having such a laugh right now."

"Ye mean, if *they'd* bought ye a holiday instead o' *me?*"

"Aw, what's it like up there on that cross, Paddy? Nice view? I'll make sure to pay ye for my half, if that's what has your nose out o' joint."

"No, it isn't."

"Why bring it up then?"

"Because the way you're acting, ye don't seem to be the slightest bit grateful for all o' this!"

"All o' what, Paddy?! Your riveting company?!"

"Your fuckin' tan for one thing!"

"Oh thanks. Every time I see meself in the mirror, I'll be thinking o' ye."

With tempers worsening, and an early return to the hotel being the wisest course of action, we decided to stick to our plan, and headed to the late-night bar. Amidst the bar's party atmosphere, we sat amongst the other tourists, dirty looks and seething silences aplenty. Each round of drinks induced another round of arguing; the drunker we got, the bitterer it became. As the floor filled, she had a hankering for a dance.

"Will ye dance with me?"

"Ah, I'm bollocksed, Steph. I can hardly stand."

"I suppose that means ye won't be getting it up for me later?"

"Piss off, will ye!"

"Yeah, maybe I will, Paddy. Maybe I'll find someone who'll ride me senseless!"

"I pity him if ye do," I replied smugly.

She slapped me.

"Fuck you, Paddy!"

"Yeah, go on, Steph, make a show o' yourself! Ye have it down to a tee!"

"Ye know what, I'm fuckin' done with you, Paddy! I've been done with ye for ages. I didn't even wanna come here with ye!"

"Yet ye were quite happy to have me pay for it, weren't ye?! Fuckin' bitch!"

She went for another slap. I caught her hand and held it aloft as onlookers watched the scene unfold. I let her go and said, "I'm going for a piss. Do whatever ye want."

In the toilet, I looked at myself in the mirror, seeing a red streak across my cheek, before I splashed water on my face. The generic dance music pounded through the walls as a Brit pleaded with the occupant of the sole cubicle.

"Hurry up, mate, before I shit myself."

I made my way back to our table, thankful she wasn't there, presuming she was in amongst the crowd of dancers. When the song ended and a few of them returned to their seats, I saw her. She had her arms wrapped round another bloke and her tongue down his throat.

Fuckin' cunt! Little fuckin' slag!

I rose to my feet, picked up my pint and barged through the dancers to get to her.

"Here, have one last drink on me, Steph, ye fuckin' slapper!"

A flick of the wrist. An upturned glass. A shower of lager raining down upon her. She shrieked and yelled every obscenity in her vocabulary at me, as the lager ran from the crown of her head to her waist. As I admired my work, a bouncer grabbed me from behind and escorted me from the building in a headlock, saying something to me in an eastern European language which I assumed was an instruction to clear off.

I plodded up the road tiredly before I found a bench that, with the hotel seemingly a lightyear away, I decided would be my bed.

Amongst the revellers, the myriad of languages, the singing, the shouting, and draped in the warmth of the balmy Majorcan night, I drifted off.

I heard broken glass being swept and opened my eyes. I momentarily enjoyed the luxury of bewilderment as to my circumstances before the previous night's episode formulated in my mind. I lay squinting at a cloudless sky, hearing the multilingual conversations of ramblers. A tap on the shoulder. A dark Spanish head leaned over me, blocking the sun like an eclipse.

"*Señor, muévase por favor.*"

He gestured to me to move on.

"I'm just lying here, mate."

"*Muévase ahora.*"

He placed a hand on his baton. No more words were needed. I slowly lifted myself from the bench.

"*Veta a casa.*"

With a head begging to be decapitated to end its torture, I set off on the arduous walk back to the hotel, stopping only for a can of coke in a shop. Two long gulps saw it emptied. Its journey down my throat was almost pleasurable. Its sweet taste was a shot of adrenaline into my system.

Stalls were being erected, prowlers looked for bargains, the tanned ones in their second week, the pale ones having just arrived, the red ones a few days in, men in shorts with no socks, women in shorter shorts with incumbent tank-tops, sunglasses hiding hangovers, flip flops galore, the strict dress-code of the Spanish holiday.

Where is she? Are we finished? What'll I do?

I knew the answer to the second question. I had no desire to try to reconcile with her and I was certain that the feeling would be mutual. We were done. I reached the hotel and for the first time that week, its peculiar smelling pool and shabby lobby were a welcome sight. At the apartment, unsure of what scene was awaiting me, I opened the door furtively. Silence.

"Steph?"

No answer.

Thank Christ.

I took comfort from a cup of tea as I endured a medieval battle being fought in my head. My mood soon altered from weariness to anger.

Fuckin' cheek o' that slut! What now?

With our bus to the airport due to depart in a couple of hours' time, I was clueless as to her whereabouts.

In your man's bed no doubt!

I didn't care.

Fuck her!

I refused to call her. She could stay in whatever hole she'd crawled into. The thought of facing her, of that acrimonious exchange, and of bickering with her all the way home, made me hope that she wouldn't return. I lay on the couch, apathetic and inert, wishing the bus would leave earlier to expedite my departure and diminish the chances of her walking through the door at any moment. Every set of footsteps that I heard ascending the stairs, I thought was her. But two hours later there was still no sign of her. Having packed my suitcase, I hastily made my way down to the lobby and handed the key to Torres.

"If a girl asks for me later, *Señor* Torres, tell her I've left."

"You leave without her, *Señor?*"

"With a bit o' luck."

"Ah I see, *amigo*. The women, hard work! My wife, she say we need new house, another car, another baby, a new this, a new that – it never end! *Dios mío*, I go *loco*, *Señor*!"

"Well, I wanna get home before I go *loco* meself… Here, ye can take these back," I said, handing him the packet of Viagra. "Save them for a more deserving cunt."

I bid the affable chancer farewell and climbed aboard the awaiting bus, the departure of which was being delayed because of the driver having to wait for a couple who'd gone back up to their room to collect forgotten belongings.

For fuck's sake, will yis come on! She'll probably arrive any second!

With us finally on the road, I saw the same faces from a week prior boarding the bus. Their glum expressions were those of holidaymakers whose week of bliss had come to an end. My even glummer face was that of someone whose week of torment couldn't end sooner. I stared out at the passing scenery, my prior admiration for it now absent. The only sight I was delighted in seeing was the airport when the driver woke me from the sleep I had fallen into, or rather that my hangover had pushed me into.

As I sat in the departure lounge, I began to question my actions.

Maybe I shouldn't just fuck off without her?
Maybe I should ring her, just check if she's okay?
Maybe we could arrange another flight?
Maybe we can talk things over?
Whoa, whoa, whoa! Talk what over?

I doubted the doubts enough to doubt the value of doubting.

My morose appearance was at variance with those around me. A cheerful family talked about their holiday as a snuggling couple whispered to each other. Three blokes were laughing at each other's stories of their antics as a group of women were huddled around a camera, browsing through and admiring their photos. I was too lost in my cyclical thoughts and too relieved to be leaving to be envious of them.

The announcement to board rang out.

For the first time in my life, cold, wet, windy Ireland and her patented grey sky seemed a paradise.

One of her prodigal sons was returning home.

Chapter 18
Imbibing with His Holiness

My misadventure abroad had left an acrid taste in my mouth. I returned to Irish soil jaded. The bullish half of me was missing, presumed dead, last seen on the island of Majorca where its remains were believed to be buried. I hoped the familiarity of Bray would resurrect it. I got off the bus at Castle Street; a gasping fish thrown back into the sea.

Defiant working-class accents shouted over the incessant monotone roar of a jackhammer as it scattered dust across the shopfronts. The street, gridlocked with roadworks, was the venue for the latest meeting of the county council's 'Digging a Hole' committee. There was one man to design the hole, a second man to dig the hole, a third man to measure the depth of the hole, a fourth man to administer the tools for digging the hole, a fifth man to ensure health and safety was adhered to in the hole, a sixth man to direct the traffic surrounding the hole, a seventh man to fill the hole, an eighth man to review the first man's design to improve the next hole, a ninth man to supervise all of the aforementioned jobs involved in digging the hole, and a tenth man to receive the ire of everyone who had a pain in their hole with the hole.

Obscenities flew in all directions, car horns blared, strangers exchanged friendly nods, others traded scowls, and dogs went about their business. All the while, the irresistible whiff of chips emanated from Tardelli's take-away. They were the sights, sounds and smells of home.

Back in the house, I offered only the sparsest details of my week with Popey and the lads, who they'd been told I was holidaying with. The lie, I initially told myself, was born out of a want for privacy. But I knew it was because I felt they hadn't been overly enamoured with her on the few occasions they'd met her. Therefore, it suited me to make them believe that it was nothing more than a casual arrangement that would run its course. She had never properly acquainted me with her own family, probably for the same reason. In retrospect, it was the only thing we'd had in common. If they suspected there was more to tell than I was letting on, they were discerning enough to let the truth be.

Having retired to my room for a lie down, she was all I could think of.

Is she still in Spain? What's she doing? Who's she with? That fella? Someone else?

I didn't want to care, but I did. I was tempted to send her a message. The urge would come and go as I did my best to allay it. I knew a good night's sleep in my native bed would rejuvenate me physically. My mental recuperation was another matter, however. Part of me eagerly awaited returning to work; its normality, I reckoned, would be the appropriate medicine. Another part of me dreaded it.

That pub, those eejits, their shite talk.

The following morning, I dragged myself out of bed, tempted to crawl back into it. I watched the kettle boil without realising I was doing so. Its click extracted me from the trance I was lost in. Spreading butter on my toast seemed an almighty effort, as did eating it.

The job managed to keep my mind from straying too often. Any time I allowed it to, it wandered down the potholed dirt road back to Stephanie Heffernan. Weeks after my return, I still hadn't heard from her. I knew we were finished, but I still sought closure. The further my mind wandered, the more I questioned whether it was closure I sought or an indication that what we once had could still be had again.

I vowed not to contact her, and as time passed, it became apparent that neither of us was willing to lay the first stake to mend the broken fence.

My bullish half had yet to perform its much-expected resurrection. Assuming the blonde demon possessing me was the reason for its desertion, I attempted to have her exorcised by means of a reliable source.

"Ah, Paddy, how's things?" said Popey over the phone.

"All good mate, yourself?"

"No complaints. I'm on the bog here, Paddy. What's the craic?"

"Do ye want me to ring ye back in a minute?"

"Ah, you're grand. I can talk and shite at the same time."

"I'd say so, ye talk shite often enough. Ha ha. I was just wondering if ye fancied a pint. We're due one. I haven't seen ye in ages."

"Have ye ever known me to turn down a pint, Paddy? When and where?"

"Eh, not O'Connell's anyway, I see enough o' that kip. How about the Waterfront?"

"Em… Uh… Jesus… Sorry, Paddy, I'm giving birth here… Fuckin' hell, I need a midwife… Gimme a second… Aw, there we go… Christ, that was an ordeal… Where did ye say?"

"The Waterfront. How's tomorrow at say, eight?"

"I swear, I'm after losing half a stone down the jacks… Yeah, that's sound, bud. Talk to ye then."

"Spare me the details, will ye. Ha ha. Grand, see ye then."

Popey returned from the bar, a pint in each hand.

"There ye go, Paddy, get that down your neck. So, any news in your world?"

"Ah, just tipping away in O'Connell's. You?"

"I've started an apprenticeship as a mechanic."

"How'd ye get that?"

"The fella me da goes to was willing to take me on."

"I was looking to do something like that, but I couldn't find anyone. So how are ye getting on?"

"Ah, its hard work, there's a lot to learn, but it's interesting."

"So, will ye be the mechanic for Ferrari now rather than Bray Wanderers' star striker?" I asked jokingly.

"Well, ye know all about me knee."

"Ah, the famous knee," I said, laughing.

"Yeah, well, that fucked that up… Ferrari? You know me, Paddy. Why bother climbing the Sugarloaf when ye can climb Everest?"

"Because the auld Sugarloaf is handier. But you're right, Popey. I *do* know ye, and I wouldn't bet against ye."

I laughed as I sipped my pint, realising how much better it tasted when drunk in the right company.

"I haven't heard from the lads much, have you?" he asked.

"Nah, they all sort o' went their own ways once we finished school, didn't they?"

"Yeah. We should all meet up one o' the weekends. It's nearly a year now since we were all together."

"Are ye still with herself?"

"Sharon? O' course! Sure, who else would put up with the pair of us? Between me, you and our two pints, I think she could be the first and last notch on me bedpost."

"Ye serious?"

"Would I joke about such a thing? I don't know whether it's something to celebrate or mourn. I mean, me bedpost has room for plenty more notches. Sharon's awright, but she's not…"

"Not what?"

"She's not wild in the sack. She won't do things that other girls might. I wouldn't mind doing a bit of exploring. Ye see me predicament?"

"Ah, the girls ye have in mind are more hassle than they're worth. I'm speaking from experience. The last one I was with was up for anything, but her demands in the sack extended to everything else, ye see what I mean?"

"I get ye."

"If I was you, I'd stick with what I have. Better the devil ye know, Popey."

"You're a wise head on young shoulders, Patrick Dempsey, ye know that?"

I laughed again. Only Popey would ever be heard making such a statement on my behalf, and only he could manage to somehow make it sound credible.

"You'll be the best man at the wedding, Paddy."

"And the best man to blame for the divorce. Ha ha."

"So tell us, what happened with your one ye mentioned?"

"Ah, we went to Majorca. It was a disaster. I ended up coming home without her."

Popey's mouthful of drink dribbled out one side of his mouth as he shook in laughter.

"Aw, ye think ye get on grand with someone, Popey, and then ye live with them. Different ball o' shite altogether! If we hadn't gone, I might still be with her… Shame in a way."

"Are ye mad? It's a blessing in disguise. You're better off finding out when ye did, rather than pricking about with her for God knows how long. Leave her be, for fuck's sake."

He offered his casual critique between two guzzles of his pint, as if it was bereft of any significance. But his advice provided certainty where there'd been only doubt, closure where there'd been a gaping wound, and a friend's voice at a time when I was exasperated from hearing the silent voice in my head.

"That's what ye need, isn't it, Paddy?"

"Ah yeah, an auld chat."

"A few pints, I meant."

"Yeah… a few pints."

I offered to buy the next round, an unspoken token of my appreciation for his exorcising prowess that he'd wielded in his own genial way.

As days passed, she became nothing more than a memory. My bullish half, however, was still elusive. Long after she was exorcised, I still felt lethargic. So much so, that I began to re-assess my initial assumption as to its origin.

Was she the cause or the scapegoat?

I became frustrated with a life that was so unexceptional and so homogenous with those of others, that I could hardly distinguish it from them. Wake, wash, work, home, dinner, sleep. Wake, wash, work, home, dinner, sleep. Wake…

The effervescent 'Rambling One-Man Band' from yesteryear was now the 'Stationary One-Man Band,' playing apathetically to an equally disinterested audience on a street full of impersonators. I negotiated a small pay rise in O'Connell's in an attempt to scratch the itch and started looking for alternative employment, convinced that it was O'Connell's increasing banality that formed the crux of my lassitude. I drifted through the remainder of 2007, waiting for something to re-energise me.

By 2008, I was twenty and living in my own head more than the world outside of it. I could spend hours scrutinising thoughts ad nauseam, a once innocuous habit which was now morphing into a debilitating one. I often wandered the streets of Bray, envious of the insouciance of its denizens. Obsessing over the reasons for obsessing was exhausting work. Something was askew. I ploughed on regardless, hoping to flush it out of me.

So incarcerated was I in my own head, that I paid little attention to anything that was going on around me. But when the country fell victim to an economic earthquake, the devastating aftermath of it would prove to be impossible to ignore.

Chapter 19
The Death of a Patriot

Since the mid-1990s, Ireland's cherished Celtic Tiger had been the country's pet, tasked with the job of guarding the country from the recessions that had crippled it in prior years. We never asked ourselves how long our beloved pet would live, nor how we'd cope with his eventual loss, or how we'd replace him. Instead, we opted for the easier option. We convinced ourselves that this tiger was immortal, that this tiger would look the grim reaper in the eye and laugh at the ludicrousness of mortality. So obsessed did the country become with its tiger, it's a wonder that he didn't become a national symbol alongside the harp and the shamrock or become a mythological figure like Cú Chulainn and Fionn MacCumhaill.

But by the autumn of 2008, the repercussions of the collapse of the Lehman Brothers Bank in the US, meant that our Celtic Tiger was only weeks away from being slain.

Through a virulent cocktail of ill-judgement, naivety and arrogance, Ireland had left itself open to be devastated by the burgeoning global financial crisis. The economy's growth was no longer being driven by exports, but by an unsustainable property price and construction boom. Personal debt had increased with 'credit' having become the vogue word of the nation. Prudency had been upstaged by indulgence. The banks, through their lending practices, had fuelled the boom and had overexposed themselves to the property market and the construction industry in the process. All of this gave rise to a property bubble that had become so big, it was only a matter of time before it burst. What was once a real economy would soon show itself to be a cheap counterfeit, with the most catastrophic consequences.

Our 'esteemed' politicians, when warned about the fundamental defects in the structure of our booming Celtic Tiger economy and of the risks inherent with these defects, had facetiously laughed off such exhortations and decried their propagators as heretics. But the roars of laughter in Leinster House were no longer heard when the ramifications of the financial crisis began to be felt. The construction industry imploded, the property bubble burst, and the banks were left on the verge of collapse, saddled with debts to the tune of billions. After it was announced that the country was in recession, the government issued an unlimited guarantee of all debt to six banks to prevent their collapse and that of the country, which would eventually cost over €40 billion. This bank guarantee and the bankers involved, would become the favourite topic of conversation at every level of Irish society; on every bar stool, at every bus stop, anywhere where two Irish people happened to come in contact. The guarantee ensured that generations of Irish still to be born would be repaying the debt of their ancestors. The bankers became the country's villains, while the patriarch and matriarch of Ireland, unemployment and emigration, reintroduced themselves to the national psyche, after a much-celebrated hiatus.

It seemed there were two Irelands. There was us and there was them, the haves and the have nots, the accountable and the unaccountable, the lawful and the lawless, the humble and the smug, the patriots and the traitors.

Amongst the patriots, was the greatest of them all. The once powerful beast that built the country was now enduring the last few painful minutes he had left before death would graciously end his suffering. The priest had just administered the last rites as the politicians, the bureaucrats and the great and the good of Irish society provided a bedside vigil in his final moments, hoping that he'd give them one last bit of advice before he passed on.

The great animal lay in the bed, a forlorn shadow of his former eminence, hooked up to machines, his body frail, his speech slow and laboured. His huge paws which once carried a country lay limp over the side of the bed. With his eyes squinted, he beckoned the Minister for Finance over to him. The Minister leaned in close as Ireland's greatest patriot of the late twentieth century, whispered in his ear in a dying voice, "I warned ye about the bankers!"

The Minister nodded in acknowledgement and shot stern looks across the room at his advisors, delegating the blame to his colleagues.

"That you did, Our Honourable Beast. Shame on us for not listening."

"And that property bubble! One hundred percent mortgages! How many times was I giving out about them?"

"We were too busy getting rich, Oh Great Wise One. We took our eye off the ball."

"Bankers, politicians, tax dodgers. I knew yis would be the death o' me eventually!"

The Minister held his huge paw in his hand.

"Be at peace, Oh Great Patriot. You've done your fair share. We'll look after the house when you're gone."

"Yis couldn't look after a shaggin' doll's house!"

The noble beast never minced his words. The Minister offered no argument, his silence acknowledging the truth that had been spoken.

"It'll be very challenging without ye. The budget is gonna be tricky, the cabinet meetings, those EU summits, the election… Oh, Christ, the election! If we're lucky, we'll be back sitting on county councils, complaining about dog shite!"

"You lot were still sitting on county councils, arguing about what shade o' white the road markings should be, when I was building that economy! All those years o' toiling and what do I have to show for it? What legacy do I have?"

"Well, there's the new roads, Great Leader. We'll always have them. They're not going anywhere."

"Exactly. Going nowhere! Only leading to ghost estates and deserted towns."

"We'll see out the next few years as best we can. There'll be austerity, but we'll get through it."

"Ah, I could never even spell the word austerity! What about all the young people whose education I funded?"

"They may have to emigrate, but we'll dress it up as work experience. We'll get a few o' them back eventually when things pick up."

"Ah, Christ, they were the future. Now the Brits and the Yanks will reap the rewards of all me work! Why did I bother with yis at all?!"

"You were always loyal, Oh Great Master. We'll build a statue of you on O'Connell Street."

"So I can be covered in pigeon shite like poor auld O'Connell?"

"We'll get a youngfella on an intern scheme to clean it every week."

"Aw, for fuck's sake!"

"Before you pass on to receive your eternal reward, Great Leader, could you share one last piece of wisdom with us?"

The tiger rolled his eyes in exasperation.

"Unemployment will skyrocket, Oh Great One. Any last tips?"

The great patriot's eyes narrowed, and one last breath was exhaled, before he spoke his final words. "Tell them all to become politicians. It's worked out well for you lot!"

On that last sentence, the tiger's eyes closed, his breathing came to a halt and the beep of the machine confirmed his passing. The gatherers bowed their heads solemnly in momentary respect before scurrying out the door, lest there be any finger pointing.

The death of the Celtic Tiger brought an end to the most triumphant era in the history of the state and would be the harbinger for the most agonising. The prosperous Ireland I had grown up in was now unemployment-ridden, debt-ridden, and was struggling to stand on its two feet. It was the drunk at the bar, happy to retell old tales of better times if you were willing to put a drink under his nose.

The economic crisis distracted me from my own ruminations as the realities of the recession loomed.

It wasn't long before the security of my own job came into question. O'Connell's still attracted a crowd on Friday and Saturday nights, but the pub was worryingly quiet during the week. Even some of the regulars like the Kennys, Willie Clarke and Pete Robinson were frequenting it less often. Only Billy Hughes maintained his normal routine. Now our favourite customer, he'd have to stab someone to be refused service.

The Christmas period proved to be the major earner that Doyle had hoped it would be, with hardly an empty seat in the house some nights. The buoyant atmosphere was redolent of times past, as were the arguments at the bar as the old gang reunited to air their grievances about the recession, each of them now an amateur economist.

At home, the Christmas festivities provided temporary relief from the anxiety of the incertitude. I could see January 2009 in the distance and looked at it in trepidation through my fingers. What I saw was an empty O'Connell's, the Christmas crowds already gone, the floor clean from the lack of footfall, innumerable sparkling glasses waiting to be filled, the silence of closing time now the sound of a Saturday night, plying Billy Hughes with drink to ensure I'd be paid at the end of the week.

Another one, Billy? One more, Billy? One for the road, Billy?

Your wife? Ah, she'll be grand, Billy. I'll ring her for ye.

By January 2009, the dole queues lengthened to 326,000 people. Unemployment would continue to rise steadily to 15% given time. Youth unemployment would eventually hit 33%. The daily news became a collage of protests, strikes, shots of dole queues and of young people leaving Dublin airport in search of a life.

Another generation were being ousted from their own country, while those responsible for the exodus watched on from their lavish homes that they built on the back of their enormous salaries. Ireland had become unrecognisable to the imperious country that it had been only a few months prior. This was a country from a bygone age, usually witnessed through old black and white newsreels or read about in history books. This was our parents' and grandparents' country, not ours. Our Ireland was to be a small-scale adaptation of 'The American Dream.' We, like previous generations, would make the grim discovery that behind this image crafted by a minority, lay the reality to be lived by the majority.

Politicians quarrelled in parliament as they used the crisis to further their own political careers.

In O'Connell's, we never spoke of layoffs, as if broaching the matter would be akin to opening a pharaoh's tomb and becoming stricken by its curse. By refusing to confirm that there wouldn't be layoffs, Doyle inadvertently confirmed there would be. It motivated us all to work harder over the following weeks to prove our worth.

On a Friday afternoon in late February, Doyle called me into his office. I feared the worst when I walked in and saw the serious look on his face.

"Have a seat, Paddy… Ye probably know what this is about." He waited for a reply.

I said nothing.

"With the way the economy is, our turnover has reduced dramatically. Our ability to create revenue has diminished. This means that we have to restructure the business and exercise cost-saving measures… meaning that…"

"When am I finished?" I interrupted abruptly.

"Two weeks. I'm sorry, Paddy, I really am."

His apology was as meaningful to him as it was meaningless to me.

"Why *me*? I've been working me arse off!"

"It's last in, first out, Paddy. Nothing personal."

"I'll take a pay cut!"

"The ones who are staying will be taking a pay cut. It's our only hope o' keeping afloat."

"I'll work free overtime… I'll…" My voice was imbued with desperation.

"Me hands are tied, Paddy. You've been a model employee. I know that doesn't mean much, but there isn't much else I can say. If things pick up and you're still available, you'll be the first fella I call."

"How long do ye reckon that could be?"

"Months, a year maybe, a couple o' years, who knows? I wouldn't be betting on it being soon if I was you."

"Do I get any redundancy?"

"No, sorry, Paddy. Ye haven't been working here long enough to qualify for it."

"Right, well, that's that, I suppose," I defeatedly remarked.

"Unfortunately, I'm afraid it is. Again, I'm…" His hands offered a gesture of apology this time.

My dejected nod acknowledged it.

I worked apathetically for two weeks, suffering the staff's sympathy, which hid their delight for not having met such an unfortunate fate themselves. I questioned whether the last two weeks' pay was worth enduring the patronisation of their vacuous kind words or the humiliation of being at a party to which I was no longer invited. While they laughed amongst themselves, I despised the merriment that they enjoyed at my expense. In my bitterest moments, I despised *them*.

By the end of the first week, I couldn't wait to get out of the place. On my last day, Doyle met his final obligation. He reached into his desk drawer and pulled out an envelope.

"That's your P45."

Ye can wipe your arse with it!

"Thanks." The word stumbled out of my mouth and fell face first onto the floor as I pocketed the envelope.

"I'm sure you'll find work, Paddy. Be patient, keep the chin up. Kiss arse when ye have to and kick arse when ye have to."

I wish he'd shut the fuck up!

I know an arse I'd love to kick right now!

He held his hand out.

"Best o' luck, Paddy. Give me a shout if ye need a reference."

We shook hands and parted ways amicably. I made for the front door like the premises was engulfed in an inferno and headed up Bray Main Street.

Fuckin' cunt! No fear o' that prick being laid off! Worked me bollocks off for nothing!

What the fuck do I do now?

It was a question that never seemed to tire of my company.

I surveyed the main street. Its transformation in recent months was staggering. In every direction I could see *For Sale, Closing Down Sale* and *To Let* signs that denoted the times in which I was living. Closed shutters were abundant. The mood in the town had altered. It was palpable in every shop, in every passing conversation, on every face. The life of the town was helplessly pouring down the drain. This was recessionary Ireland; the economic cold turkey we were promised we'd never suffer. It was the Ireland of old, dug up and displayed for the benefit of those who were fortunate enough to have missed out on the previous recession. 'The Good Ship Employment' had sailed its last voyage and was retired because of irreparable damage. I now sailed on 'The Good Ship Recession,' a ship so flawed in its design, only a miracle could prevent its imminent sinking. The one lifeboat it offered its aggrieved passengers was emigration.

I reached my destination at the top of the main street. It was a place the Celtic Tiger had us believe was fictitious. Alas, as I sought its refuge, its existence became indisputable. I entered the doors of the social welfare office and was directed to hatch number five to sign on the live register. I explained my circumstances to the clerk on the other side of the glass, as he scribbled the details. With the stroke of a pen my self-worth was written off. Its loss was a necessary sacrifice in return for the state's handouts. A pernicious trade off.

I was unemployed, an economic statistic, one of the 326,000.

When I arrived home, I dreaded the revelation I was about to make. I hadn't informed the family that I was being let go, as I'd half hoped that Doyle would change his mind in the two weeks or would discover a gold mine beneath O'Connell's cellar.

"How was work, love?"

"Grand, Ma… while it lasted."

"What do ye mean?"

"I've been let go."

"Ah no! You're joking?"

My silence confirmed to her that I wasn't.

"Aw, I'm so sorry, love… Listen, don't worry, something will come up."

"Yeah, something."

"I'll get ye a cup o' tea."

The auld *cupán tae;* the Irish mother's cure to all of life's problems.

I sipped the tea and feigned interest as Ma talked about jobs and courses before she eventually copped that my mind was elsewhere.

"Ye awright, love? Love, are ye awright?"

"Yeah grand, Ma… I was just thinking… That's a grand cup o' tea."

Chapter 20
A Changing Landscape

A few weeks had passed since I became unemployed. Without a job, the one thing I did have was plenty of time at my disposal, which I spent traipsing the streets of the town, watching road sweepers, bin men, and sole traders going about their daily business, creating an affectation of normality amidst the recessionary reality.

I led myself to the door of the Waterfront, despite having told myself that I was walking along Strand Road purely for an evening stroll and a mouthful of sea air. There's nothing like alcohol to reassure you that all is right with the world, before convincing you that all is wrong with it.

"A Guinness, Eoghan, when ye get the chance."

I devoured the first two pints before slowing to avoid suspicion. With each gulp, I could feel the drink sand the sharp edges of my emotions. I'd let it sand away until there was nothing left.

The news was on, reporting the country's latest afflictions. Every story was about the recession. There was no getting away from it. Its associated terminology was a new language we were unwillingly learning, some of us already fluent. We could hold a conversation about the weather in our new native tongue of Recessionish.

"What's the forecast for tomorrow, Paddy?"

"Well, we have to take into account seasonal changes which have made for a fluctuating state of affairs in the recent quarter's temperature figures, Jimmy."

"I see, Paddy. And with those seasonal changes taken into consideration, how confident can we be that tomorrow will see an increase or a decrease in the temperature?"

"The market data suggests that there'll be a three percent rise, but there is a one percent margin of error."

"I see, I see. And what is the market value of an increase in temperature?"

"Well, hopefully a warmer day will bring much needed streams of revenue to struggling small to medium enterprises that are facing possible insolvency, Jimmy."

"How so, Paddy?"

"Well, there'll be more ice creams eaten, more bags o' chips bought at the seaside, the pubs will sell a few extra pints and tourism will increase once word spreads that the sun has got lost in Ireland. It should provide a healthy boost to our ailing economy. And that combined with our twelve and a half percent corporation tax rate will provide further incentive to multinational companies to base themselves here. All in all, it should see our Gross National Product and our Gross Domestic Product rise. This will create jobs, reduce unemployment, lead to a decrease in emigration figures, and in turn, grow the economy further, leaving this economic downturn behind us."

"Jesus, that's fantastic, Paddy! And we'll get all that just from having a few sunny days?"

"Ah yeah. But this is Ireland, remember? Look out your window tomorrow morning."

"Why?"

"'Cause it'll be fuckin' raining!"

"Desperate altogether, isn't it?" the man beside me remarked.

I nodded in agreement with a mouthful of Guinness.

"I was about your age when we last went through this in the eighties and here we are again. Back to square one. If ye learn one thing about this country as ye get older, mate, it's that it goes around in circles. Last year's news will be next year's news."

I had enough drink in me to make me social, but not enough to be incoherent. I offered my 'astute' economic assessment of the situation.

"Load o' bollocks, isn't it?"

"Ah, it is. Especially for you younger lads. Straight from school into the dole queue. What sort o' banana republic is that? What about you? Are ye…"

"I was laid off."

"Ah, me commiserations. Both for that, and for having to pass the hours with an auld eejit like me… If it makes ye feel any better, you're in no worse a position than meself. I'm a bricklayer, *was* a bricklayer, but the only thing being built in Ireland now is a shaggin' debt!"

"What are ye gonna do?"

"I haven't a clue, mate. There's big money in Australia for fellas like me. If I hadn't the wife and kids, I'd be gone like a light. Make a few bob, then come back when the mess is cleaned up. But with me couple o' little nippers and herself, sure, I'm stuck here. You on the other hand, you're a young lad, you've nothing tying ye down here. I'd get out while I had the chance if I was you. The next few years could go by in an instant and what will ye have to show for it? Fuck all. You'll be sitting here in four years' time, having the same conversation with some other eejit, no job, no money, no prospects, nothing. I was in the same boat in the eighties, I hung around, ever the optimist and all that shite. If you're young, you've everything going for ye, mate. Ireland's a write-off. It makes for a decent postcard, that's about it."

"Ah, its early days yet."

"Fuckin' too right it is, and wait till you see what's around the corner!"

I stared at the television, its pictures supporting his opinion, adding muscle to his skeletal words.

"Charlie Keane's the name."

"Paddy."

Upon our handshake, he produced his wallet and insisted on buying the next round, which was soon followed by another. The drink soon hindered our ability to discuss the finer points of Irish economics and led us down a side street where the craic was aplenty, and all troubles could be put aside until the following morning.

"So, what has ye here by yourself, Paddy? Have ye no young one to drown your sorrows with?"

"Not at the moment."

"How come? There's plenty o' them around. You're in your prime. Don't waste it... Look at the arse on your one over there. If ye had any sense, ye'd be introducing yourself to her."

"If I had any sense, I wouldn't be here."

"Sure listen, if you're gonna be on the dole, ye might as well make the best of it. You've been laid off, ye haven't been castrated, for fuck's sake."

After another couple of pints were drunk, he was finding it harder to turn his thoughts into sentences.

"My missus… great woman… fantastic woman… when she wants to be… and a right… when she… and ye could get either one at any given time. We argue about everything. The other day…" He placed his fist over his mouth, swallowing hard. "The other day, she was talking shit about some shite, and we ended up arguing. Before ye know it… we go off on a tangent arguing about something else…then something else. Then we start arguing about what it was we were arguing about in the first place… Do ye know what that is?"

Before I said anything, he answered his own question. "Marriage, that's what that is." He was about to speak and then gulped. "I'm telling ye, putting that ring on their finger is like…like signing your own death warrant… Steer away from the altar as long as ye can, Paddy. That's me advice."

He then finished his pint in one go.

"And with those words o' wisdom… I'm afraid, I'll have to leave ye to your own devices… Herself will be wondering where I've gone… I only popped out for a bag o' spuds."

He gingerly rose from his stool, struggling to put his arms into his coat.

"Remember what I said…"

"About marriage?"

"No, no, about this country… Don't let it drag ye down with it."

Off he went. A row was probably awaiting him at home. As I amused myself with the thought of it, I imagined being like him in twenty years' time.

The character at the bar?
The fool at the bar?
Laughed with?
Laughed at?

Having left the Waterfront, I bumbled down Quinsborough Road and over the bridge, turning left onto Lower Dargle Road. The night's stillness was broken by the odd noise; a cat running into a bush, a television in someone's bedroom, the patter of footsteps in the distance behind me. My eyes were focused on the path as I tried to keep my legs within its margins. The footsteps behind me sounded closer. I could distinguish two sets. My eyes were still fixed on the path. Closer again. I passed under another streetlight. Beside my shadow I saw two others cast on each side of it. Instantly, I became aware of what was happening. Fear and adrenaline coursed through me. Before I could think of something to do, I felt a punch to the jaw. It knocked me off balance, my drunken legs struggling to hold me up. Another punch to the side of the head followed. The two grabbed me and pushed me against the wall.

"Give us your wallet!"

A pair of menacing eyes glared at me. The other pair glanced anxiously to and fro.

"Ah, lads, for fuck's sake. I've been laid off!"

"You'll be laid off by the time we're done with ye! Where's your wallet?!"

"Up your ma's gee!"

Another punch, hard into the stomach. I was winded and wheezing. The street was spinning around me.

The anxious one spoke.

"Do ye want us to kick your fuckin' head in?!"

"Yis can suck on me fuckin' head, yis cunts!"

Another hard blow to the face, its impact ensuring the fight wouldn't go the distance. I tried to swing back but my arms were held back by one of them. I did the one thing I was still capable of doing; I spat, only for my hogger to miss my target completely. I was flung to the ground, where I received a brace of kicks.

"Quick, Martin, his pockets!"

He discovered my wallet.

"There's a fiver here."

"A fiver?! Ye would have to pick someone on the fuckin' dole. Let's go!"

"A few coupons too."

"Take them! Come on the fuck!"

"Leave me the coupons at least, will yis?" I pleaded in pain.

I could smell his breath as he leaned in close and released a hogger of his own that landed under my eye. As an attempt to silence me, it worked.

"Fuck's sake, Martin! Come on, stop arsing about!"

They fled, leaving me at the foot of a wall. Pain permeated every part of my body. I felt like a wreck. I didn't have the strength to lift myself off the damp ground. I closed my eyes and found relief.

I felt a pleasant sensation on my neck, along the side of my face, touching my lips. Warm, comforting, arousing. The inimitable touch of a woman. I imagined her beautifully shaped figure wrapped round me, her long hair resting on my chest, her ample breasts pressed against me, her luscious lips working miracles. I let out a soft groan, mumbling, "That's it… Yeah, right there, hun… Don't stop."

Her tongue journeyed back down my neck, the intensity soaring. I opened my eyes to look at my seductress. Brown hair, dark eyes, floppy ears and a wet nose.

A fuckin' dog!

Its tongue drowned me in its slobber as its two paws pinned me to the ground. I pleaded with it to stop, without having the strength to resist.

"Get off him, Sammy!" I heard a man say.

He hurried over, pulling the dog off me.

"Sorry about that, mate. He's a handful… Jesus Christ!"

"I got a hiding," I said, feeling absolutely battered from the combined effects of the assault and the hangover.

I looked around me. A dawn sky offered me some sense of time.

"Do I look bad?"

"I'd say no worse than ye feel."

He offered his hand and managed to pull me off the ground.

"Do ye need to go to the hospital?"

"Nah, I'm just a bit bruised… I just need to get home."

"Where's home?"

"Only around the corner."

"Ye need me to walk ye round?"

"Ah no, I'm fine, I'm fine."

"Do ye want a lift to the Garda station?"

"Nah, they got nothing off me."

"Even still, just to report it, ye know?"

"Ah, I'll go up later. You head on. I'll be grand."

"Okay. Well, look after yourself, mate. Get home and get some rest."

He took his dog away with him, whose stubby legs made the effort of walking look easy as I struggled to negotiate a few hundred yards. I entered the house and collapsed onto the couch. I started to hear movement above me, followed by the sound of someone descending the stairs. I knew by the gentle steps being taken that it was Ma.

"Where've ye been, Patrick?!"

"Defending me title, Ma," I muttered, as I raised my head from the pillow.

"Good God! Did ye fall, love?!"

Did I fall? Yeah, onto someone's fist.

"I got a few digs, Ma."

"John, get down here, will ye!" she shouted up the stairs. "Paddy's had the shite knocked out of him!"

Lumbering thuds came down the stairs. If I hadn't known better, I'd have thought we'd taken in an elephant as a lodger.

"Jesus, Mary and Joseph, Paddy! Did some young-fella catch ye with his mot?"

"Will ye show some concern, John!"

"I am concerned!"

"What happened, love?"

"He has a head on him like a fuckin' panda bear, Aoife. We know what happened to him!"

"John, will ye… Where? When? Patrick?"

"I got jumped on…two lads…up the road…"

"Did they get much?" Da asked.

"A fiver."

"They did that for a fiver?!"

"And me chipper coupons."

"The half-price fish and chips ones? Fuckin' scumbags! Did ye not tell them you're on the dole?"

"Well, he hardly had his P45 handy, John!"

"I *did* say it to them!"

"I'll say one thing, Paddy boy, the country's really gone down the shitter if they're having to resort to mugging you!"

Da's unique brand of sympathy was strangely welcomed.

"It's not funny, John… Aw, ye poor thing, love. I'll turn the hot water on for ye for a shower. Would ye fancy some breakfast?"

"No, I've no appetite."

"What about a boiled egg?"

"No thanks, Ma."

"Porridge even?"

"Nah."

"Corn flakes?"

"For the love o' God, Aoife! Will ye let the lad be! He'll have a pain in his bollocks listening to *you* as well as pains everywhere else!"

"I'm grand, Ma. Honestly."

"The fuckin' women, son. They see one black eye and ye'd swear ye were diagnosed with Ebola."

"Ah, it's terrible, John. He loses his job and now this," Ma said sympathetically.

"It's nothing major, son. You'll be right as rain in no time. I'd say ye'd murder a cup o' tea, would ye?"

"Yeah, Da."

"Aoife, will ye get him a cup o' tea? Let him oil the auld machinery… I wouldn't worry about those chipper coupons, son. That Tardelli cunt must pick his fish from a fuckin' goldfish bowl, I swear. And as for his chips! There's so few o' them in the bag they get lonely."

Appreciating that he was trying to cheer me up, I wanted to laugh but didn't have the energy to do so.

"True," I replied wearily, forcing a smile.

The hot water washed away the dried blood, but the pain and the self-pity were harder to scrub away. My legs were buckling under my weight, and I leaned against the wall of the shower for support, closing my eyes, letting the water work its magic. I could have stood there all day. My only motivation to step out was the hot water turning lukewarm.

I dried off. Bruises had appeared on my ribs and back. A lump protruded from the back of my head, while the mirror reflected the face of somebody who'd been beaten, not just physically, but mentally also.

I put on fresh clothes and returned to the sitting room where peaceful rest eluded me because of Claire's hankering for every minute detail of the incident. All I wanted to do was sleep. It seemed that I was happiest when doing so, free from myself and from the rest of the world.

A week later, my bruises had healed. Being unemployed meant that I'd been able to recuperate at home. The house had become a cell. I'd lived like a vampire, reluctant to walk the streets in broad daylight, only venturing outside at night. In the empty house, I'd spent the last few days listening to albums that were becoming part of my soundtrack to unemployment and writing my latest song, *The Life of a Banker.*

Oh Éire, my Éire, my infallible mother
who bore me and fed me from her nurturing breast.
My devotion to thee shall never waver.
I'll dutifully serve thee at your behest.

Your only riches are your days of yore.
Your greatest triumphs were glorious defeats.
Now you wander your barren land,
starving and hopeless, on blistered feet.

The time is nigh to take flight from your nest,
for your measly rations will suffice no more.
The coming dawn will alight the sky,
into which I'll mercifully soar.

I see my future in the world of banking.
On the road to Dublin, I begin my trek.
You'll hear from me, Mother, when I've made my fortune.
I'll write you a letter on the back of a blank cheque.

Oh Mother, my apologies, it's been so long!
You're probably thinking I've forgotten you.
I meant to write, but time is money,
and sentiment has no monetary value.

Oh Mother, if you could only see me now,
awash with riches and hungry for power.
How proud you'd be of your wealthy son,
as I bask in the opulence of my ivory tower.

Oh Mother, on occasions, I reflect on the past.
Your indigency is a stain on my tailored suit.
Such shame is yours and not mine to bear.
While I dine on caviar, you subsist on rotten fruit!

I dare not speak of my impecunious mother
to my banking brethren or their alluring wives.
My plebeian upbringing is the cross I carry.
Its revelation would negate my meteoric rise.

There's idle talk from a begrudging few,
of the folly inherent in our surging gains.
As they warn the nation of a looming crisis,
we'll count our money and sip champagne.

Oh God Almighty, the news is tragic!
Lehman Brothers has gone bankrupt.
Without its pockets to fill our own,
this bank is doomed and sure to erupt!

There's fear of layoffs and whispers of fraud,
as fingers are pointed and alibis are crafted.
Our saving grace is our hold on the nation.
If we crash, the state's death cert will be drafted.

We'll invite the Minister of Finance for tea,
and remorsefully inform him of our predicament.

As he berates us for our haughty imprudence,
we'll play our trump card and engineer a covenant.

Oh Mother, thank heavens, there is a God!
We're no longer liable for the billions we owed.
Your benevolent government has bailed us out,
meaning that you, not us, will reap what we sowed.

Oh gracious Mother, I had planned to return,
for fear of eviction, insolvency and arrest.
But your citizens have aided me in my hour of need,
relieving me of my worries and stress.

But the bailout has come with a moralistic price.
I've been ostracised from the very country I built.
From the fringes I'll rekindle my life of old,
awash with excess and bereft of guilt.

Oh Mother, I'll visit you when I've a minute to spare.
My triumphant tales you must surely hanker.
But I'm busy purchasing a holiday home in France.
Such is the burdensome life of a banker.

Having now served my sentence under self-imposed house arrest, I deemed my release worth celebrating. An hour later, music was blaring and cans were being drunk.

Fuck the rest o' them! Let them have their poxy jobs!

Unemployment wasn't all gloom. I could buy happiness and self-respect for a small price. I was king of my own world; a world that didn't stretch beyond the confines of my skull.

The news came on. Predicting its misery, I turned off the television.

When my supply of cans ran out, I grabbed my coat, keys, and wallet, and was off down the street, heading for the nearest pub after O'Connell's.

I could feel myself plunging into the filthy pool of idleness and becoming accustomed to its foul water.

Chapter 21
The Constitution of the Idle Man

The gulf between the employed and the unemployed lies in routines. The longer one is unemployed, the further away the ideal of a daily routine drifts to the periphery before the very concept becomes alien, and one inevitability succumbs to living an idler's life. The urge is repelled in the initial weeks, but the onset of fatigue after countless esteem sapping rejections from employers, soon leads to one subscribing to and abiding by 'The Constitution of the Idle Man.'

This constitution when adopted, outlines the rules and obligations that must be adhered to, in one's newly acquired half-life. They are as follows:

- Early rising is forbidden. It's the practice of the employed. Embrace your mattress's comfort, the warmth of your blanket and the shelter that your bed provides from the world beyond the four walls. It is your haven. Learn to respect it. Sunrises are only to be witnessed when struggling home in the wee hours after a night of revelry. Early nights are also strictly forbidden. You must readjust your body clock to suit your employment status.

- Countless hours of television must be viewed every day. The television is a portal to a different world; one replete with sports stars, actors, musicians, foreign cultures, drama and possibilities. The escapism it provides will allow you to temporarily forget about your tedious existence.

- Your daily contact with the outside world must be limited to bar flies and any of your unemployed brethren.

- Your entrepreneurial endeavours must be limited to applying for competitions on television shows, placing a bet, or buying a lotto ticket.

- You must make a valiant attempt to find work that doesn't exist. The demoralising daily rejection erodes your self-esteem and ensures that you know your place in society, God forbid you become possessed with any notions of grandeur.

- You must indulge in regular alcoholic binges. They'll provide an escape from the day-to-day drudgery. You'll justify spending your dole on drink by insisting that by doing so, you're putting money back into the economy which will help to rebuild it.

- You must maintain a daily exercise routine of aimless walks through town for the purpose of getting out of the house. This will help you to retain your fragile sanity.

- You must undertake regular counselling sessions from the local voluntary psychiatrist, also known as the barman. He has a wealth of experience in dealing with every problem that has befuddled mankind and is the very man to point you in the right direction in times of strife. The cost of a couple of pints is all he'll charge you for disclosing such wisdom.

- You must accept that unemployment is a female repellent. The most patient woman in the world will tire of you, your lifestyle and your lack of money. The exception to this rule is a woman who is also unemployed and therefore may sympathise with you. This can also be problematic as your shared unemployment leads to a suffocating courtship. It's like marriage without the taxation perks.

- Lastly, if questioned about your current employment status, you must never refer to yourself as being unemployed. The word must be extracted from your vocabulary. You're either 'looking to start a new career,' 'taking a year out,' 'in between jobs,' 'in transition,' or any other euphemism that refrains from using the 'U' word.

Job seeking was an act of climbing an insurmountable wall. I'd either fail in getting my two feet off the ground or scale its mammoth height to within inches of my goal, only to fall to my death.

Like previous generations whose fate it was to become cannon fodder on the battlefields of the world, we were the generation whose fate it was to become economic cannon fodder. We were on the frontline, first to charge and first to be slaughtered, while the instigators of the war stood on the hillside, watching the slaughter from above, trying to think of a clever way of putting a positive spin on the proceedings.

"Thank Christ we're up here, Minister. God Almighty, it's carnage down there!"

"It's that bad? How will we explain this catastrophe?"

"Minister, why don't we tell them that it'll be over by Christmas? It worked in World War One."

"I'm not paying ye a six-figure salary to regurgitate some spiel from a hundred years ago. We need something fresh... something snappy...something simple enough for them to understand but vague enough to not mean anything."

"You're right, Minister. Let me think... Ah, I've got it!"

"Go on."

"We tell them that what we are experiencing at the moment is a...transitional period."

"Oh, excellent!"

"And that's not all. There's a whole story to be told, Minister."

"I'm all ears."

"This is how we tell it... With the death o' the Celtic Tiger, this transitional period was inevitable. But if we follow our current austerity-based strategy through to the end, we'll come out the other side and will witness...wait for it... the Celtic Resurrection!"

"Ah, now that's fabulous! That's why you're me spin doctor."

"Think of it, Minister. We can use it as our slogan for the election, have it on all our posters. 'Let us guide you in the direction of the Celtic Resurrection!'"

"Ah, brilliant! It has another five-year term written all over it! Come on, let's leave this crowd to annihilate each other. I think a celebratory drink is needed and perhaps a pay rise for your good self?"

"Ah, Minister, you're too kind!"

"Don't have the audacity to say ye don't deserve it! Would ye like an extra one at the front or an extra zero at the end?"

"Any chance I could have both?"

"Sure, I'll give each of us both!"

"Isn't it a great auld country all the same, Minister?"

"Ah, that it is. We'll make a toast to the Irish Republic!"

If there was one comfort, it was that I was not alone in adopting 'The Constitution of the Idle Man.' Hundreds of thousands of people throughout the country were unwillingly abiding by its rules.

With emigration soaring, my generation was being decimated at a frightening rate. Those of us who believed we'd survived the worst of it and that the country was nearing a recovery, settled into a life of obscurity, worthlessness and idleness, hoping that our just reward for enduring such, was that we'd be reserved a place at the front of the queue at the Hill of Tara, for when the Celtic Tiger's long-lost cub would come to claim his late father's throne and deal out the new jobs he'd brought with him to the waiting masses.

We would become a generation whose expertise on daytime television and social problems was unrivalled, but whose curriculum vitaes had so many holes, a reading of them was akin to watching the entire youth population of Ireland lining up, pulling down their underwear and collectively bending over. We'd be the problematic generation who'd be doing the country a favour if we left with the rest. We'd be the nagging child that would never shut up. We'd one day be the impoverished old codger sitting on the bus, staring vacantly out the window at the world hurtling past, sombrely reflecting on a life that had hurtled past, our only possession obtained from which, being the envy we'd have for the ebullience of the youngsters sitting beside us. We'd be the punchline that induced their laughter. The futures they'd find would be the ones we'd lost, the very ones we'd spent decades trawling the streets for. It wouldn't be beneath us to drop to our knees and beg for them to be returned to their original owners.

A few drinks, however, could always be relied upon to shake off the 'unemployment blues.' If I was to live through this recession, I was determined to make it the best recession since records began.

Chapter 22
The Diary of an Idler

The monotony of my daily routine was such that any awareness of what day of the week it happened to be was lost within the endless cycle of repetition. Time was a mechanism used by the employed in their parallel universe. It was their system to ensure the effective management of their day. It got them out of bed and made them rush out the door. It determined the length of their lunchbreaks and appointments. It indicated the end of their working day and when the next bus would arrive. It was used to calculate their wages and their pension contributions. It found its way into every crevice of their lives.

In the vacuum of unemployment, time doesn't exist. The clock stops upon signing on the live register and doesn't start again until you've signed off.

What follows is one week, that could be multiplied by fifty-two, to chronicle a year in the life of the unemployed.

Monday

Unable to find the willpower to get out of bed, I eventually rose at eleven and watched a psychiatry show, thinking I'd learn a thing or two. There was some fat young one prattling on about her bulimia. She would've been some sight if she wasn't bulimic!

I changed the station. Ads. One for hair loss treatment. I inspected my own hairline, thinking that while one recession had cost me my job, the other was costing me my hair.

I channel hopped through cooking shows, lunchtime chat shows, old sitcoms and dreadful new ones. I felt hungry. Beans on toast. No effort in its cooking nor eating. More television, a quiz show. Questions so easy that they hardly warranted prizes. A holiday show. Two Brits looking for a flat in Spain. They were looking for a place where the locals spoke English, where there was a British bar, British food, British people to mingle with, British television and a Spanish beach.

A cup of tea was required. A lack of milk led me to go to the shop.

I was standing in the queue as another till opened. The man at the back of the queue darted across to the new till. I slouched my way over and told him that as I had been in front of him previously, I should also be ahead of him in this queue. He politely retorted that this queue was a new queue, therefore he was entitled to be first. I informed him that from my perspective, this queue was a continuation of the previous queue, so the previous positions should be maintained, in the interest of fairness. I sought the opinions of other customers, only to find they didn't share my irritation. Their indifference made me question whether I would've deemed the matter to be of any importance before I became unemployed.

A dripping thought of a pint formed a puddle in my head. Aware of how much I'd contributed to the

Waterfront's coffers over the previous weekend, I ignored the temptation.

That night, Claire had us watching a show called 'Philip or Philomena?' A man named Philip underwent a sex change to become Philomena, then a year later he changed his mind and wanted to become Philip again. Rather revealing. Poor Philip had believed that womanhood held all the answers to his problems, only to later realise that he had underestimated the complexity of the female species. He hadn't planned for the hormonal mood swings that had him craving the simplicity of manhood, which he realised he'd taken for granted.

Did nobody warn him?

Tuesday

I was awoken by Ma and Claire bickering about the length of the latter's skirt. Da's voice was noticeably absent, his experience with the opposite sex teaching him to adhere to a strict policy of neutrality on such matters. I had an urge to ring the auld bell down below. I found a video on the phone. The opening credits rolled.

'Dick Hardon's Plumbing Adventures, starring Dick Hardon and Rebecca Cumming.'

Knock knock.

"Hello."

"Hi, Miss. I'm Dick Hardon. You called me yesterday. I'm here to fix your leakage problem."

"Oh, aren't you very forward! You're late."

"I've been busy all day, Miss."

"Oh, I bet. You must be worn out. I hope you can look after one more woman's needs."

"I certainly can, Miss. I can go all day."

"Is that so? How will you fix it?"

"I have all the tools, Miss. I know what I'm doing."

"Oh, I bet you do, big ones too, I'd say! How long will it take to repair?"

"Well, that depends on how bad the problem is, Miss."

"Oh, it's very bad, Mr Hardon. I've been getting so frustrated lately."

"I could be here a couple of hours. I'll know once I inspect the problem."

"Well, the sooner you do that, the better then. Tell me, Mr Hardon, how much will all this cost?"

"It'll depend on the workload, but we could be talking around two hundred dollars, Miss."

"Wow, that's a lot for a lady like me."

"Well, I offer a premium service, Miss."

"Is that right? Is there any way we can reduce that price? Are you flexible at all?"

"Not in the slightest, Miss."

"So I see, Mr Hardon! How on earth will you be able to work with that in your pants? I'm not the type of lady to leave a man in that state."

"What about the leaking pipe, Miss?"

"Oh, Mr Hardon, that's not the only thing leaking. And it seems it's not the only pipe in need of some attention!"

Rebecca Cumming stripped him off and managed to surpass her performance from the last video I saw her in, 'Tony the Carpenter and his 9-Inch Drill Bit.'

I got up to discover that the television was on the blink. So, to give myself something to do, I took Buddy out for a stroll down Pearse Road, along Lower Dargle Road and back through the park towards Castle Street. Age had claimed much of the vigour of our once feisty canine. The devilment was still there, but he lacked the vitality to demonstrate it. In his prime, he'd strut up and down the park, flirting with the bitches. Now, a mouthful of fresh air and a sniff would suffice. We sat together in search of whatever scraps of tranquillity could be found with the obligatory winos on a bench nearby. The dripping hadn't stopped. The puddle was now deeper.

As I was tying Buddy to a bollard outside the shops at Castle Street, people walked past me with an urgency that hinted that they were the employed. The time that I possessed so much of, was the very thing they had a shortage of. I happily would've traded some of my time for some of their wages.

With a sliced pan and a packet of ham, I headed down Green Park Road, turned onto Ardee Street, then onto Dargan Street. I opened the front door and heard two voices. I listened cautiously, fearing the house was being robbed.

"*I thought I told ye to leave town.*"

"*I ain't going nowhere!*"

"*You're gonna leave town now, whether walking or in a box... Your choice, old friend.*"

"*You've never fired a gun in your damn life. It takes a man to kill a man.*"

"*It takes a fool to underestimate a man.*"

"*Well, I'm gonna turn around now and head into that bar. You do what you have to do.*"

"Don't try me, partner!"

"It's a coward who shoots a man in the back."

"And an even bigger coward who stabs a friend in the back!"

BANG!

An old western. The television was working again. It would thankfully save me from an afternoon of introspection.

At dinner, the family spoke of their day. They tried to engage me in the conversation. I was beyond engagement. So removed were their lives from mine, mine from theirs, the most I could muster was an occasional, "Oh right," "I see," or "Oh yeah."

More television followed dinner before I went to bed. Another day in the books. No different from the previous one.

Wednesday

The soul-destroying, morale slaughtering, demoralising time of the month. Signing on day. My monthly trip to the social welfare office to sign on the live register, to show them I was still alive and looking for work. The routine ate away at the remnants of your self-esteem, and reminded you, in case you'd forgotten, that you were nothing, a broken-down engine not even worth scrap value.

I stood at the back of the queue outside the building in the rain, getting drenched with my cohorts, feeling like we were the dregs of society.

Having made it inside, I kept my head down, not wanting to be recognised, but my curiosity was piqued.

I glanced around me for familiar faces, either hoping they'd offer some sort of reassurance that I wasn't the sole victim of such circumstances, or out of a spiteful delight found in dragging everyone else down with me. I spotted a few. Liam Mulligan stood afar. Liam or 'Lolli' as he was known, was a welcome St Brendan's representative. He was nicknamed 'Lolli' because of his resemblance to a lollipop. His stick thin figure which could fall through a crack in the footpath, was accentuated by a massive head which somehow nestled on his feeble frame, and his body, in a miracle of anatomical engineering, seemed to cope with the weight. His head didn't seem so big anymore. He'd grown into it. The more I looked around, the more I saw. Cian Buckley, another St Brendan's man, was to my right. Brendan Fitzpatrick from down the road was a few bodies behind me. Mousey Keating was over on the far side, his voice unmistakable as he argued with the man behind the glass. Mousey's presence made me wonder how the old gang were faring in the drastically changed country we were now residing in.

For such a large congregation, the silence was only interrupted by the occasional cough and the pelting rain. It had all the joyous atmosphere of a morgue. All we were missing was a corpse. Any of us could've played the part of one, our faces ashen, our bodies stone cold. Only the hushed conversation that started up between two women ahead of me suppressed such musings.

"It was our anniversary last week, Louise."

"Did he remember?"

"Ah, did he fuck! He claimed he did, but I was dropping so many hints the week before, I nearly had to hoover the fuckin' things up. Well anyway, we agreed to keep it small 'cause the money's tight, ye know? So, we got me sister to look after the kids so we could have a romantic meal at home. We bought each other small presents too."

"Ah, that sounds lovely."

"Ah, hear me out first, Louise! This is my Dessie we're talking about. If he did something right, there'd be something wrong!"

"Ah, he's not that bad."

"Now don't you be sympathising with him, Louise Redmond! You don't have to live with his antics. It doesn't matter what ye ask him to do. If he was in charge o' the crucifixion he'd forget to bring the nails!"

"Sure, he's no different than the rest o' them. So tell us, what happened?"

"He insists on doing the cooking. He's been watching all these cooking programmes lately and fancies himself as a bit of a chef. Now, wouldn't ye think he'd cook the kids' dinners during the week with all this knowledge he's acquired? Ah no, what does he do? He teaches the kids what he's learned so *they* can cook *his* dinner!"

"So, he's doing the cooking and…"

"And o' course, what happens? He has the steaks on, he forgets about them, and they get burned to a crisp. So, he comes out with these steaks and presents one o' them to me like it's a culinary masterpiece or something. I said to him, 'Dessie, I can't eat this, it's like a lump o' coal.' He goes, 'I thought ye liked your steaks well done?' 'Well done? I'll break me teeth trying to chew on the thing,' I said. Then he goes, 'Ah, it's not that hard.' I said, 'I'll belt ye across the head with the thing, Dessie, and ye can judge how hard it is!'"

"Well, the thought was there at least. My husband's idea of a romantic evening is turning the telly off for an hour and lighting a poxy candle as he drinks his cans. So anyway, what did yis do?"

"I said, 'Never mind the food, let's just have our few drinks.' I had no appetite anyway. He says, 'No, I need something to eat. I can't have sex on an empty stomach.'"

"He said what?"

"Ah yeah, that's nothing unusual for my Dessie. And the cheek of him assuming he had a guaranteed ride. That little pecker of his has more confidence than it has inches."

"So, what then?"

"He wanted a chipper. I wanted a Chinese. He starts going on about a special they're doing in Luigi's, that it's the last night for it..."

"Ah, for heaven's sake."

"So, we start arguing... Any romance has gone out the window by this stage, Louise. Anyway, I gave in, the chipper it was. Let him save his few shaggin' pennies! I swear, if he had his way, he'd be down by the Dargle fishing for the fuckin' things!"

"Ah, that fella o' yours is a fuckin' nuisance."

"So, he arrives back from the chipper. Then as we're eating away, he tells me I'm looking gorgeous, that he prefers how I look now as opposed to ten years ago."

"Ah, that's lovely. I wish I had a fella like that."

"I ask him what he means. He says I'm more womanly looking now. I'm a bit fuller looking. He loves me bigger arse, me bigger boobs, me rounder face. I was like, 'What?!'"

"So would I be!"

"'Are ye saying I'm fat, Dessie?' I ask him. He says, 'Ah no, I like a bit o' chubbiness on ye, that's all. It gives ye a nice pair o' cheeks.'"

"Which pair o' cheeks? Is that a compliment?"

"Ah, Louise, in *his* head, I'm sure it is. I ask him, 'Do ye think I've a fat arse, Dessie?' He says that I've an arse that he loves, and he doesn't care why it's gotten bigger. He just loves it. Have ye ever heard anything like it, Louise?"

"I thought my fella was bad."

"So, I said to him, 'Since when do ye have a thing for arses?' He goes, 'It's not a thing. I just appreciate a well-rounded arse, that's all.' Louise, his exact words were, and I quote, 'I don't care how you've got your new arse, love. I just like it. It's like when I'm eating me rashers – I don't care whether the pig was shot or had his throat slit, I still love what's on me plate either way.'"

"Was he comparing ye to a pig? That's the strangest compliment I've ever heard."

"That's my Dessie for ye. Sure, things only got stranger from there."

"Go on, tell us."

"We swapped presents. I got him some clothes. What does *he* get *me*, Louise? Me beloved husband, what does he get me?"

"What?"

"A dildo."

"A dildo?"

"Oh yes, a dildo."

"Ah, *he's* a fuckin dildo!"

"And not just any dildo, he tells me. The 'Pleasure Deluxe,' no less. The biggest and best apparently. Ten inches of relentless pleasure, so it says on the box."

"That sounds awright to me. I'll take it off ye if ye don't want it. Ye can give Dessie me regards."

"Ah, ye wanna see this thing, Louise. It's like a fuckin' anaconda. It's a weapon. Ye could rob a bank with this yoke!"

"Have ye used it?"

"Have I fuck! I'm scared what it'll do to me! He told me he bought it for me for when he was away. I mean, ye'd hardly notice him when he's in there, let alone miss him! He said it would spice up our sex life. I asked him did he get the huge one for me huge arse. He told me they had smaller ones, but the big one was the same price, so he wanted value for his money. Typical fuckin' Dessie! I swear, he wouldn't feed the ducks without keeping account o' how many pieces o' bread he'd thrown in."

"Well, if I was you, I'd be putting it to good use. Dessie may have scored an own goal. His little fella might be the next in line to be made redundant. Ha ha."

"And well overdue too. Ha ha… I'll pop over to the euro shop when I get out o' here."

"For what?"

"The auld 'Pleasure Deluxe' is just like Dessie – batteries not included! Ha ha."

"Ha ha."

"God, it's hard to believe it's been ten years… Ah, I do love him. He's just an eejit. But he's my eejit."

The girl at the front of the queue, having signed on, turned to the awaiting faces. Her head was stooped as she wrestled her social welfare card into her purse. Her woolly hat was pulled down over her brow, and with it, her black-rimmed glasses disguised her. She trudged past the next few people in line, retracing her steps to the back of the queue; the walk of shame that I too would soon take. It was a walk of about thirty yards that felt like thirty miles, in which everyone you knew seemed to converge in the one line, notifying the entire room to your presence with an amiable and unwanted, 'How are ye?'

As she approached me, her gaze shifting from the floor to the door, there was no mistaking who it was. Rachael Dowling. The girl with all the brains and aspirations was unemployed. The vindictive side of me enjoyed it, deriving satisfaction from the irony of Her Royal Highness standing in a dole queue with the person she once thought she was superior to; the same person she once foresaw loitering at the bottom of the career ladder while she climbed it, awaiting the view from the top. And yet, there she was.

The sympathetic side of me struggled to be heard, its voice a faint whisper amidst the double helping of *schadenfreude* I was treating myself to, which appeared on my face as a subtle raising of the eyebrows. Her face was one at odds with those around her. She didn't belong there.

With punctured self-esteem, I gauged my presence, and that of the rest, to be expected. We were destined to be casualties of the recession. But Rachael Dowling was a size ten foot in a size nine shoe. She thought she was above this. She *was*. A smidgen of sympathy found a crevice to crawl through. Her lofty ambitions were those of a different person to the one before me. As she walked past me, we refrained from locking eyes, both of us pretending not to see the other. Part of me hoped she'd tap me on the shoulder or say my name. When she did neither, I felt an urge to turn around and take a quick glance, but I didn't for fear of her catching me in the act.

Seeing her had the effect of transporting me back to a time when ambitions and futures had value, when the innocence of youth knew nothing of the despondency of adulthood. I longed for those days. I saw myself with her. Not the current embodiment of me; a younger, naive, charismatic, nonchalant version. I regretted ignoring her, cursing myself as I waited impatiently for the man ahead of me to sign his name. As he passed me, I rushed to the counter, card in hand, and quickly wrote my signature.

"Your next sign-on day is…"

"Yeah, yeah, thanks."

I fumbled with my wallet and rushed out the door into the car park. She was nowhere to be seen. Out on the main street, I glanced left and right, barely keeping my head still long enough for my eyes to register what lay before me. She was gone.

I felt my mood change abruptly as my socks absorbed the water from the puddle I'd stepped in. I found a perverse pleasure in knowing she could no longer look down on me with ease, and in imagining what her parents thought of their precious little princess, now that she was reduced to playing in the same sandpit with a playmate they once deemed unfit for her company.

As I plodded along the main street, I questioned the motive of my pursuit. I knew it wasn't her I was chasing; rather, a former life, a former me, a former country. I was chasing a time warp in which I could relive the same couple of years continuously, never having to face any future upheavals.

I sat at home, drying my feet, watching the rain pepper the window, dwelling on the stark contrast between then and now.

I didn't believe in depression. Self-pitying claptrap. The avocation of the weak. Its 'sufferers' were sympathy seekers. God help them if they had a real problem. But then again, not believing the earth was round, didn't change the fact that it *was* round.

With a change of clothes, and with the morning downpour giving way to a mild afternoon, I was out the door again. Just the thought of a few pints helped to clear my head.

I sat at the bar of the Waterfront, chastising myself for chasing after Rachael Dowling, as if she was anything worth chasing. Thankfully, she hadn't witnessed such a pathetic display. If she had, the news of her family being murdered wouldn't have been enough to wipe the grin off her face. Seeing her standing in that queue alongside me, almost made the recession worthwhile.

The drink was much better company than she was. It cheered me up and ensured my enjoyment in a way that she never could.

That night, I took my alcohol-induced high spirits with me to bed, hoping they'd still be lying with me come the morning.

Thursday

I channel hopped through midday television until I found two American good-for-nothings with enough ink on their bodies to rewrite the Book of Kells, arguing over a child's paternity like it was a dispute over whose turn it was to do the washing-up.

"Natasha, I know ye slept with Dominic! I followed you to his apartment one night."

"Ye what?"

"Ye heard me!"

"I was only going over to meet Naomi."

"Ye couldn't have been. She wasn't there that night."

"How do ye know?"

"Oh, I'll tell ye how I know, because she was with me that night!"

"You were BLEEP Naomi!"

"Yeah, only 'cause you were BLEEP Dominic! Was he worth it?"

"Yeah, he BLEEP was actually. He has a BLEEP BLEEP on him like an elephant's trunk!"

"Is that right? Well, maybe his trunk has a lot to answer for!"

"What are you saying?"

"I'm saying, if that's Dominic's baby, I ain't paying for it!"

"You ain't been paying for it anyway!"

"Why would I? So I can save him a fortune?"

"Oh, so our baby is just an expense to ye, is it?"

"It is if it's someone else's!"

The host interrupted them to introduce Dominic to the stage, who was greeted with a chorus of pantomime boos before making his contribution.

"Don't be trying to pawn off your kid on me, Jake! Take some BLEEP responsibility."

"I should take some responsibility?! This is coming from the guy who's been BLEEP my woman!"

"I could say the same for you, but you're welcome to BLEEP that skank Naomi. We've traded girls, Jake. Everyone's happy, so what the BLEEP is your goddamn problem?"

"My BLEEP problem is I'm raising a kid who's probably not even mine!"

"Well, he ain't mine! We used protection…most o' the time."

The host interrupted them again.

"Now folks, look at the picture of baby Jake Jr on the big screen. Let's have a vote. Hands up those who think he looks more like Jake… Okay, and now, hands up those who think he looks like Dominic… Hmm, I think its fifty-fifty. Folks, both Jake and Dominic have taken paternity tests and I have the results in this very envelope. We'll reveal who indeed is the father of baby Jake Jr after this commercial break. Don't go away. We'll be back in three."

I changed the station. A farming programme. In the middle of watching a cow giving birth, I heard something being posted through the letterbox. It was the local newspaper. I leafed through it; my attention being drawn to an article about the building of a new supermarket being mired in planning issues. A local councillor stated that the supermarket would provide an essential service to the southern end of the town and would also lead to the creation of much-needed jobs locally. Another councillor was quoted as saying, 'It's bad enough that we are losing so many jobs, but now we are doing our upmost to chase them away!'

There was a knock on the door. I opened it to see two smiling gentlemen in suits standing before me.

"Hello, sir," they greeted in unison.

"How are yis?"

"Very well… We've called to talk to you about Jehova," the elder of the pair said.

"Jehova?"

"Or God, as you may know him."

"Ah, right… So, what's he up to?"

"Now that's an important question you ask, sir."

"It is?"

"Indeed. Where does Jehovah fit in our contemporary society? How can he help us in the uncertain times that we are living in?"

"Was that the question I asked?"

"Yes, and a fascinating question too."

"So, what's the answer?"

"The answer is through prayer and through our reading of the bible. Tell me, have you ever felt the presence of Jehovah in times of strife?"

"Well, I had a problem with the telly the other day and when I arrived back it was fixed, just like that. It was a miracle, like the loaves and the fish."

"I see. And what about in a more personal way? In your daily life, have you felt him offer clarity when you've been overwhelmed by confusion? Does he guide you in the right direction?"

"Well, I remembered to sign on yesterday. Was that because o' him?"

"If you felt his presence, well then, yes. Jehova's work comes in all shapes and sizes, from the spectacular to the mundane."

"Can he help me get a job?"

"He can help you make peace with yourself. He can help you to accept your failings. He can guide you down a spiritual path which will make you a better person, and in turn, a better employee…so yes, he can help you find employment."

"Eh, I was thinking more in terms of a few hours' work in the church, painting it, cutting the grass outside… What's his hourly rate? Would he give a decent reference?"

"Well…"

"I have to say, you're not selling this Jehovah fella well at all. What about Jesus?"

"What about him?"

"Well, was he any use as a carpenter?"

"Why do you ask?"

"Well, if ye think about it, the disciples were following him around, scribbling down everything he did from saying prayers to taking a dump, but never a wrote a word about him making any furniture. Bit of a cowboy perhaps? Do ye reckon if Jesus was around now, he'd be on the dole with the rest o' the builders? He wouldn't look like much of a Messiah standing in the dole queue, would he?"

"Jesus saw himself as being equal to all men."

"What, going around claiming to be a king? Ah, he was a bit fond of himself now in fairness."

"He had a calling, a purpose in life!"

"Ah, I'm not criticising the chap, fair play to him if he was. I admire anybody who's in love with themselves. I wish *I* was. I fell out o' love with meself years ago."

"When?"

"A few days after leaving the womb. I more or less had enough o' meself by then. Things had been going grand for nine months until the midwife pulled me out."

"I sense a great void in your life, my friend. There's an emptiness there that only Jehova can fill."

"You're right, mate. Do ye know what it is? Pussy! I haven't had a morsel in ages. I'm gagging!"

"Ah, the love of a woman can indeed aid a man on his spiritual journey."

"I had a dream a few nights ago. I was hanging on a cross with Jesus and the other two lads beside me. I had a raging boner sticking out o' me towel and there wasn't a woman in sight to sort me out. Me hands weren't much use to me either, them being tied to the cross. I was in agony. I asked Jesus what to do."

"And what did he say?"

"He said, 'Don't worry, Paddy. Mary Magdalene will be here in a minute. She'll sort ye out.' What do ye think that dream means?"

"I think it's your subconscious telling you to allow Jehova to play a greater role in your life. I think you are lost in a dense wood, searching for higher ground to view the landscape from above and assess which road is the wisest to travel."

"Ye got all that from me dream?"

"Yes, and from what you've said. We meet gentlemen like you all the time. Many young men are seeking more from life that the materialistic world around them can't offer. Only Jehovah can... Here, take this pamphlet. We'd be delighted if ye'd join us in our Kingdom Hall, where you'll meet others just like you, who can attest to the difference Jehovah has made in their lives."

"Oh, I'll be there, front row. See yis now," I said, closing the door on them.

Devoid of the winning lotto numbers, the pamphlet quickly found itself in the bin.

Thursday was both the high and low point of the week. Dole day. It was similar to the sign-on day but with the consolation of being furnished with cash to make it more bearable.

I waited in line in the post office on Quinsborough Road. Queues and unemployment went together like fire and smoke. I envied those with letters and parcels. My new ambition was to one day use the building for its actual postal service; quite a climbdown from my teenage aspiration of being a wealthy musician.

I had my card in hand. On it was printed my new identity, 2788744T.

My plan as such was to keep my head down, hand over my card, sign my name, get the money, avoid any chitchat and get out. But as if trying to intentionally sabotage such a plan, the clerk, against the laws of subtlety, counted each note aloud for the rest of the queue to hear.

"That's twenty, that's seventy, now a hundred, one twenty, one twenty-five, one thirty, one thirty-five, one forty and…"

He reached into another drawer for coppers.

"Forty-one fifty, forty-two, one hundred and forty-three euro, there ye go."

By the time I had the money in my hand, my pride could be found hanging from the ceiling. I mumbled a thanks and hurried out like I'd robbed the place. In a way, I had. The most productive thing I'd done all week was to buy a sliced pan and a packet of ham.

No more than fifteen minutes after I put the money in my wallet, I was taking it back out and handing it over the bar of the Waterfront.

Friday

I visited the job centre as a token attempt at doing something constructive, only to find that it was bleaker than ever before. There seemed a better chance of me finding a sack with a million euros in it, than there was of me finding a job.

I wandered the streets, my forte in life, remembering the nonchalance I once possessed when I walked through them as a schoolboy. The shop front signs of former businesses had been taken down. Once bustling chain stores sat across the road from empty cafes. Barbers swept floors bereft of hair. There were half-price sales, sales on the half-price sales, early drinkers in pubs, early drunks sitting on a wall, cans being swilled and empties being crushed, mouth almighties jawing to other mouth almighties about God Almighty knows what, the employed busy being employed, the unemployed busier being unemployed.

I came to the Carlisle Grounds, taking note of the fixtures' board.

TONIGHT'S MATCH
BRAY WANDERERS V ST PATRICK'S ATHLETIC
KICK OFF: 7.45PM

The ten-euro ticket would be money well spent in exchange for a temporary disruption of my monotonous routine.

That night, I was sitting amongst Bray's diminutive band of loyal supporters whose fervour couldn't be curbed by the empty seats surrounding them. Irish Football wasn't about capacity crowds, mesmeric teams or flamboyant players. It was escapism. Lost in an atmosphere unbefitting the sparse congregation, my voice was both contributing to and being drowned out by the chorus of cheers, boos, shouting, singing and slagging. The beating drum reminded me I still had a pulse. Football at this level was a brotherhood. I was amongst my own. This was the one place where we still had an identity, where disconsolate eyes rose from the ground temporarily. It was a place where the recession could be left at the creaking turnstile and all your pent-up infuriation could be unleashed. This was real religion. This was *our* church, where elation and anguish were just a kick of the ball away from each other. This was a town awakening for ninety minutes. This was the drudgery of Irish football in a half empty Carlisle Grounds, and I relished it.

I had found a seat near the halfway line, with the dugouts to my left and a floodlight pole to my right, obscuring my view of both goal ends.

As the match went on, the referee's performance came under vociferous criticism from the home supporters.

"Ah, fuck off, ref!

"That was never a free!"

"Ye fuckin' daft cunt, ref! He was looking for it!"

"How much are they paying ye, ref?!"

Also to be heard were snippets of 'expertise.'

"Ah, why is that young O'Byrne lad playing up front?! He was sucking on his ma's tit half an hour ago!"

"That prick is free down the wing every time… Jesus Christ, Bray! Will yis put the little bollocks in a wheelchair!"

"Jesus, Mary and Joseph! Yis couldn't score in a fuckin' brothel!"

"Ah, for fuck's sake, Bray! Me auld one would've stuck that one in with her handbag!"

Half-time. Nil-all. The drama in the stand had surpassed that on the pitch.

I scurried out the gate at the half-time whistle along with many of my compatriots for a few refreshments in Smith's across the road. With only a fifteen-minute interval at your disposal, a well-executed drinks break was a marvel of time management and alcohol consumption. It afforded you the appetite to suffer another forty-five minutes of footballing dross. The matches always seemed

more exciting in the second half, the crowd more buoyant, and the ref always a bigger bollocks than he'd been
in the first half.

A swift exit from the ground would ensure that you'd
be served a couple of Ronan Smith's already-poured pints
of Guinness that would be lined up along the bar like
a battalion awaiting an impending incursion. If truly
determined, a third pint could be downed. Although,
with the battalion obliterated by then, the time it took to
place your order, for the pint to be pulled, rested, topped,
and for it to be knocked back before the commencement
of the second half, made the undertaking a risky gamble.

Even riskier was the chipper break, in which a Friday
evening queue in Leonardo's around the corner, could
cost you the first ten minutes of the second half. With
there being a prohibition on outside food being brought
into the ground, to assist the sales of the club's own over-
priced offerings, Leonardo's take-aways had to be smuggled in. With the unmistakable whiff of chips, a burger
or a kebab emanating from the bulge under your coat, a
scrupulous steward could easily catch you and force you
to gobble your food outside the ground before permit-
ting you to re-enter.

With two pints drunk, I darted back across the road,
just in time for the re-start.

The seat beside me remained empty until fifteen
minutes into the half, when its occupant returned, shaking his head at me in exasperation.

"It's unbelievable, mate! They had me standing outside like an eejit, eating me chips and battered sausages.
Your man says to me, 'Ah, the rules are the rules.' The

rules me hole… I swear, ye can't take a shite in this country anymore without there being a rule on the correct way to wipe your arse!"

"I hear ye," I agreed, laughing.

"And where were all these rules for the bankers?! I guarantee ye they're not standing out in the cold, trying to shove battered sausages down their throats!"

"Probably on some beach somewhere getting a tan, I'd say."

"Ye say right. And it's not Bray beach. Jesus, I wish it was. We could fuckin' stone them to death. Here we are, only a few years from the centenary of the Easter Rising and what do we have to show for it? Debt, unemployment and emigration, that's what. And what did they die for anyway? So that we'd have the freedom to be screwed by our own? Those bankers, I swear, they'd sell their own children if they got a decent offer for them… Anyway, come on the fuck Bray!"

The second half was as enthralling as the first. My eyes strayed. Amongst the dispirited looking supporters leaning on the wall behind the goal, one familiar face stood out. I walked towards that end of the ground and approached him from behind.

"How come you're not playing, Popey?"

"Ah, Paddy, how are ye keeping?"

"Same as everyone else, shite."

"This auld match isn't up to much, is it?"

"Ah, it's the pits. What are ye up to these days?"

"Fuck all. The apprenticeship went up in smoke. They couldn't afford to keep me on. What about you?"

"Nothing, mate. It has me head done in at this stage."

"I know, I'm the same… How's the gang?"

"I'm useless at keeping in touch. Last I heard they were working or in college or whatever. But that was then… How come I never see ye out and about much?"

"Ah, I don't be out that often, money and all that, ye know? I prefer getting a few cans. Are ye still hanging around your usual haunts?"

"Ah yeah, I'm not gonna let a recession stop me from enjoying meself. You shouldn't either."

"I'll try to bear that in mind," he said impassively. "Did ye ever get back with your one?"

"Stephanie Heffernan? Christ, no. I took your advice, Popey."

"*My* advice? The blind leading the blind. So, you're on the market then?"

"Ah, not really. I think I'm better at playing the field rather than committing to anyone, ye know what I mean? I've a bit o' acting the maggot to get out o' me system before I go down that road again. Are ye still with Sharon?"

"Nah, that fizzled out. She couldn't put up with me anymore, so she said."

"Have ye picked any winners since?"

"Nah, I haven't been trying to."

"Why not? What happened? Did ye finally manage to pull the knob off yourself? Ha ha."

He offered a perfunctory laugh and turned his head, ignoring the question.

"Well?" I asked.

"Ah… I just amn't bothered really," he eventually replied.

I'd noticed a change in his appearance. He'd put on weight. But it wasn't just the weight. He looked tired. Maybe that's what the weight does to you. Then again, I probably did too. Maybe that's what unemployment does to you.

We continued chatting amidst the shouts, but with the initial pleasantries fulfilled, he became more distant, more concentrated on the game. As the match entered its latter stages, still at nil-all, the crowd bade for one last attack on the St Pat's goal. Bray pushed an extra couple of men forward for a corner in injury time. The ball was cleared down the wing, and the little bollocks who should've been put in a wheelchair, made a darting run down the sideline, dribbling past two Bray players to get into the box, and with a perfect strike, nestled the ball into the bottom corner of the net. A moment of disgusting beauty. The sounds of the groans and curses were that of a town deflating.

The final whistle was blown, amplified amidst the silence of the crowd.

"For fuck's sake, Bray! Same auld shite!" I said, hearing similar opinions being voiced around me.

I expected Popey to be livid, but he was quiet and motionless, his stare still fixed on the pitch as the players were leaving it.

"Are ye in shock, Popey? I don't know why ye are. Same auld story!"

No answer.

"A fuckin' draw would've been a good result," I heard someone say behind me.

There was nothing like a bad result to unearth the masters of hindsight, the engineers of 'what could have been,' the architects of 'how things should have been done.'

"Are ye coming for a pint, Popey? The Waterfront will be black. We'll find ourselves a couple o' fine looking ones."

"I'll go for a quiet one with ye in O'Connell's, if ye want?"

"I wouldn't give that shower the steam o' me piss!"

"Somewhere else then. I just fancy a bit of an auld chat. I'm not really in the mood for…"

"Would ye listen to yourself! You're like an auld one. Did ye bring the tea and biscuits with ye? Ha ha. I want a bit of action tonight. I have me good shirt on. I don't want to have ironed it for nothing."

"Fair enough."

"So, are ye coming to the Waterfront then?"

"Nah, I'll give it a miss. I'll get a few cans."

Popey muttered something as I watched the Bray manager berate the ref as he left the pitch. When I turned my head, he was gone. I could see him amongst the supporters heading for the gate, but decided to leave him be, seeing that our respective paths for the night ahead were diverging. His inconspicuous exit was unlike him, but a bad result could have that effect on you.

Sitting at the Waterfront's bar, I had a hankering for Popey's company. We were overdue a recessionary drink, but Popey, much like myself, was his own man. He'd find his own mischief without needing his hand to be held.

Two hours, a few scoops and a couple of flirtatious glances later, the match and Popey had already been forgotten.

Saturday

Even though every day was a Saturday, the day still had a special appeal. It was comforting to lounge on a day, knowing that everyone else was lounging with me. Normality. For once I was no different than the employed. I rose to their level, or rather, they sank to mine.

The day, as was customary, began with a full Irish. Four sausages, two rashers, two cuts of black pudding, two cuts of white pudding, fried tomatoes, fried mushrooms, hash browns, a fried egg, half a loaf, and plenty of tea.

Of course, such a meal couldn't have been savoured if not for the invention of the pig. It was a sacred animal in Ireland. Its sacrifice for the greater good of the Irish nation was akin to the self-sacrifice of the leaders of the 1916 Rising. They fought for the country – the pig fed the country. It was responsible for putting more food in the mouths of Irish children than any government, charity or church. So much so, that its contribution to Irish life was commemorated by its placement on the half-penny coin. A worthy recipient of such an honour. The Celtic Pig would've been a more pertinent moniker for our much-ballyhooed era of affluence.

The day was spent watching television. For the first time that week, it warranted being viewed.

Saturday night was my primary drinking spree. Any others that preceded it during the week were mere training sessions for the main event, a warming up of the liver for the coming battering. Amidst the Waterfront's hectic scene of singing, dancing and romancing, was the dreary sight of me at the bar, scouting what was on offer.

The usual array. Young and gorgeous, out of my league. Forty somethings and formerly gorgeous, in my league. Young and average, possibly in my league. Young and fat, a league below me. I'd aim for one of the young and average, I'd settle for a forty something, and if all else failed, I'd offer myself to one of the patrons whose body was the only thing as big as their craving for male attention. My most recent dalliance had been with such a rotund woman, and it was an experience I had pledged not to relive. But my carnal cravings were such, that this night would test the feasibility of that pledge.

The women danced as I stood, mingled as I kept to myself, and were jubilant as I was stoic. I tried to catch the eye of one of them. She was young and semi-attractive from a certain angle when under a generous light. I waited for a signal. Nothing. She was immersed in the song. When she'd order a drink, I'd line her in my crosshairs and take her out like the sexual assassin I fancied myself as being.

She soon staggered towards me. A flirtatious collision was imminent. She ordered a vodka and coke. I watched her pour the coke into the glass, the time it took to rise to the rim being my quickly diminishing window of opportunity. I panicked, devoid of ideas. Charmer's block. She paid by card as I remained speechless. Someone from behind her pushed forward, half of her drink spilling over my shirt.

"Oh, I'm sorry, hun!" she said, holding what was left of her drink.

"You're grand, no bother."

"Aw, look at ye! Your shirt's destroyed!"

"It'll dry in a minute. Don't worry about it."

"Aw, it was your man behind me… What are ye drinking? I'll get ye one."

My charm may have abandoned me, but I'd been adopted by luck.

"Would ye go away out o' that. Sure, you're after losing half o' yours. What are ye drinking? I'll get *you* one."

"Ye are not! I'm buying. I owe ye for the shirt."

"Ye don't owe me anything. I'm buying… and we'll call it even if ye drink it with me. There's an empty table over there."

I caught a glimpse of a middle-aged fat woman. She gave me the dreaded 'Finger Point of Doom,' the patented signal of the middle-aged drunk woman who wants you. I ignored her and escorted my night's catch over to the far corner of the lounge, fearing that the menopausal behemoth was in hot pursuit. I positioned myself with my back to her, hoping she'd look elsewhere.

"What's your name?" I asked.

"Michelle, and yours?"

"Paddy."

"So, do ye often come here by yourself, Paddy?"

"Now and again. I like going out by meself. The night's less predictable."

"Such as randomly bumping into someone like me?"

"Maybe," I responded, trying not to give too much away.

"Ye fancy yourself as bit of a man o' mystery, do ye? I can see right through ye."

"Is that so? So tell us, what am I thinking then?"

"You're thinking o' how long ye should wait before ye make a move," she said, offering me a saucy smile.

"Is it that obvious?"

"No more obvious than ye leering at me when I was dancing."

"Well, ye must've been leering at me too, if ye caught me," I said, steeped in alcohol-fuelled swagger.

"Maybe I was," she replied, offering me that smile again before she leaned into me, reached round the back of my neck and made *me* the recipient of the 'Attack of the Lizard.'

We endeavoured to converse thereafter, but the blaring music and our inebriation led to most of our babbling being lost in translation.

"Do ye wanna stay long?" she asked.

"Nah, I hate that song. Do *you* like it?"

"What I'd like is for you to show me what you've got in your pants!"

"Sorry, Michelle. I haven't the legs for a dance."

"I said – your pants!"

"France? I've never been there. Have you? I've only been to Spain."

"A lane? I'm not riding ye down some lane, hun. I've a flat. I live with me mate."

"Nah, it's not too late… They're still serving… What do ye want?"

"I want you… in me bed."

"Ye want to be fed? Yeah, no bother. We can go to Leonardo's."

"I bet you're big!"

"Nah, not too big. I'll just get a small burger. I'm not that hungry with the drink."

"Do ye have a condom?"

"A coupon? I had a few o' them but a pair o' lads robbed them."

"I can't wait to taste ye."

"I know, same here. Their burgers are lovely."

Closing time. We both struggled to our feet, making numerous haphazard attempts at finding our way out the door.

"We'll get a taxi back to mine."

"We can walk. A bit o' fresh air will do us good."

"I'm not walking anywhere in these heels."

"Take them off."

"I'm not walking in me bare feet. I'll step on a syringe or something."

"I'll keep an eye out for syringes."

"Are ye that tight, Paddy?"

"No, I just thought we could have a romantic walk."

Sensing her irritation, I opted to acquiesce to her taxi. We hailed one down and hopped in.

"Where are we going, Michelle?"

"O'Byrne Road."

Off we went as I made small talk with the African driver.

"How are ye getting on these days with the recession?"

"Ah, it's tough. There aren't as many people going out, but I'm getting by – just about."

"Paddy, tell him he can join us in bed."

"Michelle, sssh… Yeah, some o' the pubs have gone fierce quiet."

"Paddy, tell him I've never been with a black fella before."

"I'll tell him to fuck ye out o' the car if ye don't shut up!"

"Paddy, I've never been with…"

"Neither have I! But I'm not harping on about it, am I?!"

"I think I'm gonna be sick, Paddy."

"There's a hundred-euro charge, my friend, if she gets sick in my car," the driver warned me.

"If ye think I'm paying a hundred quid for your puke, Michelle… Stick your head out the window."

We arrived at our destination and got out of the car. After a few attempts, she managed to unlock the door. Screams, moans, and pleas of "Gimme that big boy!" emanated from the bedroom.

"Is that your mate? Fuckin' hell, is she being murdered in there? Your man must have a tool like a sledgehammer."

"Come on, let's join them."

"Join them? What do ye mean, 'join them'? I can't do it with two other people watching."

"Why not?"

"I just can't. It's bad enough with the person I'm with watching, never mind anyone else. The best sex I have is by meself."

"They're not gonna be watching. They'll be too busy."

"Let's just do it here on the couch," I said, as I began to strip her.

With the sexual Olympics in full swing in the next room, I was determined to outperform my competitor

and come home with the gold. There was but one problem. With hours of drinking behind me, Little Paddy
was as scuttered as I was. His attempts at standing up
straight were as lethargic and as comical as my own. Even
when given a helping hand, he couldn't amass the energy
or wherewithal to wake from his drunken slumber. She
stared at him in bewilderment.

"What's wrong with it?"

"It's just the drink. It puts it to sleep."

"Well, wake it up."

"I can't just wake it up… It does its own thing. He's
his own man."

I can never understand why achieving an erection
can't be as simple as raising an arm. A design flaw in the
male anatomy if ever there was one.

"Ah here, give it to me," she ordered, as she grabbed
Little Paddy. His head disappeared and reappeared like
an indecisive mole before he eventually woke, refusing to let a night's drinking make him miss such an
opportunity.

"That's more like it," she said. "Ye think *she's* loud?
Wait till ye hear *me*."

Between her and her mate's panting and screaming,
and the groans of the other chap, it was like spending a
night in an insane asylum. My pursuit of the gold medal
ended when I could still hear the noises of the other
pair emanating from the next room, long after I gave
all I could. Nevertheless, 'Little Paddy' had discovered
another new land, arriving on shore to plant his flag, having sailed through choppy waters to get there.

Sunday

Awoken by her exhalations, I was reluctant to open my eyes. With consciousness came realisation, consequences and a hangover. The world of sleep was a far more forgiving place. It postponed whatever the inevitable was. But wanting to make a swift exit, I opened them. Her naked body was lying beside mine. I sat up, running a feeble hand through my hair, waiting for my brain to awaken. With a mouth that felt like I'd swallowed sand, I went to the sink and guzzled three glasses of water before returning to the sofa to dress quickly. My jeans were caught below her right leg. I gently pulled them. Her mouth opened. I stopped. After a moment, I slowly pulled again. As I released them from beneath her, to my horror, the legion of loose change in my pockets crashed to the wooden floor, clinking and rolling all over the room. Her eyes opened wearily.

"Why…why are ye dressed like that, Paddy?"

"Like what?"

"You've your coat on but no trousers."

"I was feeling nippy."

"Trying to fuck off more like it."

My lack of a response confirmed her suspicion.

"So, what do ye wanna do?" I asked.

"What do ye mean?"

"Well, do ye want me to hang around? Make ye a cup o' tea or get breakfast or something?"

"Go on home. I don't mind."

"Are ye sure?"

"Jesus Christ, Paddy! I want to see the back o' you just as much as you want to see the back o' me. Go on, get out o' here before Leanne wakes up."

I put on my trousers and shoes and made for the door.

"Paddy, don't forget your change."

"Ye can keep it."

"Are ye that eager to escape?"

"No more eager than you are to get rid o' me," I replied, as I made my second attempt for the door.

"Before ye go, Paddy…a word of advice… Next time you're planning on doing a runner, hold your jeans upright," she said, smiling.

"Will do," I said, smiling back, before I evacuated the building promptly, delighted to have escaped without contracting the relationship virus. I had no doubt that she carried the same strain of it as Stephanie Heffernan, and I knew that a second bout of that would be even deadlier than the first, with unemployment exacerbating its effects.

Sunday was the day in which my week of drinking caught up with my body and forced it to shut down for some overdue rest and recuperation.

My initial exuberance after a successful night of womanising was soon deflated by the unavoidable comedown, both physical and mental. It left me with no desire or ability to do anything other than sit in the armchair in the sitting room, staring vacantly out the window, letting sleep come and go as it pleased. The television was on. Ma, Da and Claire were coming and going. Everything was as it normally was, except me. I was like a semi-conscious sloth, best left alone. I was unable to entertain company or perform even the most menial tasks. Eating my dinner was a chore. Chewing was an effort, as was having to listen to the conversation round the table. The ecstasy of my one-night stand was already forgotten. I ate what I could and scooped the remainder into Buddy's bowl, returning to my armchair with a cup of tea, taking comfort in the knowledge that a night's sleep was only hours away. The following day, the merry adventure would start all over again.

In a sombre mood, I could summon the powers of hindsight and question the week that had been, the week that would be, whether a dead end lay ahead, or what, if anything, lay ahead. But as quickly as I could ask the question, I could just as quickly dismiss it. I felt like an old punch-drunk boxer climbing through the ropes for one more fight.

Another week awaited me. Monday morning would see me rejuvenated, ready to scrap with the recession once again.

Seconds out, round twenty-five.

Chapter 23

Dead Amongst the Dead

I was lying in bed, half awake, watching specks of dust floating in a beam of light that had snuck through a gap in the closed curtains. I turned onto my back, offering my attention to the cobweb in the corner of the ceiling. The resident spider was patrolling the domain of its web like a sentry, reaching the edge, before it began weaving further, enlarging its kingdom before me.

Sweep it?

No, leave it.

The elegance of its construction was a testament to the eight-legged architect's artistry. Surrounding it were cream walls, the colour accentuating every stain on them.

Paint the room?

Books and albums were scattered everywhere. They formed columns across the room, soaring from the floor, literary and musical skyscrapers, waiting to collapse at the slightest touch.

Rearrange them?

Even the most trivial odd job would prevent the mind from atrophying. My dirty clothes lay in piles at the foot of the skyscrapers.

Must put on a wash.

Any washing powder?

Have to buy some.

A trip to the shop; a great adversary of time. It'd kill at least twenty minutes.

Such menial tasks maintained my sanity and steered me away from unemployment's brand of insanity, one in which you didn't lose your mind, instead, it wouldn't leave you alone. Every day, I provided an audience for its doubts, for its intrusive thoughts, and afforded it the ability to unhinge me at any moment. With no job and little human interaction to distract me from it, it consumed me whole. Losing my mind would be a pleasure, a relief. I half envied those who did.

Dust, cobwebs, spiders, stains, painting, books, albums, shopping, washing powder. Such mundane thoughts were occupying my mind before the call came.

My phone rang. At the slight prospect of the call being a job offer, I pounced on it.

"Hello?"

I cleared my throat of its croakiness.

"Paddy?"

A girl's voice. Meek.

"Yeah, who's this?"

I asked the question knowing the voice sounded familiar.

"Rachael."

"Rachael Dow… Rachael, how's things?"

I spoke the words in a more benevolent tone than intended.

"I'm okay, Paddy, you?"

"Ah, getting by, ye know yourself."

What does she want?

What do ye think?

After all this time? No. She doesn't want to…

O' course she does! Don't bite. Let her tail dangle between her legs.

"Listen, Paddy… I, eh…"

"I meant to say hello to ye the other week when I saw ye in the dole office, but I wasn't sure whether ye wanted me to. I wasn't ignoring ye. It was just…"

"Never mind that, Paddy."

Oh, never mind? She wants a clean slate, does she?

No, I don't know what she wants.

Ye know very well what. Let her apologise for every-thing. Don't give an inch till she does!

"I don't know what to say, Paddy."

Oh, I'll write the script for ye, no bother! First line, 'I'm sorry, Paddy.' Second line, 'Will ye take me back, Paddy?'

"Ye don't have to say anything. What makes ye think I'd even want to take ye back?"

That's it, play hardball!

"Sorry, what?"

"Ye heard me!"

"Paddy, what are ye talking about?"

Her voice was a hybrid of confusion and anger.

"Ye know very well what I'm talking about! Us!"

"Jesus Christ, Paddy! I'm not ringing about that!"

Less confusion, more anger.

"Well, why the fuck *are* ye ringing me then?!"

I found the tone that I wanted to use earlier.

"Oh my God, have ye not heard?"

"Heard what?"

"About Alan."

"Popey? What about him?"

"Aw Christ… Paddy, he's dead."

I heard the words and distrusted my hearing.

"Say again?"

"He's dead."

The words individually made sense, but collectively were nonsensical.

"What do ye mean he's…"

"He's dead. Gone. Fuckin' hell, I thought ye knew!"

There was no ambiguity in her words. They offered no loophole. I felt a shortness of breath, a dizziness, an urge to shout, punch the wall, claw at my skin, rake my fingers through my hair, cry in anger. My hand trembled as I held the phone to my ear.

"I'm so sorry, Paddy."

I tried to compose myself enough to ask the questions that came to me, one after another, in a flurry of panic and bewilderment.

"Jesus, what happened?"

All I heard was her breathing.

"Rachael, what happened?"

"He killed himself… That's what I heard."

A wave of shock silenced me. I could hardly think, let alone speak.

"Are ye still there, Paddy?"

"Yeah, I'm here. Jesus Christ, Rachael. How do they know it was…?"

"They found him unconscious in bed with empty pill packets beside him. His da called an ambulance but it was too late. He was long gone."

"Holy fuck… When did this…?"

"Yesterday. I'm so sorry. I wouldn't have told ye over the phone. I thought ye'd have heard."

"No, not a word."

"What was the matter with him?"

"I've no idea. Last time I saw him was a couple o' weeks ago at a Bray match and he seemed fine. Well, not fine… Well, he was awright but, I don't know… I don't know, there was something about him, something not right. He wasn't like he normally was. But, why the fuck would he… Was there a note?"

"Not that I've heard of… I was talking to some o' the lads. They can't make heads nor tails of it. No one can. He must've been suffering. Poor Alan. God love him… His poor ma and da, Paddy. Jesus, how will they cope?"

"God help them…and his two sisters… I just don't believe this, Rachael. This is beyond…"

"I know, I know. I heard it from one o' the girls. I thought it was a sick joke."

My tremulous inhalations and exhalations were all I could muster in retort.

"They're having a wake, Paddy. I'll let ye know when as soon as I hear."

"Thanks."

"Do ye wanna meet up? To talk?"

"There's nothing to say, is there? I mean, nothing that'll change anything."

"I suppose not, but if ye wanna talk, ye know where I am, okay?"

"Yeah, o' course. Sure, let me know about the wake, and I'll see ye then."

"Yeah… Ye were a good mate to him, Paddy. Yis were a right pair o' scallywags."

I dug up a half-hearted laugh from somewhere.

"That we were."

"Listen, don't do anything daft, Paddy."

Is she really gonna lecture me now?!

"No, no, I'm grand. I just need a minute to take it in… Do ye reckon I should go to the house?"

"I'd give them space. Wait till the wake."

"Yeah, probably best."

I wanted to get off the phone.

"Listen, Rach, I'll talk to ye later. I just need to get me head round this."

"Yeah o' course. Take care."

I hung up, feeling as if I was in a dream, one that I couldn't wait to awaken from. I closed my eyes and opened them again, only to see the spider still in its web, confirming what I already knew.

What was wrong with him? What was so bad that he….

I couldn't even bring myself to say the words.

Why didn't he talk to someone? Did he have anyone to talk to? Was he alone? Was he embarrassed? Did he do something?

Of all the questions, one repeatedly gnawed away at me, which I fervently tried to ignore.

Why hadn't I spoken to him?

I had an inkling something was awry when I met him. I knew he wanted to have a quiet drink with me. Maybe he felt he'd met the right friend, at the right time, in whom he could share his torment. That friend was more interested in gallivanting round the bars on the seafront in search of a one-night stand, hoping to find pleasure between a slut's legs while Popey ruminated about finding solace in his own demise. I suddenly felt responsible. The reactionary emotions of confusion, anguish and anger were superseded by the far more potent emotions of guilt, shame and regret. I wrestled with them for hours. At times, I'd win the argument.

I'm not fuckin' clairvoyant. He wasn't himself that night, but sure, neither was I!

Moments later, I'd lose the argument.

Ye fuckin' idiot! Did the poor chap have to spell it out? Ye ignored him for some local slapper!

Later in the day, I began to blame Popey.

Ye selfish gobshite, Popey! Fuckin' top yourself 'cause you're going through a rough patch? Half the country's going through a rough patch! And your ma and da, your sisters. What about them? They're left behind to clean the mess. They're left wondering. We're all left wondering. And we're all supposed to be guilty and carry that guilt round with us for the rest of our lives? Ye hated your life? Mine's so fuckin' irrelevant it doesn't even warrant being hated, but I still don't go and do that!

I then imagined Popey lying lifeless on a cold, steel mortuary tray. Another image; his body being butchered in the autopsy. Not even the crude incisions or the sickening sound of the saw cutting through his chest, would incite a reaction from his lifeless remains. The worst image, the most disturbing; Popey's mother finding him in his bed, calling him, no response, tipping him, no response, curiosity turning to concern, seeing the empty pill packets, concern turning to fear, shaking him, shouting at him, fear turning to despair, his face drained of colour, his body stiff, his mother standing over him, her tears dripping down on his face, running down his cheeks as if they were his own, her wail travelling throughout the house, the thud of his father's feet as he runs up the stairs, the horror etched on his face as he sees his dead son in his wife's arms. The moment they'd relive perpetually evermore. Supplanting even that, was the image of Popey gazing at the pills, the rationale seeming so logical, the decision being made, the pills being consumed, lying down and waiting, reliving his life in mere minutes, afraid, lonely, exhausted, still waiting, thoughts of his family, feeling uncertain, wondering if it was too late to change his mind, fear and anxiety fading, heavy eyes, the urge to sleep, the room darkening, the end.

The images haunted me. I couldn't get them out of my head; nor the realisation that when I'd needed his counsel, he had given me his time and advice. When he sought the same from me in return, I gave him nothing. There was no getting away from the undeniable truth that I hadn't been there for him.

I couldn't summon a single tear. I felt an onus to demonstrate my sense of loss, a physical outpouring of emotion, a fitting show of respect for the deceased. But I'd spent so long containing my emotions, that a dramatic displaying of them seemed beyond my capabilities.

I sat in the sitting room, remembering some of our antics and daft conversations.

"Paddy, I need your help tonight?"
"With what?"
"I'm trying to get into that club down the seafront."

"And?"

"Well, they won't let me in 'cause they know I'm not eighteen."

"And?"

"Paul Murphy told me the way to get in is to go up to the entrance holding hands with another fella and pretend to be a pair o' poofters. They'll let ye in 'cause they don't want ye complaining about them being anti-queer. Paul said it works every time."

"He's only having ye on, Popey."

"He's not. Him and Richy have done it, so he says."

"So, you're asking me to do it with ye?"

"Yeah."

"Would ye get offside, Popey! Ha ha. I'm not going up to the bouncers holding your hand like a fuckin' knob jockey!"

"No one's gonna see us."

"And what if they ask questions?"

"Like what? I'll just say, 'This is Paddy, me lover, me sexual partner, the recipient o' me cock.'"

"The recipient o' your cock?"

"Well, I could leave that bit out. I'll be subtle. I'll throw in a few hand gestures, camp it up a bit, ye know."

"How can I subtly tell ye to fuck off, Popey! Ha ha. Find someone else to be your recipient."

I laughed aloud remembering the episode before it buckled under the weight of its own poignancy. An anecdote never to be re-enacted; a life never to be relived. Gone forever. The finality of it was petrifying.

Why?

The unanswerable question. The irrelevant question. He was dead. Answers were nothing more than snippets of information to satisfy my starving curiosity, to soothe my festering guilt. No amount of answers would resurrect the dead, nor change the unchangeable.

Alan Pope. Dead at the age of twenty-one. His reasons would accompany him to the grave. I thought of saying a prayer for him and his family. For the first time in my life, I appreciated the lure of God and hoped that it existed, that there was a heaven, and that Popey was still amongst us in some parallel realm which only death allowed us mortals to enter. I'd never said a prayer voluntarily. I sat on my bed with my hands joined.

Please God, if you're up there somewhere, let Popey in and look after him, will ye… And look after his family and…

I stopped abruptly.

This is fuckin' daft!

My religious awakening couldn't contend with the concoction of grief and anger that had overtaken me.

A person, a life, a future, a friend, the closest thing I had to a brother, now reduced to a statistic; a contributor to the national figure for male suicide spoken of on the news. Nobody would know his name. He'd be indistinguishable from the rest. Dead amongst the dead. His rotting corpse like all the others. Twenty-one years of life. An eternity of death.

What if there isn't anything else?

I dreaded the wake and the funeral.

Why both?

It prolonged the agony.

When Ma, Da and Claire arrived home, I didn't utter a word to them about Popey. I didn't have the appetite for the drama, nor the patience to listen to another round of the same questions I'd been asking myself all day.

At dinner, I silently nibbled at my pork chops and lumpy mashed potatoes. I was somewhere else, far removed from the table at which I was sitting.

"And how was your day, Patrick?" Ma innocently asked.

"Grand."

Chapter 24

A Grim Reunion

"Doesn't he look lovely, Bríd," the woman said.

"He does. He's always been a handsome boy."

The two of them stood by Popey's coffin, admiring the corpse like it was a priceless ornament on a mantlepiece, touching its hand gently. Their voices fell silent as they mouthed a prayer in the dim light cast from a lamp in the far corner, before stepping aside for the next mourner. A middle-aged man stepped forward and placed his hands on the side of the coffin. He swallowed hard, blinked continually, fighting back the tears. One escaped and he rid himself of it before it reached the bottom of his nose. He leaned in and whispered into the corpse's ear, rose, and then walked away rubbing his eyes. Another man. Young, in his thirties, a young girl by his side, no more than seven.

"Alan, I don't know what to say… I'm lost for words, mate… I know you're up there and if ye put a good word in for me with the main man, sure we might see each other again someday."

"Is Alan dead, Daddy?"

"He's passed away, love."

"Away where, Daddy?"

"Heaven."

"Will he meet Tickles?"

"O' course he will. Tickles will be delighted with the bit o' company."

"I bet he'll be wagging his tail, Daddy, and jumping all over him."

"That'd be him awright."

"How do ye know he's in heaven, Daddy?"

"'Cause he was a good boy. Good boys go to heaven, just like Tickles."

"Why didn't we have a party for Tickles, Daddy?"

"It's not a party. We're just saying goodbye…and because Tickles was a dog… Come on, love, other people are waiting."

The procession continued. They were of all ages, some smartly dressed, others underdressed. There was no bawling, just very discreet displays of pain.

The cramped sitting room was accommodating a dozen or so people at a time, faces drifting out as new ones emerged. A conveyor belt of misery. A table of sandwiches, biscuits, cups, tea bags, glasses, and bottles of stout and lager, stood against the window, a focal point for mourners, offering them a more appealing view of the adjacent house on Green Park Road, than the coffin placed against the opposite wall at the far end of the room. I had stood beside it, towering over the body within it. Above it, were the communion and confirmation photos of the three children. A young twelve-year-old Popey was sitting in his oversized confirmation suit with a disobedient tuft of hair sticking out the side of his head. His smile was so joyous and so effortlessly portrayed, that the boy bore no resemblance to the corpse lying before me. The made-up pallid face, the closed eyes that shut out the life around it, and the redundant body gave it the appearance of a waxwork of Popey. The disparity between the two was frightening. My vigil had been without words. I looked at the still face with eyes that were seeing death for the first time. In its presence, I felt guilty to be alive. I slowly stepped away from it, wanting to sprint away.

His father was sitting in a worn leather armchair in the corner nearest to the coffin, immaculately groomed, a cup of tea and an unbitten sandwich in each hand, staring into space as mourners shook his hand and tried to engage him in conversation. I had approached him when I arrived to offer my condolences, but beyond telling him how sorry I was for his loss, I hadn't known what else to say. I'd wanted to apologise for not being there for his son and for the role that I'd convinced myself I'd played in his death. But I couldn't bring myself to tell him about it, both out of shame and knowing that such a revelation would be nothing more than a selfish attempt to assuage my sense of guilt, through his forgiveness. Unable to endure another second of the excruciating silence that had been lingering, I'd let someone else take my place next to him, to repeat what I and everyone else before me had already said.

His mother, conversely, was playing host, constantly going back and forth between the sitting room and the kitchen; refilling the kettle, washing dirty cups and glasses, and replenishing the supply of food and drink. She patrolled the room, asking if everyone was alright for this or for that, hiding her anguish behind a dead smile, keeping herself busy. Her movements were such, that I couldn't get hold of her for a moment to rehash what I'd told her husband. But my dread of that very rehashing was such, that I didn't overly exert myself in my attempts to grab her attention.

His two sisters, one older and one younger, stood awkwardly by the table, receiving embraces, kisses and commiserations, nodding their teary-eyed heads upon each introduction, while receiving the occasional request from their mother to help with something.

It seemed that the couch had been moved closer to the door to make space for the coffin, while kitchen chairs had been placed along the opposite wall at each side of the fireplace. The modestly sized room struggled to cater for such a gathering, as the family struggled to handle such an occasion. I was sitting on one of the kitchen chairs, hidden behind a couple of mourners. Mere minutes since my arrival, I was already finding the grieving unbearable. The room was doused in pain. The occasion was to nobody's benefit. It was like an act of self-harm to punish ourselves for what we had done wrong, or what we thought we'd done wrong.

I grabbed a bottle of lager from the table. Muttered conversations circulated.

"So tragic."

"So young."

"God love him."

"Such a nice boy."

Out of earshot of the family members, I heard whispers.

"How did he…?"

"Pills."

"Good God!"

"Does anyone know why?"

Paul Murphy, Rory Davin and Seán Walsh entered the room and went over to the coffin, the three of them speechless as they stared into it. Other lesser-known students from St. Brendan's arrived after them to begin their shift of grieving as those who preceded them slowly clocked out. Some of the girls wept, much to my chagrin, for I struggled to remember any of them ever having said one word to Popey, his portly appearance never warranting their attention. There seemed to be an air of superficiality in the room as the corpse of Popey had friends the living Popey hadn't known of. The whole occasion seemed a charade. My own presence was beginning to feel pointless.

Richy Talbot was next to arrive, seemingly the most capable mourner of the younger crowd, an amateur undertaker, easing his way around the room like a dejected ballerina, making the necessary handshakes, his despondent face the picture of bereavement, while his smart suit and tie looked tailormade for the occasion. Rachael Dowling then made her entrance and hastily offered her condolences to the family members. She gravitated towards the old gang by the coffin, tears quickly welling, arms being offered around her.

Another contender for performance o' the evening!

Fancying a bit of food, but not a school reunion centred around a corpse, I found myself back at the table. As I was deciding which sandwiches to pick, I heard Rachael say my name and turned to her.

"Awright, Rachael?" I greeted.

"Ye holding up?" she asked.

"Yeah, you?"

"I was, till I saw him just there. It's so sad to see him like that... What could've happened, Paddy? I never thought he'd be the type to... He was always so cheerful."

"Isn't that what ye always hear with these things?"

"True."

"Do ye want a drink?"

"No. I didn't come here for a drink."

"And what? I *did*?"

"Paddy, please! It's not the time or the place to be listening to your..."

The gang sauntered over to us, and in doing so, aborted the argument.

"Shocking lads, isn't it?" I said.

"I was heartbroken when I heard, Paddy," said Richy. "Such a lovely fella... Jesus, what was wrong with him? I mean, to do that!"

"I haven't the foggiest, Richy," I answered honestly.

We stood in a circle, unaware of what to say next. It dawned on me that grieving was a skill. Some were better than others. We were hopeless. We were bereft of anything meaningful to say. Maybe we were too young, too inexperienced or on some selfish level, too preoccupied with our own tribulations, but death, it seemed, was a conversational dead-end which we couldn't get past.

We sipped our drinks silently, our eyes fixed on the coffin, as if waiting for Popey to jump out of it, in tears of laughter, having successfully fooled us all. The ultimate wind-up. If it was a joke, the punchline was well overdue.

"Are yis staying long, lads?" I asked, just as something to say.

"Nah," Seán answered. "I just wanted to see him before he's…"

We all nodded.

"What are ye doing with yourself these days, Paddy?" Rory asked, all of us undoubtedly grateful to him for changing the subject.

"On the dole, you?"

"Same."

"What about you, Richy?"

"In college. Me da was hoping to have something lined up for me in the bank for when I finish, but the recession has fucked everything up. His own job there isn't even secure."

Paul and Seán told similar tales of anticipated degrees that would lie in their bedroom drawers as they stood in the dole queue in the near future.

"Meself and Seán are thinking o' going to Australia after we finish college," said Paul. "See if we can find work over there if there's nothing here… Mousey's the same. He was saying he might be going over to Canada. He has a brother already over there."

"Speaking o' Mousey, any sign of him?" I asked.

"Ah, he was here earlier," Paul informed me.

"What about Mick Dolan? I haven't seen him in donkeys."

"Ah, ye wouldn't want to see him, Paddy. He's gone off the rails. Last time I saw him he was strung out on God knows what. Last I heard, he'd been arrested for robbing some auld one's house."

"Jesus, that bad?" I asked, surprised, but not shocked.

"Sure, no sign of him here. Couldn't even be arsed to show up to pay his respects. Selfish prick. He'll be the next one to go. Fuckers like him are walking the streets and there's that poor lad over there in a box!"

There was a disheartening realisation that all of us had probably come to. That being that any aspirations we'd had during our schooldays had been shattered. Our lives weren't unfolding as we'd naively foreseen. None of us would have predicted back then, that in a few years' time, we'd be mourning the death of Popey, fearing the death of Mick Dolan, and that there wouldn't be a job amongst as some of us contemplated leaving the country in search of new lives.

Then there was the aimless journey that *I* was on, convincing myself that something would soon appear in the distance and provide me with a destination. The unspoken truth was that it wasn't just Popey's death we were mourning in that moment, but the death of what should have been, of aspirations. The single corpse didn't account for the collective loss of lives amongst us, or rather, lives that were never given the chance to be born.

With the requisite mourning duties performed, each made their excuses, said one last goodbye to Popey and gradually made for the front door. Rachael and I were the last two remaining.

I opened another bottle.

"So, what were ye up to before the recession?" she asked.

"I was working in O'Connell's. You?"

"I started the psychology course and hated it. I stuck at it for a while but eventually dropped out. I was working here and there until recently."

"Ye should go back to do something else," I advised.

"I would if I knew what. Unemployment's a great motivator."

"Maybe not for everyone," I grimly remarked, looking over at the coffin.

"Do ye reckon that's why he…?" she whispered.

"I know he was excited about the apprenticeship. It must've hit him hard to be let go. Then there was your one, Sharon. She ended it with him. I got the impression that he wasn't taking it well but, then again, they're hardly reasons to… There must've been something else…"

If I'd spoken to him that night, I could've found out!

"…but who knows? It could've been anything. Ye think ye know someone like the back o' your hand, but ye only know what they tell ye."

She nodded in agreement. "And what about you? Ye looking after yourself?"

"Why wouldn't I be?" I asked defensively.

"No reason, just asking. How's the family?"

"Same as ever, I suppose. Yours?"

"Likewise."

We were wandering aimlessly around a conversational maze, so I broached the topic we'd been avoiding.

"It was a shame the way things worked out…me and you, I mean."

"Ah, Paddy, that was ages ago now, forget about all that. This really puts stupid shite like that into perspective."

We both glanced at the coffin.

"Yeah, it does."

She hugged me. In doing so, she had an even greater effect on me than she'd had when I'd bumped into her in the social welfare office; her touch reminding me of when we were together, of times past, of better times. It was enough to wash away any resentment I still harboured; enough to make me want her again. I thought about how I'd been happier with her back then, and of how I could rediscover that happiness if I was with her again. I gambled and went for it.

"Listen, Rachael, would ye be interested in… maybe…"

I was interrupted by the sound of her phone ringing.

"Sorry, Paddy, I'll have to take this."

I listened to the fragments of conversation.

"Yeah…okay… I'll be out shortly… See ye in a minute." She hung up. "Paddy, I've to go. Me boyfriend's waiting outside."

"Boyfriend?"

"Yeah, Ian."

It was like a bullet ripping through me and exiting out the other side, leaving me fatally wounded.

All my bitterness, anger and resentment returned instantly, waiting impatiently for the call to be unleashed. Not only did she have a 'fella,' but she'd gone out of her way to inform me of such, as if she'd read my mind and decided to sadistically quash my delusional notions of reviving a bond that was as dead as the corpse behind me.

"Sorry, were ye gonna say something, Paddy?"

"No, nothing…never mind."

"Listen, I best be off… It's been nice seeing ye again… I just wish we'd all met under different circumstances."

"Same here."

"Sure, I'll see ye at the funeral tomorrow."

"Yeah, see ye then."

"Go easy on them," she said, pointing to the bottle.

Go fuck yourself!

"I'll say goodbye to Alan and the family before I go."

He'd tell ye to go fuck yourself too if he could!

I watched her lean over the coffin, planting an ostentatious kiss on his forehead.

Christ, where's the puke bucket?

I reclaimed my seat and felt like hurling the bottle against the wall.

Murmuring, handshakes, silence, hugs and crying. I could no longer stomach it.

Get out o' here!

I still had to pay my respects to the rest of Popey's family. I didn't want to face them. Especially his mother. I couldn't look her in the eye, knowing that I'd tactlessly spurned her son's cry for help.

I grabbed another couple of bottles, brushed through the black-clad bodies, and without once looking back at the monument of death at the far wall, I left the corpse, the family and the whole horrific scene behind me.

I walked briskly from the house as if anticipating a mourner to emerge from it and call me back, obstructing my escape. Slugging the bottle, I heard one voice from which there was no escape.

You're a fuckin' coward! Ye didn't have the bottle. The only bottle ye have is in your hand!

I knew how to silence the voice and erase the whole episode from my brain. My walk home was diverted across the bridge, along Seapoint Road, and onto Strand Road.

Sitting at the bar of the Waterfront, the thought that I was using Popey's death as an excuse for a session arose.

I'm having a drink in his honour. Yes…in his honour.

And since when do I need an excuse anyway?

The night was young. I'd hit the drink hard. I needed to.

I began downing pints quickly, each one eroding thoughts of Popey, the corpse, the family, Rachael, guilt and whatever it was that I was trying to dress up as a life.

At closing time, I staggered out into a swirling world and crossed the road to the promenade to sit down. Hearing only the mellifluous waves spilling onto the shore, I was soon lying down and fast asleep.

Chapter 25
A Sullied Farewell

The waves crashed as I walked along the shore bare-footed, the wash engulfing my feet. The high sun darkened my pale complexion while lightening my dark reflections. Children played and dogs barked as I skimmed stones, watching the ripples radiate towards me. An idyllic scene. An unreal scene. Suddenly it disappeared. All that was left of it was the sound of the waves crashing. Echoes of a dream.

The wet tapping of raindrops on my head had woken me. I opened my eyes only for a sterile scene to be revealed. The light rain ensured that the promenade was empty. The sky was a blanket of grey clouds, the darkest of which hung ominously over Killiney. I shivered in my wet clothes as I felt the onslaught of a gruelling hangover. The urge to vomit was relentless. My tolerance wasn't. The first expulsion landed on my jumper, before I leaned forward and unloaded the remainder of the orange discharge onto the ground, wearily watching the rain dilute it.

Bereft of the energy to lift myself from the bench, a task that felt like lifting a thousand tonne weight, I closed my eyes again, head in hands, trying to rediscover the serenity of my unconsciousness. An empty mind, one unburdened by thinking, was made elusive by the very act of seeking it. I felt the rain begin to ease as my thoughts ran amuck.

The wake, Popey, the corpse, the family, Rachael, unem-ployment, the funeral...

Shite, the fuckin' funeral!

I checked the time. I'd be late. The panic induced an adrenaline rush that enabled me to lift myself off the bench and begin the arduous walk to St Peter's Church in Little Bray.

I trudged down a muted Strand Road, only the most dedicated joggers and coffee drinkers populating the dreary scene. Turning left onto Quinsborough Road, I lumbered towards the railway crossing, trying in vain to beat the descending barriers. Half of me was grateful for the respite they provided, the other half of me cursed my luck, conscious of the time.

I waited. In the distance, the murmur of a train could be heard approaching. Moments later, it roared into view, before decelerating into the station. The barricades rattled and raised. I walked on, turning right onto the main street, over the bridge, through Castle Street and onto Dublin Road. Passing the bookies, I remembered the tip the barman had given me.

Pearse's Gunner Eye at 12/2 at the Curragh. Ye'd be an eejit not to put a few bob on it.

And an even bigger eejit to listen to him.

I entered the newsagent beside it, desperately craving food and something sugary to wash it down. The headline of one of the newspapers summarised the state of the country.

Calls for a general election increase as unemployment soars

As I read it, I heard a familiar voice. Looking up from the paper, I saw my neighbour Frank Griffith standing in the queue with his back to me, yapping away.

I haven't the head to be listening to him. If he sees me, he'll keep me talking all morning. I'm already late.

I exited the shop swiftly. The 'fruit and veg' shop was next door.

Even a banana or something would be better than nothing.

"Just the one banana, is it?" the shopkeeper asked.

"Two, thanks."

"I've lovely new apples in from…"

"Just the bananas, thanks."

"Can I interest ye in these oranges on special offer?"

"The bananas will do, thanks."

"Anything else?"

"Nothing else."

"Are ye feeling awright, mate? You're looking a bit…"

"No, I'm just a bit… I had a few drinks last night. I'll be grand. Just give us the…"

"Ye haven't puked up your vitals outside, have ye?"

"No, I haven't. Will ye just give us the…"

"There isn't a morning I'm not out there with the bucket, I swear. I'm convinced that boozer instructs them to puke outside *my* door… What was it ye wanted again?"

"The bananas! Will ye give me the shaggin' things before I go bananas!"

"Ah, the very things. Fifty cent when you're ready."

"Here, there's fifty cent in that."

Gobbling the bananas, extracting their fuel, I turned into the grounds of St Peter's church. Just inside its front door, still out of view behind a parish notice-board, I patted my hair, took off my vomit-stained jumper and rolled it up under my arm. I listened to the Mass, taking a moment to collect myself, reluctant to leave my hiding place. Knowing I couldn't postpone it any longer, I fought the urge to remain hidden, and came out from behind the noticeboard, scurrying like a rat to the nearest pew at the back of the church, hoping I wouldn't be seen.

Looking around, I saw both familiar and unfamiliar faces. The coffin lay in front of the altar, looking as congruent in its current surroundings as it looked incongruent in the house the day before. Its closed lid unsettled me. There was no escape, no regression, no progression. Nothing. It brought finality. I imagined the corpse lying in the coffin as the lid slowly closed, light gradually dying like one final sunset before darkness enveloped it.

Popey's elder sister stood at the pulpit with her reading in hand.

"A Reading from the Book o' Wisdom," she said in a trembling voice. "The virtuous man, though he dies before his time, will find rest. Length o' days is not what makes age honourable, nor number o' years the true measure o' life; understanding, this is man's grey hairs, untarnished life, this is ripe old age. He has sought to please God, so God has loved him; as he was living amongst sinners, he has been taken up. He has been carried off so that evil may not warp his understanding or treachery seduce his soul; for the fascination of evil throws good things into the shade, and the whirlwind of desire corrupts a simple heart. Coming to perfection in so short a while, he achieved long life; his soul being pleasing to the Lord, he has taken him quickly from the wickedness around him. Yet people look on, uncomprehending; it does not enter their heads that grace and mercy await the chosen of the Lord, and protection his holy ones. This is the Word o' the Lord."

"Thanks be to God," we responded.

A hymn and another reading. Popey's younger sister now stood at the pulpit, and began speaking hurriedly, betraying her unwillingness to be cast in such a role.

"A reading from the first letter of St Paul to the Thessalonians… We want you to be quite certain, brothers and sisters, about those who have died, to make sure that you do not grieve about them like the other people who have no hope. We believe that Jesus died and rose again and that it will be the same for those who have died in Jesus: God will bring them with him. We can tell you this from the Lord's own teaching, that any of us who are left alive until the Lord's coming will not have any advantage over those who have died. At the trumpet o' God, the voice of the archangel will call out the command and the Lord himself will come down from heaven; those who have died in Christ will be the first to rise and then those of us who are still alive will be taken up in the clouds, together with them, to meet the Lord in the air, so we shall stay with the Lord forever. With such thoughts as these you should comfort one another. This is the word o' the Lord."

"Thanks be to God."

Another hymn, as forgettable as the last.

The priest, a frail-looking elderly man, slowly walked to the pulpit. From this embodiment of fragility, came a voice at variance with its host; empowered, authoritarian, erudite, parental, eloquent, emotive, captivating. It was a voice of loss, hope, forgiveness and sympathy, from a man whose acute mind was as polarised from his withering limbs as the gates of heaven were to the fires of hell.

"The Lord be with you," he said.

"And also with you."

"A reading from the Holy Gospel according to Matthew."

"Glory to you, Lord."

He paused before he spoke. "When he saw the crowds, Jesus went up to the mountain and after he sat down, his disciples came to him. He began to teach them, saying:

Blessed are the poor in spirit, for theirs is the kingdom of heaven.

Blessed are those who mourn, for they will be comforted.

Blessed are the meek, for they will inherit the land.

Blessed are those who hunger and thirst for righteousness, for they will be satisfied.

Blessed are the merciful, for they will be shown mercy.

Blessed are the pure in heart, for they will see God.

Blessed are the peacemakers, for they will be called children of God.

Blessed are those who are persecuted because of righteousness, for theirs is the kingdom of heaven.

Blessed are you when they insult you, persecute you and utter every kind of evil against you falsely because of me.

Rejoice and be glad, for your reward will be great in heaven. This is the gospel of the Lord."

"Praise to you, Lord Jesus Christ."

Having heard that gospel reading many times before, this was the first time that it resonated with me.

He spoke again. "Dear Brothers and Sisters in Christ, I am fortunate enough to have known the Pope family over the years in which I've served in this parish. It was my predecessor who had the honour of welcoming Alan into the Catholic faith two decades ago, and I am humbled to have the honour of celebrating his funeral mass and his life, here today."

He paused, coughed, surveyed the congregation, and continued: "When I first heard the tragic news of Alan's passing, I'm sure my reaction was the same as all of yours. Firstly, I was deeply saddened. Secondly, I thought of his family. And thirdly, I asked myself the question, 'Why?' It's a word that has no doubt been on all our minds these last few days. It's also a word that can lead us down a troublesome path. It can create doubt and can make us question ourselves. We begin to wonder if we were there when he needed us, and if we could've done more. Such questions need not ever be asked. Knowing how much you all cared about Alan, I can say with certainty that there isn't a single person here who wouldn't have given him all their time and attention if he sought their counsel. Let us not think, 'Why?' Our attempts to understand his decision only strengthen the grip that our grief has on us. So, in this time of sadness, when we are feeling the agonising pain of our loss, let's not seek comfort in answers which we'll never attain, but in our unyielding hope that Alan has only left this life for another, as Jesus did in the resurrection."

He paused again as he allowed his message to be absorbed.

"Alan was as witty as he was smart, as mischievous as he was innocent, as respectful as he was a jester, and as loving as he was loved. He was a well-admired, friendly young man, and a credit to his family. I've heard so many anecdotes of him, all of which are so typical of a young man carving his way in the world, and indeed, dealing with the tribulations that life presents us with along the way. For these reasons, we should not fixate on Alan's last moments on this earth, but rather celebrate the twenty-one years of his life that preceded them. It is, itself, a long time. Long enough to accumulate a trove of precious memories to cherish. It is these memories, not regrets, that you should mull over as you celebrate the life that was, and the life that we pray forever will be. Let us entrust our faith in God the Father and pray that he welcomes Alan into his kingdom, into paradise, where we hope we will all meet him again one day."

The ensuing silence was the unspoken acceptance of the faint hope he offered. My throbbing head desensitised me to the occasion, preventing me from having any emotional reaction to his words.

The priest continued talking, his words being reduced to random sounds as my headache thwarted my efforts to listen to him. With eyes that were feeling heavier with each prayer that was recited, I watched people shake hands, hoping that none of them would approach me.

As the organ started up, the congregation left their pews to receive Holy Communion. Without sufficient will or piousness, and conscious of my dishevelled appearance, I remained seated.

With clasped hands and my head tucked into them, I was hiding more than I was praying, drink-stricken more than I was grief-stricken. I looked up to see Mousey Keating receiving communion and watched him chomp on it like he was chewing gum as he returned to his seat. Then Her Royal Highness Rachael Dowling stepped forward. At the end of the queue was Richy Talbot, his dapper appearance hiding the injuries he sustained to his ego when his high horse threw him off its back. The priest then introduced Popey's father. He rose from his pew, walked studiously towards the altar and slowly genuflected as if he'd rehearsed the whole routine in his head a thousand times. His grace was impeccable until he reached the pulpit. He fiddled with the microphone, mouthed to speak, stopped, inhaled, licked his lips, and looked over at the priest who gestured to him to take his time.

"I... I..."

Another inhalation.

"I've never been accused o' being a great man o' words, so you'll have to forgive me if I ramble on... I've a few things written down here that I scratched out and rewrote, and as I was listening to Father Devlin's homily, I started looking down at me scribbled writing, wondering how I'm supposed to even make sense of it, let alone follow Father Devlin's beautiful words."

He paused to nod at the priest in appreciation. The gesture was reciprocated.

"When I looked down at me scribbles, Alan came to mind. I was forever on at him during his schooldays about his lousy handwriting. Even the teachers used to say it when we met them. I always said to him that if he ever wrote a masterpiece, it'd be mistaken for a painting, with all the squiggly lines all over the place."

There were muted laughs from the pews.

"And I think o' that now and think to meself, his handwriting wasn't awful, it was distinctive. And as daft as that sounds there's truth in it. It was something that was uniquely his, like a signature or a fingerprint."

He closed his eyes for a moment and spoke again.

"I could stand here and talk about his love o' football and his sense o' humour, but couldn't I be saying the very same about anybody? That's why the handwriting came to mind. And it got me thinking that, as the years pass, hopefully I'll start to remember more and more little things like that. I suppose it's something to look forward to. It's not much I know, but there's a comfort o' some sort to be found in it."

He paused again as if trying to form his thoughts into sentences.

"This funeral would have to take place a year from now for us to be able to speak of our loss in some coherent manner. But something I've learned in recent days is that time is a tricky customer. It's foolish to look too far ahead, and having taken great comfort from Father Devlin's words, I think it's even more foolish to look back. I remember me own da, God rest his soul, had an auld saying he used to come out with whenever he was in a philosophical mood after a few pints. He'd say, 'Son, if we were supposed to be looking back all the time, the Good Lord would've put eyes in the back of our heads, rather than in the front.' He was dead right. And without wanting to repeat what Father Devlin said, for he said it much better than I ever could, if there's anything we can do for Alan now, it's to live the lives that he'd want to watch us living from wherever he is now… I won't pretend that a few kind words will help ease the pain, because they won't. And I won't pretend that I won't entertain the 'what ifs' now and then, because I will. The pain of his loss will remain with us for the rest of our lives. In a way, I want it to. I know that sounds… I don't know how it sounds, but as long as it's there, it feels as if some part of him is still there. I'm almost dreading the day when I don't feel it 'cause I'm scared that will mean that I've forgotten him."

He closed his eyes again, tried to speak in a quivering voice, stopped, swallowed and continued: "Finally, thank you all very much for coming today. It's unfortunate that it takes such a tragic occasion to bring us all together, but sure, isn't that always the way… Alan shared a bond with each and every one o' ye. I ask o' yis today before we leave this church, please don't let his passing break that bond. Spare some room in your mind for him. Let him come and go as he pleases. It would mean an awful lot to us to know that he still lives on through the thoughts and the conversations of his friends. If ye'd like to share a memory of him with us, or if ye wanna have a chat about him, by all means do. Call to our house anytime. Our door will always be open… Let me just finish by saying that, Alan…" He stared despondently at the coffin. "… the two days in which you came into this world and left it, were the happiest and saddest two days of our lives. If you sought happiness, I hope you've found it. Our pain in this life is a small price to pay in return for your happiness in the next life."

A tear fell from each eye. He nodded to the congregation and walked briskly back to his pew, receiving a solemn applause.

If ye'd like to share a memory of him with us, or if ye wanna have a chat about him…

Yeah, did ye hear about the time he tried to seek counsel from me?

I didn't! Oh, yis must've had a great auld chat, did yis?

If I'd sinned, this was my atonement. Mental and physical pain duetted in an all-out assault on me as I listened to the profusion of prayers and hymns. Enduring Catholicism with a hangover was a punishment befitting Catholicism itself.

The priest spoke again. "Before we go our separate ways, let us take leave of our brother. May our farewell express our affection for him; may it ease our sadness and strengthen our hope. One day we shall joyfully greet him again when the love of Christ, which conquers all things, destroys even death itself."

He sprinkled the coffin in holy water before the smell of incense wafted to the back of the church, an aroma that would forever remind me of Popey's funeral thereafter.

"Into your hands, Father of mercies, we commend our brother Alan, in the sure and certain hope that, together with all who have died in Christ, he will rise with him on the last day. We give you thanks for the blessings which you have bestowed upon Alan in this life: they are signs to us of your goodness and of our fellowship with the saints in Christ. Merciful Lord, turn towards us and listen to our prayers: open the gates of paradise to your servant and help us who remain to comfort one another with assurances of faith, until we all meet in Christ and are with you and with our brother forever."

"Amen."

"In peace, let us take our brother to his place of rest."

All rose as the coffin was mounted on six shoulders and carried down the aisle, Popey's father, the chief pallbearer. His wife and daughters trailed behind, his elder daughter comforting her distraught mother and younger sister. Their tears displayed a pain that only their own eventual deaths would end. The congregation slowly followed. Faces I hadn't seen since leaving St Brendan's passed by. Popey's former girlfriend Sharon was amongst them.

Fuckin' cunt, Sharon! Where were ye when he needed ye? Where was I?

Last to exit, I stood awkwardly amongst the crowd outside as they commiserated with the family members.

I decided I couldn't face the burial. I'd fall into the grave, throw up into it, make a scene of some sort. It'd be better if I wasn't there. I'd already paid my respects.

Out from the crowd, Her Royal Highness pounced.

"Paddy, where were ye? I didn't see ye."

"I got delayed. I was a few minutes late."

"Nursing your hangover, were ye?" she asked scornfully. "The whiff o' drink off ye!"

"Yeah, I had a couple o' bottles at the wake, big deal," I replied defensively.

"A couple? Ye look like ye were out till all hours this morning! The fuckin' nerve o' ye, Paddy, arriving up to your friend's funeral hungover!"

"Language, Rachael, you're outside God's gaff."

"Don't you dare lecture me, Paddy! You're a disgrace! Ye don't give a shite about anyone, not even yourself!"

"I gave more of a shite about that lad lying in the coffin than the rest o' yis combined!"

"Is that right? So much so that ye arrive up to his funeral in this state! Ye would've been better off staying home!"

"Well, that's exactly where I was about to go before ye started hassling me."

"So, you're not coming to the burial then?"

"Not unless I can throw you in on top of him."

"Go and…"

"Go and what?"

She leaned in close enough to kiss me.

"Go and fuck yourself, Paddy! That's what!"

She walked off. I cursed her quietly as I heard someone mention something about a reception upstairs in O'Connell's.

My planned journey home was abandoned as I crossed the pub's threshold for the first time since I'd been made redundant. My pledge to never set foot in the place again was cast aside, out of respect for the occasion or out of necessity for myself. Standing inside the doorway, I felt nothing. It hadn't changed. Familiar furniture, familiar heads, familiarly quiet. Death was bringing life to the place.

I caught Daragh's attention. *He* still had his job.

Blew enough smoke up Doyle's arse, no doubt!

"Ah, Paddy! Long time no see. How are ye keeping?"

How the fuck do ye think I'm keeping, ye brown nosing twat!

"Never been better, Daragh. Ye still stuck in this kip?"

"Ah, still hanging on."

Hanging on the end o' Doyle's knob, I'd say!

"Any luck with work, Paddy?"

"Sure, who needs it? It's great craic on the dole," I said sarcastically.

He smiled awkwardly.

"So, what brings ye in here at this hour?"

"The same thing that brings everyone into this shit-hole," I replied, taking my wallet out of my pocket.

"Are ye okay to be drinking, Paddy? Ye seem a bit…"

"A bit what? I've just come from a mate's funeral. Do ye want me doing a stand-up routine in the corner?"

"Oh, you're with the Pope family. I see, me apologies. What will it be?"

"Guinness."

"Go on upstairs. I'll bring it up to ye."

With a couple of pints down my throat, I could feel the hangover slowly fading like an old photograph, before I added another brace of pints to tear the faded photograph into shreds. By the time the other mourners started to arrive, I felt re-energised.

The gang came up the stairs and found a table by the wall. I was sitting at the bar, my pint and sandwiches the only company I craved. Popey's family were scattered around the room, conversing with relatives and friends as best they could, given the circumstances.

Must give them me condolences.

Seán Walsh waved me over to their table. I was about to decline the invitation when I saw Rachael remonstrating with him in objection, which made me change my mind.

I brought my pint, sandwiches and haughtiness with me, pulling up a stool between Paul Murphy and Richy Talbot. Rachael was sitting across from me with a lad, averting her eyes from me.

The new fella, I assume.

They extolled Popey.

"Ah, wasn't he a character all the same?"

"They broke the mould with him, awright."

"I miss the poor auld divil already."

"Jesus, seeing him being put in the ground like that…"

I feigned interest as I brooded and glared at her latest 'fella.' There was something about him. Maybe it was his quiff, or his perfect fitting navy suit which put my own appearance to shame. Most likely, it was the way he was commiserating with the gang, a phony performance for someone he hadn't even known, for someone who would've ridiculed his ostentatiousness and made him the target of a joke. I was sure that the lads were thinking the very same thing.

I should tell that fuckin' prat what we all think of him!

I said nothing, busying my mouth with another sandwich, while surveying, analysing, critiquing, disliking and despising the character in my line of sight.

Anecdotes of Popey were being told, some heralding a smattering of a giggle, others sending the gang into convulsions of belly aching, jaw straining, eye welling, lap slapping laughter.

It was Paul Murphy's turn.

"Remember the time when we were in first year, when Popey put a thumb tack on Mr O'Kelly's chair. O'Kelly was scribbling some mathematical horseshite on the board with his back to the class. Popey snuck up from behind and carefully placed the tack on his chair. He tiptoed back to his seat with O'Kelly none the wiser. So, O'Kelly starts shitting on about his *obair bhaile* at the end o' class. He wouldn't sit down! We were nearly coming in our jocks with anticipation. Then he leaned over his desk, pulled back his chair, put on his glasses, and dropped his fat Kerry arse onto the seat.

'Jesus, Mary and Joseph!' he shouts with a head on him like a snake's after crawling up his arse. Ha ha. He jumps out of his chair, turns around and we see the tack stuck in his left arse cheek.

We're breaking our shite laughing and there's O'Kelly rubbing his arse trying to find the tack.

'What are yis laughing at?!' he barks.

Silence. Not a word. Ye could hear his tack drop.

'What are ye laughing at, Murphy?'

'Nothing, sir!' I said.

'Something tickling you, Walsh?'

'Nothing, sir,' he says.

Then O'Kelly goes, 'I want to know who put that tack on me chair, and I want to know within the next minute. If I'm not told, there'll be double homework for everyone. Understood?' We're all nodding away like fuck. 'Well?' he says. Nobody says anything. 'We're obviously keen for extra homework tonight, are we?' he asks. We're dying at this stage, trying to keep our poker faces on. 'Dempsey, am I amusing you?' he asks.

And Paddy goes, 'Eh, no, sir.'

'Then wipe that constipated look off your face!'

'Yes, sir,' he says.

So, then O'Kelly starts walking laps o' the room, inspecting our faces. He gets to Popey. 'Did you wake up with that face on ye this morning, Pope?'

'What face, sir?' Popey says.

'The stupid one I'm currently looking at, Pope!'

'Eh, yes… I mean, no, sir.'

'And why is it that you seem to be finding this little incident funnier than everyone else, Pope?'

'I'm not, sir…honestly.'

'I have a suspicion, Pope, that you're the comedian who put the tack on me chair!'

'It wasn't me, sir. I swear to God!'

'Ye know what happens to liars, Pope? They get triple homework. You'll be on your pension and you'll still be doing me sums! I'll give ye one last chance to own up to your little deed. Ye can have ten seconds to mull it over. Ten…nine…eight…seven…' We could see he was rattled. 'Six…five…four… Time's running out, Pope. Three… two…one… Time's up. Now what do ye have to say for yourself, Pope?' Popey was bricking it.

'I didn't do it, sir,' he says.

'Is that so, Pope? Now, do you take me for some sort o' fool? An auld Kerry *amadán*, is it?'

'No, sir.'

'Do ye take yourself for a fool?'

'No, sir.'

Now here's the best bit.

O'Kelly leans in close to him and shouts, 'Well, only a bloody fool would put a tack on his teacher's chair and then still have the box o' tacks sitting on his own desk!'

Ye wanna see the head on Popey. Ha ha. And we're all pissing ourselves laughing.

O'Kelly roars, 'Silence! Or I'll have every single one o' ye down in the principal's office!'

Popey doesn't know what to do.

'Someone must've robbed one o' them out o' the box, sir,' he says. Ha ha.

O'Kelly's in his element. 'And who was that, Pope? The tooth fairy, I suppose?'

'Eh... eh... eh...' he goes, firing blanks. Ha ha.

It's fuckin' Christmas for O'Kelly. 'Triple homework for you tonight, Pope, and give me your diary. I'll be writing a note to your parents.'

'Ah, sir, they'll kill me!'

'That's not half o' what *I'd* do to ye if ye were *my* responsibility! And there'll be double homework for the rest o' yis! Yis can have great craic finding the humour in that!'

We all turn around to him, fuming, and we're all muttering, 'Ye fuckin' eejit, Popey!'"

The gang's laughter was at odds with the lugubrious conversations around us, but it was no less reverential. Even in death, he still had us smiling. Everyone except me. I was so consumed by my disdain for the prat sitting across from me, that nothing else mattered.

Mousey laughingly introduced another tale of misadventure.

"That reminds of a time when…"

"I meant to say to yis…" the prat interrupted.

I wasn't amused. I exerted myself to be unamused.

Any excuse!

"Sorry, mate, I wanna hear Mousey's story if ye don't mind," I said. "Whatever ye have to say isn't so important that it can't wait two minutes."

"No, it's awright," Mousey said.

"No, it's not awright," I replied. "We're here to remember Popey, not to provide this prick with an audience."

"This what?!" the prat asked.

"Ye heard me! Today's not about you, pal, so just shut the fuck up and let the chap finish his story!"

"Who do you think ye are, talking to me like that?!"

"Don't bother with him, Ian," Rachael interjected.

"Who do *I* think *I* am? I'll tell ye who I am. See that pain in the arse you've your arm around? I'm the one who broke her in for ye!" I boasted.

The words enraged him. He rose from his seat like a defending champion ready to educate a naive contender in the sweet science.

"Don't get yourself excited, pal. I'm not interested in her. Been there, done that. You're welcome to her. I'll even tell ye how she likes it!"

He lunged forward. I dodged and pulled him to me, knocking the glasses off the table, the last round of drink spilling before the first round of punches started flying.

I clattered him on the cheek before he caught me on the side of the head. I wobbled before thrusting myself on him, the fight degenerating into a wrestling match as the gang tried to separate us, amidst Rachael's pleas for us to stop. Daragh then became involved, pulling us apart with the help of the others.

"What in the name o' God is going on here, Paddy?!" he demanded to know.

The mourners stared at us in silent disbelief. Eyes wide. Mouths open. Lethal looks that would kill a rhino. The family amongst them. The priest in there too.

"This bollocks had a swing at me!"

"Ah, me arse! Ye were spoiling for it!" the prat refuted.

"Right, you pair are barred immediately. I want no fighting outside either!"

I was apoplectic.

"Barred?! So, I'm not good enough to even drink here anymore, am I not?! I bet ye couldn't wait to see the back o' me as soon as I walked in that door! Are ye afraid I'll take your job? Ye needn't worry, Daragh. I don't suck cock as good as you. Even *she* doesn't!" I said, pointing to Rachael.

"Paddy, out!"

He turned to the prat.

"And you can leave a few minutes after he's gone."

"Thanks a lot, Paddy!" Rachael said angrily.

"He started it, Rachael! Ye'd want to be careful with him and those fists."

He was ready to engage again but she held him back.

"You're a fuckin' embarrassment, Paddy!"

Before I had a chance to respond and tell her what I really thought of her, Daragh intervened again. "I've already told ye to leave, Paddy. Now go, before I call the guards!"

With a concoction of adrenaline and alcohol rushing through me, I barged out and headed down Dublin Road. The breeze that was blowing through my ripped shirt sent a chill through me but couldn't cool my boiling temper.

Barring me! As if I'd want to set foot near the dive anyway!

Only Ma was home. She called from the kitchen.

"Paddy, where have ye been all this time?"

"I stayed with someone after the wake. I'm just back from the funeral."

"God love that poor family," she said, emerging from the kitchen. "What happened to your shirt?"

"Ah… some eejits were scrapping in the pub, and I tried to break it up."

"Scrapping?! With the family there and all? Who rears these gobshites?"

"I'm gonna lie down, Ma. I'm exhausted."

"Want anything?"

"No, I had sambos."

The soft bed was ecstasy after the damp concrete of the promenade. The last twenty-four hours were still too raw to evaluate the severity of the destruction I'd left behind me. I spared myself the burden of introspection.

Another day's work.

But that day would come, and when it did, I'd wish it never had.

Chapter 26
The Unholy Trinity

In the days after the funeral, I smugly waited to receive a series of messages on my phone, the lads showering me with their admiration for the honourable stance that I had taken. They never came. Neither good nor even bad ones. Nothing. My performance was being erased from their memories, and me along with it. It seemed like they were disregarding me, and that they were treating me like I was a social pariah who was best avoided.

Taking her side?! Fuckin' wankers!

As days became weeks, and as I offered my mind a much-needed break from the dastardly liquid, my certainty of having been wrongly convicted began to diminish.

I began to review the episode with increasing clarity, hindsight painting a hideous picture, very different from the majestic work of art I'd first seen. My righteousness opened the first act before it stepped aside for sheepishness, which stole the spotlight in the middle act. Embarrassment then took to the stage in the final act, before the unholy trinity of guilt, shame and regret delivered a stellar performance in the final scene to bring down the curtain. I was left crestfallen, raging at my antics and at the absurdity of my willingness to play the victim.

To have exacerbated his family's pain by provoking a scrap, and to have treated his death as an opportunity to rile up Rachael Dowling, ate away at what little self-respect I still had. I was aghast. To recollect my behaviour in O'Driscoll's was to remember a scene in which the protagonist looked like me, sounded like me, but was an imposter, someone I couldn't reconcile with my present, rational-minded self. I was flummoxed as to how to repair the damage, nor did I know if it was even repairable. My reputation was in intensive care from a self-inflicted wound, my ego in a similar state, lying in a bed alongside it. No visitors. The only company they had was each other.

The ego it seemed, was the more dogged of the two, still clinging on to life, for when the obvious idea of ringing round and offering a healthy serving of apologies reared its contrite head, the head was mercilessly decapitated without hesitation.

Apologise?!

Get on me knees and beg for their forgiveness?!

No chance! I wouldn't give them the satisfaction!

Fuck them! Let them ignore me. I never heard from them anyway!

The ego was making a Lazarus-like recovery, as my reputation died quietly beside it.

I spent the coming days constantly ruminating, unable to ignore the fact that the longer my sobriety was lasting, the more intense the feelings of mortification were becoming. I knew a few drinks, a little session, would dilute my sense of abasement. I craved the resilience that alcohol had forged in me, the certainty of righteousness it had offered, and its ability to rescript the whole episode to my liking, or even just to enable me to forget it all ever happened. Temptation lay in the off-licences, in the endless plethora of pubs in Bray, each of their entrances offering me an exit. Each one was capable of rebuilding my pride and self-esteem, constructions which would be far sturdier than anything I could build by myself. It was tantalising. Harrowing. It was an excruciating battle between my willpower and my urge to reclaim the moral high ground that sobriety had pushed me off. It was increasingly becoming a mismatch and it wasn't long before my willpower surrendered to the lure of the Waterfront.

It took five pints before I rediscovered my certainty of having been wrongly treated, replaying the role of the victim with aplomb, even trumping my previous performance.

Someone sitting at the bar attempted to ignite a conversation. I lent him a nodding head, the thoughts inside of which were tolerable for the first time since before my ill-conceived flirtation with teetotalism. I feigned interest as he kept talking.

"Ye see, the world isn't actually round. Well, it's not a sphere, I mean. It's an oblate spheroid. And o' course, they were convinced it was flat back in the day and they were all terrified o' falling off the edge of it. Little did they know that if it *was* flat, ye couldn't fall off the edge, even if ye wanted to throw yourself off it. Gravity would pull ye to the centre of its mass. Even trying to *get* to the edge would be like climbing a cliff… Manhole covers are round 'cause that way they can't fall down the hole… Ye see, what actually makes a boat float is that the density o' the boat is less than the density o' the body o' water that it's sitting on… The only way we're gonna visit other gal-axies is using wormholes. Ye create one by bending space, making a shortcut for yourself… No mention of aliens in the bible… We can't see light. What we see are objects reflecting light. That's why space is pitch black, despite the billions o' stars. There's nothing up there for their light to reflect off… Ye know where the term 'crocodile tears' comes from? The auld crocodiles start crying when they're killing something. And all it takes is an elastic band to keep their mouths shut. Isn't that gas?"

Pity an elastic band wouldn't keep your mouth shut.

I impatiently waited for him to empty his verbal bowels, before he drank the rest of his pint and left.

"Same again please, Eoghan, when you're ready."

Halfway through another pint, I felt a tap on my shoulder. I turned round to see a familiar stranger. His eyes were sunken and lifeless. Teeth were rotting in his mouth. Sharp cheekbones jutted out from a pale face that hardly disguised its inner skeleton. A scar ran down the side of his face at an angle. He stared at me with a sickly smile that was half endearing, half threatening.

Mick Dolan.

He was almost unrecognisable. If I had passed him on the street, I wouldn't have noticed it was him. I'd been told about Mick's debauched lifestyle at the wake, but we hadn't crossed paths since I last needed him for drink. Judging by his appearance, what I'd been told was true.

"Jesus, how are ye keeping, Mick?"

"Ah, getting by, mate, ye know yourself."

"Have ye finished that apprenticeship?"

"Ah, I packed that in ages ago. It wasn't worth the hassle. Your man was getting on me case all the time. I eventually told him where he could shove his fuckin' spanner. I was working in one or two places for a while… I'm on the dole now. What about you?"

"The same… Here, what are ye having?"

"Bulmers."

I ordered and allowed him a mouthful of it before I addressed the untimely death of our mutual friend.

"Did ye hear about Popey?" I asked.

"Yeah, fuckin' tragic. I only heard after he was buried. Nobody said a word to me about the funeral or anything."

"Ah, you're joking?"

"No word of a lie. Wouldn't ye think they'd pick up the phone?"

"And there they were, having a go at ye for not being there!"

"Is that right?"

"Yeah, right shower o' cunts the lot o' them!"

"They probably didn't want me there."

"I don't know, Mick…maybe."

"They were probably afraid I'd arrive up in some state and cause a scene."

"Don't worry, I covered for ye on that one. They still got their scene."

"What were ye up to?"

"I got into a scrap with Rachael Dowling's fella in O'Connell's. The prick was mouthing off, then threw a punch at me. I let him have it."

"Fair play to ye."

"At least one person's grateful. The lads didn't say a word. And I haven't *heard* a word from them either."

"They're the same with me. They're showing their true colours now. The only one worth a curse amongst the lot o' them is in the ground… Fuck them, Paddy. I wouldn't waste me time thinking about them."

"Dead right. Sure, ye wanna see Paul and Seán hamming it up with the mourning. Fuckin' joke! They didn't give a fuck about the chap when he was alive."

"Aw, I could imagine. If I dropped dead tomorrow, they'd be the same."

"Ah, they've changed," I said, as I gulped my pint.

"They have awright. Fuckin' shame," he agreed, as he endeavoured to empty his own glass in a timely fashion.

"Some o' them are planning on leaving," I said.

"Where?"

"Australia and that."

"I don't know if I'd be allowed into the likes of Australia."

I didn't ask why. Everything I'd heard answered the question for me.

"I'll see how things pan out here anyway," he said. "You?"

"Same. I'll have to get something soon though. I haven't a pot to piss in. Shag all to be doing with meself. If it wasn't for this kip, I'd be climbing the walls."

Mick's gaze shifted left and right, the corners of his eyes bloodshot, before looking beyond me at the front door.

"Did ye cut yourself shaving?" I jokingly asked.

"What? Oh, that?" he asked, pointing to his scar. "Ah, I owed someone a few quid."

"Jesus. Did ye pay him?"

"Eventually, yeah. He would've given me a proper knifing if I didn't," he said, without a hint of hyperbole.

Even Mick's speech had changed. Every sentence was languid. He was fidgety too. His legs kept twitching beneath the bar, as if acting of their own volition.

"Ye taking care o' yourself?" I asked, concerned. "Knives and money… It sounds a bit…"

"Ah, that was ages ago. Just something that got a bit out o' hand. He was the wrong fella to be owing money to, let's put it that way."

I asked my next question hesitantly, unsure of how far I should proceed in satisfying my curiosity.

"What do ye… What do ye be taking?"

"What makes ye think I do be taking anything?" His tone suggested that I'd caused offence.

"Nothing… I just meant, eh, if ye were…"

He revealed that sickly smile again.

"Ah, the usual."

I began to feel uncomfortable in his company.

"The usual?"

"Coke, ecstasy, acid, whatever's going. That stuff's healthier."

"Healthier?"

"Well yeah, it keeps me off the smack. Keeps me mind off it anyway."

I had so many questions I was reluctant to ask. As if sensing that, he spoke more about it.

"I know what you're thinking. I just started doing it for a bit of a buzz, that's all."

"Were ye doing it long?"

"Long enough. I had to make an effort to knock it on the head though… For me ma and da's sake at least. I owe them a fortune."

"How are ye faring?"

"I'm on a good run these last few weeks. Woke up with a mad itch this morning though, so I'm getting meself sorted with the other stuff, just to dull it… What about you?" he asked, as his eyes wandered over to the door again.

"Me?"

"Yeah, do ye take anything?"

"Nah."

"Ah, give over, Paddy. Ye don't pass for a choir boy."

"The odd joint, I suppose. That's about it."

"Ye serious? I could give ye something that'd blow your mind."

"Christ, I don't need it blown. It's bad enough as it is."

"Ye'd have no worries. Ye'd just get lost in your own little world."

"I've always been lost in me own little world, that's the problem. If ye can give me something to help me find me way out of it, I'll take it," I said, laughing uncomfortably.

He focused his attention on the door for a third time.

"Ye looking for someone?" I cautiously asked.

"Yeah, just waiting for a mate."

I said nothing. I could piece together the mystery of his sleazy appointment without further probing.

They were right about him.

I thought of offering some advice and found the prospect amusing.

Take advice from me? I wouldn't even take advice from me.

He looked over my shoulder and nodded. I turned my head to see that a dodgy looking bloke had entered the pub, who I assumed was the aforementioned 'mate.' After catching Mick's attention, he went into the toilet.

"Be back in a minute, Paddy," Mick said to me before doing the same.

Assuming that Mick was buying drugs, I contemplated knocking back the rest of my pint and leaving before he returned to the bar. Something stopped me. A minute or so later, the 'mate' re-emerged from the toilet alone and quickly exited the premises. Mick soon reappeared too and returned to his stool. I said nothing as I pretended to be watching the television.

"Got meself a rake o' shite," he confirmed, as his sunken eyes started to rise out of their sockets. "Want some?"

"No, you're grand," I answered uneasily.

"For free, I mean. I'm not gonna charge a mate for a little taster… Here, have a look."

He dipped his hand into his coat pocket.

"Nah, you're awright."

"Are ye not curious?"

"Well, yeah, but…"

"But what? You're dying to try something. I know the look… Go on. Ye could do with the buzz. I'd say you've had a rough few weeks. I'll tell ye what's what and ye can take your pick."

Part of me absorbed his words, yearned the refuge of his offer, and wanted to experience its high. A voice told me to accept his gift. It assured me that in it, lay the missing ingredient, the cure to my woes. Another voice. Desperate in its tone, distraught. It begged me to resist the hollow pleasures he tantalised me with. He looked furtively around him – a habit, it seemed, and then slowly began to pull his hand from his pocket below the bar. I felt a rush of excitement, like that of a kid entering a toy shop to finally buy the toy he had been saving up for; the one that had been unattainable for so long. But as I considered accepting Mick's special offer, I glanced up at his emaciated face. I heard the second voice again, screaming at me to decline it.

"Ah, you're grand, Mick, honestly… I'm going for a slash," I told him, as a means of giving myself a minute away from him to compose myself. As I returned from the toilet, he was getting up to leave.

"Right, Paddy, I better head."

"No bother, Mick. I'll see ye again," I said, hoping that I never would.

"Drink up that pint before it gets warm," he instructed, patting me on the shoulder as I sat back down on my stool.

"No fear o' that," I replied, gulping it as he left the bar.

My own company thankfully befriended me again. The tales about Mick had been validated. The lad I remembered was just that, a memory. Through addiction, bad decisions and ill-chosen comradeship, he had degenerated into the very person that his younger self would have disparaged. His journey from being one of the lads in St Brendan's to becoming a local junkie, had been made in just a few short years. Once viewed with respect, he was now looked upon with contempt. Even entertaining his company brought unwanted attention, as I noticed a couple of suspicious looks being given to me after he left.

For all his failings, I sympathised with him, for I saw him dig his first shovelfuls of the hole in which he now stood. None of us did or said anything then. Once he was on hand to ensure that we had drink and hash, we were happy to respect whichever road he chose to walk down, provided that we didn't have the misfortune to bump into him on it. We saw the signs, deemed them to be counterproductive to our needs, and promptly ignored them.

Just like Popey.

And yet, he had been condemned, not a kind word spared for him, handed a life sentence by a jury of hypocrites who had given him the shovel to dig his hole, back when their social lives required him to do so.

Wankers!

I was no better. Amidst the guilt I carried for Popey, my conscience found room for Mick. Except Mick was still alive, could still be reined in from the netherworld in which he rambled. But the coward in me feared getting too close to him, feared that my willpower wouldn't be strong enough to resist a taste from the illicit menu he'd place in my hands, feared that it would provide such a euphoric escape that one taste of it would leave me craving more, feared that I too would enter the netherworld. I wasn't a million miles away from it as it was. I'd leave him be, give him the time and space to make sense of himself. In essence, I'd do nothing.

Half an hour after Mick's departure, my mood began to change. I felt calmer, more relaxed as a warmth flowed through my body. As I basked in its pleasantry, long overdue, a slight tingling sensation overtook it. Unfamiliar. I let it run its course. I felt different but couldn't define why or how. My heartrate increased as my temperature rose. Another minute passed before I lost track of time, or it lost track of me. It ceased to matter, ceased to exist. I was disconnected from my body. I drifted away as I looked at myself sitting at the bar. I felt no urge to comprehend the sensation. A notice on the wall. Its letters were starting to move, jumbling around to form different words. The lights in the room were almost blinding. Their colours changed from white to yellow to red to orange. Then they mixed together as if dropped into a glass of water. Each colour gave off a scent. I could close my eyes and smell each one. Rays of light travelled around the room in dizzying motion. The floor's wooden boards moved up, down, left and right. I moved with them, gliding back and forth. The far wall pulled away from me until it was nearly out of sight. The room widened and narrowed continuously, constantly shapeshifting. Rectangle, square, oval. The people looked strange. The whole room was pouring down a sinkhole. I was weightless.

"Sorry, you've had enough tonight, Paddy."

The words exited his mouth. I read them as he spoke. The sound echoed off each wall. Liquid poured continuously from the beer taps, spilling to the floor like a waterfall. Tributaries of orange, blue, green and pink, formed a multicoloured stream flowing towards the door. Peculiar faces with glasses in hand were ready to dip into it.

Me first.

I leaned over the bar and put my mouth under the tap. There was no taste from the yellow liquid, but I could hear it, like strings building towards a massive crescendo.

That man again, waving his hands, making shapes, painting letters in the air. G… E… T… O… U… T… I dropped to my hands and knees by the stream, lowering my mouth into its current. The taste varied with every mouthful. A figure approached, empty glass in hand, wanting a drop. No. It was mine. I found it. I'd mark my territory. I stood by the stream, unzipped and another tributary flowed into it.

I heard a voice.

"Get out now! You're barred! Don't ever come back!"

I followed the stream out the door. The night sky was illuminated by a white light being cast from the moon. I heard voices everywhere. Blinding lights. Music from something led me somewhere to find someone. I couldn't stay still. Sights, sounds, tastes and smells pulled me in every direction. Everything was amplified. I'd died. This was heaven. It existed.

Where's God?

"God, where are ye? I've arrived!"

I saw a figure in the distance. I ran to it.

"Are you God?"

"Am I what?"

"God."

"No, ye just missed him, mate. He was here a minute ago having a pint with Moses."

"Which way did he go?"

"He went to the loony bin. Go there and you'll find him. They'll look after ye."

I frantically ran to the next person.

"If this is heaven, where's God?"

"Heaven? This kip at closing time? More like hell. Ha ha."

Hell?

The colours, the lights, the ambience, all seemed so heavenly. Misled. Fooled. Everything altered instantly. The light faded. The sea was red. Voices whispered in my ears, taunting me. A dark shape loomed in the distance. An ominous creature. An acolyte of Satan. He stood before me, seven feet tall.

A claw grabbed me. I broke loose from his grasp. Another demon emerged from the shadows.

Him!

The personification of evil. The creator of sin. The master of condemned souls. The Lord of the infernal kingdom. The nemesis of the Almighty. His depraved black eyes stared at me intently. A malignant grin appeared on his scorched face. I fled.

The acolyte and his master, ready to claim my soul, galloped after me. I ran and saw a circle of light on the horizon. Heaven. Salvation awaited me. I jumped the fence and ran down the beach to the shore. Just as I was about to swim to heaven, the devil grabbed me, dragging me back into the depths of hell.

"Get your hands off me, Satan, ye bollocks!"

"Will ye relax for Christ's sake!"

I wrestled and threw a punch at him.

"Let go o' me, ye evil cunt! I'm going to heaven!"

"If ye call me that one more time, you'll be going to heaven quicker than ye think!"

Resistance was futile as he took me deeper into his realm, from which escape seemed impossible. I paced restlessly. Holes appeared in the walls and then disappeared once I tried to step through them. Another one appeared above me, but I couldn't jump high enough to reach it.

As hours passed, an overwhelming sense of dread permeated me. I was doomed, destined to languish for eternity in Satan's dungeon. Despair strangled me. I could feel it grip my throat and squeeze. I finally lay down. I'd never felt as apathetic, as empty, as inconsolable in my entire life. I could empathise with Popey, why he did what he did. I could never live with such anguish. I wouldn't last a week. I saw him. He was standing there. Motionless. Scornful eyes. Not a word, just looking at me. Judging me. I was scared to approach, too ashamed to look him in the eye. I turned my head. Then, he was gone. I cried. My once sturdy dam had collapsed, finally succumbing to the unrelenting pressure behind it. I wanted to end the pain. I couldn't kill myself – I was already dead. I closed my eyes. Images still appeared in the darkness. I ignored them until they ignored me and allowed me to slip into unconsciousness.

Chapter 27
The Morning After a Night of Hell

I woke to discover that I wasn't in my bedroom. I wearily looked at my confined surroundings. A steel toilet was in the far corner. Attached to it was a sink. The bed I was lying on was secured to the wall beside me. There was a small, barred window just below the ceiling.

Christ, I'm in a cell! Why?

I had a few pints. Then?

I met Mick.

Then?

I banged on the door.

"Hello… Anyone there?"

No answer, but a cheerful whistle to the beat of heavy footsteps.

"Hello?"

"Hold your horses before I lose me rag with ye."

Keys jangled before the door creaked open.

"Have ye retuned to the mortal realm, Mr Dempsey?" the portly Garda asked.

"What? Why am I here?"

"Ye were arrested last night, that's why."

"Arrested?! For what?"

"Ye don't remember?"

"Do I want to?"

"Ye exposed yourself in a pub, urinated on the floor, and when we got a call in relation to your behaviour, ye assaulted the Garda who was trying to arrest ye."

"You've mixed me up with someone else!"

"I think *you* were mixing Garda Thornton up with someone else from what I was told. Now, was it Santa or Satan? I'm nearly sure it was Satan."

Satan? Oh no!

"Yeah, 'Get your hands off me, Satan, ye bollocks!' I believe it was."

"Aw, for fuck's sake. I thought that was a dream!"

"No, it was real alright."

"Aw, God Almighty."

"That's the very man ye were looking for apparently."

I rubbed my eyes as I feared the possible consequences.

"What happened? I was only drinking and then… everything went a bit…strange."

"Whatever you're taking, I'd knock it on the head before it knocks *you* on the head."

"I'm not taking anything. Maybe I had a panic attack or something… Maybe I *should* be taking something."

"Listen, son, I'm no doctor, but running around thinking you've died, gone to hell, and have the devil and his mates chasing after ye, aren't normally the symptoms of a panic attack. A hallucinogen, I'd guess."

"No, I don't remember…"

"Were ye with someone?"

"No, I was…"

A thought stopped me mid-sentence – Mick's offer.

Did I take something?

I had no memory of having done so. I was adamant that I hadn't. Then, another thought. His parting words.

Drink up that pint before it gets warm.

Mystery solved.

That fuckin' gobshite put something in me drink!

"I was spiked!"

"Isn't that always the way?"

"Honestly! I bumped into a mate, not a mate, a fella I know. I left me drink to go to the jacks. He must've…"

"I'd review me drinking buddies if there's any truth to what you're saying."

I was infuriated, dumbfounded by Mick's stupidity. Whether meant as a joke or a favour, he had driven me to the brink of madness before the brink of madness led me into a cell.

"What the fuck was he thinking?"

"How are ye feeling now?"

"Like me brain's been raped."

As I cursed my luck for having bumped into him, a more pressing matter arose.

"So, what now?"

"Well, ye swung a dig at a Garda."

"It wasn't a dig. I was only pushing him off. I didn't mean to… It wasn't *my* fault… I mean, what would *you* do if the devil was hounding ye?"

"Usually I'd take her out for a bit o' grub," he joked.

"I didn't know where I was or what was happening. Me head was all over the gaff. Listen, I'm sorry. I really am!"

I thought of the consequences of an assault charge against a Garda being brought against me. I'd be found guilty in the space of time it took the judge to put his wig on, cremating my already deceased reputation, sabotaging any chance I had of finding work.

"What made you attend the Waterfront Lounge on the night in question, Mr Dempsey?"

"I wanted to drown me sorrows, sir."

"I see. Do you recall a previous occasion when you were socialising in O'Connell's Public House and you became involved in a physical confrontation, Mr Dempsey?"

"Eh, I do, yeah."

"You seem to be involved in your fair share of melees, Mr Dempsey."

"I didn't start that one, sir."

"That may be, but witnesses say you instigated the argument, Mr Dempsey."

"Well, he was a bit of a git, sir."

"A git?"

"Yeah, a bell-end."

"I see. And the member of An Garda Síochána that you assaulted, was he also a 'bell-end,' as you so crudely put it?"

"No, he was the devil."

"The devil, you say?

"The devil indeed. Have ye ever met him?

"I can't say that I have, Mr Dempsey."

"Well, take a dose of what I was on, and you'll meet him."

"And you plead not guilty to the charge in question because of your state of mind under the influence of this drug, Mr Dempsey?"

"Yes, sir."

"Now, Mr Dempsey, that's akin to a drunk driver running someone over and then pleading not guilty to it because he was drunk."

"Ah, but ye'd want to see the devil, sir. It's one thing reading about him but seeing him in person! Oh be to Jaysus, I nearly scuttered me cacks!"

"Nevertheless, Mr Dempsey, it's still a lousy defence.

"So it seems… Is it too late to claim insanity? I'd have a stronger case."

"Ye could give me a warning and let me go," I humbly suggested.

"I'll tell ye what, I haven't the patience for any more paperwork. Ye seem a good lad, you've no priors, and taking into account your story, I'll let ye go… But I don't wanna see or hear of ye again, ye understand?"

"Yeah. I mean, yes, sir."

"If I catch ye causing any trouble around this town again, it'll be a different story, alright?"

"Yes, sir."

"And if you're gonna get high, take something that doesn't require a shaggin' exorcism!"

"Yes, sir."

He walked me out of the cell and down a corridor to the reception area, where he handed me my wallet.

"Listen, I, em…I appreciate it, Garda…"

"Costello. No worries, son. I've actual criminals to chase after. I haven't the time to be dealing with auld eejits like yourself."

"I'll see ye so."

"Ye bloody well better not see me again! And if I was you, and I spotted Thornton down the street, I'd cross the road."

"I'll owe him a pint if I bump into him."

"He might take ye up on that offer. Ye won't miss him. He'll be the red fella at the bar with the two horns and the tail hanging out the back of his stool. Now go on, get out, before I change me mind."

A night in a cell certainly served as motivation to never return to one. It was the life of a caged rat. All you had was an abundance of time to think. Sleep was the only escape, allowing you to dream about being elsewhere before you reawakened in your ten-foot box. Hell didn't need a devil, fire, or sinners. Four walls and a locked door could achieve the same effect.

How have I got to this point?

Having suffered severe cognitive molestation, such dispirited self-questioning was unavoidable as I sought to ascertain where my life was going. I didn't have anything that could masquerade as an idea as to what I would do with myself.

My optimism, which had provided balance on the seesaw that was my state of mind, had stepped off in the wake of my antics, sending me plummeting to the ground. Abandoned by it, I felt a magnification of the gloom that the lack of a job, opportunities, and a life, had begotten. The only positive thought I could scavenge was that perhaps I'd reached my nadir and that things couldn't possibly get any worse.

Dragging myself home, I'd never appreciated my freedom, nor its worthlessness, as much as I did along that walk to Dargan Street.

Chapter 28

Paddy vs Goliath

Still not a word. Three days since, and not as much as a murmur regarding my exploits. But as I quietly celebrated having been spared the whip of mortification, unbeknownst to me, the rumour mill was operating at full capacity. Witnesses' accounts were being recorded and cross-referenced to verify them, leading to the formulation of a single narrative that was being published to all interested parties. Before long, I became bombarded with messages, each critiquing my performance, milking it for every ounce of humour that it contained.

"Pissing on the floor, Paddy? Get your dog to toilet train you!"

"I heard ye had a date with the devil, Paddy. How was he? I hope you made him wear a rubber! Ha ha."

"Fighting the devil on Bray seafront? Ah, you've lost the plot, Paddy. Fuckers have been put in straitjackets for less! Ha ha."

"Exposing yourself, Paddy? From what I heard there wasn't a whole lot to expose! Ha ha."

"Giving the devil a few slaps, Paddy? Fair play to ye.. The auld Catholic education wasn't completely wasted on you. Ha ha. Have you given any thought to becoming a priest? It's your only chance of finding work! Ha ha."

I thought about responding, but then figured that a reaction was the very thing they wanted. Instead, I deleted their messages from my phone, just as they had deleted me from their lives.

Tossers!

I headed to the Waterfront, wary of showing my face, but equally keen to move on from the incident.

"The usual, Eoghan, please."

He looked at me as if I'd grown a second head since our last meeting.

"Do ye not remember our conversation the other night?"

"Which one?"

"The one involving me barring ye!"

"Was that not said as a laugh?"

"As a laugh?! Ye started drinking from the taps. Then ye took a piss on the floor! I'm not having that carry-on, Paddy."

"Does that not go on every night?"

"Maybe in your house it does!"

"Someone spiked me drink. I wasn't me usual self."

"Ah, would ye pull the other one! Do ye know how many times I've heard that?"

"It's the truth. You're letting all sorts o' dodgy characters into this place these days."

"Oh, so it's my fault, is it?"

"Well, it's not mine."

"Listen, I'm not the one who took me mickey out."

"Ah, ye'd swear ye never saw a fuckin' mickey before!"

"I had women swearing they'd never come back!"

"Ah sure, let them off. It won't happen again, I promise."

"Too right it won't happen again 'cause you're barred! End o' story!"

"Ah, that's a fuckin' disgrace, Eoghan!"

"*You're* a disgrace!"

"I've given some o' the best years o' me life to this place and how am I repaid? Ye bar me and call the guards on me!"

He rolled his eyes in amusement.

"I've heard it all… Will ye go and take your little sob story somewhere else, where ye might find some gombeen who's willing to listen to it."

"You've some bloody cheek, Eoghan! I've been one o' the few people coming in here during the week. I've kept ye in a job. Ye'd be on the fuckin' dole if it wasn't for me!"

"Is that right, Paddy? Funnily enough, that never crossed me mind when I was mopping up your piss!"

"That's not as bad as having to listen to your bullshit!"

"Well, ye won't have to listen to it anymore. There's the door, Paddy. I don't wanna see ye in here again!"

"Good, ye won't! The next time you'll see me is in the fuckin' dole queue, and I'll be grinning from ear to ear at ye, ye prick!"

I burst out the door.

Fuck him! He's welcome to the kip!

It wasn't long before I found a new watering hole on Quinsborough Road; Dunphy's Bar, the place of refuge for those who found themselves barred from everywhere else; a 'delightful' clientele waiting to be discovered.

A string of weary heads hung over the bar, their idle eyes sparing me a glance as I entered. Mutterings passed as conversation, gruffness passed as cordiality, the stained eighties wallpaper passed as decor, and the pint of flat black water passed as Guinness.

Nice, cosy, little dive, this is.

Nostalgia was already tormenting me with memories of balmy summer evenings hunched over the bar of the Waterfront, drinking my woes away as the socialisers mingled. The two pubs which had unburdened themselves of my presence had once been the nucleus of my existence. Both were now scratched off my list of places of interest for drinking or for potential employment. At my current rate, a third pub being scratched off wasn't beyond all possibility.

In my head, I was on my own little island, detached from everyone else, and becoming ever more inconsequential. In the story of 'Paddy versus Goliath,' Paddy would win by forfeit, as the giant wouldn't even bother to show up for the fight, deeming his opponent to be such an irrelevance that the contest didn't warrant his time.

With my pint in hand, Dunphy's, I told myself, wasn't without its own charm. I rolled my eyes at the thought's absurdity. When there's nobody left to cod, one must resort to codding oneself.

Chapter 29
New Year's Revelation

New Year's Eve
Mullin's Inn

The demise of 2009 was worthy of a celebration. Between unemployment, the recession, Popey, the funeral and the arrest, the year had stripped me bare and lashed me with the cat of nine tails fifty-two times. All I had by the end of it was a besmirched name and a barrel load of regret.

In my war against the recession, I was being pummelled. My earlier notions of 'having a good recession' now seemed as ridiculous as they were delusional. My pledge to 'see out the recession,' to forgo travelling beyond these shores, had by now shown itself to be nothing more than vacuous patriotism sprinkled with a smidgen of naivety. The longer I was out of work, the harder I knew it would be to find it. Employment in Ireland was now an old boys' club. You had to know someone who knew someone to stand any chance of even getting an interview.

My enthusiasm in celebrating the death of the year that had been, contrasted with my reluctance to celebrate the arrival of the new year. To do so was to partake in a charade, and those who did were second-rate clowns enamoured with their roles in the economic circus. I couldn't stomach such superficial festivities anymore. The last twelve months had led me to become increasingly cynical. I embraced it. Cynicism made you question and scrutinise everything. It made you wary of people. It sharpened your mind, one which had been blunted by years of unwavering optimism. The optimist wouldn't last the distance in this recession; neither the pessimist. They were at opposite ends of the spectrum but walked together towards their own undoing. Cynicism was the skill of finding a balance between optimism and pessimism. The cynic was a chameleon who could adapt to any environment. He'd be the only survivor of this economic apocalypse. As the last horde of Irish boarded the final ship that was to cast away from its shores, he'd traipse the austerity-ridden wasteland that they were leaving behind and eke out a living from whatever he could scavenge.

I felt disdain for those around me. They were like death-row prisoners giggling away as they were brought to the electric chair, revelling in their ignorance.

Seconds to midnight.

"Ten…nine…"

Why am I subjecting meself to this?

"…eight…seven…"

I should've stayed in.

"…six…five…"

They must be launching the first Irishman into space.

"…four…three…"

Sending him on a mission to find jobs in the cosmos.

"…two…one…Happy New Year!" the patrons exclaimed as they shook hands, hugged, and kissed.

Amongst the voices behind me was a girl's that I recognised.

"I don't believe it!" she said. "Would ye look at the heap o' shite the cat dragged in. Paddy fuckin' Dempsey!"

I turned around on my stool to see the physical form of torment standing before me.

"Aw Christ... Awright, Steph?"

"Ye haven't lost your charm, I see. God, I haven't seen you since... When was it last? Oh yeah! Since the time ye fucked a pint over me in Majorca!"

"Has it been that long? Jesus, time flies in a recession."

"I've a good mind to pour this over *your* head," she said, raising her drink aloft, "but unlike you, I've actually got a bit o' class."

"Yeah, just a bit. Not enough for anyone to notice. Ha ha."

"Oh, you're all smiles and jokes now, are ye? I suppose if I hang around till you've another few pints on board, I might see a repeat performance."

"The fuckin' neck on ye, playing the victim. I came back from the jacks and there ye were, having it off with some prick. How'd ye expect me to react?"

"Aw, give over, Paddy. Ye were miserable. I'd been tolerating your mood all week. I'd just about had enough of it by that point. I'm not gonna apologise for trying to salvage what was left o' me holiday."

"Oh, *your* holiday? Ye mean the one *I* paid for?"

"Oh God, change the record, will ye! You and your money. I swear, you're as tight as a nun's arse."

"Speaking o' money, how much did that eejit cost ye in the end, after ye missed the flight?"

"Missed the flight? I avoided it. I needed to be stuck next to ye all the way back to Dublin like a hole in the head. I stayed a couple o' days longer with Robert, if ye must know. We had a great time. He was the opposite o' you. Real social, full o' life, big lad on him too. Jesus, I was nearly afraid to ride him. I thought he'd puncture one o' me lungs… So, to answer your question, it cost me a few quid, but it was worth every fuckin' penny."

"Is that right? And how's Robert these days?"

"It was just a holiday romance."

"Really? I never would've guessed. There I was waiting for the wedding invitation to arrive in the post."

"Oh, you're so witty," she said sarcastically. "Ye know, if ye'd bothered to ring me the following morning, I might've considered giving ye a second chance. But I knew ye wouldn't. I even said to Robert, 'That selfish muppet won't even pick up the phone, I guarantee ye.' And wasn't I right?"

"What do ye mean, 'giving *me* a second chance'? I'm the one who should be giving *you* the…no, thinking about giving you…no, being the one who'd be giving the second chance if I wanted to give ye a second chance… which I don't!"

"What?"

"Ye know what I mean."

"Paddy, if you think I'd want a second chance with you of all people, ye must be on another one o' your wacky trips… Yeah, I heard about that. Ha ha. I never doubted it was true. As soon as I heard, I thought, yep, that sounds like Paddy."

"How did *you* hear about that?"

"A friend of a friend. Ye know what they say, Paddy – if ye can't take the thrill, don't take the pill."

"Well, I didn't have much of a thrill, I can assure ye."

"You never have much of a thrill doing anything. That's your problem in life. Ye suffer from what the doctors call 'miserable arsehole syndrome.' The state o' ye, sitting there by yourself on New Year's Eve, being all anti-social."

"I'm not being anti-social. I'm being pro-individualism."

She put her eyes up to heaven.

"God, to think I used to go out with ye. I'm scarlet for ye."

"You don't need to be scarlet for me, Steph. I'm well capable o' being scarlet for meself, thank you very much. I've had plenty o' practice. Ye don't get chased around Bray by the devil without learning a thing or two about mortification, trust me."

"Oh, I trust ye. You're the expert on the subject… God, I don't know how I put up with ye for those few months, I really don't."

"I've had to put up with meself for twenty-one years. A few months? That's a walk in the park."

"No, me life since breaking up with you has been a walk in the park."

"What are ye talking about? Ye didn't break up with me!"

"Oh, you think *you* broke up with *me*?"

"I know I did."

"Ye did in your shite! Ye think that throwing your toys out o' the pram and pissing off home without me was breaking up with me? No, no, no, that was when I decided to break up with *you*!"

"Well, we'll have to agree to disagree. Either way I saw the back o' ye and I'm delighted."

"Yeah, ye really look it, Paddy, brooding away there in your little bubble o' misery."

"I was happy in me bubble until you came over and burst it."

"Ye'd rather sit there by yourself letting that little brain o' yours drive ye mental, wouldn't ye? That's so typical o' you. God, you're such a dry shite."

"I'd rather be a dry shite than a mouthpiece talking shite!"

"Well, take your pick, Paddy – ye excel at both. What brings ye here anyway? Was your bar stool stolen in the Waterfront? Ha ha."

"I got bar– bored with the Waterfront. I fancied a change o' scenery."

"Oh, is that why ye took a piss on the floor? 'Cause ye fancied a change o' scenery from the toilet? Ha ha. I suppose whoever was there can count themselves lucky that it was *only* a piss. It wouldn't be below *you* to pull down your jocks, squat down, and have a hefty shite for all to see. That'd be more your style."

"Ah yeah, that's me to a tee, Steph."

"I heard ye were let go from O'Connell's too."

"Christ, are ye spying on me or something?"

"As if! I was down there recently and saw no sign o' your mopey face, so I asked the barman. I'm surprised it took them that long to sus ye out."

"Well, it didn't take me too long to suss *you* out. What is it ye want? Have you just come over to annoy me or what?"

"I just thought I'd say hello, seeing as I saw ye. Me new year's resolution is to clear the air with me former fellas."

"That'll keep ye busy all year so."

"Well, at least one of us will be busy then… Listen, I'm with the girls over there, so if ye wanna join us for a drink rather than sitting there looking like you're about to do yourself in, you're welcome."

"As if I'd wanna get stuck with you and that gang o' tarts. The state o' yis. The fuckin' table wouldn't want to be seen with yis. Ha ha."

"Suit yourself, Paddy. Do me a favour though, will ye?"

"What's that?"

"Don't mention me name in your suicide note if ye wouldn't mind. Spare me the embarrassment. Ha ha."

Her remark stung.

"If ye knew what I've been through lately, ye wouldn't be making wisecracks like…"

She was already walking away.

I think you're this, Paddy. I think you're that, Paddy. I think, blah, blah, blah! What does she know? Her opinion is about as relevant as her own arsehole! A chimp trying to open a can o' beans knows more about what he's doing than that gobshite does about fuckin' anything!

They were sitting in the corner. Stephanie and her three stooges. Two of them took up most of the circumference of the table. The other one had so much fake tan on that she looked orange, and had a tattoo of Chinese writing going down her leg. Their cackles rang out. I was undoubtedly the source of their amusement.

Maybe one of her mates fancies me. Maybe that's why she was inviting me over.

Some chance o' me subjecting meself to one o' those yokes!

Maybe she still has a thing for me. Maybe she wants to give it another go.

No chance o' that either.

As I amused myself with the horrid thought of being stuck in their excruciating company, my attention was drawn away from them to a girl at the far end of the bar ordering a drink. I eyed her head to toe, toe to head, left arm to right arm. The blokes at the bar paid no heed to her. Their unwanted attention was being squandered on the short skirted, generously chested, boisterous alternatives. Perhaps her slender frame didn't possess the curvature they craved, or maybe her reserved demeanour indicated a disinclination to offer herself to their shallow desires. Their disinterest only served to accentuate my interest. She tossed her light brown hair over her shoulder and walked from the bar with her drink. To my horror and delight, she sat down at Stephanie's table.

She's with them!

The offer to join them resurfaced, now more tempting to accept.

I have to go over.

No, ye can't go over. What about your pride?

What pride?

She'll have gotten the full debrief on ye already.

All the more reason to go over.

Steph'll cut ye down in front of her!

Better that than behind me back! I'm going over.

You'll regret it!

I'll regret if I don't!

I navigated through the legion of revellers, squabblers and singsongers, and arrived at their table to hear them engrossed in their jaw exercises.

"How are yis?" I interrupted.

They looked at me quizzically. Stephanie smirked.

"So, you've decided to join us after all?"

"Well, if yis are stuck for a bit o' company, I thought it'd be rude not to."

"If *we're* stuck for company? Aw, never mind. Girls, this is Paddy. Paddy, this is Karen, Sorcha, Denise and Kelly."

Kelly.

I dragged a stool over and squeezed in between Stephanie and one of the bigger girls. I was dwarfed beside her. She had arms like tree trunks and a belly with its own gravitational pull. I could foresee myself being reluctantly dragged into her orbit if I wasn't careful.

"How do ye know Steph?" the orange girl asked me.

"She was me mot a while back."

"Ah, don't say it like that, Paddy," Stephanie butted in.

"What do ye want me to say?"

"We were…a thing for a while…for a time…a short time."

The hatchet job has started already. She's quick out o' the traps, I'll give her that.

The best form o' defence is attack!

"It was more than that, Steph… She was in love with me… It was one-way though. She just wasn't me type."

"Would ye give over, Paddy! Not your type? Anything with two arms, two legs and a pulse is *your* type!

Ye wouldn't say no to a granny on her deathbed. If she died in the middle of it, ye'd still be going at it. Then again, she'd only need to stay alive for ten seconds anyway. Paddy breaks all the laws o' physics in bed, girls. He comes faster than the speed o' light. Ha ha."

Oooh! That was a good one. I'll give her credit where it's due.

I glanced at Kelly. She'd smiled at the remark. I was losing ground.

"Dead right, Steph. Ye hardly think ye were worth any more o' me time than what ye got? Those ten seconds felt like ten hours!"

Ha ha. That's put ye back in your box, Steph!

"How come ye never mentioned Paddy before, Steph?" her other mate beside me asked.

"Paddy's not someone ye can just casually bring up in conversation. He's someone you've to experience for yourself, to try to make sense of in your own time. He's still trying to figure himself out, God love him."

Oh, she wants to go down that road, does she?

"I think she took the breakup much harder than I did. It's still a bit raw for her. I've moved on. I'm not one for holding grudges. I'm a glass half full sort o' fella."

"As long as I've known ye, Paddy, you've never wanted to spend the money to even fill the glass halfway."

She's really upping the ante now. This is heading straight for the 'Paddy's on the dole' turn off. I can see the sign up ahead.

"Well Steph, that's relative to how many times I used to have to refill your glass. I swear, girls, she eats and drinks like an alcoholic horse."

Have a nibble on that, Heffernan!

My eyes were fixed on Kelly. Still not a word from her.

"So, what do ye do, Paddy?" the girl opposite me asked.

Fuck! Of all the questions she could've asked. This is a setup. She's in on the act.

Stephanie butted in again.

"What does Paddy do? Ha ha. He eats, drinks, sleeps, shits and sands his auld plank. Isn't that right, Paddy?"

"Amongst other things."

Retaliate quickly. Show no mercy!

"She's one to talk, girls. I feel sorry for that arse o' hers. It has the misfortune of belonging to someone who couldn't be bothered scratching it. Ha ha."

Kelly had the face of someone trying not to laugh. Our eyes met and neither of us seemed to want to look away. When she did, it was only for a moment before she looked back at me again and caught me still staring at her. I didn't flinch. I maintained my gaze as if she was the only other person at the table.

"Did you hear me, Paddy?" Stephanie asked.

"What?"

"Are ye deaf? I'm going up for drinks. What are ye having?"

"I'll get them. It's my round."

"Since when do *you* have a round?"

I ignored her jibe.

"Is it the same again, girls?" I asked, directing my gaze at Kelly.

Hers was the only voice I sought. Along with the others, she replied. Three words.

"Yeah, thanks, Paddy."

I wanted a third, a fourth, a sentence, two sentences, a conversation. I stood at the bar impatiently, fearing someone would snatch her up while I waited to be served. Stephanie approached me.

"Do ye not think I know what you're up to?" she asked.

"What do ye mean?"

"Ah, Paddy, ye do think you're so clever when I can read ye like a book. I know exactly what you're doing."

"I don't even know what I'm doing, so how the fuck could you know?"

"Ye only came over 'cause ye saw herself."

"Who?" I asked innocently.

"Ye know very well who… Kelly."

"Her? No."

"Yes."

"No."

"Yes."

"Maybe."

"She's way out o' your league, Paddy."

"You know shag all about me league."

"I know enough to know that she's not in it."

"Listen, why don't you look after your own shite and I'll look after mine, awright?"

"Oh, don't worry, I will. It's just at the moment your shite is mixing with mine because she's me friend's friend. She was messed about by her last fella, and I don't want her to get messed about again by you."

"Well, the way you're running me down, there's no fear o' that happening."

"Ah, don't be so sensitive. I'm only having the craic with ye."

"Well, take your craic somewhere else, will ye. I'm drowning in your bullshit over there."

"Good. I'll be giving her fair warning about ye."

"Ye jealous?"

"Jealous? Ha ha. Of what? Count yourself lucky if she even remembers your name."

"When I set me mind to something…when I'm serious about someone…you just watch me."

"You've never been serious about anyone in your life."

"That's 'cause I've never been with anyone worth being serious about."

"Oh, is that so? Well, I'll tell ye what, Paddy, I won't say one word to her good *or* bad. Fair enough? But if I get the slightest whiff of any o' your carry-on, I'll let her know about your night with the devil, Majorca…"

"Yeah, yeah… Is she seeing someone?"

"No. But we're heading to the Waterfront soon, so hopefully she'll meet some fella there who isn't an eejit named Paddy."

"That kip will be black. Would yis not stay here a while longer?"

"Oh, that's right, I forgot. You're barred, sorry, bored with the Waterfront, aren't ye? Aw, that's such a shame."

That it is.

"Now, if ye don't mind, Paddy, I'm gonna say hello to that fine-looking fella over there. Tell the girls I'll be back over in a minute."

I claimed a seat beside Kelly on my return. Stephanie's absence was a blessing.

With a bit o' luck she'll hit it off with him or just talk him to death.

As the other girls performed autopsies on their previous 'fellas,' with everything from their waistlines to their hairlines being published for public consumption, I tried to drag Kelly away from their conversation and into mine, conscious of the ticking clock.

"Your name is Kelly…?"

"Lawless," she said, smiling at me.

"So, have ye had a nice Christmas, Kelly?"

"Ah yeah. Quiet though… Tonight's me first night out in a while."

"Money and all?"

I hoped the answer would be a yes. A fellow member of the 'Unemployed Fraternity' would view me with eyes that looked ahead at me rather than down on me.

"No, not because o' money… Because of a fella."

"I see," I replied, unsure if I should enquire any further, not wanting to be nosy.

"I was with him for a while… It turned out that he was the fella of half a dozen other girls too… After I found that out, I was never really for up for going out… Anyway, for another night?"

Her face was one which betrayed her desire to talk about something else.

"Yeah," I agreed.

"Ye never said what it is ye do," she said, just as I thought I had successfully dodged the question.

"Did I not? Ah, this and that."

"Working?"

"No."

"Studying?"

"Eh, no."

"Any idea what you're gonna do?"

"No, well, yeah…kind o'."

"Like?"

"I don't know…not sure yet."

This is like the world's worst job interview.

"It's awright. I'm not judging or anything."

I offered a bashful smile.

"Being unemployed is all the rage these days," she joked.

We let our smiles linger longer than they needed to, as if it was the first time either of us had smiled in eons and had only just rediscovered how to do it.

"What about you?"

"I'm a nurse."

"Makes sense."

"How come?"

"Ye come across as the nursing type…ye know, considerate and all."

"Do I really or is that just a line?"

"Ah no, honestly. Me line would be something like – I bet ye look great in the uniform."

"Oh, very original," she said playfully. "Come 'ere, there must be something that you're good at."

"Ah, I don't know… Causing mischief, maybe. I'm a great man for a bit o' that."

"When you're not causing mischief, what do ye like to do?"

"I plan me mischief."

"You're a hard man to get a straight answer out of."

"I was a politician in a past life."

"There's a job for ye! Get your foot in that door and you'll be on the gravy train."

"Could ye imagine me mug on posters around the town? Ha ha."

"I could. They'd be something decent to look at for a change."

"Yeah right," I replied dismissively, rolling my eyes.

"What do ye mean 'Yeah right'? Are ye not great at accepting compliments?"

"I suppose I'm just not used to receiving them."

"Don't let the whole job thing knock your confidence."

"It probably already has," I said, before realising I'd disclosed more to her than I intended.

"I've been there. It comes back though," she assured me, before saying, "You've real dark eyes, kind o' sad looking."

Unwilling to commit to any further disclosures, I joked my way around her observation.

"That's me tortured artist look that I'm trying to cultivate."

She offered me a look that told me she knew exactly what I was doing.

"Ye still haven't told me what you're good at. Everyone's good at something. Honest answer this time."

"Honestly? Nothing."

"Ah, I'm sure we can find something… Happy New Year, by the way, Paddy."

"Yeah, Happy New Year," I replied, my face undoubtedly that of a child who comes down on Christmas morning to discover an extra present.

As we conversed, I hoped a tornado had torn the Waterfront to smithereens, or that it had been closed because of a rat infestation. Anything to prevent her departure.

"Are ye ready to head down to the Waterfront, Kelly?" the orange girl asked.

"Yeah sure. What about you, Paddy? Ye coming with us?"

"Eh, no. I'm feeling a bit tired to be honest. I might head on home."

"I'm not that arsed meself, but I don't wanna be letting the team down. Where's Steph?"

I looked across the bar to see Stephanie consuming her conquest like she'd just come off a hunger strike.

"He must be this week's catch," she said.

"Poor fella, has it all ahead of him. I don't know how ye put up with her."

"Ah, she's okay in small doses… Well?"

"Well what?"

"Well, are ye gonna let me leave without getting me number?"

"Maybe I will."

"You're worse than me at playing hard to get."

"I told ye I wasn't good at anything," I said jokingly.

I got her number before her gang showed her to the door. She walked behind Stephanie as they were leaving, before turning around and mouthing the words, 'Call me!'

For the first time that night, I welcomed the new year's arrival, hoping that 2010 would prove to be my renaissance.

Chapter 30

The First Works
of the Renaissance

"Have ye given any more thought to it?" Kelly asked.

"To what?"

"To what you're gonna do… Well?"

She asked the question as if expecting a blueprint to be offered in response. I had nothing of the sort. In the last few years, there was no other question that boggled my mind more than that. The weight of the question crushed me, its strength overpowered me, the consequences of my inability to answer it frightened me. I could make a better attempt at answering a question regarding the origin of the universe, its mind-blowing complexity paling in comparison.

It was as if I hadn't moved an inch since the question was first hurled at me in St Brendan's, or that I had unknowingly walked a circular path and was left baffled, having ended up where I started.

"I'd do anything, I suppose. The pub was awright. I'd do that again if there was a job going."

"I'm not asking ye what ye *would* do, I'm asking ye what ye'd *like* to do."

In the brief time I'd known Kelly Lawless, I'd come to realise that she was quite adept at drilling holes in the verbal wall that I'd constructed in front of me and peeking through them to see what was on the other side. It was a skill she required, as getting me to open up was like pulling a shipwreck from the bottom of the ocean.

"All I ever wanted to be was a footballer or a musician. I hadn't the feet to be a footballer or the hands to be a guitarist."

"What about your brain?"

"What about it?"

"Ye can use that, can't ye?"

"I have been. That's what has me where I am."

"You're still dodging the question."

"I *answered* your question. I had pipedreams. Once I realised that's all they were, I had no plan B. Anyway, what ye want and what ye get in this country, are two different things. If I'm offered a job cleaning the shite off the streets, I'll take it."

We stopped talking for a moment in reverence to our surroundings. It was a typical January Saturday afternoon in Little Bray Park. An intermittent wind lifted fallen leaves from the moist grass, juggling them in the air before allowing them to fall back onto the ground. The footpath was being dotted with the first drops of rain that the gloomy sky had been threatening us with. Children played football with jumpers for goalposts. The park was their stadium, the hum of the passing cars was the roar of the imaginary crowd that they were playing in front of. I envied them. At first, I didn't know why. Then I did. Childhood. Innocence. Blossoming dreams. Unbreakable ambition. They were too engrossed in the present to ever lend a worrying thought to the future. I was once one of them, possessing the same unbridled aspirations, the same unabating insouciance. A different time, a different country.

We'd arranged to meet for a walk. I'd found it a daunting prospect and hoped that the walk would just be the necessary journey needed to cross the threshold of a local pub rather than the local park. But whether it was because of her company or my nostalgia, I had no inclination to move. Drink couldn't have been further from my mind.

"We used to spend our lives down here when we were younger, just playing ball all day," I said. "We had a rule – if ye kicked it over into the river, ye had to go in and get it. Fuckin' nightmare. Ye'd be wading past old nappies, bicycle wheels and God knows what else. I realised I wasn't gonna be a footballer when I had to hop in for the hundredth time. I swore I'd never hit the ball in again when I came out one time with a pair of old manky Y-fronts wrapped between me toes."

"Oh God! I'd be screaming. Ha ha."

"I wasn't far off that meself. Ha ha. Ah, good memories all the same."

"Don't get too bogged down with them though."

"It's hard not to when it feels like you've already lived your best years… Since Popey – Alan, a mate o' mine, killed himself, everything's been going pear-shaped… Then, sometimes I think it was already going pear-shaped before that, and here I am using his death as a handy excuse."

Without having consciously decided to do so, I was disclosing myself to her. Maybe it was because I believed that she saw through my bravado, or that I had run my race and needed someone to lean on at the finish line. Then again, perhaps it was because so much of my ego had been crudely severed to the point that I no longer possessed the ability to care about what anyone thought anymore. Whatever the reason, she was picking the locks to doors that I'd vowed to keep shut. The shipwreck was slowly, painstakingly, rising from the ocean floor.

She said nothing, as if prompting me to keep talking.

"I met him not long before he did it. He wanted to go for a pint, have an auld chat and that. I didn't go with him 'cause I wanted to go motting down the seafront instead. It's eaten away at me ever since, I swear. I mean, the one time he fuckin' well needed me, needed a mate – where was I? … I knew there was something up with him. It fuckin' kills me to think of it. The 'what ifs.' What if I had gone for a pint with him? Would he have spoken about what was bothering him? Would he still be here? Everything's boiled down to one decision. His life's over, me own life's whatever the fuck it is, all because o' that one poxy decision!… I try not to think about it, but if I don't, I feel guilty 'cause it feels as if I'm sweeping him under the carpet, ye know?"

"You're not sweeping him under… That was his choice, Paddy. Ye could hardly watch over him twenty-fours a day. You've to accept his decision and live your own life."

"What life?"

"Ah, don't 'what life' me! Aren't ye sitting here with your health at least? That's more than some people have… You're not the only one with regrets."

It was my turn to offer the silent prompt. She hesitated for a moment and then spoke. "Me da was doing the dirt on me ma a few years ago. She found out about it from a mate o' hers who saw him with your one. Before Ma even got the chance to confront him about it, he arrived home one day and told her he'd met someone, and he was leaving. Just like that. No talking it over, no arguing, no drama, nothing. Ma was shocked. She begged him to stay, told him she'd forgive him, offered him a fresh start. He didn't care, his mind was made up, so he said. He hadn't even the balls to tell his children. He wanted Ma to pass on the message to us. And then, one day he was suddenly gone. Poor Ma was forced to tell us what happened... It was weird how quiet the house was after he left. Ma was just drifting through the days, saying nothing, putting on a show, but I could tell she was struggling. She'd spend half the day looking at her reflection, inspecting wrinkles, wearing extra makeup, asking us if she looked attractive, never mentioning a word about Da, good or bad. I suggested to her that she talk to someone, and she laughed it off. I think she always thought he'd return. Da was still trying to stay in touch with us. He even asked me and me brother and sister to have dinner with him and herself. It was as if he was deleting Ma from his life, like she'd never existed. Anyway, we didn't go. I told him where to shove his dinner and that I never wanted to see him again, that he was as dead to me as Ma was to him... The next time any of us spoke to him after that, was a couple o' years later when we found out he was dying." Her face was smeared with the pain of recounting the time.

"Dying?"

"His brother called to the house one day to tell us... Pancreatic cancer. The doctors had caught it too late. I know the way Da was. He was probably ignoring the symptoms for ages. That would've been typical of him. If his head fell off, he'd be convinced he'd wake up the next morning with it reattached… We went to see him in the hospital. God, there wasn't a pick on him… He told us he hadn't much time left and apologised for everything. We forgave him and told him we loved him. Then he told us that if he'd known he was on borrowed time, he never would've left us. He said that missing out on his last couple o' years with us was a regret he'd take with him to his grave, and that he'd give anything for a bit more time with us… After that, we never really mentioned anything to him about dying. We just reminisced and talked about what we'd been up to since we last spoke to him, that type o' thing. He was trying to keep the conversations upbeat, so we went along with it… The following week, he started to slip in and out of consciousness, so it became harder to talk to him. Ma had the last proper conversation with him before he passed away."

She dabbed her eyes with her coat sleeve.

"And where was your one?"

"Ah, they'd broken up before he got his diagnosis. Da had been living in some tiny flat by himself before he went into hospital."

"Did she ever visit him in hospital?"

"I don't know. We never saw her there. We never asked him either. None of us wanted to talk about her, including Da… We did see her at the funeral though. She kept her distance from us, thank God, 'cause me sister would've unloaded on her if she'd approached us… During the funeral, I began finding it harder to justify not talking to him after he left us. Then I remembered what I'd said to him about him being dead to me. What I'd give to take that line back... I started to think that we'd committed an even worse act than he had, by denying him his last couple o' years with us... Is any o' this sounding familiar?"

"Yeah, very... How are yis now?"

"Well, that was a good while ago. We've moved on, but it still feels as if we're in the middle o' rebuilding something at times. Ma still withdraws into herself now and then. I know the signs. When I see them, I go for a walk with her or something... Whenever we talk about Da, we try to avoid talking about the last two years of his life. There's not much point in dragging it up... Well, there hasn't been until now." She dabbed her eyes again.

"Shite. Sorry, I didn't mean to..."

"When I found out me last fella was riding half o' Bray, it brought it all back. It made the breakup hurt even more than it should've. I don't even think I was that upset over him, it was more the memories it stirred up that I was upset about. I suppose I was experiencing how Ma must've felt, that feeling o' worthlessness, ye know?"

I know it like the nose on me face.

I offered an arm round her, knowing that my best words would probably be inadequate.

"Anyway, I'm saying all this 'cause you're sitting there gobbing on like you're the only person who's ever had something worth moaning about. I wasn't sure whether to tell ye or just give ye a slap across the head," she said, smiling.

"It's nice here, isn't it?" I said, attempting to lighten the mood.

"Yeah, we should come here more often."

We.

"Yeah, we should," I concurred, placing my hand on hers.

She leaned her head on my shoulder.

"Kelly, why are ye interested in me?"

"Why wouldn't I be?"

I could think of plenty of reasons, but not a better answer. I leaned into her and debuted my latest kiss, the 'Smooch of the Besotted.'

"Are ye right?" I asked her as the rain got heavier. "I don't want ye catching a cold over me."

We walked to the bridge where we said our farewells. She broke through a queue boarding a bus and was out of sight, but not out of mind. Journeying home, the troublesome thoughts that so often provided me with their company, were quelled in the afterglow of her presence. Their ability to dig their nails into my brain lessened, their stranglehold on me loosened. Not knowing what lay ahead, I was content to cherish such a frame of mind for however long it lasted.

Chapter 31
The Fall of the Great Wall

With her warmth that even the gloomiest of Irish winters couldn't nullify, with her sense of humour that rivalled my own, and with her knack for resuscitating my self-esteem with the odd offhand complimentary remark, there'd be no retreat from wherever I was heading.

Unemployment caused days to either creep by at an excruciatingly slow speed, or to hurtle past with nothing but daytime television to show for their existence. With her, a steady pace was attainable. She was dismantling the great wall of Paddy Dempsey, brick by brick.

There was still the niggling voice warning me, doubting her sincerity, fearing commitment, lambasting me for ignoring the harsh lessons learned from my prior experiences. The voice still found a somewhat ardent listener, but its concerns were beginning to seem more and more frivolous. I began to ruminate less and strove to live outwardly rather than inwardly. I was reluctant to claim that she made me happy, for it implied I was previously unhappy. I'd never judged myself as such, but then again, my understanding of happiness and unhappiness had been completely muddled, lost to an impassive emotional state which was engineered to do nothing more than survive, only being able to overcome the limitations of its design courtesy of copious amounts of alcohol.

Having climbed Bray Head one Saturday afternoon, we sat at the base of its cross for respite.

"I used to come up here the odd time when I was mitching from school," I told her. "Perfect spot to hide away for a few hours."

"What would ye do to kill the time?"

"Nothing. I'd just sit here thinking and looking at everything going on down below."

"That's where your troubles started so. You with a pinch o' thinking is a recipe for disaster."

I wrapped my arms round her and watched the town below us illuminate and darken as the sun went in and out of the clouds.

Ant-like people walked along the seafront as dinky-like cars drove up Strand Road. The town was different from up there. It was just a view; a magnificent one. The closed shops, boarded-up houses, dole queues, mortgage arrears, defaulted loans, faces of disenfranchised youths, austerity, squandered futures, and the air of dejection, were all absent. Some of its shabby estates were the picture of cleanliness from so far above, while its shadier residents were indistinguishable from the rest. The realities of the recession were hidden away, out of sight. The view amplified the town's qualities while masking its scars.

Out to the south-west, the Wicklow Mountains stood imperiously above everything else within sight, not lending themselves to subtlety, with their rugged magnitude dwarfing the town below them. To the north, Dublin City. A mirage of hope. A graveyard for opportunity. The capital city of unemployment. The towering chimneys at Poolbeg were a fitting metaphor for it; iconic and redundant in equal measure. Bray was a slapper of a town straddling the Dublin-Wicklow border, throwing one leg over each county, willing to offer itself to whichever had the deepest pockets.

To the east lay the Irish Sea. Beyond it was Britain. Our long-held animosity towards her, a once intrinsic facet of our national identity, was now drastically depreciated in value, no longer being a national asset but rather a liability, now that the begging bowl was being dusted off after its much-trumpeted furlough, for any of her spare coppers. Likewise, Britain's aged right hand of imperialism was now tucked in its pocket as it cordially offered its left hand of rapport. Two countries still in the midst of a divorce proceeding were realising that amicability was more profitable than acrimony. Historical grievances could be forgotten for the right price.

The scene was an idyllic backdrop for a conversation that was long overdue. I'd been deferring it as I waited for the opportune moment, afraid of her response, fearful that I was being hasty. When a strong gust of wind passed, I took it as my cue.

"Kelly, ye know the way we've been seeing each other a bit?"

"Yeah."

"Are we...ye know... a couple?"

She smiled before replying, "Well, I'd hate to think that we've been spending all this time together for nothing."

"Me too," I said, smiling back at her, before I kissed her on the forehead.

As the wind became stronger, I deemed it time for us to get down onto lower ground.

"Come on, let's walk to Greystones," I suggested.

"Greystones?"

"Yeah, it's only a few miles. We can get something to eat, then get the bus home."

Greystones; a town so close to Bray geographically, but the antithesis to it socially, politically and economically. Even religion differentiated them, with Greystones' meagre Protestant minority being the largest of any town in the state, enough for it to garner the moniker of a 'Prod Town.' The term was thrown about derogatorily by Bray's finest barstool Catholics, all of whom could be found on any given Sunday in their own houses of worship, with their pints placed in front of them and their worries left behind them.

We descended from the summit and started off along the cliff walk, beneath Bray Head to our right and above the precipitous cliff faces to our left. For so long, I had felt like I was standing at the edge of a cliff, anxiously wondering if it would erode beneath my feet or if a passer-by would push me off it. In her company, such thoughts seemed unworthy of my attention. As she interwove her fingers with mine, I realised that as much as the sea was reshaping the contours of the coastline ahead of us, she too, was reshaping *me*.

"We'll have to mind our Ps and Qs out in this place, Kel. They can spot a pair o' shitkickers from a mile away."

"A *pair* o' shitkickers? Speak for yourself! Ha ha."

"Ah, who are ye codding? You're as much a shitkicker as me."

"I am not! Ha ha."

"Guilt by association, I'm afraid."

"Oh, I see. And tell us, how many other girls have ye turned into shitkickers?"

"Girlfriends, ye mean? Two."

"Well, one o' them I know… How'd ye end up with Stephanie? Yis are complete opposites."

"The high maintenance girls tend to be attracted to me. I provide a roof over the head o' their bullshit."

"And the company of your own. Ha ha… What about the other one?"

"Rachael Dowling? Ah, she was the opposite. She'd put years on ye. She'd need an instruction manual on how to enjoy herself."

"Jesus, the life o' the party beside me," she said in amusement.

Our bantering saw us leave miles in our wake in what seemed mere minutes. In the distance, Greystones began to slowly emerge as we traversed the meandering coastline.

"So, did ye always wanna be a nurse?"

"Yeah, I was lucky in that sense. Some o' the other girls didn't know what to do with themselves after school. A few o' them still don't."

"I'm the chairman o' that club… It must be great doing something ye wanna do. Not to mention, having a proper qualification."

"There's nothing stopping you from getting one too."

"With the way things are, it wouldn't be worth the paper it's printed on. It'd only be a one-way ticket out o' here."

"Even with a one-way ticket you're still going somewhere. It's better than having no ticket at all."

"Do ye ever think that there's something out there for ye waiting to be grabbed, and ye just have to figure out what it is first?"

"Do you?"

"Sometimes. Trying to figure out what it is though, is like trying to do a jigsaw with your eyes closed."

We walked the last few hundred yards of the cliff walk in the thick of a fog which had surrounded us, before following a back road that led us to the town's harbour and its array of bars and restaurants.

We rested our spent limbs on a bench overlooking the sea as darkness began to fall. In the distance, a ship sailed by. Its light travelled towards us through the fog, letting me know that there was something out there on the horizon.

"Come on, Kel. Let's get a bit o' grub. Me belly's starting to talk to me."

Chapter 32
Altering Reflections

First to wake, I sat on the edge of the bed looking at her while she slept, remembering some of the previous times when I'd awoken next to a girl. The local strumpets, hangovers and escape plans that were so intrinsic to those occasions, were now thankfully absent. I had managed to revoke my membership of the 'casual encounters club' before impregnating one of its members. Thinking back to one or two of them, I laughed at the thought of having come away from such encounters with my health still intact, and not having to meet the boss of bosses prematurely and be chastised for my dissolute ways.

"Jesus Christ, Paddy! Ye weren't supposed to be here for another fifty years!"

"I know, God. What can I say? Ye gave me a mickey but never gave me a brain. I was doomed from the outset."

"Oh, it's my fault, is it? Ye couldn't have put a rubber on?"

"That's against me religion, God. You of all geezers should know that."

"And is sex out o' wedlock not against your religion too?"

"Well, I pick and choose which bits I abide by."

"Ah, I see. A typical Irish Catholic so!"

"To be fair, God, I had no choice. Me little fella was famished. I nearly had him on a drip."

"Ah, Paddy, you've nothing to show for your time on Earth. I gave ye the best o' health and ye threw it away!"

"Sure, wasn't I gonna end up here eventually anyway? I was only postponing the inevitable."

"Yes, but ye only dwell in the mortal realm once. Hence why ye strive to live a full life."

"Ah, I didn't think it was all it was cracked up to be anyway, to be honest with ye, God. I'd had me fill of it… So tell us, if this is heaven, where are all the women?"

"Have I still not taught ye anything? If there's any o' that carry-on up here, your stay will be very swift!"

"Ah, come on God, I'm dead! I can't impregnate anyone, nor catch any diseases, so what's the harm? Ye only die once!"

Gasping for a cup of tea, I put on my boxers and made for the door.

"Paddy, where are ye going?"

"Getting a cup o' tea."

"Get me one."

I poked my drowsy morning mug out the back door of the kitchen with my morning cup in hand. An early spring chill ran the length of my body, summoning the hairs on my arms to attention, but I didn't care. No, I was without a care, a crucial difference.

With Kelly's mother being away for the weekend and her two older siblings no longer living at home, we had the house to ourselves for a couple of days. With the cold biting my skin, I smiled to myself, thinking that my run of bad luck had finally come to an end. There seemed to be a trail of misfortune that had led me to this moment; a series of incidents, the consequences of which had placed me in her vicinity on New Year's Eve. I appreciated the irony of it as I made my way upstairs with the cups, before climbing back into the bed.

"I thought ye'd gone to India to make the tea."

"I was just catching a mouthful of air."

"The only thing you'll catch out there is a cold."

"Sure, haven't I a nurse to look after me, if I do?"

"You may pay me."

"Ye never mentioned a fee last night. If I knew I was paying, I would've asked ye to dress up."

"This'll be the last time you're in this bed, Paddy, if you're not careful," she jokingly remarked.

"Do ye know what I was thinking? I was thinking of all the circumstances that had to fall into place in order for me to have met ye."

"That's fairly deep thinking for this time o' the morning," she said, sipping her tea.

"It's true though. Strange when ye think about it. If just one link in the chain was absent, we wouldn't be having this conversation."

"Are ye trying to tell me that fate brought ye to me, Paddy?"

"Well, fate may have brought you to *me*. Lousy luck brought me to *you*."

"Listen to *you*! Ye must've heard that line in some film."

"I can romance with the best o' them, I'll have ye know."

"St Valentine himself lying beside me."

"What did *he* do to become a saint? Don't ye have to perform a miracle?"

"Men buy women flowers in February because of him. That's enough of a miracle. Why do ye ask anyway? Are ye thinking o' becoming one? You're too contrary."

"Contrarianism is a very underrated trait. I'm not too contrary, only dabble in it now and again. The odd fix once in a while is grand… Saint Patrick the second, patron saint of contrarianism. It has a ring to it."

She rubbed her eyes, yawning.

"Jesus, Paddy. Ye talk some serious shite in the morning."

"I know. This is the random nonsense that does pop into me head."

I'd rather that than Popey rotting in a box.

The thought came from nowhere. The image followed immediately after. It startled me. I tried in earnest to erase it from my mind.

"Paddy, what's the matter?"

"Ah, nothing… Just thinking about Popey."

"Don't be if it drags ye down. It's of no benefit."

As if I've a choice.

"Well, haven't I got you now to pull me back up?" I said, unsure as to whether the comment was meant jokingly or with the utmost gravity.

"And who's gonna pull ye back up if I'm knocked down by your da's bus tomorrow?"

"Ye won't get away from me that easily. I reckon you've another fifty years o' your sentence left to serve."

"Paddy, if that's your idea of a marriage proposal, God only knows what the ring is like."

"No, it's not me… Why, would ye?" My tone unconsciously changed.

"Would I what?"

"Ye know, if I asked."

"Well not now."

"Later, I mean."

"Ah, that's cheating asking me like that."

"It's not. I'm just getting the lay o' the land."

She smiled before saying, "Never mind the lay o' the land. Ye know what I'm interested in right now?"

"What?"

"Breakfast. Go on, stick us on something."

"I want to meet your family," Kelly nonchalantly said to me that evening, as if her words had no more weight to them than a sliotar. But to me they had the mass of a small planet. Not wanting to reveal my disinterest in the idea, I opted for the 'acknowledge and change the subject' strategy.

"Oh really? I've a question for ye. If ye had to choose, would ye rather be blind or deaf?"

"Deaf... So?"

"Would ye rather..."

"I'd rather ye stop changing the subject, Paddy!"

"What was the subject?"

"Ye heard me. I want to meet your family."

"Well, em... I don't know..."

"What do ye mean, 'I don't know'?"

"Ah, I find that family stuff awkward. Why would ye want them knowing our business anyway?"

"Christ, I didn't realise we were a state secret. Do they know about me?"

"Well...not really, no."

"Ah, Paddy, why haven't ye told them?"

"I just haven't got around to it. I was waiting for the right moment to break the news."

"Fuckin' hell! Ye'd swear ye were telling them some-one's died!"

"Everything in its own time. That's all I'm saying."

"Well, never mind… Listen, I've an idea."

That sounds ominous. They were probably Hitler's very words when he thought o' the final solution. 'Ich habe eine Idee!'

"Okay, what?"

"I think I should meet your family for dinner, and me ma could come too. We'd meet each other's parents. It'd be a lovely occasion."

What?! The mother too! Two disasters merging to form one colossal hybrid of destruction!

A lovely occasion? It'd be a fuckin' abortion!

The events of recent times had created a gulf between my family and me. I had subconsciously placed them in the back seat, as I sped dangerously down the wrong side of the road. Family affairs had become of little interest to me, and playing 'happy family,' even less so. But I tried my hand at altruism long enough to appreciate that, so far, I had taken more from our relationship than I had given, and that the imbalance needed to be addressed. I knew I could rekindle some of my old magic, recite a hackneyed incantation, and create some concoction of a story regarding the family being on holiday, the house being renovated, Da being too busy with work, the dog having contracted syphilis, or any of the endless excuses that my imagination could provide. But I didn't. The longer I was with her, the longer I wanted it to last. I knew she could attract the attention of lads who had jobs, substantial bank balances, cars and prospects that

I didn't have. I had no idea of the length of my shelf life, but if Popey's death had taught me anything, it was to rid myself of the 'what ifs.' If she was to wake one morning and decide that she wanted to break up with me, I was determined to ensure that it wouldn't be down to a lack of effort on my part, or over trivialities such as the occasion she had proposed.

I recalled sitting at Rachael Dowling's dinner table as her parents interrogated me, doing their upmost to make me trip over my own lies. They needn't have bothered. I'd eventually tumble to the ground ignominiously, having been tripped by the outstretched leg of the recession.

I wouldn't permit Kelly to be the target of such scrutiny. I was old enough now and belligerent enough to tell any naysayers which orifice they could insert their opinions into. Not that I foresaw such a happening. My family, long accustomed to my aloofness, to my lack of companionship, would welcome her into our modest abode. It was never them, always me. Unemployment isolates you to the point that isolation becomes the norm. It erodes your self-esteem until you're convinced there's something wrong with you. It acclimatises you to a routine that makes you fearful of any situation that exists beyond the parameters of that routine.

I ignored the niggling voice that for so long was the conductor of such feelings, directing the orchestra as it played its doubt-ridden concertos to an audience that was now decreasing with each performance.

"Yeah, sounds great. I'll say it to them."

She smiled and rested her head on my shoulder. The weight, for once, was welcomed.

Chapter 33
Feeding Time in the Zoo

Saturday evening in the sitting room. Claire was exercising her thumbs on her phone, Ma was engrossed in a book, Da was complaining about having paid his television license because there was nothing to watch, while Buddy offered him a tilting head before he rolled onto his back for a rub.

"Come 'ere to me, ye little bollocks, and I'll give ye a rub, seeing as you're the only one o' them that's listening to me," said Da.

Buddy ambled over delightfully at his master's request, his eyes closing in pleasure as he received his reward for his attentiveness. Da always had a soft spot for Buddy, a dog that he liked to say was a four-legged version of himself, with their mutual affability and sense of humour. Buddy, ever cute in more ways than one, knew how to exploit this fondness for his own benefit.

"Is there anything for dinner, Ma?" I asked.

"Not much. Throw on a fry for yourself."

"Awright. It's just, well, someone's coming over."

"Does he not have food in his own gaff?" Da asked.

"Well, it's not a he... It's a she."

"A girl?" asked Ma, with a look of shock on her face.

"What girl? Do I know her?" asked Claire.

"Is it your mot? Is that what you're trying to tell us, Paddy boy?"

"Eh… Well, she's a friend…who's a girl… She's coming over for dinner tonight with her ma."

"She's what?!" Ma asked, the look of shock on her face morphing into horror.

"Yeah, they're coming over in an hour or so."

"Ah, for fuck's sake, Patrick!" she said, using a profanity that she reserved only for the most deserving occasions. "The house is a mess. There's nothing to eat. I've nothing to wear. Why are ye only telling us now?!"

"I forgot to mention it. Sure, how much notice do ye need? They're only coming over for a bit o' grub. I thought ye got the shopping."

"Relax, Aoife. It'll be grand," Da assured her.

Once Da insisted that something would be 'grand,' it was usually an indication to the contrary, but his calming influence was welcomed.

"I'll fly down to the chipper and get a few fish and chips," he cheerfully suggested.

"Ah, John, I'm not having people coming over for dinner and giving them a bloody take-away. What will they think of us?!"

"Well, they better think something good 'cause they're getting a free fish and chips out o' me!"

"This is bloody ridiculous, Patrick! You've had all the time in the world to tell us and ye leave it till the eleventh hour. Typical you!"

"Kelly wouldn't want a big thing being made of it. She just wanted to meet yis."

"God, I could strangle ye, Patrick, I swear! A nice girl wants to have dinner with us, and she ends up being subjected to this family's carry-on. God love her!"

"God love her is right!" Claire said. "How much is she charging?"

"You shut your mouth, Claire! Who's talking to ye?" I snapped.

"I can't wait to see her ma's face when she's given her fish and chips," she said, laughing.

"Claire, that's enough from you!" Ma barked. "Now help me clean this place up."

"Do what your mother asks, Claire," Da instructed.

"Ah, John, I could've made a lovely roast and veg!"

"Well, aren't they getting seafood instead?"

"Seafood?! John, are ye for real?"

"Well, I'm not gonna squat down and pull the fish out o' me arse, Aoife. I mean, it'll be some geezer that's come from the sea."

"John, it's hardly…"

"It's seafood…in batter, with chips, a garlic sauce, and a few onion rings on the side… And this Kelly young one, would I know her to see from me bus route?"

"Ye might. She gets the one-four-five into Vincent's. She's a nurse."

"A nurse, no less," said Da, sounding impressed.

"John, will you clean the kitchen while we clean the sitting room. Patrick, you help him, and try not to blow it to smithereens while you're in there if it isn't too much to ask."

Ma frantically inspected the sitting room upon hearing the doorbell, then inspected herself in the hallway mirror, before opening the door.

"Oh, hello, You must be the gorgeous girl he's been talking about for ages, and this must be?"

"Caroline. Nice to meet ye."

"Likewise, Caroline, come on in. Let me introduce yis to everyone… This is me husband John."

"How are yis, ladies?"

"That's me daughter Claire, and beside her is Patrick."

"How are ye, Caroline?" I greeted.

"Lovely to meet yis," Caroline replied enthusiastically, as I critiqued her appearance with matching enthusiasm. *What a cracker!*

"Sit down there, ladies. What will yis have?" Ma asked.

"A coffee would be great," said Caroline.

"Do we have coffee, John?"

"Not that I know of, Aoife."

"We've no coffee… How about a cup o' tea?"

They both nodded.

"Do we have milk, John?"

"Em, enough for one maybe… And we've no sugar."

"I'm sorry about this, ladies. You'll have to forgive me for the disorganisation. Patrick, ye see, operates on a different wavelength from the rest of us. Ye'd think he'd tell us yis were coming over for dinner with a few days' notice, but my Patrick's brain doesn't function like other brains. He decided to tell us about your visit an hour ago, so I'm sure yis can understand."

"O' course, Aoife. To the male brain that makes perfect sense," she quipped.

She sounds like a raving feminist. Christ, I hope it's not hereditary.

"And we haven't really anything for dinner, so how does a take-away sound?"

"Fine," they both said in cheerful unison.

The colour in Ma's cheeks softened.

"I told ye they'd love it, Ma," I interjected, receiving a death stare from Ma for my troubles.

Da inhaled, like he was ready to give a grand oration.

"Right, well is a smoked cod and chips awright with everyone?" he asked, as he rose from his seat.

"Yeah, yeah."

"Grand so. Sure, I'll pop down now. Will ye come with me Paddy to give me a hand? Let the ladies chat amongst themselves for a few minutes."

"Eh…right, yeah."

"Pick up some coffee, milk and sugar, John…and a bottle o' wine too… Is white awright, ladies? A bottle o' white, John."

In the car, as we headed over to Castle Street, Da complimented me in his own unique way.

"Jesus, son, you're punching well above your weight with that young one. Fair play to ye," he said, smiling. "And the mother! I'd say she'd make even the most impotent man defy gravity for one night… Where's the husband?"

"Dead."

"A widow? God Almighty, she'd probably kill a man for a decent lash. Ye wouldn't know your own name by the time she'd be finished with ye."

"What did ye need me for? It's only a few bags."

"I was doing ye a favour. Ye don't wanna get stuck on your own with all the women, trust me. They'd chew ye up and spit ye out. I wouldn't even recognise ye on me return."

"I suppose."

When we returned to the house, Ma asked Da to bring the food down to the kitchen, but Da thought otherwise.

"Sure, we may as well have it here, Aoife. The kitchen's in rag order."

"I thought yis cleaned it?" Ma queried.

"Ah, we got a start on it, but it's still a bit… It's nicer up here," Da informed her, as Ma eyed him suspiciously, poking around for an ulterior motive.

"Yis can pull that coffee table across. Me, Paddy and Claire can eat off our laps."

I could sense something pre-planned in Da's words.

"Is that okay, ladies?" Ma asked, before Da took the initiative and dragged the coffee table across to them before they answered. Again, the look of suspicion from Ma, as Da pretended not to notice.

An air of normality had thankfully pervaded the visit as Ma conversed with Caroline while Claire and Kelly were like two pen-pals who'd met for the first time. Da and I found ourselves captivated by our fish more so than our company.

"Jesus, that's a cracking bit o' cod isn't it, ladies? The auld fish should be proud of himself," Da critiqued.

"This beats a roast beef, Ma," I innocently blurted, before receiving her death stare again.

"What time is it, Aoife?" Da asked.

"Half seven, John. Why?"

"I was just thinking about the match."

"What match, John?"

"Rovers are playing Bohs. It's on the telly."

Aha! I knew he had an ulterior motive!

"Oh, are they? Good for them."

"Yeah, a big game, ye know?"

"I see."

He's flying a kite, gauging the reaction, looking for support.

I don't want to miss the match either, but I'm not gonna be the sacrificial lamb, not a hope.

"I was thinking…"

Oh Jesus, he's going for it. He's a brave man. Or a very stupid man. We'll soon find out.

"What were ye thinking, John?" Ma asked, looking sternly at him.

"Well, seeing that we're in the sitting room and all…"

"Yes?"

She's really torturing him. This is cruel. This is a human rights violation.

"Would any o' you ladies mind if we put the…turn on the…watch the…"

"Watch what, John?" asked Ma, her sternness unabating.

Aw, this is cringing!

"The eh…the thing…the telly…the match."

He's entered the jungle. There's no way back now!

"The match, John? Really?"

"Yeah, I'm sure Paddy would want to watch it too, wouldn't ye, Paddy?"

The cute fucker! He's dragged me down with him. I hadn't even said a word.

So, this is what the jungle looks like. Quite the place. How do ye get out o' here? Anyone?
Don't say yes!
"Well, em...if Da wants to watch it, I won't object."
Right back at ye, Da!
He had a resigned look on his face that acknowledged my victory over him. His next move was crucial. I watched as he and Ma stared at each other. They were having an intense argument without saying a single word.

"Then again, if you ladies would rather chat, I'm sure we could give it a miss."

Ah, the coward! With the enemy in sight, he decides to retreat.

Ma looked appeased.

"We don't mind, do we, Kelly?" Caroline asked.

"No, not at all. Stick it on."

He's manipulated the support of the majority. What a political stroke! The man's a master politician! Ma's boat has been torpedoed. She's sinking fast.

"Well, if nobody minds, well then what harm, I suppose," Ma said in a false cheerful tone, trying to conceal her anger.

"Grand so," said Da, with a head on him like a child who'd tasted chocolate for the first time, before he switched on the match.

"There's a great atmosphere here tonight in Dalymount Park for this league clash between Bohemians and Shamrock Rovers. The teams are set. The referee looks at his watch, blows his whistle and off we go!"

"So, how's the nursing going, Kelly," Ma asked.

"Aw, busy…always busy."

"Did ye hear that, Patrick? Busy!" said Ma. "You'll have to look up that word in the dictionary."

Oh, she's having herself a wee dig, is she? Why me? I was a mere pawn in the operation.

Da's having the last laugh now. He's a cunning foe.

"Hopefully, I'll be busy soon enough," I half-heartedly replied, not wanting to engage with Ma any further on the matter.

"Are ye working yourself, Caroline?" she asked.

"Yeah, in an office, nothing exciting, but there's some level o' security with it at least. We've had no layoffs yet, touch wood."

Just as the tension in the room began to recede, the smallest member of the Dempsey family introduced himself in his own charming, inimitable way. A nose stuck through the door; its flaring nostrils enchanted by the smell of battered fish. It was lured to the source of the smell. His head appeared first, before his small portly body followed.

"Buddy, what do ye want?" Ma demanded to know.

The timing of his visit answered her question.

"I'll leave ye a bit o' fish if you're a good boy," Da told him.

Buddy commenced a lap of the room.

"Go away, Buddy," said Claire.

"Go back to bed, Bud," I insisted.

"Buddy, you'll get such a spanking if ye bother our guests," Ma threatened.

He left the visitors until last.

"Aw, he's lovely. He's so cute," Kelly complimented.

"Only when he's looking for something," Ma dryly noted.

He put a paw on Kelly's leg.

"Buddy, stop begging!" Ma ordered.

He looked at her with a cheeky face and put both paws on Kelly's leg.

"Buddy, if ye don't get down off her right now, you'll be in your kennel for the night!"

Buddy lowered himself back to the ground, looking defeated. Then, in a demonstration of speed and agility, the likes of which I hadn't seen from him in years, he sprang upon Caroline's lap, grabbed her fish in one precision bite, swung his head back beyond her reach, and darted out the door, scarpering up the stairs.

"Ye little fucker! Wait till I catch ye!" Da said angrily.

Ma's head was in her hands as Claire offered an apology with the sound of Da scampering up the stairs accompanying her words.

"I'm so, so sorry, Caroline!"

"It's okay, Claire, really."

Finally, Ma found her voice. "Caroline, I'm honestly lost for words... This is so embarrassing...I...I..."

"Aoife, it's fine, don't worry."

Upstairs, a war was raging as Da tried to catch Buddy.

"Stay, stay, stay... Good dog... Come back here! Ye little cheeky cunt! I'll be the fuckin' death o' ye, if ye don't drop that fish! One more bite and you're going to the pound, Mister! Give. Give it... Let go. Let go right now! Buddy, I'm not gonna ask ye again!"

Then, silence. An armistice. We heard a bedroom door being slammed before Da descended the stairs. At the bottom he shouted up, "You're getting nothing for a week! No biscuits, no walks, no telly!"

He re-entered the sitting room with a flushed face.

"Jesus, I'm dreadfully sorry about that, Caroline. I'll apologise on his behalf."

"Honestly, forget about it. I love dogs. I know what they're like, trust me."

"I mean, I don't know what his fuckin' problem is. I told him I'd leave him a bit. Ungrateful little arsehole, that's what he is! You have him spoilt, Aoife, that's the problem."

"*I* have him spoilt?! Says himself who was massaging him earlier like he was about to run in Shelbourne Park! I'll tell ye what the problem is with him, John. He's just like all the men in this family, he has the male Dempsey gene!"

Ma's face was now that of someone who'd surrendered.

"I don't suppose ye want this back, Caroline?" Da asked, pointing to the fish in his hand.

"O' course she doesn't want it back, John, for fuck's sake!" Ma snapped.

"Awright, awright! I was just asking! Here, ye can have mine, Caroline. I only took a few bites out of it."

"Ah, thanks for offering, John, but it's really not necessary. You enjoy your dinner."

"Ah no, it is. We look after our guests in this house, don't we, Aoife?"

Ma could only shake her head at Da's words.

"Well, I was enjoying the fish, so…"

"Good woman yourself. Tuck into that... So, what were we talking about before our little friend interrupted?"

Just as Da was salvaging the situation, the whimpers of Buddy travelled through the house.

"Ah, listen to him up there. He's upset," I said.

"Oh, he's upset, is he?!" Ma said. "Not half as upset as he'll be later when I spank his hairy arse black and blue!"

"Ah, Ma, listen to him crying. He knows he was out o' order. He's sorry," I insisted.

"Ah, ye can't be spanking him at his age, Aoife," said Da. "He's an auldfella. It'd be like spanking an old man... Isn't he a gas dog all the same?"

"I'm not finding his brand o' humour very funny at this particular moment, John."

"I mean, his legs are giving out on him, he's half blind, half deaf, yet his appetite for a bit o' mischief is as healthy as ever... Gas little character."

We finished our dinner.

"Mmm, that was lovely, wasn't it, Kelly?" Caroline remarked.

"Yeah, delicious," Kelly agreed, as she looked over at me, struggling to maintain a straight face.

Ma stood up.

"I think a drop o' wine would go down well, ladies."

Nobody disagreed.

"Where did ye leave the wine, John?

"It's in one o' those bags beside ye."

"It's not."

"It has to be."

"Well, I'm telling ye, it's not. There's milk, coffee, sugar and biscuits in one bag…and there's more milk, coffee, sugar and other bits and pieces in the other bag."

"What?! Paddy, you were supposed to pick up the wine in the off-licence."

"I wasn't. I said I'd go into the shop for the coffee, milk and sugar while you were in the chipper."

"No, I said I'd fly into the shop and get all that after I came out o' the chipper."

"Ye didn't. You said ye'd go into the off-licence after ye came out o' the chipper."

Ma's head fell back into her hands. She exhaled before speaking.

"So, yis didn't pick up the wine? Jesus, one o' the few things yis were asked to do! I mean, did yis not notice yis had the same stuff?" she asked in bewilderment.

"Well, we had bags. Da, I thought your bag had the wine in it!"

"I thought yours had the wine in it!"

"So, there's no wine, but we have two jars o' coffee, two bags o' sugar and two litres o' milk! That's just brilliant, isn't it? I suppose I should count meself lucky that yis didn't arrive back with two bags o' magic beans!"

"We were up to our eyes, Aoife. We had to look after milk, coffee, sugar, wine, bags o' chips, fish, onion rings… and there was only the two of us," Da argued.

"Ladies, again, I'm sorry about this."

"Not at all, Aoife. Don't be silly," Caroline responded.

In her, I was beginning to see the source of Kelly's affability.

Da rose from his seat again.

"Anyone fancy a cup o' coffee? We've loads o' that."

We all looked at each other and smiled before we burst out laughing.

The rest of the evening passed without any further incident. The conversation was kept light, unemployment and the recession given a well-deserved night off. If I felt there was a danger of them rearing their ugly austerity-ridden heads, I studiously steered the conversation down a side road.

By ten o'clock, the pair had had their fill of the Dempsey family for one night, maybe forever, and made for the door.

"It was great meeting yis. We must do this again sometime, a second attempt," Ma said, as she ushered them out.

"Absolutely. We'll have to have yis all over at ours," replied Caroline.

"Sorry about all the carry-on."

"It made the evening, Aoife. We'll have a hard act to follow to make our one as memorable as yours. Ha ha."

"For your sake, I hope it won't be. Ha ha."

I waited impatiently for Ma to close the door, hoping to end the night positively.

"Bye."

"See yis all."

"Bye, see ye later."

"Good luck."

"So long."

Finally, the door closed, with Ma leaning her back against it.

"Thank God that's over with. What a disaster!" she bemoaned.

"I thought it went well, better than I expected," I gaily announced.

"Patrick, you'll be doing yourself a favour by doing *me* the favour of not testing me bloody patience! And as for that dog, I swear, I'll have him put down, and you along with him!"

"Ah, Ma, ye'd hurt his feelings if he heard ye saying that about him!"

Da untucked his shirt, giving his belly it's freedom back, as he flicked through the stations, before commenting, "I told ye it'd be grand, Aoife, didn't I?"

Chapter 34
Mount Paddy

Despite spring's arrival, the country's economic winter showed no signs of ending. I continued to take my reserved seat on the unemployment merry-go-round, sending off countless job applications, before my enthusiasm was met with silence, or at best, a courteous response thanking me for my interest but highlighting my lack of experience, or my lack of qualifications. Always a lack of something. Never a lack of nouns stating what that something was.

With the country stuck in a blocked toilet and our politicians the plumbers that were charged with the gargantuan task of unblocking it, any hope of a recovery lay in the distant future, if at all. The jobs market was a dog fight, and I was like a poodle having to scrap with German shepherds. My stubbornness could motivate me to suffer another dozen laps on the merry-go-round until I was dizzy, but Einstein's definition of insanity was seeming ever more pertinent. A change of course was imperative. I had to step off the rusty fairground attraction and reacquaint myself with the dreaded world that I had once been so eager to escape from. I made the decision, having accepted its unavoidability. I'd go back to education.

The notion wasn't as foreboding as I imagined it would be. Maturity, perhaps. Desperation, more likely.

What'll I do?

The question threatened to sabotage my plan in its infancy. I needed the input of the more reliable brain of my other half.

"Ye read a fair bit... Why don't ye do something that involves writing, like journalism or..."

"Journalism? Nah, I'd be no use at that."

"How do ye know? You're very observant, that's half the job."

"Yeah, but I don't have much to say about anything."

"Not much to say? Paddy, ye never shut up! And you're always moaning about the state o' the country and questioning everything. All you've to do is put it all down on paper."

The longer she talked, the more she talked me into it. She sold it like a canny saleswoman, introducing the idea, then supporting it with her unique selling point to capture my interest, before getting into the finer details to finalise the deal. She could sell water to a fish.

"Ye could apply for a diploma course, they're easy to get into, and then take it from there."

"Are there jobs in it though?"

"Well, it'd keep ye busy for the time being anyway. Ye'd be doing something that interests ye for a change. What else are ye gonna do? Wait until the country recovers and crawl back behind the bar of a pub? How long will that be?"

I let the idea off the leash and let it potter about my brain, awaiting the doubting thoughts to stick their claws into it and tear it apart, before performing an autopsy on it and concluding that it was a woeful idea. But the thoughts never came.

"Yeah, I might do it. It'd be interesting anyway if nothing else."

For the first time, I felt that the serpentine road upon which I trudged was leading somewhere, to something. To have even the first draft of something, induced a zeal within me that unemployment had rendered dormant. I clung to the aspiration while clinging to her who sowed it and, without whom, I'd still be subservient to the unholy trinity, an authoritarian regime which punished me for any displays of fervour, indicting me on acts of heresy.

After numerous attempts, I was finally conquering the perilous Mount Paddy, a mountain that dwarfed Everest in its enormity. Having climbed carefully, wary of the dangers of a misstep, I reached its once elusive summit. As I stood on it, exhausted, but in awe of my feat, a disturbing realisation suppressed my jubilance. From there, the only way to go was down.

Chapter 35
An Abject Toss of a Coin

Of all the ideas I'd ever had, it was by far the most audacious and without doubt, the most intriguing of them all. It was an idea so mammoth, that when the doubting voice offered no opposition to it, I coerced it into offering a token argument to convince me of my folly.

Once it had acquainted itself with me, it didn't feel like a foreign concept, but instead, like something that had been hibernating in my mind all along, just waiting for the right moment to rise from its slumber. It was an idea that refused to dilute itself, catering only to extreme outcomes. It would either be the start of a new life or the end of a life, my greatest decision or my biggest mistake.

She was my cane. The longer I strode with it, the more reliant I was on its support, the more I feared it being stolen from my grasp. Love was an ambiguous word, too generic to accurately describe my vehemence. Love had stepped off the bus at the previous stop. I was obsessed with her. There was only one way in which I'd truly satisfy my obsessive cravings, only one means by which I'd strengthen my grip of the cane and ensure I'd never fall.

It was now June. Six months since New Year's Eve.

How long can I wait? A year? Two years?

I was impatient, or perhaps distrusting, for I feared that her eyes would wander. Time was my nemesis.

It was a ludicrous idea, but great ones always were. The besotted romantic in me, or the obsessive, thought nothing of the obvious financial hindrances. I imagined the romantic scene on Bray beach at dusk. With one arm slung round her, I'd rummage in my pocket with my other hand and pull out the ring.

What do ye think, Kelly? Will ye?

Oh, Paddy darling, my love! I was wondering when ye'd ever ask!

Nothing to it. It'd be achieved with less effort than it took to piss without wetting the seat.

Kelly Dempsey. A cracker of a name.

I imagined the scene again, trying to do so from her perspective rather than my own.

Will I what? Marry ye?! Have ye lost your marbles, Paddy?! You've no money, no job, nowhere to live, and where in the name o' God did ye get that ring?! It looks like something from a fuckin' Christmas cracker!

When reality strikes, it does so with the force of a cannonball. In all my certainty of the necessity of my proposal, I had failed to consider that she socialised with reality more in one day than I did in a week, and that the impulsiveness of it would undoubtedly leave her more bemused than elated. Maybe time was my ally, I thought, and that the passing of the coming years would see our bond strengthen as well as my job prospects improving with a newly acquired qualification. It might even see the first sprouts of an economic recovery rising from the ground. Time could extract the element of uncertainty from the proposal. I came to a compromise.

The original idea was abandoned. Instead, I'd assure her of my unfaltering commitment to her and speak about my intentions for us in the future. I hoped that it would be enough to prevent her eyes from exploring while also sparing me the burden of having to marry her sometime soon. It was such a simple plan that I reckoned it couldn't possibly fail. I mulled over it, double checking for any tripwires that I may have missed. All clear.

But, if I'd learned anything in recent years, it was that in the life and times of Paddy Dempsey, there was always something that could go wrong. If I hadn't found it, it was because I hadn't looked hard enough!

Finding myself in such a lavish restaurant stripped me naked before covering me in a blanket of insecurity. The higher social standing of those around me made me suspect that they eyed me dubiously as an interloper. The menu, which read like Marie Antoinette's shopping list, was being discussed effusively by them.

So, this is how the other half live.

"What are ye gonna have, Paddy?"

"Napoleon's balls, for all I know."

"This one sounds nice."

"Never mind if it sounds nice. With a French name, beans on toast would sound nice."

I caught the attention of the hovering waiter.

"How may I be of assistance, sir?"

"We were just wondering if there's anything in particular that ye'd recommend?"

"Oh, I'd highly recommend the *Côte de boeuf.* It's a beef rib for two, served with blue cheese butter, sautéed girolle mushrooms and potatoes. An exquisite dish, sir."

"Do ye wanna go for that, Paddy?"

"Yeah, go on."

"And to drink?"

"Whichever wine is best suited with it," Kelly replied.

"I know the very one."

I bet he does. It won't be the cheap bottle o' piss I have in mind.

Off he went, as I earwigged on the conversations circulating around me, wanting to learn the language of the elite. Property, work, stress, holidays, cars. A different world. Its appeal wasn't without an ugly materialism that being unemployed made me both crave and despise in equal measure.

"Jesus, Kel, you fit in here. I stand out like a wart on a knob end."

"Sssh! Ye *do*, talking like that!"

"Did ye hear your man over there mention the bonus he got? *He's* having himself a decent recession. He's probably a banker."

"And I suppose you'd turn it down if you were him?"

"Well, no…but it's not as if *he* needs it, is it? All *he's* short of is a second garage for another Merc. What a wanker!"

"Jesus Christ, Paddy! Bankers and wankers! Can we change the subject?"

It was her birthday, so I'd decided to dispense with a large chunk of that week's state handout to celebrate it appropriately. I'd also hoped that the occasion and the setting would provide a perfect backdrop for my marriage manifesto. It had been painstakingly worded and was now due its recitation. I was eager to deliver it, but also fearful of her sober response, thinking that the exorbitantly priced wine could prove to be a shrewd investment.

We ate and drank, my mind wandering from the conversation at hand, as I watched her lips move, her expression change, only hearing the voice in my own head as I entertained last-minute changes to my manifesto. I caught words likes 'jobs' and 'opportunities' as I wrestled with my linguistic quandary. Given time, I felt I'd phrased it as best as my grasp of the English language would allow and that any further editing was futile.

I drank a mouthful of wine to prepare myself before I noticed that Kelly's face had changed. She looked worried. Rather than ask what was troubling her, I reckoned my manifesto would return a smile to her face.

Say it, say it, say it now!

"Kelly, yourself and meself have been seeing each other for a while, right? Well, I just wanted ye to know that I really love ye. I'm serious about us, and I hope that we'll get married someday. And don't worry, I'm not rushing or anything. I don't mean as in next month or next year, just…ye know, at some point down the road, when I've a few quid in me pocket."

Bullseye!

Her brow furrowed.

"What? Paddy, were ye not listening to what I said?"

"To what ye…?"

"I'm moving to Australia."

My mouth opened to speak, only for my bottom lip to sag listlessly. It was as if she'd reached down my throat and pulled out my tongue.

"You're what?! Why?"

"I've just told ye. 'Cause there's better pay for nurses over there. They're offering loads o' places to Irish nurses. The wages and the hours here are a joke. I'd be mad to turn down the opportunity. There's no reason for me to stay."

"Am I not a reason?"

"Ye are…but…"

"But what? I'm not enough of a reason?"

"Ye are, Paddy. It's just that I have to think o' meself too. I don't want to end up like…"

"Like *me*, ye mean!" I tried to restrain the anger in my voice.

"I didn't say that!"

"Ye don't have to! What about everything I just said? Is that all one-way?"

"No, o' course not!"

"Well then?"

"Well then, what?"

"Why are ye leaving?"

"I've just told ye…twice. We're going around in circles."

After all her talking, a few lousy Aussie dollars were all that was required for her to dump me like an overdue shite.

Fuckin' bitch!

I got up to leave.

"Where are ye going?"

"Home. If you're dumping me, I'm not hanging around," I said, rising from my chair.

"Oh, sit down, Paddy! Who said I was dumping ye?"

"Well, it's the same thing. Either way, we're finished!"

"It's not the same thing. Will ye sit down and hear me out."

I took my seat and awaited her spiel.

"Paddy, I agree with everything ye said. Ye think I want to head off to the other side o' the world and leave ye behind? That's not what I want. What I want is… I was hoping…hoping that ye'd come with me."

My anger was supplanted by confusion.

"Go with ye? Nah, I can't."

"Why not?"

"This is me home. There's me family and…I don't know, I just can't! Anyway, I don't have a trade or a degree or anything. They'd be quick enough showing me the door."

"Ye can stay for a year on a work visa."

"Awright, and after a year?"

"We can cross that bridge when we come to it. At the very least ye'd have a year to make some money."

"Sure, what would I do down there?"

"More than what you're doing here!"

"What if I go and it's not for me?"

"Well, at least come with me and find out. It'd be an experience, an opportunity."

"There could be better opportunities here that I'd miss out on. Things'll pick up eventually."

"What opportunities? There's nothing keeping ye here, Paddy. You're a smart fella. Why should ye waste your life here, sitting around watching telly all day? You're better than that."

"It may be a shite life, but it's *my* life and it's about the only thing that I can claim is mine!"

"Well, isn't that all the more reason to come with me?"

"And where would I live?"

"With *me*. One o' me friends is over in Sydney. She's raving about the place. Her flatmate's moving out, so…"

"Can ye promise me you'll want to come home after a year?"

She hesitated. "I don't know, Paddy… You're looking too far ahead. A year's a good bit away."

"And Australia's even further away."

"God, ye'd swear it was a different planet the way you're going on!"

"It might as well be! And what about me plans for that course?"

"I'm sure ye could do something similar over there."

"What about your ma?"

"Please don't bring me ma into this to suit your argument."

"Well, you're making sure to *avoid* bringing her into it 'cause she doesn't suit *yours*."

"She won't be alone. Me brother and sister will still be here, and I'll be in contact with her all the time."

It was as if she had foreseen my reaction and had prepared answers for every question that she knew I'd ask and solutions to every problem she'd expected me to present.

"Well, you've obviously been considering this for a while, so why am I only finding out about it now?"

"'Cause I'm only after getting the visa. I applied for it a while back."

"So ye knew the whole time that ye'd be leaving, but ye kept playing me along anyway!"

"It wasn't like that! I wasn't sure whether I'd get it or not. I didn't know where I stood. And the closer we were becoming, the harder it was to bring up."

We reached a stalemate. A silence ensued. She had presented her case, and I, mine. Where we were to go from there, I had no idea. Her face was lost somewhere between anger and disappointment. I imagined mine was a mirror image.

"When are ye planning on leaving?"

"Next week."

"Well, send me a postcard, won't ye?" I said sarcastically.

"Aw, Paddy, please don't be like that!"

"Like what?"

"At least sleep on it."

"I don't need to. I'm not going. This is home."

"You're the one always complaining about the place!"

"Yeah, but I don't think the grass is greener everywhere else!"

Unbeknownst to me, my raised voice had attracted the attention of others. The waiter approached our table.

"I'm sorry, sir, but I'm afraid you're disturbing some of our guests."

I turned to him and used him as an outlet for my anger.

"Tell me, *sir*, what's the French for 'fuck off'?!"

He was momentarily taken aback before replying, "I'm afraid if you continue to speak so loudly, I may have to ask you to leave."

"No need. I was just about to!"

Kelly was sitting across the table from me with a face that was reminiscent of the faces that stared at me after the fight in O'Connell's.

"I can't believe you're being like this about it, Paddy."

"And what way did ye expect me to be?"

"Given your circumstances, I assumed ye'd want to come with me."

"Well, ye assumed wrongly."

"Paddy, don't let this bloody country dictate your life."

"I'm not gonna let *you* dictate me life!"

"If that's what ye feel I'm doing, then fine! There's nothing else I can say."

I rose from my seat again, leaving the bill on the table.

"I'm off."

"Don't leave like this!"

"I'm not the one leaving, you are!"

As I stepped away from the table, she muttered, "Ye know I love ye, Paddy."

"If ye really did, ye wouldn't be fuckin' off to the other side o' the world when I needed ye most."

"That's unfair!" she protested.

"Yeah? Well, so is life. That's something I've learned the hard way recently."

With that parting remark, I exited the restaurant, leaving behind the fear of a new life for the familiarity of a stagnating existence. I conceitedly expected her to chase after me. A hundred yards down the road, I glanced back. She wasn't there.

I walked along the main street with a battle of conflicting emotions raging inside my head, all scrapping to be the last left standing. I cursed her. I cursed myself for investing so heavily in her. I cursed the country for denying me a return on that investment.

Anger circled around me like a swarm of bees in the night sky, waiting to possess me. I wanted to surrender to it and let it lead me down its chosen one-way street of self-destruction. But anger required energy that I didn't possess. I was despondent. Far worse.

I arrived home, starved of the well-being that I'd had for the last six months.

I lay in bed, questioning her motives.

Is she really going to Australia or is that just an excuse to dump me?

Was I ever good enough for her?

Does she really want me to go with her or did she ask knowing I'd refuse?

I closed my eyes knowing that to wake up the next morning would be to travel six months back in time. One step forward and two steps back, the patented dance routine of Paddy Dempsey. I made a pledge to not reacquaint myself with my half-life from months prior. But I knew myself enough to know that the value of such a pledge would rise and fall relative to the fluctuations of my mood.

I would now abjectly toss a coin, the two sides of which were happiness and dejection, and bet everything I owned on it landing on the latter.

Chapter 36
Death Nurtures Life

My phone rang. A dearth of jobs and of people who I could still claim as being friends, led me to conclude that the call could only be from one person. It was a week on from her announcement, a timeframe which I had spent trying to prove my superiority over her in the stubborn art of the 'silent treatment.' My plan, if it could be branded as such, had been to deny her my presence, my voice, even my messages, until she realised I wasn't for turning. I had hoped this would make her envision her bleak future, alone in a foreign land, surrounded by a plethora of bronzed faces, but the only pasty one that mattered being thousands of miles away. I believed that offering her a taste of her life-to-be would beget an appreciation for the life she'd be leaving behind. I'd make her think that she needed me more than I needed her, that I could walk away quicker than she could hope to run away, that my future without her was more bearable than hers without me. My perseverance, it seemed, had proven too strong an enemy for her. My tales of woe, of self-pity and of self-destruction had made her underestimate me and all my powers of obstinacy. The phone's irritating ringtone was the fanfare that heralded my victory in the war of the minds. Its endless ringing denoted desperation. I imagined her humble voice as she spoke of how she'd had time to digest my opinion on the matter, and after much careful consideration, had come to realise that the merits of staying were greater than those of leaving.

"What's up?" I answered curtly, eagerly waiting to hear her contrite words.

"I was just calling to say goodbye."

Goodbye?

"You're…you're saying what?"

"Goodbye."

Bollocks.

It was *I* who had underestimated *her*. My supposed plan suddenly unmasked itself to reveal the naive arrogance that lay behind it. I tried in vain to be heard as anything but the crumbling ruin on the other end of the line.

"Wh…where are ye?"

"In the airport."

"The airport! Why didn't ye call me sooner?! We could've met up."

"If ye wanted to meet, why didn't *you* ring *me*?!"

"I thought… I don't know what I thought… So, you're definitely going then?"

"Yeah. And you're definitely staying?"

I hesitated. For the first time, doubt dipped its toe into the waters of my conviction before I held its head down in those very waters and drowned it.

"Yeah, I am." I had sought an adamant tone of voice, but I assumed my words had sounded as subdued on her end as they had on mine.

"The door will still be open if ye change your mind."

"Likewise."

"I won't, Paddy. Sorry."

"Neither will I."

Silence followed. Our staunchly held positions on the matter had led us to a conversational impasse.

"I suppose this is it then, is it?" I asked dejectedly, unable to think of anything more meaningful to say.

"Yeah, I think so… You'll look after yourself, won't ye?"

"I'll do me best."

"I'll miss ye, Paddy."

"I wish I got a bit more time with ye."

"I know… I'll keep in touch anyway," she said.

"I don't know if that's a good idea."

"Ah, don't be bitter."

"It's not being bitter. It's just… It'd be too hard if you're there but not there, if that makes sense. Every time I'd hear from ye, I'd be hoping you've changed your mind. I don't wanna be disappointed again and again."

"Yeah, I understand… Listen, me battery's about to run out. I forgot to charge the shaggin' thing. I don't know what else to say…"

Tell her ye love her!

"I love ye, Kelly… Did ye hear me, Kelly? I said I love…"

The line was dead.

Fuck it anyway!

The enjoyable life I'd been living for the last few months ended abruptly. I allowed myself to feel the sensation of two tears sliding down my cheeks before I wiped them away defiantly. To prevent any more being shed, I lay on the bed and closed my eyes, feeling them well up behind my eyelids. In the darkness, I felt myself being lured towards a debilitating presence. My new friend in waiting.

"Oh, hello there, stranger. What's your name?"

"I'm depression."

"Nice to meet ye, depression. What do you do for a living?"

"I find a person and cling to them. Then I torment, manipulate and control them."

"Just anybody?"

"Nah, I'm choosy about who."

"Are ye busy these days?"

"With this recession I'm run off me feet! But I'll find the time for you, Paddy. You'll be my most important client."

"Why me?"

"You've earned it!"

"Oh, I see. And when do ye start?"

"I already have. Do ye feel that emptiness inside ye? That lethargy? That unwillingness to face the world? That dread for tomorrow?"

"Yeah."

"That's me!"

It was as if she died. She may as well have – the result was no different. A part of me embraced the notion, for death offered closure. It spared me the false hope that would be the ruin of me and allowed me to place all my memories of her on a dusty shelf somewhere in the back of my mind.

Death nurtures life; the felled trees that become a house, the fossil fuels that heat it, the slaughtered animal that nourishes its tenants, the inheritance that enriches them. In that same vein, perhaps the cessation of the relationship would serve to benefit me in a way I'd yet to discover. But the waning light from such rhetoric found nothing amidst the darkness to illuminate. It soon faded like a dying star, a once luminous beacon of life reduced to a floating corpse, aimlessly drifting through space.

It felt like an anchor had been chained to my ankle, such was the crucifying burden that I dragged round with me. It was a burden that befriended me like a stray dog, one who sought my attention for all its perverse tricks that it proved quite efficient at performing. In the days after she left, it glowered at me menacingly as it sank its teeth into me. In the succeeding days, I let it run amuck in the hope that it would tire, knowing that to give it my attention would diminish the chances of ever seeing the back of it. To ignore it was to defeat it.

I'd received a message from her soon after she left.

'In Sydney now. Come over whenever you want.'

She'd already been shelved. I didn't respond, as much as I wished to. For my own sake I had to erase her from my memory.

I nonchalantly told Ma and Da of her departure, dressing it up as being a minor inconvenience, hoping to conceal my despair.

With the stray dog forever by my side, days were endless, sometimes bearable, other times unbearable. The stray dog stripped everything of meaning, of worth, of joy. It found a taste for my self-esteem and devoured what was left of it. It sniffed out my few interests that made my life tolerable and dropped a steaming turd on them. If Popey entered my mind, its paws frantically dug up the unholy trinity from the hole in which I had buried it. Nothing was off limits to the growling beast as it marked its ever-expanding territory.

Despite my attempts to forget her, I was still enamoured with her. Her ghost haunted me. Everywhere I went seemed to unwillingly spark a memory of her. Trying not to think of her was like trying not to breathe.

My mind was a rope being pulled to and fro in an excruciating game of tug-of-war, and I feared the coming moment when it would snap.

My half-life trudged on as weeks became months, a timeframe in which I'd hoped the stray dog would have lost interest in me and found a new friend. But it seemed to be determined to prove its loyalty to me, constantly gnawing at my perseverance and chasing people away so that it could have me all to itself. I started to binge drink again as a means of avoiding its company for a few precious hours, but the respite came at a cost. It would re-emerge in the thrall of a hangover, more menacing, more malicious and with more bloodlust than ever before.

How much longer can I take this?

I refrained from answering the question for fear of the answer.

With winter nearing, I was sitting in Dunphy's Bar one evening, asking myself the question again. This time, full of drink, I answered without hesitation.

No longer.

I thought of Popey's decision. It no longer seemed so incomprehensible. I could now appreciate the appeal of the escape it offered. Our paths were merging. I wanted to escape too, by whatever means necessary. I thought of how I'd do it. I kept thinking and thinking until my thoughts were of Popey again, and of how our personalities were homogenous only to a certain point.

Popey's final act in this world was to surrender. The stray dog had smelled his fear and made one last fatal attack. I was too stubborn to surrender to the stray dog, and too determined to find myself a pig who'd allow me to climb onto its back. I was too aware that the stray dog had befriended me as much as a result of the country's problems as my own, and that many others were undoubtedly encountering it as the recession prolonged. As the bankers and the politicians dined in style with their fellow gentry, it quietly prowled the streets, searching for its next victim. I needed to divorce myself from it before sanity divorced itself from *me*. The means of doing so was just an overdue phone call away. I had to free myself from the delusional chains of patriotism that I'd shackled myself in and was using as a convenient excuse to do nothing. I had to leave Ireland.

The only thing the country could offer me was unemployment. I had no life to speak of that could entice me to stay. The hope in the distance was nothing more than an optical illusion; a haphazard political manifesto sewn together with enough savvy spin to pass itself off as some form of coherent plan to lift the country off its knees. What would await me on the other side of the world was a mystery. But uncertainty wouldn't dissuade me. The possibility of something in Australia, surpassed the certainty of nothing in Ireland. If it was a gamble, it was the safest gamble I could take.

Alas, I still couldn't bear leaving, but I took consolation from the fact that I'd be doing so in the company of my peers. I was a paid-up member of the lost generation whose exodus would create a gaping hole in the national family tree, and whose unwanted purpose in life would be to travel the world in search of any scraps of work that other countries might be willing to offer. We'd be praised by the government in our success or commemorated by it in our failure. Either way, the state would hobble along, regardless of our collective fate.

Like so many Irish people before me, I'd seek a life that I could be proud to call mine.

The stray dog licked me and stared up at me with doting eyes, whimpering, pleading with me to stay, but I was done with Ireland. It offered me nothing but the status quo, and the status quo would be the death of me. It might have already been the death of Popey. I'd never know.

With so much of my identity entwined with Ireland and with a much-maligned yet endearing town on its Dublin-Wicklow border, to leave felt traitorous. But she was right. I *was* allowing the country to dictate my life, and I couldn't bear another year of not knowing what my fate would be at the hands of my dictator. It was agonising to think of leaving the stage on which I'd performed my most memorable roles. But the prospect of staying hurt even more. I needed a new stage, a different audience, a more accomplished play.

The stray dog was growing by the week, becoming ever stronger and more aggressive. I knew, given time, it could overpower me. I feared Popey's fate. I'd learned from the harrowing finality of his decision, the dangers of tolerating the intolerable for too long. His tragic end would be the tinder to ignite my new beginning. Death nurtures life.

Chapter 37

The Buyer Becomes
the Seller

Eager to inform Kelly that I'd found God and that he was an Aussie wearing a cork hat, I re-read the message she had sent me after she left and began to type.

"Is that offer still…"

I stopped. Since her departure, I'd cast her in the role of the damsel in distress awaiting rescue from her loneliness. But time passes, and in doing so, it changes lives, circumstances, people.

Maybe she's already forgotten about me.

I hesitated. I foresaw the reply informing me of her new 'fella,' of how she'd waited patiently for me and couldn't put her life on hold for me any longer. But even such a gut-wrenching reply would be better than never knowing.

I wrote.

"Is that offer still on the table?"

I waited impatiently for a reply before she wrote back to me the following day.

"Sorry…"

With that one word, the stray dog was ready to pounce on me before I read on.

"Sorry for taking so long to get back to you. Work was mad. Yeah, of course the offer's still on the table! Are you coming over?"

In an instant, the stray dog was put down. My devoted, sadistic companion was no more.

My broad smile must've been like one from a childhood photograph. To stretch my cheeks in such a fashion almost felt alien. I wrote back.

"Yes. Don't know when. As soon as possible."

If only telling the family would be as easy.

All four of us were watching television the following night.

"Oh, by the way, I meant to tell yis something," I said, knowing that there was no point in waiting any longer to deliver the news.

"What is it, love?" Ma asked.

"Ye know the way I was saying that Kelly's in Australia?"

"Yeah," she said.

"I was thinking o' going over."

"For a few weeks?"

"Well…"

"How would ye afford it?"

"I'd be staying with Kelly."

"And what about the flight?" she asked.

"I can afford it, one-way."

I had accidently dropped the guillotine blade.

"One-way?" Ma asked.

"Yeah."

At that moment, I felt as if I had torn her heart out and laid it on the table for her to witness its last beat in the brief moment before she died. Her ensuing silence stung. I would've preferred her to lambast me over the folly of what she deemed as being an impetuous decision. Anything but silence. It indicated that she couldn't offer legitimate opposition to the idea, knowing full well my predicament. But more so, it was a tell-tale sign that she was upset. Her attempt at hiding her emotions was the very thing that exhibited them.

"I can get a visa to live and work over there for a year."

She hesitated in replying. "Is it what ye want?"

"Yeah."

"Will ye be happy over there?"

Now it was my turn to hesitate. "More than I am here."

"Don't be going over there thinking that ye have to, to appease us."

"I'm not, Ma. I want to. I'll make a few quid and..."

"Money's not everything either. We can give ye a few bob when you're stuck, can't we, John?"

"O' course we can, Aoife, but he's a young man now. He wants to make his own way."

"I know he does. It's just that it's not what I ever envisioned for him when we were rearing him. I saw him as a...a... I don't know... Doing something that didn't involve him emigrating to the other side o' the world."

"Sure, some of his schoolmates are probably in the same boat," said Da.

"They are," I confirmed.

"This place will drive him to the madhouse, Aoife. It's a man's nature to wanna fend for himself. Not being able to do that messes with your head. You women wouldn't understand."

"Says the man who has his dinner handed to him every evening! I've never heard such horseshite in me life, John!"

I could sense an argument arising and interjected promptly. "And anyway, it's not like I'm going to the dark side o' the moon. It'll only be for a while. I'll keep in touch and all that."

I found myself delivering Kelly's pitch. Ma was now the unwilling recipient of it as I had been months previously. But just like me, I was sure she'd come around to it.

"Is she gonna look after ye?" she asked.

"Ah, the million-dollar question, Paddy boy. Those manky cacks won't clean themselves."

"I should talk to her meself, just to run over a few things."

"Jesus Christ, Aoife! The poor girl will change her mind about him by the time you're finished babbling."

"Ma, she doesn't want a lecture about me washing and ironing!"

"And I suppose you're gonna do it yourself? That'd be a first. I don't want ye looking like some tramp over there."

The Irish mother was a peculiar creature. She wouldn't want her son expecting to be mothered by his other half, but she'd be the first to scrutinise his appearance and utter the words, 'Is she not looking after ye?'

The reality of the opportunity that Australia presented to me was dawning on her.

"When are ye planning on leaving?" she asked.

"Kelly told me it takes a few weeks to get the visa organised."

"So, we've a few more weeks with ye anyway."

"Jesus, Ma. I'm not dying!"

I tried to think of something to say to lighten the mood before Claire shoehorned herself into the conversation.

"Aw, you're so lucky, Paddy! The weather, the beaches…"

"There's nothing lucky about it, Claire. Don't be daft!" Ma barked. "This bloody country! It was the same for *our* generation, me parents' generation and me grandparents' generation. I don't know why we don't just give birth to the kids abroad in the first place and save them the price o' the bloody flight!"

"Ma, when Paddy leaves, can I have his room?"

"No, Claire. What's the point? Your brother will be home in twelve months' time.

I couldn't bring myself to lie to confirm her statement, nor to be honest and contradict it. I said nothing, hoping that my silence was ambiguous enough to be left open to interpretation.

Chapter 38
The Prison of the Dead

October 20th, 2010

I was to leave around midnight for an early flight to London which would bring me to Singapore, before setting off on the final leg to Sydney. I didn't have much baggage, bar what lay between my ears. I could picture myself having my head weighed before boarding the plane. I stuffed my clothes and anything I deemed essential into a suitcase. It pained me to forsake my array of books and albums. So much of my life was interwoven into their prose and lyrics. Part of me wished to leave them as a reminder of where home was, as an enticement to tempt me to return, an eclectic treasure chest buried for safe keeping, its location marked on the map for its eventual unearthing in time to come.

All I had left to do was to wait. I double checked everything. Passport, ticket, visa, wallet. I treble checked – quadruple checked. I flicked through the television stations, not being able to focus my attention on any of the programmes. I started to restlessly walk up and down the house. My mind was running ahead of me. I'd killed so much time so effortlessly over recent years and yet there I was, struggling to see off a few hours. I couldn't relax. I knew a few pints would settle me but the thought of arriving at the airport in a drunken stupor made me dismiss the idea. By the early evening, I had to get out of the house to expel some of my energy. Walking over the bridge onto Quinsborough Road, my mind was a pendulum, swinging perpetually. Despite never having been more assured of the validity of my decision, I regretted its unavoidability more than ever. Nostalgia was penetrating what I thought to be an impenetrable will to leave. I began to wonder if my decision had been made in haste.

Is it too late to change me mind?

When I reached the Carlisle Grounds, I expected to be pulled to the bottom of its deep reservoir of memories, but my attention was curiously drawn to the lofty Celtic cross that lay outside its walls, commemorating Bray men who died in the Great War. Having been encouraged by their politicians to fight in it, on the premise that doing so would be in the national interest, their sacrifice was quickly forgotten. Those who survived returned to a country that was determined to erase them and their dead comrades from its history, deeming them all as being an embarrassing blemish on the face of *Kathleen Ni Houlihan*. In some capacity, I could relate to the indignance they must've felt as their country turned its back on them. In need of material to inspire new folk songs and wanting to trim the fat that was so detrimental to her economic anatomy, it was now my turn to be spurned by the *Sean-Bhean bhocht*.

I crossed the train tracks and walked along the seafront. The summer throngs were gone. In their place were closed tuck shops along a deserted promenade, and a lawn that was still recovering from the departed carnival. Its once boisterous pubs were quietly sitting in the shade as the sun slipped behind their rooftops. I soaked in as much of the scene as I could before emigration banished it to memory.

As if to guard myself from the temptation to change my mind that I knew my surroundings would provoke, I thought of the homeless man I once encountered. At fifteen, I was naive, buoyant, and ignorant of a parallel world populated by those who weren't. Yet, on that day, I saw the antithesis of my unworldliness. I saw the consequences of making too many mistakes and squandering too many opportunities.

Still homeless?

Still alive?

Alone?

My memory of him in his bedraggled state, seeking someone with whom he could share his affliction, now seemed more affecting than it did then. Perhaps it was because I feared the worst for him, or probably, selfishly, because I imagined myself as him, trudging along the seafront, possessing nothing other than a bottle of whiskey and scant hope. I still wasn't him by a distance, yet I feared I was becoming him, as if that day I had met an apparition of my future self who had come to warn me of what lay ahead.

Barry Cunningham!

If Popey's death alerted me to the dangers of staying, and Kelly Lawless offered me a means of leaving, Barry Cunningham gifted me the willpower to ignore the last-minute doubts that were troubling me.

I gazed at the horizon, knowing my uncertain future lay beyond it. At the end of Strand Road, I turned and walked up Putland Road's incline, remembering how we used to race our bikes to the top. Whoever won was owed a ten pence toffee, whoever came last had the choice of receiving a dead arm or a Chinese burn. Childhood's magic lay in its simplicity. The cost of failure was trivial. A dead arm or a Chinese burn. It was a far cry from having to choose between unemployment or emigration.

At the top, I began my journey homeward, down Vevay Road. The sun was bidding its final farewell and would lie in wait for me on the other side of the world. The main street's vacant buildings acted as a reminder as to why I was leaving. Shop owners who were fortunate enough to still be in business were pulling down their shutters, an act that perfectly captured how I was feeling regarding my imminent departure. I crossed over the bridge onto Castle Street and bypassed my turn-off for Dargan Street. I continued along to Dublin Road, which led me to the entrance to St Peter's graveyard.

I knew the deed that had to be done. I diligently roamed the cluttered cemetery, inspecting grave after grave, row after row, circling, seeing the same graves twice, retracing my steps, up, down, across, this way, that way, searching all night if I had to, the names barely visible in the dying light.

There were extravagant graves and modest graves.
Cahill, Sweeney, Fogarty, McCourt...
Immaculate ones and unkept ones.
Coyne, Birmingham, Furlong, Cowan...
Old deaths and recent deaths.
McDonagh, Nolan, Kennedy, Shaw...
Countless stories beneath my feet.
Mullen, Enright, McCann, Plunkett...

The town's history buried in the ground.
Morgan, Reid, Canning...
Pope.
The headstone was black marble with gold lettering.

In memory of Alan Pope
Feb 12th 1988 – Aug 6th 2009
Beloved brother of Aisling and Susan,
cherished son of Aidan and Deirdre.
Blessed are we who knew you in this life,
may we be blessed again to know you in the next life.
RIP

Seeing his grave for the first time neither exacerbated nor alleviated how I felt towards his death. I reread the inscription a second time, then a third time, as if trying to extract a deeper meaning from its generic words. Surrounding me were identical headstones, the inscriptions on which were probably similar. I quickly concluded that my memories of him were a far greater memorial to him than a slab of marble could ever be. Conversely, my apology wasn't the eloquent graveside oration that I'd envisioned myself delivering.

"Sorry, mate. I should've known... I don't know, if ye'd said something... I might've... Sorry about the funeral... that was just, just me making a hash o' things... I miss ye, pal. I've thought about ye every day since ye... I still can't get me head round why ye... Sure, it doesn't matter a shite now anyway..."

It suddenly dawned on me the reason, the *real* reason I didn't attend the burial. The hangover was a convenient excuse. The truth was, I was afraid to watch him being lowered into the ground to be buried for eternity, fearful that I would be overcome with guilt upon witnessing such a sight and become reduced to a blubbering wreck. I was experiencing death for the first time and was unable to bear it. I did what was instinctive to me. I turned and ran. Nothing could catch me while I was running.

"He's popular today," a man behind me said.

The voice sounded familiar, but I couldn't put a face to it until I turned around and saw Popey's father standing before me.

"Aidan, how's things?" I greeted awkwardly, knowing that the chance meeting would be my last opportunity to make amends and his first opportunity to deliver a long-awaited admonishment.

"As good as they can be, I suppose," he replied glumly, staring at the headstone as my own eyes strayed beyond the graveyard to St Peter's national school behind it, where I first met his son.

"Fine job, isn't it? The headstone," he said.

"Ah yeah, it looks the part awright," I concurred.

"The wife wanted a granite one. We ended up rowing over it, would ye believe… I suppose it's worth rowing about. It's not every day you've to pick your son's headstone."

"How have ye been getting on since…?"

"Ah, there's been bad days, I won't lie to ye. Some days I hate even coming up here. It's just a reminder of where he is and where he isn't. I usually come up with the missus, but I was just popping out to the shop and I thought o' coming up. Bit of a spur o' the moment thing."

I tried to gauge how long to wait before I broached the issue of my antics at the reception.

"This is me first time here," I confessed.

"It makes it all the more real, doesn't it?"

I nodded in agreement, not uttering a word.

"Listen," I furtively began. "I wanted to talk to ye about…"

He waved his hand in a dismissive fashion. "Forget about it, Paddy. There's nothing to talk about. We had so much on our minds that day, that little scuffle hardly even caught our attention. Ye lost a friend. We all grieve differently, react differently. Everyone's emotions were so charged, it wouldn't have taken much to set any of us off."

"I know, but I want to apologise…"

"Listen, it was one o' those days were all normality goes out the window. Yis are youngfellas. Yis haven't enough miles on the clock to handle an occasion like that."

"I don't know what was going through me head. It was like I just wanted to…"

"Lash out? Trust me, I know the feeling."

"Did ye ever…" I hesitated.

"Notice anything? No, nothing… He was a bit quieter, but that was all." He inhaled as if he was preparing to hold his breath and then exhaled with equal exertion, as if all his strength was being expelled from his body.

"What about you?" he asked me.

"Me? Nothing… Well, there was one night I bumped into him and I kind o' picked up a vibe… Thought nothing of it though… Then when I heard…"

"I know son, I know."

As if reading my thoughts, he placed an arm round me and held me to him, rubbing the back of my head, quietly speaking, almost whispering, "We'd all do things differently if we could go back in time, son."

He released me and wiped his eyes.

"Ah, it comes and goes, Paddy. You're grand one minute, all over the place the next."

"I can only imagine… How's the family?"

"Still trying to make sense of it. Still getting used to him not being round. The wife mentions him every two minutes, her way o' coping I suppose. I don't know if it's doing her more harm than good though. The girls are putting on brave faces for their ma, probably for me too… The empty chair at the kitchen table is still hard to look at. I felt like picking it up and smashing it against the floor the other night… What is it the alcos say? One day at a time."

The more we spoke, the longer we stood in reverence, the further my introspections led me to the conclusion that to speculate about Popey's reasons, to offer apologies to the dead, was all futile. He made his decision and I'd respect it. In my mind he'd live on, as entombed within me as his corpse was below me. He'd travel with me, both of us leaving the grave and the country behind. His father's voice was somewhere, lagging behind such thoughts.

"Have ye been here long, Paddy?"

"Not too long. I just wanted to say a few things before I leave tonight."

"Where are ye going?"

"Australia."

"Had enough o' this country?"

"I think it's had enough o' *me*."

"Well, better down under there than down under here," he said, staring despairingly at the grave.

Not knowing how to reply, and thinking that he probably wanted to be alone, I deemed it time to bid him farewell.

"Sure, I might see ye again when I get back," I said.

"With the country the way it is, you'll probably see me buried alongside him by the time ye get back."

"Yeah but, like ye said, one day at a time."

We shook hands.

"Best o' luck over there, Paddy. I only wish he was going with ye."

"I'll be thinking of him and your family."

"I appreciate that, son, but you think o' yourself first and foremost, ye hear me?"

I nodded solemnly.

His eyes were fixed on the grave again. In such moments he may as well have been thousands of miles away. My impending departure begot a pang of guilt. I envisioned myself lying on a beach in Australia while he remained in Bray, trying to reconstruct his demolished family life, a task as arduous as it was unenviable.

Walking away from the grave, I stopped and looked back at him. Even the caw of a crow sitting on the neighbouring headstone couldn't extract him from wherever he was lost, where he'd be forever lost, searching for answers unprocurable in this life.

I exited through the squeaking wrought iron gate, relieved to be escaping the prison of the dead, yet disheartened to be leaving its one living prisoner behind.

As I walked back home, I knew there was still one other person with whom I had to make amends. I thought about calling to her house. Foreseeing the hostile reception that I'd receive upon arriving at her doorstep unannounced, I shied away from the idea. I rang her instead. When she didn't answer, I decided to send her a message. Not wanting to grovel nor make excuses for my behaviour, I was unsure of what to write or how much to write. I settled for the shortest and most honest wording.

"I'm sorry, Rachael."

As I reached Dargan Street, I received a reply.

"Forget about it, Paddy. Take care."

It was as much a goodbye as it was an acceptance of my apology. Little did she know where I would be heading. She didn't need to know. Her implicitly expressed desire for us to move on with our lives along separate routes was shared. I sent another message.

"You too."

"Come on, Da! I'll be late!"

I was standing at the door, impatiently waiting for him. I'd managed to negotiate the final obstacle that had been placed before me earlier, in the form of our last family dinner together. It had been replete with Ma's anecdotes from years past, which she seemed to be recounting in a not-so-subtle attempt at coaxing me to stay. She dragged me down the narrow confines of memory lane, trying to beguile me with its nostalgia, oblivious to its dilapidation, and to the foreboding dead end ahead. Nostalgia was a rat trap that lured you with such memories, only to unmercifully snap your back in two.

As if spotting my indifference to her tales, she changed the nature of her pitch from the past to the future.

"They're saying that things will improve soon, aren't they, John?"

"They are, Aoife."

"And that we'll be back on our feet before we know it."

Her words were weightless. She was seeing a glass half full when the glass was empty. I once possessed that same unbridled optimism and had used it as a shield to protect me from the advancing reality. It had helped to break my fall when I plunged into the pit of unemployment. But I was on the cusp of escaping the pit and no wishful thinking or fond memories would impede me.

I was still standing at the door.

"Da, will ye hurry up!"

"I'm coming, I'm coming!"

Ma and Claire were beside me. I hugged Claire first.

"See ye in a while, sis."

"Take care o' yourself, Paddy."

Then Ma.

"See ye in a while, Ma."

"If ye don't settle in over there, or ye have any trouble, come right back. Okay?"

"I'll be grand, Ma!"

"I know you will, love... Aw, I'll miss ye... Me little boy!"

Buddy hobbled to the door. I hunkered down and held his head in my hands.

"That a boy, Bud. Don't let them tame ye while I'm gone, ye hear me?"

"Keep in touch, won't ye?" said Ma.

"Yeah, o' course I will. I'll ring as soon as I get there."

I knew she wanted to ask me to stay, but she resisted. Unsure of how long she could maintain her resistance, and if I could resist such a heartfelt plea, I turned away in haste and got into the car with Da.

"Sorry, son. I couldn't find me keys anywhere."

As we pulled away, I waved one last goodbye to them as Claire wrapped her arms around Ma.

Each mile felt like ten. We spoke intermittently, not knowing what to say. The Dempsey men weren't designed for such occasions.

As we arrived at Dublin airport, Da got out of the car with me to open the boot. After I pulled out the suitcase, he held me by the shoulders and recited what he must have been rehearsing since we left Bray.

"Listen, son, I know your ma's upset, but ye have to do what's best for you. It's your life, no one else's. This place can't offer ye anything. Go over there, make a few quid and play it by ear. And if everything works out for ye over there and ye want to stay, do. Your ma will come around. Once she sees you're happy, she'll be happy for ye. And remember, ye don't have to prove anything to us. If things don't work out for ye over there, ye know where home is. Ye could come back next week and we wouldn't think any less o' ye. But just do me one favour. Don't tell your ma you'll be back shortly if ye won't be. Ye know how she is. She'll be getting her hopes up, awaiting your return. Better to be honest about things like that, awright?"

"Yeah, no bother."

"Here, take this," he said, after pulling an envelope out of his pocket. "There's a few bob in it."

"Ah, Da, I don't want that. Thanks, but…"

"Don't be daft. Take it. You'll need a few quid until ye know your head from your hole over there."

I took it and then he hugged me. I couldn't remember ever feeling as close to him as I did in that moment.

"Would ye look at us!" he remarked as he let go. "We're like a pair o' young ones. Go on, hop on that plane before we have our fuckin' periods!"

"I'll see ye, Da."

"See ye, son. Don't forget to ring when ye arrive. Ye know what your mother's like about that sort o' stuff. She'll have me fuckin' head done in if ye don't."

"Awright, Da. Good luck."

I turned my back to him, to the life I knew, to unemployment, to the Irish Republic and all its warts.

As the plane rose, my last sight of Ireland lay outside, the night denying me a final glimpse of its lauded emerald hue. Only as I soared above the city of my birth, did I see its dazzling lights, glimpses of life engulfed by the darkness. As Ireland's illuminated coast receded, I suddenly remembered myself in primary school watching Popey trying to stifle a giggle as the class sang *Hail Glorious St Patrick*, oblivious to its emotive lyrics.

"Thy people, now exiles on many a shore,
Shall love and revere thee till time be no more.
And the fire thou hast kindled shall ever burn bright,

Its warmth undiminished, undying its light.
On Erin's green valleys, on Erin's green valleys,
On Erin's green valleys, look down in thy love."

I was now the exile. My departure would be sung about by the next generation, until their time to be exported was nigh, and so the cycle would continue. I closed my eyes, exhausted from being exhausted. I silently sang the remaining verse. Its melody was like a lullaby that could induce sleep. My ruminations however, guaranteed my wakefulness.

Chapter 39
The Serpentine Road

Walking through Sydney's streets, ten months after first doing so, I still felt as much of an outsider as I did then. I embraced my incongruousness for it reminded me of who I was. It prevented me from offering the city's residents a "G'day!" with a newly audible Aussie twang and being mistaken for one of their own.

Ireland was never far from my thoughts. In the early days, I kept abreast of the news back home and spoke to the family on a weekly basis. But being so intellectually close and yet physically so far away soon began to exacerbate my sense of alienation. At one point, I even questioned my presence in Australia and considered leaving, before logic announced its arrival into the argument, winning it by posing one simple question.

What would I do back home?

No doubt the dole queue was awaiting my return. Bar homesickness, I had no reason to leave Australia. This was home now. I didn't accept it. I never would. But the longer I stayed and the more money I made, the more frivolous that denial was sounding.

We lived in a cramped two-bedroom apartment with her friend Niamh. Kelly had already immersed herself in the Australian lifestyle when I'd arrived, and I tried my best to do likewise. However, the unforgiving heat only served to remind me how far away I was from home. I kept such thoughts to myself, being happy for her at least.

Work wasn't long finding me in the form of labouring. Niamh had been seeing a carpenter and having had my share of laughs with him in the apartment, he put in a good word for me with his foreman. But even getting a job, one of the two reasons I came to Australia, couldn't quell my discontent. If anything, the job made it worse.

I came all this way, just to do donkey work on a building site!

And so, the weeks passed. I detached myself from Ireland, as I knew my role as a voyeur, peeping through the curtains at her, would be my undoing. The phone calls home became less frequent. My interest in Irish-related matters diminished. The last news from home that I paid any attention to was towards the end of 2010, when the 'Troika' - a consortium comprised of the International Monetary Fund, the European Commission and the European Central Bank - arrived in Dublin to negotiate a bailout deal with the Irish government. The country was bankrupt. The news footage showed a trio of sombre-looking men entering the Department of Finance to construct an agreement that would commit the country to further austerity.

My reaction to it was conflicted. The bailout justified my decision to leave but it made my eventual return all the more uncertain. As usual, I was an invited dinner guest at the house of limbo.

In the wake of the Troika's visit to Dublin, I refocused my efforts on trying to forge a life from my surroundings rather than reliving a life from my memory, but the labouring was as tedious as it was exhausting. The merciless combination of gruelling work and searing heat sapped whatever morsel of enthusiasm I had by midday.

My lunchbreaks were shared with other Irish immigrants. They all told similar tales to my own as to what brought them to Australia, most of them speaking admirably about their new life, never uttering a word about returning to Ireland. It seemed that the longer you stayed, the more of a foreign concept it became.

After some time, I began to notice that certain lads on the site who'd normally speak effusively about all aspects of their Australian life, were curiously ambiguous about the circumstances of their residency. When innocently questioned regarding such, they deemed the topic of conversation to have run its course and changed the subject or went back to work. One of the lads had a word with me one day, telling me to avoid asking such questions, fearing that the site would be teeming with immigration officers by the following morning. I then understood, and from that day onwards, I listened more than I spoke and answered questions instead of asking them.

At the time, their plight wasn't of my concern, but with only a couple of months remaining on my one-year visa, it was now. I knew I wouldn't be eligible for a second visa, since I hadn't undertaken the three months of working in the sticks that was required in order to be granted one. There were job vacancies on farms, where immigrants were sought for menial work, but Kelly had been unsurprisingly unwilling to leave her nursing job and civilisation behind her, in favour of accompanying me on my unenvied excursion, becoming a farmhand in an environment akin to Mars. The alternative had been to head off on my own, like Jesus spending forty days and nights in the Judean desert, with the Irish Satan tempting me to come home. But being separated from her for such a lengthy period and having to walk away from the security of the labouring work, with no guarantee of it still being available on my return, made me opt to stay where I was.

I considered playing a game of 'hide and seek' with the immigration authorities and seeing how long I'd last before they caught me.

Which is worse, legal and unemployed in Ireland or illegal and employed in Australia?

Perhaps it was my fate to become an outlaw, a modern-day Ned Kelly, surviving day-to-day, out of view from the law, ostracised from civilised society.

I was tempted to seek advice from those I knew to be illegals, but I trusted them no more than they trusted me. A state of paranoia plagued all who found themselves in such circumstances, which was only heightened when one of the lads failed to show up for work one morning, and rumours about him having been deported began to spread.

Despite my concerns regarding my future residency status, the primary source of my disquiet was my homesickness which was getting worse by the day, refusing to be allayed by money, sunshine, or anything else that the land down under had to offer. In the past few months, Kelly and I had come to have different outlooks in relation to living in Australia. Although unnoticeable initially, the contrast between them was becoming more evident. I hadn't spoken a word about it, for her sake, choosing instead to quietly mull over it. But before long, I came to an unavoidable conclusion.

Australia's idyllic weather and beaches were that of a holiday I never wished for. Its opportunities were a form of gravity pulling me towards something I never wanted. Its affluent life seemed more impoverished than the one I'd left behind. Its currency in my wallet was my thirty pieces of silver. The means by which I'd lengthen my stay was becoming increasingly irrelevant as it offered me a prize I no longer desired. The prospect of another twelve months in Australia felt like a prison sentence. I was beginning to view the obstacles hindering my attainment of another visa as an expedient excuse to return home. I couldn't maintain my silence any longer. I decided that I'd tell her how I felt.

As I reached the bar near the hospital that she worked in, where we had agreed to meet after she finished her shift, I toyed with how best to broach the issue.

How are ye finding things here, Kelly?

I have to tell ye something, Kelly.

Is it just me or do you…

How long do ye plan on staying?

Do ye think o' home much, Kelly?

Do ye ever miss your ma?

I walked in and found her sitting by a window. We ordered drinks and made small talk for a few minutes before I abruptly changed the subject.

"I need to talk to ye about something, Kel."

"Yeah, likewise."

"What do you wanna talk about?" I asked.

"You first, what's bothering ye?"

"I was… Well, how are ye finding it here?"

"I love it."

"Still?"

"Yeah, still. You?"

My hesitation in answering the question, answered the question on my behalf.

"Do ye not like it? "

"I like it, it's just…"

"Just what?"

"I miss home."

"Well, so do I, but that's normal. The longer you're here, the less you'll think that."

"Well, that's the thing… I mean, you're sponsored, but my visa will be running out soon."

"I told ye to go to that farm down the country that was hiring people but there was no talking to ye."

"Down the country? Ye make it sound as if it's Connemara. It'd be like the end o' the world where that farm is!"

"Well, it's better than the alternative!"

"Being illegal, ye mean? That's not the only alternative."

"What do ye mean?"

"What I'm saying is… I'm saying… I wanna go home, Kel."

"You're leaving?"

"I want ye to come back with me."

"And what about me job? I'm not going home to work for half the wages that I'm getting here… Paddy, why is it when things are going well, ye have to throw in a bloody hand grenade?"

It was a most intriguing question that historians will be trying to answer years from now when they discover the lost memoir of one Patrick Dempsey, PhD in the science of unemployment.

"I'm throwing in me two cents, that's all."

"Yeah, and your two cents are senseless!"

Her lecturing tone was grating on me.

"Hang on, why is it always what *you* want?!"

"What *I* want?! I thought we both wanted this!"

"We do… We did…but…"

"So, are ye saying you're going home?"

I didn't answer. It was a conundrum deprived of an answer. I stared abjectly out the window.

"Well, I'm not planning on leaving without ye," I assured her.

"You're not *planning* on leaving without me, or ye *won't* leave without me, which?"

I said nothing.

"Paddy, I need ye here."

"I understand that, Kel…"

"No, ye don't! Because this is what *I* wanted to talk to *you* about. I've decided I wanna stay here. Permanently."

"Permanently?!"

"Yeah, I should be eligible for permanent residency soon."

"I was never planning on staying here permanently, even if I could. A year, couple o' years maybe, until things picked up back home."

"Paddy, ye knew I was planning on making something o' meself over here. Don't make it out like I'm moving the goalposts."

"But ye are! Ye never said anything about staying here permanently!"

"Because I didn't know what it'd be like, but now I *do*."

"What about three or four years?"

"The longer I'm here, the less I wanna go back."

"Ye could at least meet me halfway and think about it."

"I *have* thought about it… Do ye really miss the dole queue that much?"

"What sort o' stupid question is that? I hardly wanna go back for the…"

"But that's exactly what you'll be going back to."

"What about me family? What about your own family?"

"We'd visit them now and then, and they could come over here the odd time too."

"Visit them? Sure, I wouldn't be allowed back here afterwards without a visa. You'd get to visit *your* family. I'd be fuckin' stuck here like a prisoner."

"Ye won't be. Ye might be able to get permanent residency if I sponsor ye, after I get mine."

"How far will that be down the road? What am I supposed to do for the time being?"

"Ye just keep your head down and don't attract any attention to yourself."

"And what if I'm caught? Or what if they don't give me permanent residency after you get it 'cause they know I've been illegal for the last couple o' years? Then what?"

"If that happens, we'll return home together. I won't stay here without ye."

"You'll be bitter as fuck about it back home. You'll hate me for fucking things up for ye."

"I won't, I swear."

"And if I'm not caught or I get the permanent residency at some stage, we stay here?"

"Yeah. How does that sound?"

"It sounds like a deal that's a no-win situation for me. At least you have something going for ye over here. What the fuck do I have?"

"Me, for one. Not to mention a job."

"Ye make it sound so simple, when it isn't."

"It is!"

"Maybe for you!"

"Listen, I've told ye how I feel and what ye decide to do is your call. If ye wanna return home, I'll understand, but I'm staying here."

"So, you'll come home with me if I'm kicked out, but not if I choose to leave. What's the difference?"

"If you're kicked out, I'll know that you've stood by me and I'll stand by you in return, that's the difference… Paddy, don't end what we have by going home."

"I'm not ending anything. How is it my fault if it ends?"

"I'm not blaming ye. I'm just telling ye what will happen."

"God, I hadn't realised ye were that keen to get rid o' me! Has some doctor been chatting ye up or something?"

"If that's the way you're gonna be about it, I'm wasting me time even talking to ye!" She rose from her seat.

"Where are ye going?"

"Home… Don't get up. Stay here and do all the thinking ye need to do 'cause I wanna know."

"Know what?"

"Whether you're gonna stay here with me, or whether we're done."

She walked out the door, leaving me with her unmerciful ultimatum.

My future, my life, the very essence of who I would be, would all come down to one choice. It was a choice of such enormity that I dreaded chairing its debate for I feared both of its possible outcomes. I couldn't think straight. I needed another drink. Alcohol wouldn't find the answer but would slow my racing mind and help me to deal with the answer. I quaffed the pint, then another. I had a desire to keep ordering, knowing the volume of consumption required to enable me to lose myself in an evening of self-indulgence, in which her ultimatum would excuse itself from my company. As tempting as it was, I resisted doing so.

I started to think that this was the junction that the serpentine road had always been leading me to.

Left or right?

Turning my back on Kelly was unthinkable, but to stay in Australia was to turn my back on my own family, my own country. As much as I wanted to return home, I knew that doing so would provide scant consolation if she who mattered most to me was left behind in a foreign land, destined to become the wife of one of its fortunate natives. I questioned if happiness in Australia would forever evade me as my unceasing yearning for home invaded all my thoughts, making me bitter over the life in Ireland I had been denied.

An unwanted life or a wanted existence?

It was a question that I imagined in the form of a balancing scale, each side dropping and lifting perpetually as I ruminated over their respective merits.

A job and a wife in Australia, or unemployed and single in Ireland?

The question was rhetorical when worded as such, but its obvious answer prompted me to review my wording of it. I rephrased the question again and again, tailoring it to fit the answer I craved at that given moment, alternating back and forth endlessly.

I buried my head in my hands, hoping for and yet fearing an epiphany. I remembered what my life was like back in Ireland after she left and felt that memory push me closer to succumbing to the decision that I knew was unavoidable. There was never a choice, only a set of circumstances masquerading as a choice. A country which offered a past contrasted with one that was offering a future, albeit a future consisting of under-the-table payments, a sore neck from looking over my shoulder and suspicions of anyone who had the good manners to say hello to me. But even illegality couldn't offer a sturdy argument against it. The confusion suddenly left me, offering its chair to remorse as I accepted the solution to the conundrum. I'd join the ragtag club of Irish expats whose documentation extended as far as their site safe pass cards. I'd find a new uncertain home in the shadows of Australian society.

I looked out the window, feeling caught between wanting to leave the bar but not wanting to face the incertitude of the world on the opposite side of the glass. I imagined myself effusively telling Kelly of my decision, while secretly hoping that I'd be caught, forcing her to honour her side of the deal and accompany me home. I imagined Ma telling me how happy she was for me upon hearing of my decision, her reaction as disingenuous as the tall-tales I'd tell her to explain how I'd been granted another visa and why I wouldn't be able to visit soon.

My thoughts turned to Ireland. I was its battered spouse. Despite the abuse, I still sought the protection and familiarity of my abuser. We were unable to tolerate each other but were unwilling to divorce. I was subservient to it. I feared it would forget me, or that it already had, and that life over there would continue as if I never existed.

I imagined myself standing on Bray Bridge, watching the shallow river below flowing into the sea; an image that made me wonder how long it would be before I could do so for real.

Each time I reckon that I've reached the end of the serpentine road, another mile appears in front of me. I'll keep traversing the road until I see Bray Head's cross in the distance, until I hear St Peter's church bell ringing out, and until I finally reach Dargan Street; the lure of which is growing with each day that passes.

I know nothing of what lies ahead. Maybe I'll return home one day. Maybe I won't. Sadly, I just don't know.

About the Author

Éamonn MacCionnaith is an accounting technician from Bray, Co Wicklow, Ireland. *An Idler's Life* is his first novel.

Dear Reader,

If you enjoyed this book, would you kindly post a short review on Goodreads or on whichever store you purchased the book from?

Your feedback will make all the difference to getting the word out about this book.

Thank you in advance.

www.ingramcontent.com/pod-product-compliance
Lightning Source LLC
Chambersburg PA
CBHW030949190726
48285CB00004BB/1284